GAME OF DECEPTION

BOOK TWO OF THE GAME SERIES

STÉPHANIE C.

Be unapologetically you. Don't let the world tell you who you
are meant to be.
You tell them.

PLAYLIST

Scan Above or Click Here to listen on Spotify!

1. Slow Dancing in a Burning Room – John Mayer

2. I Could Fall In Love – Selena

3. Falling Into you – Celine Dion

4. Let Me Down Slowly – Alex Benjamin

5. Tell Him – Celine Dion, Barbara Streisand

6. Only Love Can Hurt Like his – Paloma Faith

7. Lost – Micheal Bublé

8. Someone You Loved – Lewis Capaldi

9. Lost on You – LP

10. I Have Nothing – Whitney Houston

11. Set Fire to the Rain – Adele

12. Like I'm gonna lose you – Meghan Trainor, John Legend

PART 1

CHAPTER 1

WOULD I LET THE fear of rejection cripple me, or would I straighten my back, take a deep breath, and go to him like the confident woman I portrayed myself to be? I couldn't decide.

We had been exchanging random glances for ten minutes.

He was standing by the bar with a group of men, wearing a light shark-skin gray suit and a white shirt. They all seemed to have come from a work event, appearing to have decided to continue their Friday night at this bar club hybrid, on this unusually warm night of April in Chicago.

I intended to spend the evening at home, cuddled on my couch with my cat, and watching a show until I fell asleep with the help of a good glass of Malbec. But Keisha, one of my best friends from college in New York, had convinced me to go out with her, Iris, and Amelia to *"get wasted and forget"* that Kyle, my ex, had started dating someone new and had gone on vacation with her to Florida.

It shouldn't have affected me as much as it did. I was the one who had decided to end the relationship a few months ago because I just couldn't picture myself and Kyle together long term. Kyle had started talking about marriage, and I didn't see him as the man I wanted to make that commitment to.

It didn't mean that it didn't sting a little knowing that he had moved on so quickly. In the end, I knew I had been right when I told him it was clear that we had made a mistake when we began dating. We were better off as friends.

Knowing my self-esteem needed a little boost, I had reluctantly agreed to join my friends at one of my favorite Latin bars in downtown Chicago. Iris and Amelia, whom Keisha and I had also met in college, were my very best friends from California, and they had finally made their long-planned trip to Chicago.

Unfortunately, Iris and Amelia were leaving the next day, and it had been a couple months since we had seen each other face to face, so I knew I needed to get out to see them before they left.

I had opted for a black satin mini dress with a plunging neckline and delicate shoulder straps that showed just enough cleavage to keep things interesting for the night. I coupled it with tall, strapped, open-toed sandals that flattered my dainty feet. I almost always wore heels, making the most out of my 5'3" frame. And I didn't forget my signature gold jewelry, which I always felt complemented my tan skin.

We had been dancing to our hearts' content, like we used to when we were in college in New York, consuming all the alcohol we could handle, while I flirted with some of the guys, only to lose interest almost as fast.

Still, I was determined that I was going home with someone. It felt like the right moment for me to be more fun, more adventurous, since it was the first time I was single in over a year.

And ever since I caught sight of the mystery man in the corner with his friends, I could not peel my eyes off him. After one too many shots of tequila, I was becoming impatient. My hopes that he would come talk to me were swiftly dwindling.

"Why don't *you* go talk to *him*?" suggested Keisha, pushing me a little on the shoulder. "He is clearly into you."

"You think so?" I raised a brow at her, unsure. She grinned.

"Yes! he has not taken his eyes off you since they walked in," added Iris, her gorgeous blue eyes sparkling under the club's flashing lights.

She was wearing her long soft blonde hair in a high bun, highlighting her perfect jaw and long neck. Iris was the definition of class and exuded elegance in every movement. She was the most prime and proper of our group, but she could also let go and have a fun time, especially when the four of us were together.

"Come on! He is to *die* for! He's headed for the bar, so now is your chance. If you don't hurry up, someone else will!" encouraged Keisha as the girls started laughing.

Keisha was taller than most women, with gorgeous thick black curly hair that cascaded down her shoulders. Her slightly round face and big brown eyes were complimented by her perfectly straight white teeth and brown pompous lips that widened to create the most sensual smile every time she was amused.

She truly had the most impeccable style and often chose to wear a purple dress because it accentuated the beauty of her brown skin.

But I held Keisha close to me as I considered her words. I was already a little too inhibited to stand straight, but she was encouraging me to just go up and speak to that man. A *very* attractive man.

"This shyness is very unlike you," observed Amelia, her soft honey-colored eyes meeting mine. She shoved her long brown curls away from her oval face and pursed her red pouty lips at me, leaning in as if to try to convince me further. Her gold crescent earrings flicked under the playful lights, the tone complimenting her sun-kissed skin perfectly.

"Oh, stop!" I flicked a hand in mock protest. My friends' words made me feel warm, and confidence started to take shape inside me.

"You are way too bossy to not just walk over there and get what you want," declared Keisha, knowing how to light a little fire under my feet. Iris slightly nudged me in the right direction, an encouraging grin on her face.

I loved these girls with all my heart, and since Iris and Amelia were only in town for a short time, I decided to oblige, to feed off their energy and make them proud.

"You know what? It's the twenty-first century, damn it, I'm going in!" I declared as the girls screamed with excitement, cheering me on.

My grip tightened around my gold wristlet. It took all my focus to strut to where the man was standing without tripping, and I could feel my heart beating a little faster than usual. As I got closer, another woman had already approached him, and she had no problem flirting with him at all as she pressed her very generous chest into his side.

I stopped in my tracks right behind the woman, looking back at the girls for help, not knowing what to do. I knew he had seen me, but he was purposely ignoring me.

Too tipsy to think straight, I stood there with alcohol courage fueling me, shamefully admiring his features. After all, I had nothing to lose. I trailed my eyes over his suit and white shirt, admiring how it molded against his muscles. And as I continued undressing him with my eyes, I noticed he was not wearing a tie. And I was a sucker for a man choosing to transition into a more casual suit attire after a long day's work.

As my gaze tracked back to his face, I was met with what looked like blue-green eyes, and I admired the fierceness in his gaze, his slightly crooked determined nose, his strong jaw darkened by the lack of light in the bar, and that devastatingly sexy mocking smile that had called my attention when he walked in. He ran a hand through his blond, semi-curly hair.

He raised a brow as our eyes met, and he stopped talking. He was observing me, amused. My lips curled, but I was suddenly starting to feel a little timid, as he probably had noticed me admiring what he had to offer. I wasn't generally that bold, but it was a special night.

"Pleasure meeting you." His tone and body language signaled a clear dismissal as he moved away from the woman, a glass of amber liquid in his hand.

He positioned himself in front of me, and I could feel my stomach flutter at his proximity.

"Can I get you something to drink?" he inquired with a smirk.

I had to tilt my head slightly to meet his gaze. Even with my heels, he was still significantly taller than me. "Some water would be great," I admitted. He lifted a brow but shifted toward the bartender as I leaned against the bar for some support.

"Thank you," I said as I started sipping on the water bottle he had opened before handing it to me.

I was doing everything in my power not to seem drunk.

"What's your name?" I asked, trying not to slur.

"Jake Cunningham. And you are?" He raised a brow.

"Chloe," I answered as I gulped more water.

"Nice to meet you, Chloe," he replied, raising his glass to me before taking a sip.

I found his calm yet strong demeanor intimidating. He was silently studying me, with a subtle twitch playing on the right side of his lips. I didn't know what to make of his silence, but I just couldn't look away.

"Want to dance?" I suggested as I grabbed his left hand and nodded toward the dance floor.

He seemed hesitant, but then he chugged his drink before getting rid of the glass and followed me. Dancing had always come to me naturally, so I knew I would feel confident on the dance floor.

I stopped when I found a spot in the middle of the crowd, where I felt like there was enough space for us to get lost in the music without anyone stepping on my Jimmy Choos. We were surrounded by other dancers, simply enjoying the rhythm of reggaeton. I turned around to face him as I let the sensual song wash over me.

For me, dancing was a passion. Once a song took possession of my body, that was it; nothing else really mattered. So, I did just that—enjoyed moving my hips to the rhythm, my hands in the air or caressing my body.

I could sway my hips for hours without a partner, but tonight I most certainly wanted to pull that handsome stranger into the rhythm I was so lost in.

He was just standing there, smiling, watching me have my own fun. I dared to take a step closer to him, thankful for the hand he quickly wrapped around my waist when I lost a bit of my balance. He frowned. I just laughed out loud, enjoying his strong grip.

I ran my fingers over his nicely tailored suit, enjoying the texture of it, as I slowly moved my hands towards his neck, pulling his head closer to mine. I could smell him—mixed spices with an amber or sandalwood note, teasing my nostrils and slightly arousing me.

He had a serious look plastered on his face as I got a bit closer. An unspoken invitation for him to kiss me, but he remained stoic—almost protective, still refusing to bring his lips to mine.

I gave up and leaned my head on his shoulder, my brain too intoxicated to make sense of anything.

"I think I should get you home," he announced as he moved my hair away from my face.

I just nodded, too tired to protest and too comfortable on his chest to do anything but follow him as he proceeded to walk towards the exit. As we passed by the bar, Keisha interrupted her dancing and grabbed me by the arm to make sure I was okay.

"Wish me luck," I said a little louder than I intended. Keisha stared at Jake with a protective gaze before she let go of me.

"Call me," she added before the man she was dancing with pulled her back to him.

Jake kept me close until we made it outside. The cold air hit me like a slap, sobering me just a bit. He removed his suit jacket and wrapped around my shoulders. I could feel the ground move slightly under me, but he held me until we finally got into a car and drove off.

CHAPTER 2

MY HEAD AND BODY felt heavy. I peeked around me for a second. I was wrapped in the softest Egyptian gray silk sheets, splayed out on a king-size bed. With my eyelids closed, I rolled to the nightstand on my right, my hand blindly searching for my phone. When I reached a foreign object, I groaned but finally peeled my eyes open.

I was staring at a rectangular beige lamp with a metal stand sitting on a wide black table. Across from me was a black built-in bookshelf with vases in various shapes and sizes, all white and black. Above and behind my head were a few black and white paintings with some red stripes.

It was most certainly not my bedroom.

I rubbed my dry eyeballs, then shimmied to my left. I was greeted by floor-to-ceiling windows with the most gorgeous view of Lake Michigan and the Hancock building. I closed my eyes and leaned back down, trying to remember the night before. The last thing I could recall was being at a bar with my friends.

Then it hit me... I remembered running my hands up and down a hard chest.

That man. Jake. I was in Jake's condo!

I could barely hold in my gasp when I realized I was only wearing underwear. I couldn't remember anything else or how I got in the bed in the first place.

I caught sight of what looked like a small bottle of painkillers with a glass of water next to it on the nightstand. There was a note that read *"Make yourself at home – Jake"* written in perfect penmanship.

I was mortified, but I appreciated the gesture. I pushed the heavy sheets off me and stood up, deciding it was time for me to leave. My feet landed on the cold floor, and I had to ignore the slight pain in my calves from the night before as I padded across the dark ceramic tile searching for my dress. I found it neatly folded on the dark gray ottoman in front of the bed, next to my wristlet.

I got dressed and proceeded to look for the bathroom.

If I hadn't been in such a rush, I would have been able to appreciate the luxurious masculine bedroom I found myself in. Jake was clearly very meticulous about his environment, with very simple and classy decor. The room was surprisingly relaxing even if all the colors were dark.

I finally found a black glassy door that swung open to a luxurious bathroom. As I stepped in, I noticed an oval glass sink, a large jacuzzi tub, and a big walk-in shower with a panel tower jet system. I had landed in the bathroom of my dreams.

But I knew I needed to ignore the luxuries of the space and focus on the task at hand: getting out of here.

When I found a clean folded towel, I decided a quick shower needed to occur as I could still smell the alcohol on me. He told me to make myself at home after all, and while I'd make sure to leave in a timely fashion, I didn't want to be in public in my state.

I was startled when the corner of the mirror lit up automatically the closer I got to it. I found toothpaste as well as a new wrapped toothbrush by the sink, something I was extremely thankful for as I started brushing my teeth. After I quickly showered, I detangled my wet curls with my fingers and wrapped my hair in a bun. I stared at my long face, my dark arched eyes, my slightly hooked nose, and my wide full brown lips.

"What were you thinking?" I asked myself, noticing the dark circles under my eyes. Regret filled me with unease because that was not how I normally behaved.

I scanned the room, attempting to locate my shoes, and finally spotted them by an ottoman.

It was an unusually warm first week of April, but just having the right clothes would alleviate my dreaded walk of shame. But unless I decided to look through his house in the hopes of finding something appropriate, I had to go. I pulled my phone out of the wristlet. I had eleven missed calls and twenty text messages from Keisha, Amelia, and Iris.

For the time being, I ignored them and finally walked to the door to leave the bedroom. I found myself in a hallway with more doors than I cared to count but continued to tiptoe until I reached a white porcelain-like flight of stairs. As I descended, I landed in a vast open-floor concept living room with a dark brown sofa made of leather-like material and a black piano in the center. The decor was still simple, vacillating between white and black with occasional bursts of color. All I could see was the breathtaking view of the lake.

The condo was strategically designed to be both comfortable and luxurious, while staying muted enough to allow the view to remain the focal point of every room.

I was tempted to go by the window and admire the boats floating on the glistening hues of blues, but there was no time for that.

When I spotted what promised to be the exit, I marched toward the door, determined to keep my head high. I had nothing to be ashamed of, I reminded myself. If I was a man, I wouldn't feel as if I had just done something wrong, and while I couldn't control all my emotions, I could certainly manage what I portrayed.

As I exited, I realized I was in the hallway of an upscale apartment complex. I let out a sigh of relief when I looked down the hall and located the elevators. When I finally reached the lobby, I tried to not look as lost as

I felt. Thankfully, I quickly spotted the rotating exit doors and walked as fast as I could toward where I saw taxis lining up.

It was time to call my friends, I reminded myself, opting for a four-way FaceTime call. I knew they would all want the details of the night before, and I only wanted to explain it once.

"Where the hell are you!?" screamed Keisha when she answered the phone after the first ring.

"Well, hello to you, too," I answered, a wide grin on my face, my eyes closed with a mixture of amusement and mild shame.

"We called you like a hundred times!" complained Amelia.

"Are you still with that guy?" inquired Iris.

My friends certainly weren't ones to dance around the topic. No, they were there for answers.

"No, I'm on my way home, I just left—"

"Omg I can't believe you finally had a one-night stand! How was it!?" squealed Amelia.

"Well, frankly, I don't remember much. I vaguely remember getting into his car, but it's all blurry. I woke up without my clothes on... in his bed."

"Oh wow, he wasn't there I take it? Did he leave a note?" asked Iris.

"He did. It said I should make myself at home. And he left some painkillers. He also left me a toothbrush, which was nice I guess."

"Ugh men, such assholes!" exclaimed Keisha.

"But that was the point, right? A good time with a stranger, no commitment?" offered Iris.

"Yes, that was, if only I could remember. But anyways, I'm almost home, and I need to catch up on some emails."

"Do you want me to meet you there so we can go to your dad's party together?" asked Keisha.

"Ugh, fuck! I totally forgot it's today," I uttered, checking the time. "Okay, it's only one, I have time. Karla is coming over to do my hair and makeup, and she is bringing her assistant if you want to join? I meant to tell you sooner. She should be at my place at three."

I found Karla when I attended a friend's wedding a couple of years before and ever since, I hired her once or twice a year to get me ready for big events, and this party was promising to be the biggest of them all.

"Yes! Oh, the perks of having such a fancy friend!" teased Keisha.

"Haha! Please—it's one of the many perks we both share in life, and you know it," I laughed. "Sorry, girls," I added for Iris and Amelia, as they were flying back to Mexico this morning.

Amelia owned a hospitality management company that recently expanded internationally. Since Iris was an interior designer, she was helping with the design of a new hotel the company was opening in Mexico.

"I really wish we could stay longer," sighed Amelia, "but with that new hotel, it's been nonstop meetings and calls, and Iris is getting annoyed."

We laughed, with Iris shaking her head, holding her laugh to seem offended.

"How dare you! How do you want me to pick the perfect shade of paint all the way from here!?"

"She makes a fair point," I agreed.

"Yeah, got to find that perfect shade of white," teased Amelia, causing another uproar of laughter amongst us.

"Don't listen to them!" I defended, unable to hold back the tears of laughter. "They don't understand how many fucking shades of white there actually are!"

Keisha and Amelia lost it again, at my and Iris's expense, the conversation being a running joke since Iris and I had taken two months to pick a shade for my house.

"Oh, and did you get that guy's number?" asked Keisha once we calmed down.

"Hm, I don't think so. Not that I'd ever have the nerve to call him. I was so drunk, and I'm sure I made a fool of myself. Anyways, see you soon! All of you!"

With that, we hung up the phone, but I kept my headphones in, the sound of music distracting me from my thoughts.

As I was driven down the street, I started to remember small details from last night. Making it back to Jake's place—laughter—and perhaps a kiss. I vaguely recalled him laying me in his bed but was still unsure if I just slept or if we had sex.

Luckily, there wasn't much traffic on Lake Shore Drive, so twenty minutes later, I was finally turning the key into the entry door of my house in Bronzeville.

I raced through my beach-house-french-country-themed foyer and formal living room and went straight up the stairs to the master bedroom.

I sighed out of relief in being in familiar grounds. After removing my heels, I slid my dress down, waltzed through a pair of French doors, and tiptoed into my wide, custom-made walk-in closet. I grabbed a set of ivory lounge pants and light sweater day wear.

My meticulously ordered closet always made me happy. Being organized was indeed my favorite hobby, as it made me feel in control.

It might have been a bit superficial, but looking at my precious handbags and shoes displayed on white lit shelves behind glass doors usually forced me to slow down, take a breath, and appreciate all I had accomplished in life.

Now that I was in comfortable attire, I headed back to the room, and gave myself just a few moments to absorb everything that happened in the last twelve hours.

I slid beneath my puffy off-white down comforter and rearranged my decorative pillows—beautifully hand-embroidered cream-colored pillowcases—so that I was comfortably settled in my king-sized bed.

The sunlight filtered in from the oatmeal color linen curtains, highlighting the simplicity of my bedroom. While I didn't have much décor, I loved the solace I found in this space of mine.

At the end of my bed sat a long ivory chair with a matching ottoman by the window. It was where I lounged when I read a good book before bed. My two matching off-white nightstands housed the light pink and white lamps I found at the little antique store I stumbled upon one weekend after brunch with the girls.

I loved the pop of color they provided the space. Two green paintings I bought one my first trip to Italy sat between the French-style windows.

I heard a purr followed by a meow. My Tortoiseshell kitty strolled in the room and rubbed herself sweetly against my ankles. Penny was the love of my life. I was what they called a failed foster. I took her in from an animal shelter as she waited for dental surgery, and within ten minutes of her roaming around my house, all shy but curious, I was done for.

The second her procedure was over, I adopted her. We were still together five years later.

"Hey, baby," I cooed as I stood to pick her up and carry her to my bed to pet her. "You're not hungry, are you?"

My spoiled girl had an automatic feeder and a filtered fountain water dispenser, but she also loved her treats. And I pampered her more than I should. I leaned towards my nightstand where I kept my Toblerone bars and her favorite Greenies treat. I got her a couple, set them up on a napkin, and deposited her on the floor to enjoy them.

She was the only one allowed to eat in my room besides me, and in my case, only a chocolate bar or ice cream. She devoured her treats and jumped back on the bed to make donuts, on top of me of course.

We had been living in this house for two years. It was my dream home, except for the fact that I still lived in Chicago.

I loved the city but hated the winter and had strongly considered leaving town after I graduated from University of Chicago Law School five years prior, but my family lived in Illinois, in the northern suburbs, and I wasn't ready to get too far from them.

Instead, I bought three big empty adjacent lots in Bronzeville, a predominantly Black neighborhood. It was meaningful to be going back to the place where I had spent the first ten years of my life before my parents moved to the suburbs, for me and my brother to attend private school not too far from where my father had found his dream job.

I hired a team of architects, engineers, and interior designers to build me a four-bedroom, four-bathroom, three stories, and an overground basement paradise in my parents' old neighborhood.

That was when I had hired Iris, to handle the interior design and décor of my home. It had worked out in more ways than one, allowing us more time together as we worked on the project.

Iris was excellent at her job, on top of being a good friend, and she knew me very well, so it was the perfect fit.

Bronzeville was close to the lake and an easy commute to downtown, where most of the law firms are. About a year ago, I had finally caved and accepted my father's offer to join the corporation he had created, Motor Holmes Corp., as general counsel. Thankfully, the principal office was in the loop, just a few blocks away from the law firm I worked at prior, and that meant my commute was relatively the same.

I went back to my closet and started perusing through my evening dresses, looking for something suited for my father's party. He was hosting a celebratory event for his employees and friends at Motor Holmes Corp. We had just executed a deal with Listen Inc., one of the top car manufacturers in the world, to provide us with e-axles and e-drives for our electric cars.

It was my first major project for the company, and I was very proud of everything I was able to contribute to the success of the transaction.

It was going to be the beginning of a new and exciting stage in the life of the twelve-year-old company. I was extremely proud of my parents. They had come from nothing, living in a studio apartment with me and my brother when they lived in Bronzeville, to being future millionaires.

My parents had successfully pursued the American dream. After years of hard work and sacrifices, both my dad and my mother had sold all they had and moved to the suburbs. My father had secured a position there as a repairman for a car parts manufacturer. My mother had found a new hospital to work at as a nurse. Eventually, when I was in middle school, my father was able to attend college as an adult.

When I was in high school, I watched my dad earn his MBA, all while working full-time. He then quit his job and put everything he had in building his own company from the ground up. Those were scary times, but I was in awe of my parents, their resilience and dedication.

I had always been extremely invested in and curious about my father's endeavors and even shadowed him when I had time. When school allowed, and during summer breaks, I became his informal secretary, assisting him in everything I could. What had originally started with helping him manage his schedule and staying organized quickly evolved into taking second looks at and typing up corporate governance documentation as well as contract templates for negotiations.

I spent a lot of time 'playing lawyer' as my dad had teased—researching the law, interning in the business and legal departments at Motor Holmes, and I fell in love with the profession in the process. Eric, my brother, also had been helping and developing a passion for law. He had pursued a very successful business career first, though. Eventually, the law bug was too hard to pass, and his passion had evolved into chasing the thrill of arguing in court, while I preferred drafting clean, clever legal languages in contracts. Or murky ones, when appropriate.

My parents' strength and tenacity inspired me so much that I was able to secure a scholarship to Columbia University and obtain a B.S. in English and business as double major in three years.

After having the time of my life in New York during my college years, I moved back to Chicago to attend law school and be closer to my parents. As the company became more successful, my dad was able to take a lessened workload. He chose to dilute his ownership down to 40% and gave the remaining amount to the other four stakeholders in the company.

What had set my father's company apart from others' car engineering was his early investment in the integration of a motor, gearing, and power electronics into one equipment located between an electric vehicle's driven wheels, an e-axle. The focus was on one of the primary equipment that transformed the energy from batteries to propulsion power. In that process, and to speed things up, we had acquired a small company in Michigan, complimenting the plant in Glenview Illinois.

The tech reduced how much power a vehicle required, allowing it to drive much longer and accelerate in an efficient manner. The technology helped minimize manufacturing costs and render electric vehicles more affordable. The company had obtained the right patents to protect the inventions and protected the trade secrets to remain competitive in the market.

The new model was set to launch over the winter. The company was about ready to go to market with its new product. Business was about to explode because I landed the exclusive contract with Listen Inc., a previous client I had worked for and built a relationship with when I was a law firm associate.

I smiled to myself as I remembered my father's shocked expression when I gave him the news. About six months after I joined my father's company, I had reached back to Listen Inc., and after a long, stressful six months, they were executing a four hundred-million-dollar exclusive contract with Motor Holmes. Sometimes I'm still in disbelief of what I had achieved in less than a year.

I had big dreams for Motor Holmes, and my dad knew that with me by his side, in just a few years, the value of those shares would grow substantially if we took the company public.

I settled on a long off-shoulder burgundy chiffon evening gown with a thigh-high slit and a long trail. Satisfied, I laid the dress on my bed and went to the third floor and rooftop to sit and relax my mind in preparation for the chaos of the night.

That was my favorite room in the house to write. Nothing beat being on the third floor, feeling the sun on my skin within the privacy of my rooftop. The neighbors could not really peek in even if they wanted as the house was the highest on the block. In the area I had a big beige couch and a coffee table—which doubled as a working table for me to write my novels—that were surrounded by floor-to-ceiling windows and a skylight that let all the natural light in.

The other half of the area was more of an open concept and featured a retractable roof. It was my favorite place to entertain guests. A bar grill combo was off to the side, and a jacuzzi was located at the other end.

Keisha and I spent many weekends there, sometimes joined by Iris and Amelia, enjoying the view and the jacuzzi. We shared our dreams, hopes, and disappointments under both the sun and the moonlight. The memories we had created were priceless.

I had also purchased the lot across from my house, to keep my view intact. My brother had called me spoiled, but I had worked too hard to deprive myself of anything less than my dream home. My favorite thing to do was to stay in this glass room while it rained or snowed. The calm and tranquility I felt was worth every penny.

I opened my laptop and went straight to my novel, with Penny cuddled into a ball next to me. It was my dirty little secret.

Since before high school, I had begun writing romance novels, inspired by my avid reading of Harlequin books. After I graduated college, I had submitted a few of my books to a publisher, under a pen name, to no avail. I had always wanted to be a lawyer, but my passion for becoming a published author would have been quite tempting if I had been able to lend a book deal.

By my third year of law school, I had refined my style a lot. Between the creative writing skills I had perfected in college and newly obtained legal writing skills, I then decided to give it a try again and self-publish my stories. I eventually got some traction and finally became a successful indie author.

I hadn't told anyone other than selected friends and my brother, who had always been my biggest supporters and unofficial editors. I had been shocked when I realized that my books were fairly successful, and I got to making well into the six digits every year just from my writing.

My schedule was limited due to my daytime job as an attorney, so I attempted to publish at least two books a year. It helped that I had finished manuscripts I could perfect rather than starting new ones each time. My most fond and most successful project had been the book I had written with Amelia's stories the year before, using journal entries she had drafted. Alejandro, Amelia's fiancé, had made all of us sign non-disclosure agreements before Amelia let me read those "fictional" journals.

Once I read them, I understood why. Alejandro and Amelia's love was beautiful, inspiring even, and I couldn't help but be enraptured by the way they looked at one another. But they had met under quite... unique circumstances. Circumstances that had made the fiction book beat all the records my other still successful writings had reached, even securing me a seat on best-sellers lists as a fan favorite.

When I first started at my father's company, I was working crazy hours, trying to get Motor Holmes the much-needed progress it so deserved. As I had signed the contract with Listen Inc., I was sliding into more of a nine-to-five schedule so I could focus on my writing.

My agent had been so understanding and had gone above and beyond to protect my real identity, but that also caused some limitations, as I couldn't fully tap into social media and interact with my readers on a personal level.

But I didn't want to choose one career over the other yet, so that was the best I could do. My hope was to one day be able to reveal my identity and enjoy both jobs I loved so much.

I typed to my heart's content, loosing myself in the story. My life, my friends, had always being in some part or aspects of my stories. Through reading and writing, I found an escape, traveled to different places. The lives I was able to experience through letters on a page were priceless to me. I always joked that I had lived many love stories, because I was always falling in love with the perfected male protagonists that did no wrong in the stories I wrote on paper.

In high school and in college, my avid reading kept me away from boyfriends and real-life romances. I tried not to compare my fictional men with the real-life ones, but it was hard for me to be enthusiastic about anyone I met. I could simply go home and write myself someone who made me feel alive. And more importantly, someone who wouldn't break my heart—at least, not without putting it back together at the end.

My thoughts wandered back to the man from the night before. How nice his hands felt around me, how great he smelled.

I felt desire course through me at the memory. Part of me regretted not writing my number on that piece of paper. But that was the point of a one-night stand, right? Whether we had one or not, the idea wasn't that we kept seeing each other. So, I chased the thought away and focused on my story.

CHAPTER 3

Before I knew it, Keisha was at the door with her weekender bag, carrying all her things to get ready. She had also brought a bottle of Taittinger with her, as was our tradition. I took Keisha through the formal living and dining room. We headed to the second half of the floor, to the enormous state-of-the-art kitchen.

Keisha dropped her bag in the kitchen by the back staircase while I slid the bottle in the fridge to chill.

I played some music as we made our way to the big, comfy sofa. Penny joined us, not wanting to miss out on the fun.

"I never stop admiring this house!" sighed Keisha as she petted my cat.

"You were here yesterday," I laughed.

Keisha wasn't wrong, though. I had a very specific style; most of my furniture was either beige, ivory, or other earthy colors, all mostly from a combination of Pottery Barn and Antique Farmhouse.

I loved light colors, and the only infusion of strong colors was the artwork I collected through my travels, fresh flowers, or the decoration pillows and curtains, depending on the season.

"I know, but you and Iris did such a good job with it."

"Thank you. I was mostly a very annoying client for over a year while she made my dream come true," I admitted.

I had Iris's firm on retainer as my ongoing interior designers; they came to my house a few times a year to change the decor a bit, and I was always so pleased with the result.

"I remember," teased Keisha, "but it paid off. You have so much space, and it just feels so peaceful here all the time. Not to mention that your so-called basement has a gym, sauna, steam room, and game room. You have what, like, three living rooms? Two laundry rooms and so much outdoor space! This house is a mini resort! I can't wait for all the parties you promised to throw this year."

"Me neither," I admitted. "I can finally slow down now."

Every room was basically an office I used depending on my mood, either to write or for my day job, so it all had to be perfect. And I wanted to spend as much time as I could in the little escape I had built for myself.

"Girl, you deserve it. You worked your ass off to be where you are. And it was so smart of you to build new, and in Bronzeville."

"Well, no way I could afford to have this house in, say, Lincoln Park. It would cost probably three times the price and would have been a heck of a lot smaller. And with the government giving me a good price on the lot for being a resident, it was just a no brainer. And as you know, the rich get richer in this country, so I leveraged my job in big law to get preferential interest rates. With all the discount it still came to a bit above a million bucks, but still."

"Yes, but it's already worth so much more! Do you think you'd ever sell?"

"To go where? I'm attached to my little paradise. My offer to sell you the lot across still applies, though, for when you're ready," I reminded her. "It's zoned for residential use, so I can't even build a community park there. You are the only one I would let obstruct my view," I added half-jokingly.

"I know," said Keisha, giving me a hug. "And I am oh so honored," she joked. "But seriously, one day I might take you up on that. My apartment is nice, but when I see your rooftop, I get inspired." She grinned.

I knew what she meant. She loved the space I had but for now fancied her skyline view lot more. I couldn't blame her.

About twenty minutes later, we got up when Karla called me to say she and her assistant had arrived. I opened the door for them, and all four of us headed to my bedroom, my furry ball of love on our toes.

Keisha had opted for a long white dress with no sleeves and a low back, flustering her toned shoulders. She looked like a princess, and my heart swelled a little at seeing my best friend so dolled up.

I paired my burgundy dress with gold pendant earrings my parents had gifted me for my birthday last year and kept my neck bare. Karla had tied my hair up and loosened a few fringes out to frame my oval face and slightly defined jaw. I had coupled my outfit with open toe gold Louboutins.

"You look like so pretty," complimented Keisha with tenderness in her eyes.

"You, too!" I exclaimed. "Though, I'm a bit nervous," I confessed. "My dad said he has a big announcement to make tonight. I think, or I hope, he puts me on the board."

"I am sure he will. It's the least he can do!"

"I really hope so," I added as I grabbed my phone to order a car. "It's all I want. And I want to be an officer, of course."

I took one last look at my face before we headed to the car, admiring Karla's contouring work, the light gold and green eyeshadow she had put on my eyelids, and the sheer nude to my lips.

When we finally got to the house, I grabbed my purse with trembling hands. I imagined this was how brides felt on their wedding day, and well, for me, there was no bigger event than when I celebrated my professional success.

The Uber came to a stop as a valet opened the door and helped us out. My parents had clearly spared no expense. I admired the meticulously arranged front yard and the heated lanterns along the walking path, guiding guests to the main double oak doors.

A doorman held the door for us as we got up the stairs. We were greeted by a server offering glasses of champagne neatly arranged on a tray. I was amazed at how elegant my childhood home looked.

It wasn't that it was bad before, but I had always associated that house with comfort, a place that was lived in. My mother had disposed of the old multi-colored crystal chandelier that I always hated and replaced it with an elegant iron and clear glass one in the foyer, along with adding some tasteful pottery decorations to the staircase.

I loved that house and remembered thinking that it looked like a castle when we had moved in all those years before.

Eventually, I realized that my parent's new home was the smallest and oldest on the block, but it was our little piece of heaven and vastly larger than the small space we were used to.

It was a nice three-bedroom house with an office space, a small library, a large living and dining area, and a nice big yard. Perfect for a family of four.

Over the years, the light-yellow walls had been repainted in a cream ivory color. The old furniture had also been upgraded to feature a vintage blue gray couch, cream accent chairs, and a nice oak coffee table.

The thick light tan drapes were slightly embroidered, covering see-through beige curtains. The rug was the same light green and white rug I remembered playing on, but it had been deep cleaned. The fireplace I loved sitting in front of was still there, just repainted in distressed white, covering the red bricks that had made the place look more rustic.

Iris had been hired to redecorate my parents' house after they saw the amazing work she did on mine, and as usual, she had done an exquisite job.

The bookshelf was still there, displaying all the books my family had devoured over the years. I noticed of course that the books had been rearranged, and my Harlequin collection was no longer on display. I assumed she hid them in their private library. I pursed my lips, imagining my mother realizing that I had read all those adult books when I was in high school.

I snapped out of my daze as we made it to the back of the house. Both of us paused to admire the room. It appeared that most of the guests had already arrived. I couldn't help but stand in awe at the sights before me—the long gowns and tuxes filling the room. An energy filled the space, one that you typically felt walking into a gala, but instead it was my parents' house.

Heading toward the kitchen, I soaked in the gorgeous updates made to the area. Iris and I had helped my mother upgrade all the cabinets from oak brown to off-white with glass panes, similar to what had been done for my house.

My attention was instantly captured by the dancing room right before me. They seemed to have gotten rid of the nook and the old lounge beige sofa that used to be there. Now there were guests talking and enjoying festivities. The kitchen island had been transformed into a bar, and there was another one by the bay windows opening on the wide patio they built the year before, that was also part of the entertainment space.

"You girls certainly know how to make an entrance; everyone is looking at you," said my mother from behind us.

"Mom!" I squealed, spinning around. I barely recognized her. She was in the gorgeous emerald-green gown with cap sleeves that cascaded to the floor that I had helped her pick for the party. The dress flattered her curves, and the plunging neckline emphasized the ample chest I had inherited from her. "I think they are looking at you. You look amazing!"

"Thank you, darling." My mother beamed quietly as she did a slight curtsy. "All thanks to you."

"You look like a queen, Mrs. Holmes," complimented Keisha as she gave my mom a hug.

"No, you do, my dear. You girls look so elegant; Karla really did an amazing job and those gowns, just precious!"

"Oh, don't cry, Mom!" I begged as I saw tears well up in my mother's beautiful round black eyes.

I loved this woman to the moon and back. I had grown up a daddy's girl, but when I started college, my relationship with my mother had bloomed into a beautiful friendship that I never thought possible.

My mother had given all that she was to help my dad and to put me and my brother through school, working double shifts when my dad was getting his degree to make sure there was always food on the table and her kids were provided for. I had made it my mission to pamper her because she was the rock that held our family together.

She was beautiful at 5'6" with gorgeous brown skin. Her hair had always been ear-length and permed. And while her looks were always something to admire, it was her passionate laugh and her incessant care for her children that truly blew you away.

My features were a good mix of my parents, but my gaze and facial expressions were my mother's. We had been told by family and friends that we had the same intense and expressive stare, and I enjoyed seeing my mother graciously coming of age.

I took her to the esthetician, paid for her to start a facial regimen as well as multiple salon sessions for her nails and her hair because I was finally in a place where I could treat my mother and pay her back for all the sacrifices she made for me growing up.

That precious girl time we spent together got us from being sheriff and prisoner to a wonderful mother and daughter friendship.

"I am the luckiest man in the world," announced my father as he put a hand on my mother's hips and grabbed me with the other.

"Hi, Dad," I said, hugging him back. "Nice tux."

"Thanks," he said joyfully. "It's growing on me."

"You should have seen him fighting with the bowtie this afternoon," teased my mother as she glanced at her husband, her love for him undeniable.

I always cherished witnessing how those two looked at each other. Their love was of the intensity I read about in books, a dedication that knew no limits, no boundaries.

My parents had been high school sweethearts, and my passion for romance had started right there, inspired by the little gestures I watched my parents have towards one another, like my mom doing my dad's hair and my dad bending in the middle of a restaurant to help my mother fix her shoe.

When I was in law school, I thought I had found my soulmate... until my heart had been broken in a thousand pieces, and I vowed to never try as hard again.

"You girls look so beautiful," complimented my dad without ever taking his eyes off his wife.

He was a six-foot-tall proud, slightly boisterous man of French descent, with a strong straight nose, thick, slightly wavy gray hair, green eyes, and thin lips that always pursed like he had a secret he didn't want to share.

My father never really enjoyed wearing anything other than his jeans and well-ironed work shirts. It took everything I had to get him to go for a tux, but when I half-jokingly threatened to not invite the CEO of Listen Inc. if he didn't suit up, he caved. After all, this event was to celebrate the partnership and the success that was yet to come, and he didn't want to not look the part.

My mouth softly quirked as I noticed my father's close shave and a nice haircut, a reminder that he visited a good barber shop yesterday. He had texted me with a million selfies as he tried to show me the result. I had to admit that while he still looked like my dad, the distinguished appearance he bore was that of the accomplished businessman I knew him to also be.

He wore the tux well—courtesy of Eric—with his small eyes gleaming with happiness. I felt like I could burst of joy and contentment in this very moment.

"Is Eric back already?" asked Keisha in a small voice.

I held back the urge to roll my eyes. I gave Keisha a death stare that she pretended not to see.

"His flight was delayed, but he should be here within the hour," answered my mother, directing her understanding gaze towards Keisha.

Eric was a touchy conversation between my friend and me. I knew they had a history. I did not trust that my brother wouldn't break Keisha's heart again, and I wanted to protect her from Eric's playboy ways.

We all turned and positioned ourselves as one of the photographers documenting the evening asked for a picture.

"Thank you," I voiced when he was done.

"Ah," said my father as he strolled past me, distracted by a newcomer. "I am so happy you made it!"

I saw Keisha's mouth drop open, so I swirled around to see who my father was referring to.

I felt the blood leave my cheeks as I was face to face with none other than Jake Cunningham.

"Philip, nice to see you."

"Oh, this is my daughter Chloe," introduced my dad as he let go of Jake's shake.

"Chloe, nice to see you again," Jake said, a smirk taking over his lips as he leaned in for a handshake.

I reached a hand out to meet his, praying that it was not wobble due to the nerves that were erupting inside of me.

"You know each other?" asked my father, his gaze bouncing back and forth between the two of us.

"Yes," answered Jake without taking his eyes off mine, a challenge in his stance, "we randomly met at a bar."

I was regaining control of my emotions and raised my right eyebrow to Jake in defiance.

"Glad to hear it!" cheered my father.

"Nice to see you again," I said as I removed my hand from his grasp and took a slight step backwards.

"I'm Keisha," said my friend as she shook Jake's palm, standing close to me in support.

"Jake Cunningham," he answered.

"And what an honor to be hosting you this evening," my mother enthusiastically stated as she took Jake in her arms, hugging him tightly.

"Always a pleasure, Yasmin," he answered, returning my mother's gesture.

My mouth dried out as I was quickly processing the less-than-ideal situation. A couple of days ago, my parents told me about a person who would be involved in the future of Motor Holmes…. that they were eager to introduce me to at the party. I didn't realize they were referring to someone they seemed to have a personal relationship with.

"How do you know each other?" I asked my parents, already fearing the worst.

"Jake is an old friend and a new investor in our company. Remember we spoke about him last week?" explained my father.

"Ah, I see," I managed to utter, stopping myself from clarifying that the first time I heard of this "investor" was Thursday when my dad called me from the airport on his way back to Chicago.

"It would be great if you could tell Jake a bit about your experience with us," offered my father. "He is very interested in hearing about how you managed to unilaterally get us Listen Inc. as a customer."

"Of course," I acquiesced as I forced a smile and avoided Jake's gaze. "I'll be glad to talk to Jake. I'll have my secretary reach out and put something on our calendars next week," I proposed as I finally dared to look into those now clearly blue eyes that made me feel so on edge.

I ignored my dad's frown, clearly discontent with my coldness towards his guest. I noticed my mother basically swooning as she gazed at Jake.

Great, my mother had a crush. Which I knew I would hear about later, because my mother could never pass up an opportunity to present potential suitors she had found for me.

"Keisha and I have to go welcome a few of our friends, but we'll talk later I'm sure," I said as I grabbed Keisha's arm. "Pleasure to see you again, Jake."

"Pleasure's all mine," he answered as he slightly bended his head to the left.

We rolled out of there slowly, trying to avoid running as best we could.

"Fuck!" I cursed when we made it to the bar at the end of the room. "Please tell me this is not happening!"

"Hm, well, how were you supposed to know?" offered Keisha, attempting to make me feel better.

"My dad told me about some guy who wanted to invest, but I didn't really have much more information than that, which I found weird, but I haven't managed to get a hold of him since to get more details," I explained as I nervously rubbed my forehead.

"Two shots of tequila," said Keisha when it was our turn to order.

"He must have known who I was," I declared, fire likely coming out of my eyes. "This can't just be a coincidence!"

"Let's not jump to conclusions," cautioned Keisha as she handed me one of the shots the bartender brought us. She thanked the bartender as she gently pushed me out of the line. "If you didn't know his name, why would he know yours?"

"You heard what my dad said," I insisted. "He knows that I am the daughter of Philip Holmes. What are the odds that he invested in the company without Googling me or going on LinkedIn? From what I understand, my father was considering selling him a good number of shares to entice him to join us. He must have investigated all of us before making any investment."

I stopped talking when I caught Jake staring at me from across the room as he sipped on his drink, my father chatting with him enthusiastically. I swallowed hard, unable to bring myself to look away.

For a minute, I forgot there were people around us. All I could see was that tall man in a perfectly tailored black tux, with his straight jaw, his blond hair neatly arranged backwards, who was now giving his full attention to my father.

I remembered his inhibiting smell mixed with scotch from when we danced together. Rather, when I shamelessly rubbed myself on him.

I remembered the rush of desire when I felt his strong torso under my fingers. I remembered those eyes looking at me, frowning, when we had made it to his place.

And those lips— the warmth I felt when they had grazed mine.

I felt my mouth dry and my heart beat faster.

"Are you okay?" inquired Keisha.

"Yes, I'm fine," I lied, turning to look at her.

"It's not a big deal," tried to reassure Keisha.

"No, but he will always have whatever the hell happened over my head. And the audacity, telling my parents we met at a bar. It's like he was testing me!"

"Oh no," whispered Keisha, peering past me.

I spun on my heels to follow her gaze. Jake had gotten rid of his drink, and he was walking towards us, his eyes fixated on me, ignoring the admiring looks he was getting from the crowd.

My glare was laced with both panic and admiration as he made his way through the throng of people. He looked like a lion heading towards a prey he knew had no way to escape the inevitable.

Jake stopped right in front of me. His intense stare left me feeling like I was on the spot. I could feel everyone staring at us, and all I wanted to do was melt into the ground and disappear, but I knew he wouldn't let me go anywhere.

I was regretting my attire; I had dressed for attention tonight, but I would have given gold in this moment to be invisible.

"Care to dance?" he asked as he offered me his hand.

My parents were off to the side, where I could see them observing our interaction. I hesitated, but I knew I had no choice. Unable to speak, I accepted the hand he offered as he dragged me to the dance space on the covered patio.

Jake took us to the middle of the dance floor and stopped, putting his right arm around my waist, without letting go of my right hand. I tried to focus on the Michael Bublé song that was playing from the various ceiling speakers, but I was keenly aware of his hand splayed out on my lower back.

We swayed in silence for a minute as I was starting to enjoy moving at the rhythm of Lost, one of my favorite songs, letting myself enjoy his smell. I calmed down a little bit, the moment softening my fears. I dared to look up, meeting his eyes.

"Hi," he whispered.

"Hi," I answered, more nervous than I would care to admit, a shy smile on my lips.

"I hope you made it home okay," he added, taking me by surprise.

"I did. Thank you for the toothbrush," I replied, making an effort to hold his gaze and disguise my discomfort and fascination.

He was teasing me. And I couldn't say I wasn't enjoying it.

"You are most welcome," he answered, his eyebrow slightly raised.

"I have to admit, this was the last place I expected to see my one-night stand," I dared, unable to resist.

"Is that what that was?" he asked, pulling a bit away to meet my gaze better.

"Was it not?" I asked, searching his mysterious blue eyes for an answer.

"You don't remember, do you?"

I wanted to scratch that know-it-all attitude from his face, but I coughed lightly instead.

"There might be some blank spots," I finally admitted, unable to lie.

Jake let out a hearty laugh that I wasn't expecting. I clenched my jaw, trying to keep a composed face after feeling a bit humiliated.

"Well," continued Jake, "nothing happened."

"Why were my clothes not on me then?"

"You stripped out of them." My eyes grew a bit, but he took no sympathy on me. "I don't tend to sleep with women who can barely walk or keep their eyes open."

I felt my cheeks get warm with embarrassment. "Lucky me," I mocked.

"Yes, you were." The warm green hues in his eyes started to turn to blue gray, making my body turn cold. "Any other man could have taken you home last night, and you wouldn't have been able to do anything to defend yourself if it came to that. It was reckless of you to drink that much, and it was reckless of you to leave in that state with a stranger. So, I took you with me."

Jake was frowning, clearly judging me. Who did he think he was talking to me like that?

"So, you did know who I was, or did you come to my rescue solely out of the kindness of your heart?"

Jake remained silent for a few seconds, a daring look in his eyes. I couldn't tell if he was getting irritated or if he was amused. It didn't really matter.

"I eventually recognized you," he admitted.

"And why didn't you say anything?" I demanded.

"I thought the conversation would be better suited for when you were sober," he jabbed.

My pride had had enough of that man judging me as if I was just an irresponsible child. I wanted to tell him that I had never done something like that before, precisely for the reasons he had pointed out, considering there was nothing I hated more than not being in control, but I did not owe him an explanation.

"Well, glad we had it," I said as the song was finally ending. I pulled my hand out of his and took a step back. "Thank you for the dance, Mr. Cunningham. I do hope you enjoy the rest of your evening."

I pivoted and exited the dance floor without looking back. I could feel his gaze burning the back of my neck, but I wasn't going to glance behind me. I had spotted Keisha, who moved away from the group she was chatting with to meet me halfway.

"He's a bastard" I said between my teeth, my chest rapidly rising and falling.

Keisha handed me her glass so I could drink some champagne and try to calm down.

"Scolding me like I'm some fucking child for 'being drunk with a stranger' or whatever."

"Wow."

"Yes. But at least we didn't sleep with each other; there was a reason I didn't remember, can't recall something that never happened."

"Well, that's good, right? Especially since it sounds like he will be around?" she pressed.

"Yes, that's true, just my luck." While I should have been glad I didn't have to worry about a one-night stand I couldn't remember, there was a part of me that wished I could finally say I did something reckless for myself.

"Do you think he will tell your dad?" Keisha wondered.

"No, I don't think so. He already would have, I assume. And since apparently nothing happened, what is there really to tell? I'm an adult, and I have the right to be as *reckless* as I damn well please."

Keisha's laughter calmed me a bit.

"Enough about me. Are you having a good time?"

She nodded. "I am. Good food, good booze. What else can I ask for?"

I knew but erred on the side of diplomacy. "Did Eric make it?"

"Huh? No, not yet. Not that I can tell anyways," said Keisha, looking away.

I did not push further; I didn't want to make Keisha sadder than she clearly was at the thought of not seeing Eric.

Both of us turned when we heard the sound of cutlery rapping against glass. My parents were standing on a small, elevated space by the living room, my dad lightly tapping a fork to the side of his glass to call everyone's attention towards him.

We headed to the front of the group that was amassing.

I spotted Jake as soon as I got there but pretended he didn't exist. My father gestured to me so I could join him on the small podium. I took my place next to my mother. I was surprised to see my father also call Jake, who planted himself on my father's right side.

Kyle had also joined us on the podium without being asked. He positioned himself next to me and wrapped his hand around my waist. I had somehow completely forgotten about the existence of my ex-boyfriend all night.

I stepped away from him to signal for him to remove his hand, but there was only so much I could do without being too rude or pushing my mother off the stage.

"Where have you been hiding all night?" he whispered in my ear.

"Just having a great time," I answered, a tense grin on my lips as I looked into Kyle's beady amber eyes.

Kyle looked good, the tux making his 5'11" slim body look denser. He cleaned up nicely—slicked his wavy brown hair back more than usual. His thin lips gave him a serious look. His usually very light skin was slightly tanned and red, I assumed from his trip to Florida. It still stinged a bit.

"Like what you see?" he teased.

I directed my attention to my father, who was starting his speech, not wanting to engage in a conversation that wouldn't do anyone any good.

"Good evening, everyone, and thank you for joining us today. I know that you would much prefer to enjoy each other's company than hear me talk, so I will make this quick." He scored a soft laughter from the crowd. "When I created this company twelve years ago..."

"Who is this guy?" asked Kyle.

I bent my head to see his face, and he was staring at Jake.

"New investor, so I'm told," I answered.

"And you were already dancing with him?"

"Can we not do this now?" I muttered, rolling my eyes and trying to focus back on my dad.

"... and I am now so glad that my daughter finally transitioned from big law to join us," continued my father, his head turned in my direction. A server came to give us champagne glasses as the rest of the room was also being served. "Thanks to her hard work, we now have a partnership with Listen Inc., that will take us to success we had one only dreamed of.

"Thank you Mark for your trust in us" he said, lifting his glass to the tall, well-built man with gray hair and beady eyes who was standing in the front, the CEO of Listen, "and thank you to my amazing daughter for your passion for and dedication to our success," he said as he raised his glass to me.

The crowd applauded as they all took a sip. I was a bit embarrassed, but I smiled and nipped at my drink as my father continued. "I also wanted to take the opportunity to introduce you all to Jake Cunningham our new VP, COO, and chairman of the board!"

CHAPTER 4

I STOOD THERE FROZEN as the crowd applauded, suddenly feeling a rush of cold climb through me. I couldn't believe what I had just heard, and neither could Kyle, who I felt slightly jerk next to me. I was directing all my energy into maintaining my forced smile and fake applause as I chugged what was left in my glass. I looked at Keisha, doing my best to concentrate on a friendly face. I went through the motions as my mother and father hugged me as if this was a happy moment.

No, I focused my rage on Jake, who stood behind my dad. He hadn't taken his eyes away from me and Kyle for even a second. I finally was released from my father's arms and hurried off the podium to join Keisha before I had to congratulate Jake, attempting to smile as if the events of the evening were of no surprise to me.

My body felt ice-cold, with anger and confusion coursing through me, leaving a sour taste of betrayal in my mouth. How could my father praise me for basically setting up the success of the company while giving the vacant board seat and an officer position to this stranger? He had also made him his second hand by making him the VP.

The shareholders and the directors of Motor Holmes must have elected Jake on the board and as an officer and I, the general counsel, had been left out of the loop. I hadn't even been aware that what I assumed had been a special meeting had been called and the votes had taken place. They could add a position for me, but it wouldn't have much meaning.

My imposter syndrome flared back up to the surface, making it hard to breathe. Maybe they didn't trust I could do the job, so they looked outside and hired someone they thought was better suited for the position. Maybe I was aiming too high, climbing too fast for their taste, so even after I scored them the best contract the company had ever seen, they still felt like I didn't have what it took.

I inhaled a few breaths and released them slowly to try to control my heartrate. I couldn't let anyone see that I was destroyed, least of all him. So I composed myself and threaded to Marc, the CEO of Listen Inc.

"Thank you so much for coming," I said.

"My pleasure. Sorry for being late; my flight back to Chicago this morning got delayed, and it messed everything up." he explained as he shook the hand I offered.

"No worries at all. We are just happy to have you, and I look forward to working together."

"Thank you, Chloe, me too. You are a great advocate for your father's business, and I hope he understands that."

"I think he does; we just have to do some restructuring, but you know, it's a work in progress," I forced myself to say.

Marc was clearly a bit thrown off as he probably also thought that after my success, I would be promoted to the vacant seat. I had been honest with him in terms of what I wanted my future at Motor Holmes to look like in our negotiations, and he supported me.

"I think I am going to head back home; it's been a long day for me," announced Marc after we positioned ourselves for a few pictures. "But I will see you for our lunch on Wednesday?"

"Yes, I will be there. Let me walk you out," I offered.

As Mark and I reached the exit, my father caught up to us.

"Mark, thank you for joining us this evening," he said as he shook Mark's hand.

"Of course, and you have a beautiful home."

"Thank you, Mark." He beamed.

"I am on my way out, but I assume you will join us for the lunch on Wednesday?"

"I should," answered my dad.

"Great, see you both on Wednesday then. Have a good night."

"Same to you," I said as he went outside.

"Glad he could make it," added my dad.

"We need to talk, Dad," I said after a moment, turning a bit to face him.

He looked at me like he saw the fire in my eyes. He hesitated, but he headed towards his office, and I followed him and shut the door behind me.

He rounded his desk, as he gestured to the chair, inviting me to sit.

"I'm fine," I pointed out as I stopped by the desk.

"Do you want something to drink?" he offered.

"No, thank you," I said stiffly.

The room was gorgeous, with built-in bookshelves from wall to wall, and a thick oak desk in the middle. My father's chair was a brown leather ergonomic chair I had helped him pick a few years ago, while my mother had chosen the two light brown chairs he used for guests. On the right, he had a standing bar, with various whiskeys decanting.

"You're upset," he noted.

I didn't answer, I just stared at him with all the indignation I felt boiling inside of me. I knew he wasn't very comfortable with silence.

He sighed, "I know you're mad. Please just sit, so I can explain."

"This is not the most comfortable dress—" My voice was steady but shook a bit from the rage that was building inside me. "And I'm sure your explanation will be brief, but I still have to ask... Why did you and the other shareholders give *him*—a stranger—the board position that you promised me? And why did the executive position go along with it?" I asked, still standing, my fingers clenched around the back of the chair in front of me.

"I had to. I didn't have a choice."

"What are you talking about? Did he lend you money or something?"

"No, not exactly. Listen, Chloe," he started as he approached me. "I will make it up to you in time, I swear, you just have to trust me. It's better this way."

"You could update the bylaws, add another director, I don't—"

"It's better this way, my darling, at least for now. Your time will come," he firmly interrupted.

"You haven't told me anything. Is he forcing you? Who is he? Why is he even investing at a point where we don't really need any capital?"

"No one is forcing anything, Chloe. In order for the expansion requirements to be met, to fulfill the requests from Listen Inc., we will need an influx of money. We need to go to market with the new e-axle as soon as possible, before Green Mile and Co., one of our competitors, can try to overstep us as they always do."

"We have a line of credit with the bank, Dad. I don't understand why you would bring in another substantial investor at this point in the game, and without consulting me. Why not just ask Eric? And we are so ahead with development of the new e-axle, they wouldn't be able to catch-up with us even if they wanted to.

We have the patents, we have the know-how, they don't. With the additional patent application we are preparing to file, there is no way they have the time to produce a competitive product, Dad."

"Chloe, I just ask that you be patient and trust me, just... trust me. I know what I am doing."

"And you can't tell me more than that?" I pressed.

"No, I can't, as there is nothing more to tell. Please know this is for the best, and I have nothing but your best interest at heart."

We remained silent for a painful second.

Finally, I said, "I see. Okay, well, there is nothing left to discuss." My eyes stung with frustrated tears.

"Just give me some time," begged my father in a deeper tone as I walked toward the door. "I know you want to be on the board and transition into a dual GC officer role, sweetie, and I know you deserve it. Just give me some time."

I stopped, my teeth gritting, unable to stay mad when I could spot a string of pain and desperation in my father's tone.

"Fine, Dad. I trust you, but I wish you would have confided in me. I can help with whatever it is, but you already know that. So, I'll try to wait for you to be ready to talk."

He looked relieved at my words. "Thank you, darling. I knew I could count on you. But there is nothing to worry about. This is just a new strategy I'm exploring."

I avoided eye contact, as I was still upset, and still utterly confused about this turn of events.

I swung the door open, and we both headed back to the party room. Jake was the first person I spotted; his presence seemed to take over the room, and my treacherous eyes were immediately drawn to him.

Hatred for the man filled every fiber of my being. I did not trust him. I would figure out what his game was and why my father suddenly wanted him in the company when I had never heard of him.

Jake had noticed my entrance, and he now was staring at me with a serious look on his face. I rolled my eyes and decided to look for Keisha.

I caught sight of her by the bay windows, talking to a man I didn't know. That was when I also noticed my brother Eric, standing by the bar, gawking at them as if he was about to jump and kill someone.

I enjoyed seeing Eric clearly jealous as Keisha burst out in laughter at something the man had whispered in her ear.

I strolled towards Eric. He was wearing a custom-fit dark tux with silk, his black curls loosely combed back. He was the typical tan, tall, and handsome man that girls fell in love with in all of two seconds. His black hair was curlier than mine, and he had inherited our father's green eyes.

"What has you so troubled, brother?" I asked as I grabbed his arm.

He was so distracted that it took him a second to realize I was talking to him.

"Sis!" he said, giving me a hug. "How have you been?"

"Never better," I lied. "Just enjoying our parents' lavish party for a few more minutes before I head home. I didn't think you'd make it here tonight."

"Me neither, but here I am, just in time it would seem," he said, jaw tight, looking at Keisha.

While I felt bad for him, he was the one who missed out on his chance with her.

"How's work going?" I asked, trying to distract him.

"Never better. I have a big trial coming up in the seventh circuit actually, so I'll be coming home more often in a few months."

Although Eric has amassed millions, thanks to the sale of his startup, he still preferred to dedicate his life to his work, often spending every waking hour in his office or in the courtroom.

That also meant we didn't get to see him very often. Something my mother was not fond of. I wanted more for my brother, too.

"That's great, mister big-shot litigator," I teased.

"Hey, I'm not the one who just scored a multimillion-dollar contract," he teased back with a smile.

"For what that's worth—"

"Hey," said Eric as he grabbed my hand. "I heard the announcement when I walked in. I don't know what is going on in our father's head, but what he did tonight was pretty fucking stupid. Don't let it get to you."

"It just doesn't make sense," I huffed.

"Do you want me to talk to him? I'm a big-shot New York litigator after all," he joked in an attempt to erase the pain he likely saw in my eyes.

"No, no need. I'll figure it out. You have enough on your plate."

"The American dream," he remarked before we both burst in laughter.

Eric was inevitably back to brooding, as it seemed like Keisha and the man she was talking to were exchanging numbers.

"It's been a long day," said Eric with a sigh. He drowned the last of his Manhattan, and wincing, he set his glass down on the high top we were standing by. "I'll be here for a few more days, so let's grab lunch if we can?"

"Sounds good. Just text me," I said as Eric hugged me and rushed away, glancing towards Keisha one last time.

I never figured out what had transpired between them. Keisha and Eric had met during my college years when Keisha came to spend the summer with me in Chicago. Keisha and Eric eventually attended law school at Northwestern while I went to the University of Chicago.

One night, when Keisha rushed into my apartment in tears, she confessed her and Eric had slept together, that Eric had played with her and that she regretted it, but neither one of them ever gave me the full story.

Around that same time, I had found out that Danny, my law school boyfriend of two years, had been sleeping with other women behind my back too.

We had found solace in each other and inspired one another to find the strength to focus on our careers and not on men.

Keisha asked me not to interfere with their relationship—or lack thereof. She wanted to cut all ties with Eric and make a clean break after law school. She had accepted a job at an international law firm to move to London. In London, she got in a relationship with another classmate, but it didn't last.

Every time I tried to broach the topic either with Eric or with Keisha, I had been met with silence and anger from both sides.

I had called my brother names one time and for a while I could barely speak with him. I had accepted that it was none of my business eventually, but I hated that my brother had hurt one of my best friends.

Thankfully, my relationship with Keisha remained unchanged, and when she moved back to Chicago, she seemed to have forgotten about Eric.

That was until they briefly saw each other at my parents' house when Eric flew in for the holidays a couple of years ago. They had been cordial then but one could cut through the tension between them with a sharp knife every time they were around each other.

I came back from my deep thoughts when I caught a whiff of a citrus, lavender, and sandalwood combination that had invigorated me and filled me with desire just last night.

Why was it that my body seemed to react whenever *he* was near? I felt him behind me as he brushed past me to set his drink on the high-top in front of me. He then turned to face me.

"You're not going to congratulate me?"

I just stared at his face, trying to hold back the curse I would love to shout at him. He seemed quite aware he had taken something I wanted; I was sure of it. His smug stance was just some sort of twisted provocation.

"You don't seem very pleased," he added, his gaze burning a hole through my eyes.

"Well, I don't know you. My father doesn't tend to allow outsiders in his business. And yet, here you are."

"Your father is perhaps just doing what he thinks best for the company," he offered.

I remained silent as I stood there attempting to decipher what was exactly hidden within the depths of those sharp blue eyes. My mouth suddenly felt dry, and I swallowed to distract myself and looked towards Keisha for help. Keisha had noticed my desperate glance and dismissed the man she was distracted by before coming to my rescue.

"Are you ready to go?" she asked. And I couldn't have been more grateful that she could read my mind and saved me from an incredibly awkward moment. I wasn't sure how much longer I could hold back from saying something rude to Jake.

"Yes, I am. Have a good night, Mr. Cunningham," I said in Jake's direction with a strategic tone.

We restrained ourselves from sprinting to the door and instead slowly made our way through the crowd, saying our goodbyes to different groups, before finally heading out. When we couldn't take it any longer, we headed toward the exit.

Luckily, my father had arranged for his driver to take us home once we were ready to leave.

We spotted him pulling up and rushed to get inside the safety of the black SUV.

"Well, this was a shitty night," said Keisha, blankly staring at the street as we drove through the night.

"You don't say," I agreed, with that same blank stare, exhausted despite my mind going at 1000 miles per hour toward the unknown of what tomorrow would bring.

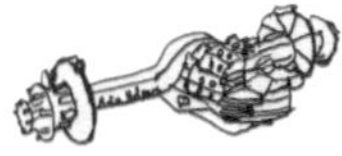

I dropped Keisha off at her apartment and was home about ten minutes after. I peeled my heels off and carried them straight to my bedroom. Then I undressed and slid into my cream comfy sweats in seconds.

Grabbing my makeup remover towelettes from my bathroom, I went up to the room on the third floor to relax and de-stress.

I opened the fridge, grabbed a box of coconut water, and started drinking straight from it. The crisp, refreshing taste of hydration after all the drinking of the past forty-eight hours was surely welcome. Once I calmed down, I grabbed a glass straw, dropped it in the box, and went to sit on the sofa, pulling a soft plushy blanket over me.

I grabbed the remote and started the show that currently filled my nights, but right now, it was just background noise. I was lost in my turbulent and confused thoughts.

This evening was supposed to be a celebration, and as happy as I was for my father's company, I felt like he had stabbed me in the back. It wasn't that I felt entitled, but I had been misled.

My father had always made clear he wanted me at the forefront of Motor Holmes. I had given up what could have continued to be a great law career at one of the most prestigious law firms in the world to work for him. And yet, when the opportunity presented itself, after I nailed the contract that would potentially change the future of his company, some stranger was rewarded with what I had been promised as mine.

I couldn't shake the feeling that something was off. My dad always maintained that Motor Holmes would remain a family business for as long as possible, even when I argued that eventually we would ideally go public, to keep up with the big players in the industry.

And yet, Jake seemed to come out of the woodwork and somehow my father trusted him enough to give him a prominent position in the company.

I had to consider that the board of directors could be behind the move. I figured they might have had concerns that my promotion—or rather evolution within my own family business—was premature, and the fact that I didn't have an MBA meant I wasn't qualified. I was convinced they just believed I was too young for the role.

My worst nightmare was people at the company thinking I was there due to nepotism. It wasn't common for someone to go straight from being a midlevel associate at a law firm to the general counsel of a company, even a mid-market company like that one.

But I had worked twice as hard as anyone in my team. While it was a bit awkward to be the supervisor of attorneys who had practiced law for longer than me, I did it with respect while exerting authority.

I had proven my worth, or so I thought, and was convinced that I had charmed the team through what I hoped had been seen as my acumen and proactive thinking, to be welcomed at the table of decision-makers. I wasn't so sure anymore.

To combat any thoughts of favoritism, I had accepted a lower salary, opting for stock instead, to show that I was serious and dedicated to the success of the company. Perhaps that was why my dad brought an outsider? Maybe he felt like people wouldn't take me seriously as a director or an officer? I shook my head, trying to get rid of those negative thoughts.

But I was nowhere near giving up. I was going to spend all the energy required to figure out what was going on, and what Jake Cunningham really wanted from my family.

CHAPTER 5

I HAD SPENT A good part of Sunday ignoring my father's calls. Instead, I spent the majority of the day sitting down in my sunroom, in my pajamas digging up any information I could on Jake Cunningham on the internet. Penny and I were wrapped in a heavy blanket as I enjoyed my favorite snap pea chips.

He was thirty-six years old, six years my senior, and was quite accomplished. It looked like he had worked for a hedge fund company for a few years while pursuing his MBA but then proceeded to run his own. Overly ambitious, even if I could relate.

He had graduated from Chicago Booth with his MBA. He seemed to have served on the board of a few companies, some of which were in the automotive sector.

His social life wasn't very well documented, but while I couldn't locate him on any social media other than his LinkedIn page, I did spot a few pictures of him at various charity galas.

I dropped my chips all over my laptop. In a few of those pictures, Jake was with *Lauren Holmes*—a beautiful aspiring Instagram model. Skinny. Blonde. Seemed like just his type.

And because she basically lived her life via her social media channels, there were tons of pictures of Jake and her attending all kinds of social gatherings, including Cubs games and friend gatherings.

While the bulk of the pictures dated from over a year ago, the latest was from just a few days ago. And the cherry on top of it all—Lauren was my cousin and childhood ex-best friend.

I snatched my iPhone to call Keisha.

"Hello?"

"Keisha, hey, are you busy?"

"No, not really. How is the snooping going?"

I informed Keisha earlier in the day that I was going to go down the rabbit hole to find out anything I could on Jake Cunningham, and she had been eager for an update.

"You will never guess who Jake has been dating... or could still be dating!" I shrieked.

"Please tell me!"

"Lauren!"

"Lauren!? Wait, no, crazy cuz Lauren?"

"Yep!" I chimed.

"Are you sure?"

"Well, he is all over her Instagram page. They have a bunch of pictures together."

"Wait, you're not joking, are you? Let me look."

"No, I swear. I don't follow her as you know, since I can't stand her, but it seems like they've known each other for at least over a year. Again, no clue if he knew that, but what are the odds?"

"Small world, Chloe, small world! How was it you never ran into them at family events? I know you guys hate each other, but she still attends those, right?"

"I mean, we see each other at family gatherings and such. I don't think she ever brought him, at least not to anything I've attended."

"Hm, well, maybe it's not serious?" she suggested.

"No clue. Doesn't matter to me frankly, but it's a little weird. Let me see what else I can dig up; I'll keep you updated."

"Sounds good. I'm about to go to dinner, so just text me."

I spent another hour looking for more, but not to find more information on his relationship with Lauren. No... I went full-blown stalker mode on Jake-in-a-tux images. I admired the way the suits were perfectly tailored to his body.

His shoulders and arms were clearly defined, and I remembered how firm they felt wrapped around me on the dance floor.

I couldn't help swiping back to that picture of him pulling on the sail of a yacht with his friends, with the air blowing through his hair, his suntan contouring his beautifully accentuated muscles. I felt a small fire grow in my belly the longer I stared at his pictures.

Lauren was in the background, and it was quite clear that she was at least a love interest. I was trying to ignore the small pinch I felt at the thought.

I wondered if he had just used me as a rebound. Or maybe it was intentionally set up by him to make my cousin jealous? I instantly felt sadness in the pit of my stomach. Growing up, Lauren was the sister I always wanted.

We were very close when we were younger. Although Lauren's father was only my father's half-brother, we saw her family quite often.

Unfortunately, Lauren's mother couldn't stand us being friends. She would constantly compare us. And while my parents tried to keep it amicable, my uncle couldn't get past it and sided with his wife. They made it clear to Lauren that she was to try to be more like me—which, granted, is a fucked-up thing to say—yet they would rub any accomplishment she achieved right in my face. Making sure to emphasize how Lauren always did it better.

Still, we tried to rise above the tension, and our friendship held strong for many years. Or so I thought, until the summer after I graduated summa cum laude from Columbia and was preparing my European trip while waiting for law school to start in the fall. Lauren was extending her break from school, after finishing her first two years of college.

I caught her pulling what looked like a few thousand dollars from an envelope in my dad's office and shove it in her purse before leaving the room.

At the time, knowing that Lauren was envious at times, and wanting to still help her, I had told my mother what I had seen in confidence, asking for advice as to what to do before my father noticed the money was gone. I had decided to just replace the sum with my savings, but as my mother and I went back to the dining room, all hell had broken loose. My father had realized his money had been stolen, and Lauren's mother had conveniently found the envelope in my bag as she knocked it over by *"accident."*

I was in shock, as it was the first time my father ever looked at me with anger and disappointment. Thankfully, my mother came to my defense, while also keeping her promise to cover for Lauren. She explained that she had given the money to me for my upcoming trip and forgot to tell my dad.

After my father apologized to me, the party resumed as normal. I confronted Lauren later, but she never admitted anything. So that was the end of our friendship. I refused to ever have anything to do with her—or her mother—ever again.

CHAPTER 6

I always hated Monday mornings, and this one was particularly stressful. I had barely slept, playing out all the possible scenarios that could come up this week at work over and over.

Attempting to distract myself, I decided a good workout would clear my head. After running on my Peloton treadmill for twenty minutes, I knew it was time to call it quits and get ready for work. I wanted to get there by 8:30 so I could ready myself for whatever was to come.

I refilled Penny's water, added some wet food on the side, and quickly got ready. I always made the time to cater to the feline that gave me so much unconditional love.

My routine was the same every morning. Whether I worked out or not, I always took the time to complete my ten-step skincare process.

Some called it overkill, but I preferred my skin healthy and hydrated. Face serums/lotion/eye cream, quality body lotion, exquisite perfume were all a must. Makeup was optional but a necessity on days I was preparing for war. And this Monday was certainly one of those days.

My hair was generally done the night before regardless of whether I was straightening it or letting my natural curls flow, but since I worked out this morning, I had to start all over and use my Dyson to straighten it and add some strategic curls to add body and levels to my cascade of honey brown hair.

I then moved on to picking an underwear set; thankfully they were all neatly arranged by my wonderful cleaning lady, and it was easy to find something silky to the touch, as well as sexy.

Even if no one could see my lingerie, it made me feel confident and empowered to look good even under my clothes.

I opted for a simple black Calvin Klein business dress with a matching suit jacket. I paired it with my nougat-colored So Kate's, and my Michael Kors Jane Large Pebbled Leather Tote Bag, in tan.

I added some shine with a simple stack of three thin necklaces, a pair of gold huggies, and three stack of delicate gold bands.

Pleased with the result, I called a car, put on my sunglasses, grabbed my Burberry coat, and met my Uber driver by my gate.

By the time I got to work, I had sent over ten emails from my laptop, setting up meetings and addressing small issues I was a little behind on.

That was the benefit of having another person drive one to work; I could commute, without the noise and discomfort of the train, while being able to kick off my workday and reduce stress in my morning. Once my Uber stopped in front of the fifty-floor high-rise where Motor Holmes Corp. occupied the thirty-seventh to the fortieth floors, I stepped out of the car quickly.

I said hi to the doormen as I rushed through the rolling doors, swiped my ID, and slid into one of the shiny gray elevators to the 39th floor. The workspaces were slick and white, with corner offices having a view of the lake. I loved our premises, as they were clean, classic, and let a lot of the natural light in, when there was any.

I turned left, swiped my ID again and swung the glass doors open. Instantly, I felt like all eyes were on me. I knew I was mostly imagining it, but I couldn't help but feel insecure. I rushed past the cubicles, to my corner office, and shut the door behind me. I didn't like the vulnerability that came with everyone knowing I didn't get the promotion.

There was one advantage of being GC, though... I got to sit in an executive office and didn't have to share a small space with someone else, as most of the staff and attorneys did.

While the previous GC didn't have a cubicle either, when I took the job, I requested that they turn one of the many meeting rooms they didn't use into my office. Nothing could beat the privacy of a closed door when needed, even with the open-door company policy.

I fired up my computer again, working through my emails as I sipped on the cup of black coffee that Margie, my secretary, set on my desk every morning.

Once again, I was thankful to be confined to the solace of my own space.

As I finally managed to focus on my tasks without thinking about Jake, my work phone rang.

"This is Chloe."

"Chloe, Jake Cunningham, how are you?"

I almost choked on my warm coffee, regretting answering the phone without looking at the caller ID.

"I'm good. How are you?"

"Great. Was connecting for our meeting today, I figured I could stop by at 11:45, you could give me tour of the space, and we could talk? I would have called earlier, but I've been at the tech training all morning."

I clenched my teeth, but I knew I couldn't avoid that unfortunate meeting. Sooner or later, I was going to have to pretend to at least treat the man with the professionalism and respect I applied towards the other directors and officers of Motor Holmes, even if it made bile rise in my stomach.

"That works. I assume you already have a badge, or do I need to issue you a temporary one for building access?"

I hoped that my sarcasm was obvious.

"I have everything I need," he confirmed.

"Perfect. See you at 11:45," I said, wanting to end the conversation.

"See you then."

I had to exercise every bit of self-control so as to not throw the phone across the room when I hung up. It wasn't nice to break company property, after all. I was thankful my father was traveling to Indiana for the day to meet with clients, as I could only handle one of them at a time.

For the next two hours, all I did was think of Jake, dreading having to interact with him again.

At 11:45 sharp, I heard a quick knock on my door. I tensed instantly. Before I was able to say anything he was in my office, in a sharkskin gray suit, a white shirt, and no tie. My spacious corner office with a lake view suddenly felt too small.

But I gritted my teeth and straightened up, forcing myself to appear as tall as possible in my beige leather chair. I placed my hands on the large thick glass table I used as a desk.

"Generally, one waits to be told to enter after a knock."

He remained in place, ignoring my comment, his hands in his pockets, admiring the lake-view behind me. After a few uncomfortable seconds of silence, he moved towards my very organized desk, positioning himself behind one of the pair of oatmeal-colored chairs on the other side.

He returned his attention to the room, his eyes trailing on my floor-to-ceiling bookshelf. I resisted the urge to hide behind my two Mac screens and stood up.

How dare he intimidate me in my own office!

He stopped his snooping and finally set his gaze on me.

"Nice office," he commented.

I raised my chin. "Thank you."

Somehow, I didn't feel like it was a compliment. It felt like he was judging me.

"Where is yours?"

"Upstairs. I haven't had a chance to go there yet."

"Of course."

He was sitting on the same floor as my father and the other directors, and some of the officers.

"Shall we?" I said as I walked to the door.

I took him around my floor, by the legal cubicles. We then proceeded to the executive floor, where I pointed him to my father's office and ignored his name on what was supposed to be my new office door. We then visited the gym and the cafeteria.

Between the tour and stopping for small talk with each other and with other employees, over an hour had passed.

Jake accompanied me back to my office. "Thank you for the tour."

"My pleasure," I said stiffly.

"And good job with the Listen Inc. transaction. Appreciated learning how you closed the deal."

"Of course." What that real praise, I wondered?

"I'd like to see the agreement and any other relevant document; can you email those to me?"

"Hm, sure, but why?" Of course it wasn't a compliment.

"Do I need a reason?"

"No, but I still assume you have one?"

Jake raised his eyebrows with a curious spark in his gaze. I stood my ground in defiance.

"It's an important contract for the company. I'd like to familiarize myself with the terms," he paused. "Is that a problem?"

"No, it's not." I swallowed hard. "I'll send it to you shortly. Anything else?"

"No, that's it. Thank you," he said as he left my office.

I resisted the urge to slam the door behind him. I suspected that he wanted to review my work, not for knowledge but to check if I didn't mess it up.

Who did he think he was, scrutinizing my work like that, especially for a done deal? But I couldn't let my pride get in the way.

I stomped to my desk and proceeded to send him the most professional email I could muster, while typing loudly on my keyboard, adrenaline changing my body temperature by the second.

———

Jake,

As requested, please find attached a zip file containing the closing book, with a TOC.

Best,

Chloe

———

Received. Will reach out if I have any questions.

Jake

Questions? About what exactly? I was fuming, but it wasn't worth it. I distracted myself as best I could by attending to actual work I had to do for the day. Jake Cunningham be dammed.

It was close to 7 p.m. when Kyle stopped by my office.

"Why is it that you are almost always the last one in the office?" he asked as he plopped in one of the chairs across from me.

Kyle was wearing a pair of jeans with a black work shirt and a black suit jacket.

"I just wanted to get ahead of some things. Makes for a much more pleasant week," I explained, "but I'm done now. Last email!"

"Good. Grab a drink with me? We don't have to go further than the bar downstairs," he added when he could tell I was about to object. "Come on," he pushed. "We are still friends, aren't we?"

I always had a soft spot for those light brown eyes and thin lips. It wasn't because I was in love with him. It was because I always saw Kyle as a sweet man, even if sometimes he acted too much like a child, like the world owed him something. He combed his fingers through his brown waves, trying to play cute.

"We are. Fine," I sighed. "Just one quick drink."

I shut my computer off, grabbed my items and slid them in my purse, and headed to the elevator banks with Kyle.

The elevator opened, with Jake inside, his right hand in his pocket, work bag in the left. He barely smirked at us, the expression not reaching his eyes.

"Hey, man," said Kyle casually.

"Hey," answered Jake, without taking his eyes off me.

I ignored them both. Jake must have known that both Kyle and I were taken aback by his joining the company with no notice.

Kyle, after all, had wanted to be like a second son to my dad, and to a certain extent he was. Kyle was the son of one of my dad's ex bosses, and even though Kyle was born with a silver spoon in his mouth, my dad still chose to give him a chance.

Kyle was never going to outshine anyone; he seemed to be a fan of doing his job but not going above and beyond. His social outings always took precedence, but my dad didn't mind.

Not everyone was meant to be at the top of companies, he had explained, and Kyle did a good enough job; he just wasn't invaluable.

I was standing in front of both men, feeling the hair on the back on my neck rise just a little. After what felt like the longest thirty seconds, we finally reached the lobby. Kyle grabbed my hand. I was surprised but wasn't going to embarrass him by brusquely removing my palm from his even if I really wanted to, so I slowly tried to detangle myself.

"Have a good night," said Kyle, showing his best smile as we walked towards the door to the bar, located behind the lobby desk.

I didn't look behind me.

Once we got inside, I let go of Kyle's hand. The hostess walked us to our usual table. Since Keg's was in the building, Motor Holmes employees were regulars at that place.

"What was that about?" I inquired as we sat down at a high-top by the bar.

"What?"

"The handholding?" I clarified, raising my eyebrow.

"Oh, that? Force of habit," he answered with a flicker in his gaze.

"I'm not sure your new girlfriend would appreciate that," I teased back half in warning.

"Who?"

"Florida girl?" I explained with a smirk.

"Jealous? As I recall, you're the one who broke up with me," he retorted, a twinkle in his eyes but seeming a little hurt.

I sighed. "Yes, I did, and so no, I am not jealous."

"If you say so," he said, drinking the water the waitress put in front of us.

"Can I bring you anything to drink?" asked the waitress.

"A glass of champagne please," I answered.

"I'll have an IPA," added Kyle.

"Can we also have some fries and mango jalapeño chicken wings?"

"Yes, perfect, coming right up."

"Might as well make this an unhealthy dinner," I explained.

"No disagreement there," said Kyle. "So, what's the deal with this dude? Jake."

"I have no clue," I admitted "I was hoping you would tell me. My dad gave me zero warning really."

"I had no idea, either. We all assumed that board seat was going to be yours after Rob retired."

"I assumed as much, as well. But no, this man showed up randomly and there we go" I stared down at my hand wrapped around my water, avoiding

Kyle's gaze, a little embarrassed. "Actually, I am not sure he showed up out of nowhere. He apparently used to date or is still dating Lauren. My cousin, Lauren."

"What? How do you know this?"

"Well, I did some research over the weekend. They are all over her social media together."

"Well, I mean that can't be a coincidence, can it? He must have known or even wondered if she was related to your dad just with the last name, no?"

"I'm sure. Doesn't really tell us much, though. No clue if Lauren introduced them to each other, but I can't imagine she would in any useful sense," I added, rolling my eyes.

"Yeah, but this is weird. We need to find out what's his plan, why he is really here," he said, his leg moving a bit nervously.

"Agreed. I can figure out how they met. I am just too agitated right now to even have a peaceful conversation with my dad."

"And you need to be my girlfriend again," he remarked behind a charming twitch of his lips.

I was taken by surprise. Every time I thought Kyle was moving on, he would say something like that. And I didn't necessarily believe him.

"Come on, Kyle, we talked about this. I can only offer you friendship..."

Thankfully, we were interrupted by the waitress bringing us our drinks and food. Kyle did not broach the conversation again and let me change the topic to how hungry I was.

It was 9 p.m. when an Uber finally dropped me home. Kyle wanted to drive me, but I didn't want to have to deal with him trying to kiss me and me having to push him away.

Kyle and I had dated for about a year and a half. I'd agreed to date him just to check the box. After Danny, my law school boyfriend, made it clear that a career woman wasn't the type of wife he wanted and told me, while high, that two alphas simply couldn't be in a relationship, I had given up on finding a soulmate.

People had the right the marry whoever they wanted, and while it made sense to take someone's lifestyle or career into consideration, the idea that I was *"too smart"*, or *"too strong"* to be wanted as a life partner had been disheartening.

The truth was that the dating scene wasn't pleasant for a successful woman with a six-digit salary.

How could it be that being financially independent made a woman undesirable for marriage? I was a proud feminist, which to me amounted to women having the freedom to choose the path they saw best fitted their happiness, whether that was staying home to take care of a family, working as if there was nothing else that mattered in life, a combination of the two, or something else. It was about freedom of choice, about being able to find happiness on our own terms.

I saw feminism as also liberating for men, even if it didn't seem like some saw it as such. I assumed some men would see my lifestyle as convenient for them as well, after all, it meant that I wasn't after them for their money; it meant I would participate at least 50/50 in all expenses as we built a life together; it meant that if I was with them, there would be no doubt that it was because of who they were, not because of how many purses they could buy me.

And yet, I found myself dating another lawyer-to-be who explained to me that he wanted women with *"less options in their lives"* just so he could feel like he was the only one in control of everything in the relationship.

While I understood wanting to be in control, I didn't understand wanting to dictate someone else's life, someone who the other claimed to love. That wasn't love, that was possession.

I also understood that without context, I wasn't going to be generating a lot of sympathies. I even had a female acquaintance tell me that I was the problem, not Danny, because I needed to *"let him be a man"* by smiling more, being more agreeable, and letting him pay the bills. I was told to downplay my success, so men weren't intimidated, so they didn't feel small.

No one seemed to care about what that meant for me, about having to change who I was to be 'deserving' of love. About feeling like I wasn't good, like I wasn't enough, like I was broken, unconventional, weird, and therefore not lovable, at least not on a long-term basis. I was the girl men went out with but didn't want as a wife.

I was disgusted and confused, my ex's words haunting me at every failed attempt at a relationship. I still dated, but for fun, and without any expectations. I needed to protect my heart, and giving up my career and making myself smaller to flatter a man's ego would never be an option.

With the passing of time, I had learned to love myself back, to be content with and proud of who I was, even if I was unwanted by some.

A man in my life would be nice to have, but it wasn't a must, or a need anymore. That part of me was gone. When I met Kyle, I had no interest in him. But when he seemed unfazed by my job or how much I made, I decided to give him a chance, but wasn't really ever able to put all of myself in the relationship, no matter how hard I tried.

I didn't want to get hurt again, I didn't think I could survive giving it all to someone again, only for that person to take me for granted, use me, and then walk away.

For two years before we started dating, Kyle had been working as the chief technology officer at Motor Holmes, overseeing the tech and software used in the day-to-day business. While he had the officer title, he wasn't really a proper executive officer of the company.

It was no secret to me that Kyle was hoping to be promoted to an actual executive officer position, but my father thought that he needed to learn a bit more in his position and be more dedicated before progressing to something more complex.

When Kyle started hinting at marriage, that was my cue to get out before it was too late. The reality was that Kyle was a bit boring to me, and that felt safe, but it didn't matter how much time we spent together if I didn't find him mentally stimulating.

And if he ever thus decided to cheat on me or leave me, it wouldn't hurt too much, but eventually I decided that my relationship wasn't fair to either of us if we were both in it for the wrong reasons.

I had been pleasantly surprised, and relieved, to realize that my father was not as heartbroken about the breakup as I thought he would be. Thankfully, since Kyle was not in the office often, the past four months since we parted ways hadn't created an awkward work relationship too much.

I had sworn after that to avoid dating anyone from the Motor Holmes, as there was no need to make my life more complicated. Of course, I had almost broken that promise I had made to myself with Jake, even if it would have been by accident. Jake... every time I thought of him, I felt a knot in my belly. The man managed to get under my skin more than anyone else since Danny, feeding me both unease and anger.

CHAPTER 7

I PULLED UP BY the building early. The weather was a bit cloudy, chilly, and rainy. After all, April was basically still winter in Chicago, even if I liked to pretend it wasn't at times.

I had to hold in the scream that almost surfaced when I saw a man standing by my desk, hands in his blue suit pockets, looking out my window. Jake turned around when he heard me.

He shamelessly perused my body—from my beige heels up to my light olive-green dress and tan Michael Kors jacket—with that infuriating smirk. I instantly felt unsettled.

I felt naked. Exposed.

He made me feel fucking naked, in my own office.

I desperately wanted to shout out to him to never enter my space without me being present, but it would be admitting that he got under my skin, and not showing emotions was something I strongly preferred when I interacted with others, especially in the presence of my enemies.

He was clearly trying to provoke me, antagonize me, acting like he owned my space, and I wasn't going to let him.

I walked over to my desk and placed my bag on the table.

"I didn't realize we had a meeting," I said carefully.

"I was just stopping by," he explained as he moved closer to where I was standing.

The fact that I had to bend my head a bit to be able to look at his face, even with my heels on, pissed me off. But I felt my heart race as I looked into those intense blue eyes, those lips too close for comfort, his smell teasing my nostrils.

I willed my legs to move, but I had lost all control. Instead, my gaze was lost in the deep pools of his for a moment. He tightened his jaw and suddenly walked away.

"I'd like for you to catch me up on the negotiation with the supplier from Indiana."

I turned to go behind my desk and sit on my chair. Of course, he remained standing, and I didn't offer him a seat.

"You are quite informed for someone who just joined the company," I mentioned, more as a suspicious dig than the compliment it may have seemed like.

He tilted his head. "I think knowing the ins and outs of the company is part of my job description."

"Hm. Well, it's going well. We are still negotiating the supply agreement. We still have a few material issues open, price and rebate terms of course being part of that, but I hope we can close most of them out today on our all-hands call."

"Perfect. Please send me the invite, as I'd like to join."

I clenched my teeth together a little more, to avoid telling him to fuck off. He had the right to be involved, but I didn't appreciate being supervised. I had been doing my job with little to no involvement from management for the past year, and I didn't need that to change.

"Of course. Anything else? I have to jump on a call," I invented, as I set my left hand on my phone.

"No, let's just connect once the call is over."

I waited for Jake to leave before I leaped out of my chair and swung my door closed. I started pacing, trying to calm down. The amount of anger I felt could burn a hole in the floor if I stood in one spot for too long.

I didn't have a call; I just wanted him out of my space.

I was ready to talk to my father. I needed to know more. I called his secretary. She told me he was to be back by three, and I would be his first appointment of the day.

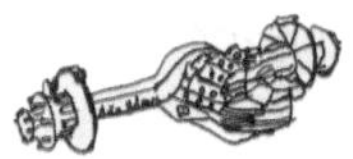

The call with the supplier was scheduled for noon. Five minutes prior, Jake waltzed into the room as if invited, pulled a chair in front of my desk, and installed himself.

"Figured we could just take the call in the same place," he explained at my surprised expression. He turned his tablet on and ignored me.

It was not the time to get annoyed, I reminded myself. Apparently, he expected me to prove my worth within the company, and I was up for the challenge. So, I dialed the number and put it on speaker.

The negotiations lasted over an hour. During the first half, I tried to ignore Jake as much as possible, but halfway through the call, I managed to put my hatred aside. I was impressed by the breadth of his knowledge of the industry and his sophisticated contributions to the back and forth.

While I was sure he was just there to annoy me, he had been quite useful on the call. We managed to work together, exchange ideas, and even laugh together as a team, to get the other side to agree to terms I had made clear we needed to have.

"Well, that went really well," I admitted as I smiled, still feeling the rush from how great the call went.

"It did. We make a good team," he added, seemingly sincere.

"We do," I acquiesced, feeling a little shy. For as much as I despised him, there was nothing more attractive to me than a man who spoke with confidence and thought.

"Would you like to grab a quick lunch?" he asked.

I hesitated, but I was indeed very hungry as I hadn't had anything except for coffee. Plus, it would be a chance for us to keep discussing strategy as I had to mark up the supply agreement and turn the draft back to the other side.

"Yes, I'm starving."

We headed down to a lovely restaurant just a few blocks north of the building. We were seated immediately because the lunch rush had already passed.

It was a quaint and simple space, with all American cuisine. I chose to sit on one of the tables on the sidewalk as the weather was a perfectly sunny seventy degrees, the sun invigorating everyone, giving us a taste of the summer to come.

"Always better to be outside when it's so nice," I explained.

"Yes, good choice." Jake nodded in agreement.

Once we ordered our food, we organically transitioned from work to a more social conversation. I refused to think about why I suddenly felt so at ease with Jake. I wasn't going to let my guard down just because I was impressed, but I had to admit that there was a small shift between us after that work call. If only I didn't find smart men so darn attractive.

"So, how was it for you transitioning from big law to working in-house?" asked Jake as he leaned back in his chair, ignoring the waitress who couldn't stop refilling our waters, to my annoyance, in what I thought was a desperate attempt to make more eye contact with Jake.

"Weird at first. It's crazy how informal things can be in-house. That was quite the adjustment. But nothing beats being able to work with my father, continue to see what he's built firsthand, and to get to be there to help him grow."

I stopped sharing; I was having a hard time reading Jake. He seemed skeptical of what I was saying, with his brow up, his eyes smaller, his intense gaze barely leaving mine.

I couldn't possibly be that fascinating, I thought.

"How did you meet my father?" I asked.

"We've been friends for years now," he explained, taking a gulp of his afternoon beer.

"Really? And how come we've never met?"

He shrugged. "I have a busy life."

I could feel the tension between us. Apparently, talking about himself was not as pleasant to him as asking me questions.

"I'm sure," I said, leaning on the table a little more.

I was dying to know more, but I didn't think that admitting my father had told me nothing about him would make me look good. So, I reluctantly stopped prying. It was clear to me that he was withholding information anyways.

I felt silly for letting my guard down and allowing myself to bond with him, just because he impressed me on a conference call.

"Everything okay with the food?" asked the waitress.

I looked up to realize she was talking to me and not Jake for once.

"Yes, the sandwich is great." I nodded.

I gave her a fake grin, quite aware that she was more so judging me for daydreaming when I was sitting across such a handsome man. Or was it jealousy because the man I was sitting accros from looked like someone that just came off the runway?

I looked up to see Jake smirking at the two of us.

"Did I miss a joke?" I asked, a little more aggressively than I intended.

"No, I just find you quite amusing."

I could feel my cheeks warming up and quickly grabbed my sandwich to give myself something to do.

"Glad you're amused," I answered sarcastically as I took a big bite of my chicken sandwich.

Jake had ordered a burger that he was already finished with.

After we wrapped up our lunch, and Jake politely declined the chocolate cookies the waitress tried to gift him, we headed back to the building.

"What kind of men says no to free cookies?" I wondered.

He smiled. "I am fairly strict with my sugar intake."

"Cookies don't count. Plus, you could have given them to me," I said with a twitch at the corner of my mouth. "I mean, come one, they were chocolate cookies. Dessert is basically the best part of a meal."

"I should have realized," he teased as we made it back.

Time had flown by. I had five minutes to get to my father's office.

"I'm going to your floor," I explained when he was going to press the button to the 39th floor in the elevator. "I have a meeting with my dad in a few minutes."

"Very well, then."

We stood next to each other, my body quite aware of him, his intoxicating smell, his arm lightly brushing mine. I scratched my throat and made sure to move a little closer to the elevator doors to get away.

Once we reached the executive floor, we both turned to the left doors, with Jake opening them and ushering me in first.

I made my way swiftly to my father's secretary in a futile attempt to put some distance between Jake and me. When I was told I could go into my father's office, he was still tailing me.

My father was seated behind his massive dark oak desk, his computer screens to his left and out of the way. He had a very old school distinguished style, all his furniture made of oak, and his chairs made of black leather. Family pictures were spread on a table behind his desk and awards were hanging above them.

Books filled the shelves to the left and right of his desk, showcasing some of his favorite authors and industry moguls who he mirrored his business practices off of. On the opposing wall was a small bar and a black leather sofa where he'd have a drink after work.

"Chloe," he said as he came to kiss me. "Hey, Jake," he added, giving Jake one of his friendly handshakes.

I observed the two men, realizing that perhaps they indeed had a close relationship. My father greeted him with the warmth he reserved for people he liked but also admired and was proud of.

A look I knew Kyle longed for but couldn't quite measure up to.

"How are you, Philip, how was your trip?"

"It was great. I think we have a good shot at doing business with those guys, and they loved the joke, thank you."

"My pleasure. Glad it was useful."

I was witnessing something I could only describe as bromance. Jake seemed like a different person: light, trustful with what looked like honesty on his face.

"I didn't realize you were in today I would have stopped by earlier to take you to lunch," said my dad.

"No problem. Chloe and I just came from lunch."

"Oh, great," my dad chimed as I gave him a cold smile, my eyebrows raised, glad he finally remembered I was in the room.

"Well, it was the least I could do after he decided to help with the Indiana supplier negotiations."

I tried hard to not have an attitude as I spoke, but I was never very good at hiding my feelings when something bothered me in my personal life.

"I am glad you are working together; I think we can do great things for this company with the projects we have coming up," encouraged my father.

"I couldn't agree more," said Jake, searching my eyes, looking like he was keeping a secret. "I have another meeting to attend, but let's grab a drink later to catch up," said Jake to my dad.

"Finally," I complained as he left, closing the door behind him.

"I am glad you are getting along," said my father as he walked to me and grabbed my hands in his.

"I wouldn't go that far," I countered, my smile softening as I felt comforted by his touch. "Now that I am more... calm about this little surprise you spun on us this past weekend, I figured I'd stop by and catch up."

"Of course," he answered, guiding me to the couch.

He unbuttoned his suit jacket and sat down. My eye warmed up as I took a good look at my dad: tired, slightly struggling to sit himself. Every now and then, through a small gesture, a wince, a weird move, a wrinkle I hadn't seen before, I was reminded that my parents weren't getting any younger.

That was a big part of why I had decided to join my dad's company in the first place, instead of pursuing partnership at a law firm, to help him relax a bit. And I didn't want my current frustrations to cause him any more stress, I realized.

"How are you doing after this weekend?" he asked hesitantly.

"So, I will be honest, Dad, I really thought you were going to promote me this weekend. I feel a bit... weird... saying that out loud, I... I don't want you to think that I feel like you owe me or... that I have some... right or something just for being your daughter..."

"No, sweetheart," he softly interrupted as he grabbed my hand again, "I know you are not like that. I know that. I am... I am sorry, I know I took you aback this weekend. I didn't mean... I didn't mean for it to happen like that..." he seemed to be having trouble to decide what to say.

My heart swelled further, wanting to do all I could to wipe that frown of concern from his face.

"It's okay, Dad, I am not mad at you, not anymore anyways, and I know you love—no, *adore* me, your favorite child," I joked with a soft laugh. "And remember you have two, not three."

My father laughed with that guttural sound that came from the middle of his stomach.

"Thank you, sweetheart." He paused. "But I do owe you an explanation. Jake is a very good friend. We worked together before when Motor Holmes used to supply Costat engines. When he was on the board there, he fought very hard for them to give a small, no-name company like ours a chance at the time, before Costat filed for bankruptcy of course.

"He is a big part of why the company stayed above water back then. I needed to add someone here with the right experience and the offer needed to be very good to entice him. It wasn't easy, as he is highly coveted, you know."

"I can tell from his experience, but Dad, why didn't you tell me any of this?" I pressed, my brow furrowing.

"Well, it happened so suddenly. We met to catch up, I got inspired to make him an offer when he explained that he was looking for a new challenge, and I had to make it appealing to beat the competition. I wanted to explain before the party, but I just didn't get the time, and this is not the type of conversation one has over the phone. I am so sorry honey.

"I have to admit, I knew you would be hurt or even devastated, but I had to jump at the opportunity of getting a brilliant mind like his in our business, and I figured that you, as my daughter, would understand and forgive me once I explained. I knew you would believe me and stay loyal to me once I apologized and promised to give you the promotion you so deserve very soon."

This was quite a lot of information for me to digest, but I was feeling a lot calmer after his explanation, and all I wanted to do in this moment was reassure my dad, even if it was still hurt by the turn of events.

"It's okay, Dad, I get it. I do. The way you did things wasn't the most Chloe friendly," I said with a chuckle, "but it's fine. You are forgiven. You are right that I will never ever leave your side. But I think there was potentially a more... creative way to do this.

"After all, you would only need one more shareholder to vote, you could add me to the board in the meantime... I know all the seats are full, but really it would just be a question of amending the bylaws."

"I will, Chloe, I will, in due time. Having a director and officer retire, bringing a new one, that's enough change for now. But I promise you, I swear, I will make sure you get involved in leadership sooner than you might think, just, please trust me. Trust that I know exactly what I am doing, and I am quite methodical, focused, and strategic in my decisions."

His tone was a bit harsher, in a clear attempt to put an end to the conversation.

Words like that confused me as it sounded like a bit of fluff. I still felt like there was more than my father was letting on, but it was more a gut feeling than anything concrete.

Maybe he was tired, maybe he knew that someone else was about to quit. Perhaps he was exhausted, making sure all the decks were aligned so his company could continue to flourish if he decided, as he had hinted to a few times, to *"take it easy and take a step back"*.

I was emotionally exhausted and accepted that this was all I was going to get from him, and perhaps I just needed to let go of what didn't really seem like an issue.

"I trust you, Dad, and I love you," I said as I hugged him. "And I am and will always be by your side; that's my promise to you."

He held me tighter, happy that we had made peace.

I left his office twenty minutes later, as I had a few other things to do before the day ended. Perhaps Jake wasn't the enemy, but that didn't make him a friend, either.

Thursday morning, I caught myself checking my makeup again while putting on just a touch of my J'adore. Penny looked at me with a suspicious gaze.

"What?" I asked defensively.

I generally avoided wearing perfume at work as I never wanted to bother anyone with any smell, but this morning I couldn't resist. I took my time to add a little more blush than usual and curled the ends of my hair a little more.

My first task of the day was the director's meeting I had been asked to attend.

I hurried into my aquamarine dress, my light beige Louboutin shoes, and my Chenille knitted sweater for the chilly morning. I grabbed my medium cream Lina leather tote bag and headed out.

I had cooled down a bit after talking to my father. Jake was there to stay from what I could tell, so I just had to get used to it. We grabbed lunch again together with Marc the day before, and whether I liked it or not, I could see what my father saw in him. He was smart, strategic, head strong, with a dry sense of humor. It's not to say that I trusted him yet, but I was no longer in panic mode about his addition to the team.

Before I headed into the meeting, I stopped by my office to exchange my sweater for my black suit jacket, more appropriate for the board meeting scheduled to start in five minutes. I felt more confident in proper business attire.

I was always a little bit anxious when I walked into the big conference room. There was a sleek, long marble table, floor-to-ceiling windows, pastries and drinks, and a big screen TV on the wall.

I chatted a bit with the directors already present in the room, until my dad and Jake walked in.

Everyone then took their positions at the table, with Jake sitting next to my father. My dad introduced Jake again as the new director to the team. The meeting only lasted an hour.

I summarized the three transactions we closed this week and touched upon a few other legal issues I wanted to catch the board up on. Unsurprisingly, Jake asked a few questions on a new customer contract I was going to start working on, and I addressed them.

"As our meeting is coming to an end," announced my father, "we've put this quarter's magazine at the center here, so please take copies if you want them. They were sent out this morning."

I grabbed one. It was my idea to create a magazine to share news and industry updates with others in our business. We could have relied on emails, but I believed a magazine on the table had more value and was more visible.

I was guilty of deleting emails most of the time without reading a word if they had nothing to do with work. And I never read the ones that sounded "interesting" that I bookmarked for later.

But I would at least flip through a magazine with a good cover when delivered to my desk. If captivated, I would read some of the articles in there. I had written some of the "New Trends" article that were featured in the magazine myself, and some had come up as topics of conversation with some clients.

As I browsed through the colorful pages, I noticed they had had the time to add a few snippets on the event my father had hosted. My heart skipped a beat when I saw that they had a picture of Jake and I that filled an entire page. It was a profile picture of the two of us when we were dancing, the crowd almost blurred in the background.

I tried to compose myself, as I pretended to continue to flick through the magazine, but I could feel my cheeks warming up. I dared to look up, to see everyone else also glancing through the pages, making flattering comments to my father about how great the party was.

I caught Jake's slight lift of his lips as his intense gaze landed on me. He clearly had been paying attention to my reaction, and he seemed amused.

Kyle was also glaring at me, with a scowl on his face.

I got up and went to my dad.

"I didn't expect to be the belle of the ball like this," I whispered in as soft of a voice as I could.

"The camera loves you, honey, you know that. Plus, I had nothing to do with that; it's all the marketing team," he said with a twinkle in his eyes.

I rolled my eyes just a bit, knowing my father was pretending not to understand what I was complaining about. If anything, he seemed overly pleased at my discomfort.

While my picture with Jake wasn't the only one taken of the dance floor, it was the one that would indeed make people stop on the page or slow down.

But there wasn't much I could do about that after the fact. I continued in casual conversation with some of the board members instead of thinking too much, fiddling with my hair just a little more than usual. As the group started to shuffle out, I packed up my things to leave.

"We do look great dancing," I heard almost as a guttural whisper by my right ear. Jake was standing right behind me.

I held my breath, my body tensing.

"We do," I acknowledged as I backed up just enough to see him.

It didn't seem as if he was mocking me, although I still felt a little defensive. I really hoped my face didn't look as flushed as it felt.

"We'll have to do that again sometime," he added in a low and controlled voice, the deep sound traveling down my spine, intensifying my pulse.

"Hm, wouldn't my cousin mind?" I snarked.

I regretted the words as soon as they came out of my mouth. I didn't intend to say that out loud, but it was too late. The side of his mouth curled up, as if he expected such a comeback and enjoyed it.

"She has no reason to," he paused, "but wouldn't Kyle?"

"He has no reason to, either," I admitted, although his statement wasn't quite as clear as I would have liked.

But I was too prideful to ask him to clarify. As a lawyer, it was in my nature to prefer specificity especially in a situation like that, and a slight part of me hoped for something I didn't want in my life at that time.

"Hm, that perfume you wear…"

"Chloe, want to grab some coffee?" interrupted Kyle as he approached us.

"Sure," I said, zoning back to suddenly remembering that there were other people in the room.

Jake's jaw tightened as he backed up a bit, hands in his suit pockets, intently looking at my ex. Kyle had been weirdly more present at work than usual. It was clear that he had not warmed up to Jake, and it was clear that Jake didn't mind or even maybe liked it that way.

"We'll talk later," he told me before he walked away, his comment about my perfume making goosebumps run down my arm.

I realized I was wearing the same one the night we met.

"What was that about?" asked Kyle.

"Just talking," I answered, as I had no intention of having Kyle get involved in anything. "Let's go grab that coffee, with lots and lots of ice."

CHAPTER 8

I LOVED A SLOW weekend. We were well into April now, and I enjoyed how the weather was progressing into warmer temperatures. Chicago was finally thawing, the trees starting to be covered in green, and my peonies and hydrangeas had begun to grow flower buds in my backyard.

It was a rainy end of the week, but I still managed to grab brunch with Keisha on Saturday. I otherwise spent the weekend attending to self-care and writing my current novel. I did all I could to avoid thinking of Jake, but not much helped. I knew I was letting my guards down with him and desperately wanted them back up.

But every time I saw him, my heart would race, and I felt off balance. And when we worked together, I couldn't help but be drawn to his cleverness and quick-witted demeanor.

I really enjoyed playing good cop and bad cop with him when we negotiated agreements. I liked the way that Machiavellian smile drew on his face when he lured the other side to exactly where he wanted them to be without them noticing. I did, though, and damn it, it so turned me on.

And there was the problem of those sensual lips I caught myself staring at every now and then, especially when they exuberated that relaxed, crooked grin. Or that chiseled masculine jawline I wanted to trace with my index finger.

None of that mattered though, as I didn't like the idea of dating Lauren's ex, not to mention that he was a coworker who still took the position that I thought was mine with no warning.

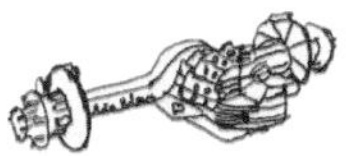

During the following weeks, as we rolled into mid-May, my resolve had been shaken daily, as Jake was always around. He was everywhere. Every meeting. Every call. *Everywhere*.

I started to develop an extra sense that told me when he was in close proximity. My nose could sniff out his scent well before he was in sight. My body tingled when I heard his voice.

The very last thing I needed was to be infatuated with that man, but there was no way to avoid him as much as I tried. The weekends gave me a break, except when he creeped his way into my vivid dreams, making me wake up wet and bothered the next day. I took cold showers, worked out, used my toys, but all it took was his intense gaze on me the next day to rile me up all over again.

By the time Friday of yet another week came around, I was ready to put some distance between us; something had to be done so I could stop looking forward to seeing him so often. And clearly, acting on my fantasies when I was alone in my bedroom at night wasn't enough.

Once the clock hit five, I changed into a fuchsia crepe cocktail dress with a sweetheart neckline, pairing it with my nude open-toe heels. I slid into my light long cream Burberry jacket and jetted out the office.

I avoided wearing more revealing clothes at work, so I didn't want to run into anyone when I did. I was meeting Keisha at a cocktail lounge in the loop. I picked a seat at the bar when I got there, hoping that a few of the people around me would leave so I could grab a stool for Keisha.

"Can I get you anything?" asked the bartender.

"A glass of your Cremant, please."

I nursed my sparkling wine and scanned the room. The crowd was as fancy and well dressed as was usual for their favorite wine bar in Chicago. The décor was mostly Victorian era, with the chance obnoxious chandelier scattered throughout. Emerald-color wallpaper with traces of gold was on some of the walls.

I loved seeing people dressed up for a night out. It certainly added to the sophistication of the space.

Perhaps I could meet a man who would distract me for a bit, help me move on from my infatuation with Jake. I smiled as some of the men made eye contact with me.

But I was getting a bit bored, and I was about to text Keisha when I realized I had my phone accidentally on silent. I had a few missed calls and text messages from her. She got stuck at work and would be very late. I sighed and pushed some of my hair away from my face.

I was already here, so I decided to wait and if Keisha couldn't make it, so be it. I'd enjoy a couple of drinks and then go home to a good book. With our jobs, we had gotten used to being stood up by each other and we were completely understanding of it. It was part of the trade, even more so as law firm associates.

"Can I buy you another?" offered a voice to my side. I pivoted just a little to meet the gaze of the attractive man who spoke.

"I'm fine, thank you."

"Are you sure? Your drink is almost finished."

"I am savoring it."

"But I'm sure you need another one. Waiter, can you bring her another one of those? And put her first one on my tab, as well."

"I already have a tab," I said to the bartender, getting annoyed.

The man wouldn't take no for an answer, as if I was either lying or didn't know my own self. I would be happy to talk to him, I just didn't want him to buy me a drink right this moment.

I hated drinking my bubbles warm, thus why I usually waited for my current glass to be done before getting more.

"Funny, I don't really know how I could have made my desire more known," I uttered with an irritated smile.

But the man seemed oblivious. Another man who appeared to be his friend waltzed up to us. They both introduced themselves, but I forgot their names as soon as they came out of their mouths.

Another one of their male friends joined us and finally made a funny joke. I was relieved that at least one of them made me laugh. I guess third time was the charm in that situation.

I quickly realized that the first man had called dibs since the newcomer was hesitant to flirt back.

Irritated, I finished my drink and chugged the other to distract myself. Iris had always told me that I was too picky. But these men were trying to impress me, talking about their cars, their beautiful downtown apartments, and for me it was the very worst way to get my attention.

I hated it when men tried to awaken my interest by showing off their money, when just telling me about something they enjoyed, or their family would do it. And yet, for some of them, if I had as much or more than them, it was over.

Because the size of their wallet was what they measured to determine the value of what they had to bring to the table. Before I could order myself a third drink, one of the men rushed to the task.

"I am quite capable of ordering my own drink," I told him between tight teeth.

"Just let me get it for you," he insisted with a smirk.

I felt like I was talking to a child. I sighed and waited for my drink, limiting my conversation to the minimum. Once the bartender brought my glass, I took a sip and lifted myself up the chair.

"Well, gentlemen, as much as I appreciated the company," I said sarcastically, "I am going to make the rounds to see if my friend finally made it. And of course, thank you for the fifty-dollar glass of Cremant—which I could've easily bought myself, but that you insisted on paying for. A word of advice for you all; next time you want to hit on a woman who made it clear she doesn't want a drink from you, listen to her. Because I can guarantee you have a better chance with her than if you keep insisting on such a silly point."

I ignored the shock that covered their faces. It seemed like they finally heard me, my words having the impact I intended, and I went on my way. I peeked around a bit but saw no sign of Keisha.

I landed at the other bar in the lounge, just standing in a corner, sipping on my drink.

"Don't tell, me" I heard behind me, "none of them were entertaining enough for you?"

I jumped and quickly swirled around to see Jake standing there, wearing a dark gray suit with a white shirt. I squeezed my eyes shut, cursing my luck.

But my body didn't listen to reason. I found myself enjoying the smell of him, traveling just on the surface of my body. After three glasses of bubbly, I was feeling very brave and slightly inhibited.

"Are you jealous?" I teased, deliberately meeting his gaze, lifting my thick lashes ever so slowly towards him.

He lowered his face towards mine.

"I've never had a problem entertaining you," he mocked, his voice suddenly deeper. I bit my cheek to keep my composure. "Just wondering why you would waste their time, let them buy you drinks if you know you are not interested."

"Well," I said, bending my head a little, my elbows on the bar surface behind me, providing support, "I call it the stupid tax. It's been my experience that many of you just get 'confused' when a girl refuses your drink, or explains very clearly that she doesn't want one or can buy herself one," I explained, shrugging my shoulder.

He raised an eyebrow, seemingly intrigued.

"These guys were basically forcing alcohol down my throat. I said no, but to them it was like I said yes. They just could not compute a rejection. Instead of admiring a girl who doesn't need a man to spend money on her to talk to her, it's more like some sort of attack to your manhood or something, where the conversation cannot proceed unless you feel like you've paid for your time.

"Just like my ex. I frankly have grown tired of caring more about the interests of men than I do my own. So, when I reject the drink but still offer to converse, if they insist, I let them waste their money and amuse myself by letting them perform their theatrics until I'm bored."

Jake laughed, a deep, guttural, fully honest sound that I didn't expect. I laughed back, feeling relieved that he seemed amused instead of annoyed.

"I can't disagree with that thought process. I take it that ex is not Kyle?"

"No, more like law school fun," I explained. "Didn't end well. I was too much of an alpha for him. His words. Can't make this type of comment up," I added at Jake's surprise expression.

"Some men are intimidated by successful women."

His penetrating stare made me feel like I was standing in the middle of fire.

"I am quite aware."

"I, on the other hand," he continued, slowly, as he took a step towards me, "find it very fucking attractive." His sensual tone caressed my skin, giving me goosebumps.

I moved back until my feet hit the edge of the bar. Jake's intense gaze made my pulse quicken as he got closer to me, holding on to the bar with his left hand placed behind me.

"You fascinate me, Chloe."

"In what sense?" I dared to ask, swallowing hard and peering up at him, my lips slightly parted.

He let out a soft groan. "I can't figure out who you really are," he admitted as he took a step closer.

I had nowhere to go. I didn't know what else to do, but it didn't matter, because I was frozen, captivated by the frown that was suddenly on his forehead and his jaw clenched as he leaned his face closer, only a hair's breadth away from mine.

"I didn't know you were trying," I answered back, my gaze drawn to those lips I desperately needed on mine.

I held my breath, wanting to close my eyes but unable to break the stare with those moss blue gray eyes, a cold fire burned in them that was holding me hostage.

He gently tucked my hair behind my left ear, then traced my jaw with the tip of his finger, stopping at my chin to lift my face toward his, our lips almost touching.

"Jake!"

He pulled back almost immediately, and my eyes widened as I tried to balance myself against the bar.

"I've been looking around for you," announced the man who interrupted us so abruptly as he shook Jake's hand.

He had just realized that he stepped into something apparently as he shifted his gaze from Jake to me, mouth open, with a curious look on his face.

"This is Chloe," introduced Jake, since his friend was staring. "Chloe, this is Tom."

"Nice to meet you," replied Tom, quickly leaving Jake's hand for mine.

"Nice to meet you as well," I answered.

"There you are!" I heard behind me.

Lauren crossed in front of me, rushing to hug Jake, positioning herself in between us as she kissed him on the lips. I felt a pit drop in my stomach. Jake removed Lauren's hands gently.

Lauren finally turned around to look at me as if she hadn't noticed me before.

"Cuz!" she squealed, wrapping her arms around me.

I was used to those facetious public hugs from my cousin, but that wasn't what bothered me.

"It's been too long!" she chimed.

"Only a few weeks," I clarified, as I had seen my cousin at my uncle's early Easter dinner.

"Feels like forever," she exclaimed, back to holding Jake's arm. "I was so excited when Jake told me you guys were working together. Small world!"

"Indeed," I acknowledged, wanting to disappear, my cheeks still feeling very warm.

Lauren was wearing an exquisite red dress, a little too short for my taste, as we were in a lounge, and not a club, but she was still beautiful.

I could feel Jake looking at me, but I couldn't bear to do the same. My heart was racing, and I was finding it hard to keep my pride unscathed. I was trying to muster all the strength I had to continue what promised to be a very awkward conversation, when I felt an arm go around my shoulders. I had never been more relieved to see Keisha.

"I'm so sorry I'm late!" Keisha apologized.

"Please take me away," I whispered as I hugged her, relief settling in.

"Hi, Keisha!" squealed Lauren, without letting go of Jake.

"Nice to see you," said Keisha sporting best smile. "Hi, Jake," she added. "I'm Keisha," she said as Tom introduced himself. "Can we please go?" she asked me before anyone else could get a word. "Our friends are waiting for us at Meister."

"Yes, let's go," I answered, eternally thankful.

"Nice to meet you, Tom. Have a good night, all," I added, suddenly finding courage to pretend to be polite.

We quickly went to get my coat from the coat check. I couldn't stop glancing in the direction of Lauren and Jake. Lauren just would not let him go. I quickly turned my head when I saw Jake searching in my direction.

We ended up deciding to go to my house for a night cap. Keisha was exhausted, and I was not in the mood for casual conversation with others. We went straight to my room to take our makeup off and get in comfortable clothes.

"Seems like you have a lot to tell me," said Keisha when we sat down in the family room.

"Meow!" complained Penny as she propped her sassy self on the blanket I was covered with. She climbed further up and licked my face, the little spikes on her tongues hurting me a bit.

"There isn't much," I lied, taking a gulp of my coconut water and gently pushing my cuddly cat down after the microneedling session she graciously provided.

"Chloe, please, I could see you were distraught to say the least."

"Fine," I admitted. "I hate that man more and more every day. And tonight, I let my guard down, just a bit... then well... Lauren shows up and makes me feel like an idiot and a bad person."

"Don't be so hard on yourself, Chloe. And we both know you don't hate him." She said that second part quick and slightly under her breath.

"He took my job, and I almost let him kiss me. What is wrong with me?" I groaned.

"The man is sexy as hell is what it is," teased Keisha. "And you were into him before all this mess."

"And he's dating my cousin."

"I frankly have a hard time picturing the man you've been telling me about with her as a girlfriend."

"Well, she kissed him. Plus, he is arrogant, rude, and always trying to supervise my work. I shouldn't have let him get so close, but it's so hard when I have to work with him every single day. It's ridiculous."

"Do you like him?" Keisha pressed.

"No, of course not! I find him attractive, but that's all it is."

"Okay, well, let's just blame whatever it is you had to drink today, and things can go back normal. If that's really what you want, of course," added Keisha, looking at me from the side of her eyes.

"That's exactly what I want. I don't need to make my life more difficult than needed with yet another office romance. Anyways, I don't want to talk about that jerk anymore. What should we watch?"

Keisha grabbed the remote to put something on, knowing when any attempt at making me take a deep look inside was futile.

CHAPTER 9

I SPENT MOST OF my Saturday in the sunroom writing, with Penny napping on my lap. It felt good, as creating stories was one of the few things I could lose myself in. That unfortunately didn't stop me from checking Lauren's social media accounts.

As I expected, she had felt the need to document her soiree with Jake. It bothered me to no end, and I was even more upset at myself for feeling a bit of a ping in my chest from seeing them together. Seemed like they had a long and fun night bar hopping.

I couldn't fathom someone that seemed as serious as Jake bar crawling but there he was, with Lauren glued to his arm like a parasite. Always the right one of course, as that allowed Lauren to show her best side in pictures as I recalled.

On Sunday, I was quite happy to leave the house and meet Kyle for a friendly early brunch at one of my favorite spots in the loop. It was the perfect seventy-five-degree day of May, and the sun was shining on Chicago.

I loved the loop and had the Uber drop me off on Wacker Drive, so I could enjoy a peaceful walk by the river before our meal. I enjoyed taking in the sight of the wonderful Chicago architecture, admiring the mix of old and new buildings, the boats parked on the river so that people could grab a quick bite or a drink.

The city was definitely coming back to life, and I was all for it.

I finally reached the restaurant, where Kyle was seated on the patio, the view of the river behind him.

After a few mimosas, I felt much better. Kyle was on his best behavior, wearing the blue shirt I had gifted him when we were dating with a pair of blue jeans and white moccasins.

"You know I'd love for you to join me in Hawaii in a month or so. It's going to be fun."

"Kyle... no."

"Do you not trust yourself around me?" he asked with his devilish smile.

"I really want this friendship thing to work," I tactfully explained.

Kyle always had an agenda in mind, I reminded myself. Ever since we broke up, it was enjoying his newfound freedom while still trying to get me back. Which to me proved exactly what I knew, that we had been together mostly for convenience.

"We'd go as friends, of course, unless you are dating someone right now who might have a problem with it?" pushed Kyle as he put his elbows on the table.

"No," I quickly answered, my head bent a little wondering what Kyle was getting at. "To both."

"Hm, you seem very... close with Jake, so I was wondering," he said, coming clean.

I drank some of my mimosa before answering.

"We are just coworkers, as you know. He seems to have an interest in the legal side of things, and so what choice do I have? My dad kind of put him above me, so I can't exactly tell him to fuck off."

"True," voiced Kyle, though he didn't seem very convinced. "He's also dating Lauren, so it would be awkward if you had something going on with him."

My lips tightened, but I focused on my drink.

"Well, I wouldn't date him regardless, but that would certainly be an impediment," I acquiesced with a sarcastic grin.

"Any dessert?" asked the waitress once she came over.

"No, thanks," I quickly answered, as I was ready to end our outing. "Can we have the bill?"

"Of course. Here you go," she said as she set the bill on the table. "Whenever you are ready, no rush."

"I have a busy day," I explained to Kyle's confused gaze.

"No problem. I'll drop you at your place. You're on my way," he replied when I looked at him curiously. "I'm going golfing today, with your dad and Jake."

"Ah, I see. A little late in the day, no?"

"Jake had meetings all morning, and your dad wouldn't go without him," explained Kyle, clearly frustrated at the intruder in his plans with my father.

Kyle's Audi stopped right in front of my house. As I suspected, he parked the car and came down, clearly expecting to be invited in. I sighed, but I didn't want to be rude, so I let him inside.

"Man, I haven't been here in so long," he exclaimed.

"I know. But I'm hosting the brunch for my dad's birthday as you know, and you know you'll be invited."

That was my attempt to try to get Kyle to leave, but he was clueless. We ended up sitting on the sofa on my patio and I had another mimosa before Kyle finally left.

I replaced the yellow dress I was wearing with my favorite light pink lounge silk set. I loved the embroidered bretelles of the t-shirt and the wide-leg flowy pants. But my favorite part were the side slit pockets. It all went with a long open front cardigan I used as a cover up when needed.

I tied my hair in a Sleeply Tie and brought my laptop to the patio, lit an almond blossom candle, and chugged some coconut water. I wanted to enjoy my light buzz with no other consequences. Penny wrapped herself in a ball on my thighs.

It was close to five when I noticed a confusing text from Kyle. He was on his way to my house, as he had forgotten his sunglasses. I rolled my eyes, as I caught sight of them on the table.

I grabbed them quickly, hoping to meet Kyle at the door and avoid having to entertain him a second time.

As I got to the entrance, the doorbell rang. I opened the door expecting Kyle, but found Jake standing there instead, his glasses too dark for me to read anything other than his tightened jaw and the frown on his forehead.

"Um, hello," I managed to utter.

I peeked behind him and saw his Mercedes parked in front.

"Your boyfriend is passed out in the back of my car," he explained.

"Who?" I raised a brow, confused.

"Kyle."

My eyes narrowed. "I see. Why is he with you?"

"It was me or Philip. I got the short end of the stick."

"I hope you are not dropping him off here?"

"Not if you don't want me to," he answered with a curious look, "but that was the request."

"Of course not. He texted me about his glasses," I explained, handing them to him.

I was conflicted between wanting to make clear to Jake that I was single, while my pride told me it was none of his business, especially considering that he was with my cousin. I chose to go with my pride.

"Anything else?" I pressed.

"No. But can you text me his address?"

"Sure," I said, feeling my pockets for my phone.

Unfortunately, I had left it in the back of the house. He didn't seem like he would leave without the address, as he needed a destination that Kyle was currently unable to provide. I held back a sigh.

"My phone is on my patio. It's a new address, so I don't know it by heart..." I explained.

"I can wait."

"Great."

I gave up and swung the door wider. Jake removed his glasses and stepped in. I ignored him and resisted the urge to run as we headed to my patio.

Jake was taking his time, admiring the artwork in my formal living area, slowing down by the well-stocked wine fridge in my kitchen. He then joined me on the patio. Penny did her adorable little strut until she reached Jake. She rubbed her whole body on one leg and then to the other. Now, Penny was always a friendly cat, but she usually hid on one of the dining table chairs when Kyle was around.

My heart swelled when Jake leaned down and tenderly stroked her head. She purred with satisfaction as she arched her back. I scratched my throat to regain my composure

"Gorgeous house."

"Thank you."

"What's her name?"

"What?" I asked, dumbfounded.

"Your cat," he replied as he scooped her up, seemingly pleased with himself. He didn't appear to mind the hair she was leaving behind on his clothes. And she upped the cuteness as she rubbed her little head on his face.

"Um, Penny."

"Hi, Penny," he said as he scratched behind her ears, her favorite spot. She was purring so loudly.

I noticed him getting close to my laptop; the last thing I wanted was the man reading the sex scene I was currently writing, so I rushed by him and shut it down.

"What's your number?" I asked, in a rush to text him.

He dropped Penny, marched to me, and grabbed my phone. She went to her feeder.

How dare he make me feel nervous in my own home? I needed to move on from the surprise of seeing him at my door immediately. I felt all flustered seeing him in my space, making it feel too small.

He typed his number and handed me the phone back, looking down at me from under his eyelids. I immediately texted him the address.

"Done."

"Not many people your age manage to afford a house like this," he observed.

"Not many people my age are as successful as I am," I countered, my jaw pointed up in defiance.

"Law firms pay well, but still," he pushed as he walked back in the house.

"Well, if you pick your firm right, bill at the top of your class, it adds up."

"It helps to have a generous father as well, I'm sure."

He wasn't the first to hint that my fortune was perhaps undeserved or handed down to me.

"What are you implying?" I asked, crossing my arms. I saw judgment in those cold eyes. "I don't know what century you come from, but I didn't accept any financial help in my career. While my friends were partying, I worked my ass off to get scholarships for school, that way I graduated from both undergrad and graduate school with no debt. And when I built this house, I was smart, I saved, I found the best price and financing I could, I was very strategic."

I tried to stop talking, but my brain had lost all control over my emotions in the moment. "I chose a neighborhood where there is so much open land its cheap to buy it. And I built my own home."

I was fuming but tried to stay calm.

"I didn't mean to offend you," he said as he approached me slowly.

"No, but you did mean to imply that I perhaps relied more than I should on my parents. And I thought it necessary to clarify, in case this was a 'you're a spoiled brat' type of comment. I worked very hard for everything I have. I was fortunate enough to have parents that made all the sacrifices for Eric and I to receive the best education we could.

"They inspired me to always aim high and never accept defeat. And I honor those principles in everything I do. This is a superb house; I am very proud of it. I made a lot of sacrifices when I was in big law, lived small, saved everything I could, to get it. I don't appreciate your insinuations."

He searched my eyes for a few seconds. "Understood."

Jake shook his head, acquiescing, almost with what looked like a new-found respect for me. I wanted more from him, an apology, anything. Instead, he just stood there and stared at me.

"You should be proud," he added, his eyes softening a bit.

I took a deep breath in an effort to compose myself, feeling some tension leaving my shoulders. I was a bit taken aback as he wasn't combative. "I am, very much. It's my little oasis."

Jake simply shook his head. No, I refused to bond further with him; that had gotten far enough already.

"Well, I assume you must get going? Wouldn't want Kyle getting your car dirty," I said with a curve on my lips.

Jake had seemingly forgotten about Kyle.

"Ah, yes," he said as he put his sunglasses back on and headed to the door. "Thank you," he added before leaving.

"Of course," I answered, annoyed at the fact that I wanted him to stay a little longer.

He stared at me for a few more seconds before leaving. I closed the door immediately but peeked out my window as he marched around his car, got in the driver's seat, and drove off.

I closed my eyes, trying to digest the past few minutes while begging my heart to slow down its rhythm.

CHAPTER 10

THAT WEEK WAS SO far the busiest of the year, and I was eternally grateful. I had a heavy number of meetings the first couple days, most off-site, giving me the perfect reason to avoid going to the building.

Wednesday was the first day I showed up in the office, after grabbing lunch with Marc to catch up on the new business relationship.

I wondered if Jake would be looking for me, but I received no emails or calls from him. He had texted me that day he was at my house to confirm Kyle had made it home safe. We had exchanged a few jokes, but I cut it off at some point. But when I got to the office, I couldn't help feeling almost relieved when I saw Jake sitting with my dad as I walked into his office to brief him on the site visits.

"Chloe! Perfect timing. Jake just stopped by to discuss his meeting with Regional on Monday," Dad announced.

"Great. How did it go?" I asked as I sat on the armchair to join the gentlemen by the sofa.

"It went as smoothly as expected," answered Jake, bending his head to face me. "Let me know if you have time to meet them tomorrow. I'd like to introduce you as the negotiations start, but they are very interested in our business."

"Yes, happy to meet tomorrow. My day is fairly open."

I had no doubt that Jake was going to land us the account. It was nowhere close in size to Listen Inc., but it was a strategic move I had pitched in our last meeting, and Jake had suggested he make the first introduction as he had a good relationship with the CEO.

The three of us talked for another hour. If Jake wasn't so obnoxious, I would have even called him my father's best decision for the company. After me, of course.

I had one last meeting for the day and was almost sad to have to leave my father and Jake. I quickly ran to my office to exchange my jeans and blue cardigan for a pair of marine color work pants and matching jacket, which paired well with my white shirt I already was wearing. I went a little more conservative with my outfit that afternoon, as I knew the executive I was about to meet had a wondering eye, and I didn't want to have to put him in his place.

As Friday rolled in, I was looking forward to a slow and uneventful weekend. I had had the longest week, and I felt drained. I also desperately needed a drink, to stop thinking about Jake and the wonderful Thursday we had spent together.

Keisha and I went to dinner at a steak restaurant, in the Fulton Market area. I loved that neighborhood; it had kept a lot of the former warehouse architecture but transformed into a fun restaurant scene, some with live music.

This was a busy night for the restaurant as it tended to happen on Fridays. I loved going out, feeding off the energy and laughter of those around me. The waitress took me to our table on the sidewalk, where Keisha was already seated.

Keisha was wearing a cute black jumpsuit that accentuated her curves, coupled with a pair of gold open-toe heels.

"Love the jumpsuit!" I complimented as I hugged my friend.

"Thank you!" she beamed back.

I had opted for a flowy light green dress, short in the front and long in the back, with buttons in the front and thin shoulder straps. The 78-degree weather was perfect for light spring clothing, and we wanted to take full advantage.

Keisha had already ordered two frozen margaritas for us. I had communicated that strong liquor was required for the night.

"Okay, how was the week?" asked Keisha as the waiter brought the steaks and various sides we had ordered.

I got busy filling our plates.

"It was long," I explained, knowing that all Keisha really wanted to hear about was Jake.

I had told her earlier this week about him showing up at my door, with Kyle passed out in the backseat of his car, no less.

"Nothing else crazy happened," I explained as Keisha was staring at me with mild impatience at my lack of disclosure. "We did spend all of yesterday together," I confessed, "and who knows if we would have also spent the evening together if Kyle wasn't waiting for me in my office when we got there."

"Why is he always there?" she wondered.

"He's been at work a lot more than usual lately... He must be able to tell something is going on, or he is concerned that Jake will replace him with my dad, or both."

I bit my lips with a guilty look on my face, immediately regretting what I had said. Keisha started laughing, enjoying my more than usual tequila-infused honesty.

I sighed as I put my fork down. "Fine," I admitted with a sigh. "I like him, okay? I can't stop myself; it's driving me crazy."

"Chloe, it's okay to be attracted to him. I mean, you were attracted to him before you even knew who he was. You broke your no one-night stand rule for him for Christ's sake. Well, you meant to anyways."

I let out a loud, frustrated sigh.

"I know! and while I am sure we didn't sleep together that night, I just... I'd like to know if it really was a coincidence."

"Ask him. You are not one to bite your tongue for anyone, if I recall. Unless you really, really like him," she teased with a smile.

"I tried that night at my parents' house, and I tried a couple more times. Nothing. He is too smart to say anything useful to me. I don't even know if that matters to be honest."

"Clo," said Keisha, grabbing my hand. "It's me. Talk to me."

My throat grew tight. "I don't know what is happening to me. I swore I wouldn't date someone from work again. But he... he's just.... I am feeling 'things' for him. I um, I fantasize..."

I wanted to run my fingers through his hair, I wanted to feel his lips.

"His voice, his smell just... it's starting to be very frustrating."

I took a sip of my drink and grabbed a bite of bread as a distraction; I was suddenly feeling overwhelmed.

Keisha was concerned, as she knew I took my work very seriously. And if Jake was distracting me and troubling me so much, it might not just be physical.

"It's more than that, isn't it?" she dared to ask.

I focused on chewing for a couple of seconds before answering.

"I don't know, I think so. I'm confused. He's with Lauren, Keisha, I... I can't. But when I'm with him, I feel like I am with an equal, I don't know how to explain, just someone I can be myself with completely, no conditions, no complex, no insecurities, on either end." I paused.

It hit different to hear myself say those things out loud. I took another big gulp of my drink.

"I have a desire to know everything about him, and for him to get to know me. It's been a while since I've had this ridiculous need to share anything with anyone. He's smart; he just electrifies a room when he is in it."

"Are you in love with him?"

"No! Of course not!" I sputtered.

"You spent over a year with Kyle, and I've never heard you talk about him like this, not even close, or anyone really for that matter, at least not since—"

"No," I interrupted. "I barely know him. I can't be in love with him. It's just... a very strong... infatuation," I declared. "It's extreme lust, I'd say. Very useful for book writing inspiration, but very inconvenient for my real life."

"Well, maybe you should just sleep with him then," suggested Keisha.

I groaned, "Ugh, no, come on."

"Why not? If all this is, is infatuation, it should go away or at least become more manageable if you sleep with him, no? He could be a total bust and then voila, no more feelings!"

"I have no doubt it would be amazing," I confessed, "but even if that could help, I am not sleeping with him. We work together; I don't need another failed workplace affair. Plus, again, he is with Lauren."

"Has he told you that? It's well known that Lauren is, how do I say, a serial dater. And obsessive." Keisha gave me a pointed look.

"Yet he is the only one she posts about all the goddamn time."

"Okay. I understand," admitted Keisha. "What are you going to do?"

"Uh, well," I sighed, "start working a bit more from home for starters. Try to cool down. Find myself a new adventure perhaps; I don't know."

I focused on my food. I felt relieved for talking to Keisha. Perhaps coming clean to my friend would lessen my confusion.

"Okay, enough about me," I said, to change the topic. "How are you?"

"Busy, that law life as you know."

"Has my dear brother reached out since the party?" I asked, purposely avoiding eye contact and giving the peas on my plate all my attention.

"Hum. Yes, but I didn't engage."

"Good!" I praised.

My brother was that one topic we always felt awkward discussing, but I was just concerned about my friend's heart and based on the looks Eric gave Keisha at the gala, I knew my brother wasn't over her.

"You know I would never judge you, right?" I offered softly, wanting nothing more than to make my friend feel comfortable to open.

"I know, sweetie, but it's about survival."

That was all Keisha needed to say for me to know what she meant.

I was at my esthetician's getting a facial, after my bi-weekly manicure and pedicure, when I noticed I had missed a call from my mother. It was followed by a text inviting me over for dinner.

"Mom," I said as I got in my Range Rover. "Sorry, I was getting a facial, but yes, dinner sounds fun."

"No problem, darling, thanks for confirming. Can you bring some of that wine I like?" she asked.

"Yep, will do. Amelia gave me a case for us to share. What's the occasion?"

"It's Memorial Day weekend, so I figured you would have some time. I miss you, and since we prepared chicken liver today, I wanted to make sure you had some. I know it's your favorite!"

"That's sweet, Mom. See you later. Is around five okay?"

"Yes, that's perfect."

I spent the rest of the day pampering myself at the spa as I had intended. I got a body exfoliating treatment in addition to the facial. After I returned home, I washed and straightened my hair.

When ready, I called myself an Uber. I had opted for a simple midi dress that stopped at my knees in a vanilla bean color. The dress had adjustable straps with bow accents. I loved the underwire cups which meant I didn't need to add a bra.

The dress had a partial front button closure and slightly embroidered scallop trims, coupled with ruffled hems. The back zipper was hidden to preserve the delicate look of the dress. I complemented my outfit with some thick gold hoops and open toe sandals. I grabbed my cross-body pink Furla purse and the wine bag when the car arrived.

I had chosen not to drive as I intended to enjoy some of the delicious California reds my mother had requested I bring. Since I moved in my house, my mom and I hosted wine tastings quite often, and I always made sure to have some of our favorites on hand.

I suspected that my mother never ordered her own wine just so she could have a reason to visit me, and I of course entertained her dearly.

CHAPTER 11

THE CAR FINALLY PULLED in front of my parents' house. I made my way in as the door was unlocked.

"Chloe, my love!" exclaimed my mom as she embraced me. "Let me help you with that," she added as she took some of the wine bags from me.

"Of course, straight to the wine," I joked as she laughed. "I brought you six bottles so you can have some left over."

"Oh yes, thank you!"

"Where is Dad?" I asked.

"In his office wrapping up some calls."

We went to the kitchen where I took care of opening two bottles. I used the aerator to pour a couple of glasses for us. This wine was one of those that seriously needed to breathe before it was at its peak, but I wasn't known for my patience.

I poured the rest in the decanter. My mother was wearing a lovely pair of white velvety pants coupled with a beautiful orange top with short sleeves and a couple of buttons in the front.

"You look very chic, Mom," I complimented.

She grinned. "Thank you."

"We are not expecting any guests, are we?" I inquired as I looked at the dining table, that was now back at its rightful place, with four place settings. "Is Eric in town?"

"Well... your father decided to invite a last-minute guest," she explained, avoiding my slanted suspicious gaze.

As someone rang the doorbell, my mother bent down to take the macaroni au gratin from the oven. "Can you please get the door? I need to get those out before they burn!"

Confused, I did as I was told. I swung the door open to Jake wearing a pair of blue jeans and a tan cardigan with a small front zipper, a beautiful flower arrangement in his left arm, standing with the sunset creating a beautiful canvas of yellow and orange behind him.

"Hi!" I squealed in a higher pitched voice than I intended, eyes wide.

"Good evening," he said with his charming smile.

"Yes," I said, swallowing hard, unable to really utter any logical sentence, as I felt as if I had gotten punched in the stomach.

I walked him to the back of the house to join my mother in the kitchen, having a mild out of body experience. I wasn't ready to spend the rest of the day staring in those mystical ocean-blue eyes.

I needed distance, for Christ's sake. Distance, and now we were going to spend an entire evening together outside of a work setting.

My mom hugged him and lifted the flowers from his arm.

"Nice of you to join us, and always with such gorgeous flowers! Tell Millie thank you for me."

My eyes were still wide open, yet I only got more confused by the second.

"My pleasure," answered Jake, as charming as I'd ever seen him. "It's self-serving, really. I get to make my mother happy that I purchase from her shop, and I get to see you smile."

"Thank you, my darling. Chloe, isn't this the most beautiful flower bouquet you've ever seen?" Mom gushed.

"Beautiful." I nodded, feeling numb.

I had so many questions but didn't know where to start. Clearly, my mother had a good relationship with Jake which would imply that my father's party was not the only place they had seen each other.

And it wasn't the first time Jake was bringing flowers to her home either by the sound of it.

I was avoiding Jake's inquisitive gaze like it would turn me into stone. Sometimes it seemed like he read me like an open book, me who prided myself on my general stoic behavior.

There was nothing I hated more than being caught by surprise and people knowing that I was missing information. I grabbed my wine glass and focused on the delicious liquid instead. I proceeded to open the fridge and unwrap the salad I had no interest in.

"Jake!" my dad shouted as he walked in and gave Jake a pat on the back. "Thanks for joining us on such short notice."

"I am not one to pass on good company and good food."

"Hi, Dad," I said, moving around Jake to meet my father.

"Hi, darling," he answered, giving me a warm embrace.

"I didn't realize we'd have guests," I muttered between clenched teeth.

"Yeah, this was very last minute, but your mother and I felt like some company would be nice."

I rolled my eyes before I could stop myself, knowing that was a silly answer that filled time while giving me absolutely nothing. My mother poured a glass of wine for Jake. "This is the wine I was telling you about," she explained, almost giddy.

"This is delicious," he said after smelling the wine and taking a sip, the sensual movement making my heart beat a little faster.

"Right? Since our last wine tasting, we've been big fans," explained my mom, looking at me.

"I didn't know you were into wine," said Jake, still oh-so-charming, intensely observing my every reaction.

"Yep," I answered in a cold tone, with what I knew to be an annoyed expression on my face.

I saw my mother sigh but ignored it. I had no obligation to be pleasant when I was feeling like I had walked into some sort of a trap.

"Jake, do you want to come with me to my office so I can show you those documents we discussed?" Dad asked him.

"Yes, let's go," said Jake before they left the room.

I slowly pivoted to face my mother, who was hiding behind her glass of wine.

"Sooooo, are you going to explain this? I feel like I am having some weird dream that I will wake up from because it makes zero sense."

"Oh, Chloe," said my mom with a chuckle, "always so dramatic. What's so confusing?"

"Mom, stop playing with me please. Why is Jake here? And why do I get the impression that he's been here more than once before?"

"Well, your dad has him over every now and then. They really like each other, you know. They discuss business mostly, but well, when he's here it makes sense to invite him to stay for dinner too. And yes, he sometimes brings me gorgeous flowers in the process."

Her glowing smile was infuriating.

"Of course it does, and of course he does," I said sarcastically. "And so, this impromptu dinner, what's this about?"

"Well," she started as she checked on the duck she was cooking, "your dad was thinking of having him over, and I figured why not invite you too? I haven't seen you since the party!"

"Playing the emotional card now, Mom?" I challenged.

"Chloe!" exclaimed my mom, seemingly offended. "No! Can't I just want to see my daughter? Now of course we also meant for the two of you to be here, to see if, well, now that you work together, if you have buried the hatchet so to speak."

"So, you want to make sure I don't hate him because dad gave him my board seat?" I demanded.

"Ugh, you are always so brutal with words," she teased, unaffected by what she likely perceived as a little tantrum. "But in part yes," she sighed as I was not backing down. "Something like that. He is a really great guy, Chloe, just trust your dad and give Jake a chance."

"Well, I'm here, so sure. I'm not going to ruin the evening if that's what you're asking. But all this, it's weird, you're acting weird. And all giddy around him for some reason. I also believe I have been on my best behavior for a while, and we actually work great together."

I stopped to stare into her eyes, still very suspicious about her intentions. "I assume you had nothing else in mind, right? Considering he's like Dad's best friend now or something?"

She almost spilled her wine in laughter. That made me chuckle as well, as I shook my head, loosening up a bit. It was just dinner, I reminded myself. And I had good wine, lots of it.

It wasn't long before Jake and my dad joined us on the patio. After a much-needed glass of wine and my mother's company, I felt more at ease and ready to mingle. I reminded myself that it was healthy to decompress a bit. The wine would help me let go of my innate distrust of others. And perhaps remove the image of Jake with Lauren I couldn't stop visualizing.

Jake seemed to be in a good mood, as well. I did my best to discreetly glance at him sitting next to me on the patio. He looked very relaxed in his casual attire, the shadow of a beard on his face, his curls less controlled than usual, the slight wind blowing them into a beautiful mess. He was even making jokes. His smile made me feel warm inside, and I felt as if this was a privilege, something he didn't share with just anyone.

I quickly took a sip when he caught me observing him. I felt my fingers itch to run through his hair. Maybe bring those full lips to that spot behind my ears and—no, I caught myself, that was enough with the fantasies.

"I'll be right back," announced my mother as she got up. "I have to check on the food."

"Let me give you a hand," offered my dad as he rose up and followed his wife.

If I didn't know any better, I would have sworn my parents left us alone intentionally.

Did I know better? I turned immediately to face Jake a little more, the alcohol in my veins giving me courage, hoping he would be a bit more honest than my mother.

"So," I started, "you come here often?"

"Yes, actually," he answered, with that devastating smile that made me want to freeze time so I could memorize every aspect of it. "Your parents have been kind enough to have me over a few times. My mother doesn't live very far," he explained, "so I am often in the area."

"Ah, that makes sense." And was a bit less suspicious. "She works at a flower shop?"

"Yes, she owns one about ten minutes from here."

"Well, the bouquet you brought is very beautiful; I like that it has all those unique flowers I don't even know the names of."

"She has an eye for these things," he replied, clearly very proud. The look in his eyes warmed my heart a little.

"Does your father live here too?" I asked.

"No. It's been my mother, my younger brother, and I for a while now," he explained, shifting to face me a little more.

"Does he live here, your brother?"

"No, he lives in New York."

"I see. Well, I would love to stop by your mom's shop when I am around here and get some for my house. Nothing like fresh flowers to brighten a room."

There was that smile again. All I wanted to do was stay just as we were, me looking into those warm blue eyes, both intimidated and fascinated by the strength that shone in their depths.

I was taken aback when Jake leaned towards me, his right hand tenderly pushing back some strands of hair from my face.

I shuddered a bit at the feeling of the tip of his fingers on my face. My breath quickened, but I was immobile, unable to move, hoping he did something else, such as run those long fingers up my...

"Table is served!" we heard loudly from inside.

Jake was the first to get up. I found the courage to do the same and trailed after him. For an unplanned dinner, my mother had outdone herself. She served a red wine duck on a bed of frites with some foie gras, my favorite.

She added a side of macaroni au gratin, some sautéed brussels sprouts, some arugula and beets salad, and some bread to dip in the wonderful duck wine sauce. And of course, chicken liver mousse as an appetizer.

I sat on my father's left side, my mother sitting across from me with Jake next to her. Thankfully, everyone was very hungry and there was just the right amount of conversation as I devoured her delicious food.

"You had quite the appetite, Chloe!" noted my mother when I slowed down to catch a breath.

"Not all women like to pretend they only live on oxygen, Mom," I answered, trying to save myself from the slight embarrassment I felt. Jake raised an eyebrow at me, as a smirk drew on his lips. He seemed quite amused. "Plus, what's the point of the Peloton if I can't eat everything I want? It's really your fault for making this taste so delicious."

She laughed, a soft look in her eyes. She knew I wouldn't stand for being teased, and she always enjoyed the fire in my eyes when I wanted to defend myself.

My father was on his best behavior, limiting the business talk to only one third of the time. He seemed so much more at peace since Jake had joined the company, I admitted, my throat slightly tightening at hearing that guttural laugh my dad had when he was having a great time and living in the moment.

When the meal was over, I helped my mother take the plates to the kitchen.

"Thank you, Mom, this was so good."

"I'm glad you liked it, sweetheart," she said with a smile. "I missed cooking for a family, you know."

That was her way of saying she missed her children. I squeezed her tightly.

"You are always welcome to come to my house and cook," I said, only half joking as I moved the rest of the duck in a container.

"So, tell me, how are things between you and Jake?"

"Um, what?" I almost dropped the duck.

"You know, professionally I mean, you guys have been working in the office together for a while now." She gave me a knowing look.

"*Oh*. Um, yes, we have. I told you, it's all fine. I can see why Dad likes him; the man knows what he's doing. I think he is a good asset for Motor Holmes if I'm being honest. Plus, he is quite easy on the eyes," I admitted.

"I am glad to hear!" she chimed, as she stopped putting dishes in the dishwasher to cast a glance at me.

"That last one is not necessarily a good thing," I added timidly.

My mother was observing me; she had that ten-step plan look in her eyes I noticed, but I didn't bite.

"There you go," I heard from behind me.

My eyes widened as big as they could. Jake was passing next to me with what was left of the dishes.

He must have heard me considering he was right there, and I wasn't the best at whispering. My heart sank just a little when he winked at me while my mother took the plates, a hint of a smile on her lips.

"Um, I'll be back. Bathroom break," I felt the need to announce, feeling like a teenager.

I avoided eye contact with both of them and rushed out, feeling my cheeks warming up. I almost sprinted to the front of the house and climbed up the stairs rapidly. I turned to the hallway on the right and opened the first of the two doors on my right.

I turned on the light as it was already dark outside, got in my bedroom, and went straight to the adjoining bathroom I used to share with Eric. It was small but had lots of cabinet space.

When I got back to my room, I instantly loosened up, enjoying the sight of the space I spent most of my childhood in. I beamed at the light-yellow walls, the white bookshelf on the left, with the TV on top, remembering when I negotiated hard for that television, after I got straight A's for a whole year.

I approached my shelf, caressing the rows of books that filled my childhood dreams. My mother had added the Harlequin books I had left in the shelves in the living room. Those books had provided me with an escape from life when needed.

Those stories had kept me away from trouble and inspired me to be a writer. I grabbed my favorite one, called Shanna. I must have read that book over a hundred times. The love story was impeccable in that one.

After putting the book down on the bed, I proceeded to the small white desk by the bay style windows. I giggled at the sight of my favorite Barbie doll, sitting next to her faithful Max Steel.

I wasn't a fan of Ken much, but Max Steel did the trick for me. I walked to my old queen-size bed, currently covered with my spring flower comforter and my favorite stuffed bunny.

I sat on the bed, close to one of the two small French country-style white nightstands that bordered it. That one still had my old CD player.

Excited, I pressed play on whatever was still in there. I got immediately lifted by hearing one of my favorite songs, *Tell Him* by Celine Dion and Barbara Kartland, taking me back to when I used to perform a concert for myself in that room. Melancholia for a different time enveloped me as I started singing the lyrics in a low voice. My poor parents; I could only imagine how loud I had gotten back in the day.

I started to skim through the book, going straight to my favorite chapter. I was lost in dreams, ravishing every word of one of my favorite love scenes when I heard a knock on the door, I had left a bit open. I turned and caught Jake walking in.

"I was sent to find you, it's time for dessert" he announced.

"Thanks," I said, a bit sad that I would have to close my book and stop my reveries. I put a bookmark in and set it down.

Jake was looking around but appeared hesitant to come in any further.

"I love coming back here," I said with a sigh. "So many memories. I miss childhood. The lack of care, the naïveté, the dreams, the songs, looking forward to the unknown without fear. All your life in front of you."

"I know what you mean," Jake remarked as he stepped in, pushing the door behind him.

He walked slowly, flipping through my books, my toys, smiling at my dolls, my desk. He grabbed my Barbie and Max Steel with a grin. I shut my eyes and hid my face behind my hands for good measure, mortified.

"They make quite the couple," he joked, taking no pity on me.

"Oh my God," I mumbled behind my hands. I opened my fingers to look at him when he laughed. "What?" I asked. "You didn't have toys when you were a kid?"

"Of course I did. I had Max Steel. I just never occurred to me to give him his own Barbie to play with."

My eyes widened as an indescribable sound left my throat. He laughed again. I, on the other hand, was horrified.

I watched as he lifted a few of my pictures and took his time studying them.

"Okay, stop snooping around," I begged. He ignored me and picked up one more framed picture before turning to face me. God, the man was beautiful.

"Paris?" It was a picture of me with the girls.

"Yah, senior trip."

"Nice."

My room seemed to have shrunk with him in it. He walked towards me but then headed to my windows, looking out.

"I heard it was quite the move when your family left Chicago to come here," he said as he finally directed his steps to the bed and sat next to me.

"It was. No child likes to leave friends behind," I confessed, my back a little arched. "But this house, it was the symbol of a new life, of my dad realizing his dreams, of my parent's sacrifice to give me and Eric a better future. It was the beginning of the family we are now, and I wouldn't trade that for the world."

Jake's intense gaze and brooding expression was confusing me. "The early days of a company are never easy, especially when someone is doing it alone."

"I know, that's why I became a lawyer, to help my dad, reduce his stress, help him take his company where I know it can go," I admitted as I put my book on the nightstand.

Jake nodded.

I continued, "Now, Eric has been trying to shove his money at my dad for a while now—trying to alleviate some of the financial burden for my parents—but he won't take it. I know it's not easy for my father to accept handouts, and that's why I am helping with my skills."

"Did you move to the city because of work?" Jake asked.

"Yes. I love this area, but I am happy I moved back to Bronzeville. It's very different from what it was before. But now I can enjoy it more, plus I get to see more diversity than both this area and downtown can offer. And I have the means to be active in the community, help make the area better, fund after school programs, help build infrastructure."

I stopped, realizing I was saying too much.

Jake was staring. He looked a bit unsettled, a frown on his face.

"What?" I asked, searching his eyes, a bit nervous as I ran my fingers through my hair, trying to understand what it is that justified the intensity with which he was observing me.

"There is a lot I don't know about you. Every time I think I've got it, you say something and amaze me all over again."

What he was saying was... what was he saying? It felt to me like he was flirting.

"Well, we've only just met. I know we met in, um, unique circumstances," I explained, allowing myself to give in a bit.

"That is true," said Jake, a soft smirk on his lips.

"I never thanked you for being a complete gentleman to someone who might have seemed a bit reckless to you. That night... I was in a special mood. I thought I needed the liquid courage to work up the strength to have a one-night stand," I admitted. "Luckily, it didn't happen," I said with an inquisitive look, inviting him to put my concerns at ease again.

"That's correct." He nodded. "Like I said, I didn't think it was appropriate. I was only looking out for you."

"Good, no point in a one-night stand one can't remember," I sighed, "or maybe that would be a good thing?" I laughed. He did not.

His voice was like velvet when he said, "Trust me, if it was with me, I'd make sure you remember. Every. Single. Detail."

The depth in his voice and the sudden severity in his tone made my body shiver.

I moved just a little closer, feeling brave enough to show him that I was interested. That I was burning for him, dying for just a touch. I felt him immediately tense, as his jaw tightened.

He sat a bit straighter. I wasn't sure if I should keep getting closer, very aware that my hand was right next to his, our fingers so close to grazing. Maybe I could just touch him slightly?

"I have to say," I started in a small voice, "while I was a bit, uh, unpleased at your addition to the business, I do enjoy working with you and I think my father made a very good decision adding you to the team."

I was trying to make peace. It was exhausting holding a grudge. I looked up, searching his eyes, assessing whether he was receptive.

I also felt quite vulnerable. It was my first and final peace offering I decided, wanting to eliminate any remnants of awkwardness between us, and potentially opening the door for more.

I shouldn't have, but I so wanted to. I was met with those crystal blue enigma's looking at me with a strict look.

"So, I've heard," he teased.

I knew he was referring to him hearing my conversation with my mother.

"It's not nice to eavesdrop," I teased, a soft quirk on my lips.

"I didn't mean to. And I do think we make a great team."

"Good."

He let out a deep breath as he bent a little closer to me.

"And for the record," he started, as he raised his hand up my left arm, leaving goosebumps in its wake, "you've also been quite the distraction for me, too."

I stopped breathing for a bit, but I leaned slightly forward, bringing my face closer to his, desperate to feel those lips on mine, wondering what they would taste like.

I could feel my hands getting warmer in anticipation, itching desperately for him to get even closer. As my eyes were closing, he let out a shallow breath, a line moving in his jaw, and he abruptly stood up. I almost tilted, trying hard to find my balance back.

He stomped to the window, his hand rubbing his mouth, as he cursed under his breath. I sat at the edge of the bed, panting, eyes wide. I needed to leave the room; I just wasn't sure my legs could support my weight in this moment.

After a few a few seconds, I regained my strength and quickly lifted off the bed. He closed the distance between us in two steps, breath heaving.

"Fuck it," he grunted, before palming the back of my head and bringing my lips to his.

He groaned in my mouth as my hands flew to his neck, my fingers finally buried in his hair.

"Sit down," he ordered. I obeyed. He ran his thumb on my parted lips as I gazed up at him.

"Those fucking lips of yours" he grunted.

He lowered his body on top of me, his arm around my waist as he lay us both down on the bed.

"Ugh," I let out as his mouth travelled to my neck, my hand still tangled in his hair.

I whimpered as he sucked on the top of my breast, slowly, deliciously. He didn't bother pulling it out, as he continued to run his hands down my body, kissing me until he was kneeling in front of me on the floor. I lifted my torso off the bed and leaned back on my elbows.

Without taking his gaze off me, he ran his hands up my legs and under my dress and only stopped when he got to my thong. He traced his thumb on my panties. I gasped.

"You're so wet for me," he rasped.

My breath quickened, but I nodded my head, confirming what he just said was true. He hooked his fingers around the delicate fabric and pulled my panties down.

He took the time, those intense eyes still scanning my face, to remove each of my feet from it. He folded it and put it in his pants pocket. I was in awe, goosebumps crawling on my skin, feeling myself get drenched in anticipation.

He gave me a crooked smile, lifting my dress to my hips. He finally broke eye contact to look at me.

There. I was bare to him, while he was fully clothed.

"I need to taste you," he declared.

"Jake…" I whispered, but he wasn't asking. He lowered his face to my pussy, sucking my clit.

"Oh!" I couldn't stop the moan that erupted from my lips, and my body vibrated under his touch.

He did it again, that time while pushing his tongue in between my lips, licking up until he was back at my bud.

I moaned again, laying down completely on the sheets. I was done for. He grabbed my thighs and parted them further. Then he held my ass and moved me to the edge of the bed, my legs around his head.

"Don't scream," he ordered before he dived back in. I brought my hand to my lips to hold back my moans.

My parents were just downstairs, and my door wasn't even locked. I was the good girl who had never snuck a guy to this house before, and while at an innocent family dinner, my coworker was feasting on my pussy in my childhood bed. But there was nothing that could make me want to end this moment.

I wanted him so much. I was so desperate for his touch, the world felt like it was in slow motion, because all I could feel was him, his tongue twirling so deliciously around my clit.

"Jake, oh God please. Please, *oh*." My hips bucked towards him, desperate for release. I was so close already, so, so close to losing it, the sensation so overwhelming and overpowering, I didn't know who I was. "Oh, I never want this to stop," I let out.

Jake came to an abrupt halt. I felt panic run through me at the idea that he wouldn't let me finish.

"We'll be right there!" It sounded like the grumbled sound came from his throat, but I was still coming back to reality, angry and sexually frustrated.

He wiped his mouth and took a few steps back. He looked angry. I assumed my parents had called to us, but I had completely missed it.

"I'm sorry, Chloe, I shouldn't have... done that."

Confusion and shame washed over me. What was he saying?

"I shouldn't have touched you like this. We are colleagues, and this was very unprofessional of me."

My cheeks were burning, and I was heaving. All I could do was stare. I had lost my voice.

"I'll see you downstairs," he declared in a raspy voice, hands shoved in his pockets, already too far from me too quickly. He stormed out of the room and pushed the door closed behind him.

I composed myself immediately, ashamed, unable to process what he had done fast enough. I got up, attempting to hide my confusion, and rushed to the bathroom to clean myself.

What had just happened? One minute he was driving me to what promised to be an explosive orgasm and the next he was apologizing to me. Was he serious? I felt so much embarrassment, I didn't know what to do with myself.

And I had to go back down there like Jake's face hadn't just been between my legs. And he still had my underwear.

After a few minutes, I managed to gain back some self-control, even though I was boiling inside. I stopped at the top of the stairs for a few seconds and forced myself to inhale and exhale a few times, before heading down, hopefully with a convincing smile that said I was already over what had just happened. Even if I knew it was definitely not going to leave my mind anytime soon.

I went straight to the kitchen, knowing my parents would be there with brownies and cake. They loved to enjoy their dessert on the patio with the heaters turned on during the cooler nights.

"Everything okay?" asked my mother, noticing my likely troubled expression.

"Yep, sorry, I had to take a call," I lied. "Need help?"

"Sure," she said, her gaze bouncing from me to Jake. "Just grab however many slices you want and let's go; your dad is outside."

I avoided any eye contact with Jake and instead focused on grabbing a very big piece of brownie from the corner and proceeded to silently eat it while wrapped up in a blanket as we sat outside.

Jake on the other end continued to be all charming and warm with my family as if his tongue hadn't been swirling my clit just ten minutes ago, his mood swings giving me whiplash.

"Chloe, I've been meaning to tell you, Jake has graciously offered to host us on a little retreat at his vacation home in a few weeks."

"Really?" I asked with a little more attitude than I intended. "What's the occasion?" I added, forcing myself to glance in his direction.

"It's a big house, and it's empty, I figured we could all use a good break," he said with a smile I wanted to rip off his face.

"Couldn't agree with you more!" chimed my mother, giving me a look, as she anticipated my potential snappy comment.

"Great," said Jake. "I'll have my assistant reserve the time on our calendars."

I rolled my eyes. There was no way in hell I was attending.

CHAPTER 12

It was close to midnight already when I finally decided that it was time to go home. My mother insisted I take some brownies to go.

"Did you drive?" asked my mom as she and my father walked us to the door.

"No, I'll call an Uber."

"At this time?" protested my father, a bit concerned.

"Yes, Dad," I answered with a slight tone. "They'll come as usual, might just take a few minutes that's all."

I couldn't wait to leave but let out a sigh when the Uber app said it would take about thirty minutes. I immediately tried Lyft, but it was the same thing. Just my luck.

"I am headed downtown," said Jake, who was standing next to me and clearly saw my phone. "I can drop you off if you want."

"No, it's all good," I rushed to say.

"Don't be silly, Chloe, it's on the way," insisted Jake, glaring at me, jaw tense.

Did he just call me silly? I shot him a murderous look.

"Not quite, it's more of a triangle situation if I recall," I added, daring him to insist further.

"Sweetie, I'd be much happier knowing you are safe with Jake," encouraged my mom, grabbing my hand as she usually did when she wanted to implore me to be reasonable.

"I have a driver," added Jake before I could retort that he had been drinking.

Of course, he knew what I was about to say before I said anything. I looked at both my parent and realized I had lost the battle, unless I had planned to sleep in the room Jake had just... No, that was not an option.

"Fine," I conceded, trying to be nice.

It would be a relatively fast drive, I told myself, there shouldn't be too much traffic at this time.

We said our goodbyes before leaving. Jake must have texted his driver because he was already outside of the black Mercedes Benz, with the back door open when we stepped out of the house.

I went down the stairs and straight in the car, ignoring the hand Jake was trying to lend me.

Jake got inside right after me and the driver closed the door. The car was as luxurious as it got, all in black leather, with specific compartments for drinks. The driver got in the car and started driving.

"I texted you our first stop," said Jake.

"Got it," answered the driver.

Jake opened a bottle of champagne, offering me a glass. I didn't want anything from him but figured that the alcohol might help me until I made it home.

Also, what the hell was he doing? Jake was back to being fun and charming, but I was hurt, and in heat apparently, and thus kept the communication to the bare minimum, and focused on the bubbles.

"About earlier, I never should have..." he began.

"I don't want to talk about it," I managed to say as my throat was closing out.

It wasn't that he was wrong... because we were coworkers, and it would be reckless to get into whatever almost happened between us back there. I didn't want to get a reputation, and Jake would have been the second person I dated from the office, even if I was dating Kyle before I joined the company. We got carried away.

Well, really, he did.

And I let him take charge. Something I didn't usually cave for.

I was still so wet for him, and if he said the words, I would put my bruised pride aside and climb on his lap right there in the back of his car. That self-awareness angered me even more.

I couldn't get past the fact that he was able to so easily walk away. No hesitation. No second thought. And, to make matters worse, he still had my underwear in his damn pocket, while I was squeezing my thighs to try to calm down.

The car came to a stop just ten minutes after we got on the road.

I looked out the now rolled-down window and spotted the most beautiful shop I had ever seen, feeling like I was immediately transported somewhere in Paris. The two-floor building looked just like a romantic country house, covered in faux pink cherry blossoms.

There was an outside yard that even in the dark looked filled with plants. I whipped around to face Jake.

"Is this your mother's shop?" I gasped, suddenly excited as I understood where we were.

"Yes," he answered with a smile. "Figured why not stop by now to get you some of those flowers you wanted."

"But I've passed by this area a million times as a child! I don't understand how she just... she transformed it into a little heaven!"

I was smitten. I basically jumped out of the car, guided by the irresistible urge to just go in. As it occurred to me that the place might be closed right now, I spun around to face Jake, who was right behind me.

"I don't think I've ever seen you so excited about anything," remarked Jake. "Except maybe chocolate," he joked.

I laughed, the tension in my stomach slowly dissipating.

"It's just so beautiful!" I whispered almost to myself. "I assume it's closed?"

"Here you are!" I heard from behind me in a slight German accent.

A beautiful woman with Jake's blue eyes, a small straight nose, and tight lips came out of the front door, her short blonde hair shimmering under the streetlight. She was wearing a beautiful flowing long blue dress with a brown belt and brown sandals.

"Mother," greeted Jake as she wrapped him in her arms.

She immediately turned to me, a warm smile on her lips. "You must be Chloe," she squealed as she embraced me.

I was taken aback and a bit confused, but I felt so comfortable around that woman that I relaxed instantly.

"Yes, I am." I looked up at Jake, who hadn't taken his eyes off me.

"I am Millie," explained his mother, holding my hands. "This one's mom," she added, bending her head in her son's direction. "He told me how much you loved those flowers he brought your mother, and since I was working late anyways it was no problem when he asked if you could stop by."

I turned a bit to look at Jake again, confused as to why he would offer up such a nice gesture after rejecting me the way he did. I almost expected to see someone else. He just smiled; with a shy smile I didn't know he was capable of having. Millie led us indoors.

I was even more enamored with the interior of the store. It was the cutest boutique I had ever seen.

The decor carried one to a different time with its golden roof. Millie sold all sorts of precious vintage items, from cute hats to ribbons, cards, jewelry. I could shop in here for hours.

"How long have you been doing this?" I wondered.

"Just a few years," explained Millie as she guided me around the shop. "I've always wanted to have a nursery. Jake finally convinced me, and he helped me buy this place. It took so much work to renovate it, but I am just so in love with it."

"It's perfect, and I am going to be here every week buying everything you sell," I said, and meant every word.

Jake seemed to also be having a great time. I knew he had been in the store probably a thousand times, but he indulged Millie and I going to every little corner of the place, with Millie sharing the same excitement as me, her new enamored customer.

"Oh, I'll be right back," announced Millie as her cellphone rang, "Ooo, I have to take this." She frowned.

"No problem!" I chimed back.

I turned to admiring the gold jewelry, unsurprised by the fact that I ended up here. Everything was just so beautiful; I didn't know what to look first at as Jake joined me.

"Each piece is unique, collected in some of her travels, attending antique sales, or through random encounters in her life."

I understood. The jewelry either worked for you or it didn't, no "*does that come in another color?*"

"I can't believe how beautiful they are. I probably shouldn't be behind the counter, especially since those are not even on sale!" I guiltily admitted, realizing I was on the wrong side of the glass cabinet.

"I don't think my mother would mind," encouraged Jake. "Let me help," he offered as he grabbed the keys that were on the counter.

Jake opened the jewelry case so I could take a closer look. He was so close, standing right next to me, that I could smell his intoxicating scent.

I wondered if he could hear my heart beating, as I felt like it was going to jump out of my chest.

"Try this one," he murmured.

Jake reached out and grabbed a gold necklace with a small antique Lavalier solid gold pendant that looked to be in perfect condition.

"Turn around."

I wanted to protest but I did as I was told, moving my hair out of the way for Jake to place the necklace around my neck.

I shuddered a bit and drew in a small breath as he gently grazed his fingers on my collarbone while securing the necklace around my neck. I looked up in the mirror. I fell in love. I got closer to see the details of the pendant.

The necklace was just so sleek, elegant, and sensual.

I was simply speechless.

"This Lavalier dates from the 1990's," explained Millie when she came back.

"It's so precious," I whispered, absolutely enchanted.

"Jake bought it when he met with a jeweler for me in France a few years back. I couldn't make the appointment and since he was in Europe he stepped in for me."

"She doesn't need the whole story, Mother," chided Jake.

I smiled and stared at him, as that was the first time I ever saw him even remotely embarrassed.

"Fine, fine, fine."

I was quite distracted by intricacies of the design of the necklace, The gold necklace featured cut diamonds set in a buttercup mounting, a river pearl, and multiple seed pearls.

We browsed through more pieces, I was fascinated by every story Millie had to share for each, whether it be an anecdote about her life or the life of a previous owner. I snapped a few pictures to send to my friends.

Millie made at least four customers tonight. Keisha was already planning her visit. That girl loved diamonds, and there were plenty of unique pieces there.

"Well, let me take you to the nursery," suggested Millie, appearing excited to get to show her babies.

She walked us to the back of the store, through two big glass doors. The nursery was really a paradise. The temperature there was slightly cooler and felt a bit humid. There were magnificent flowers and plants everywhere, with fresh cut stems in various see through fridges. From orchids to roses, to other more unique plants I had never seen before.

"Jake told me you wanted some color for your house, so here you go." Millie pushed a wonderful bouquet made of shades of white, yellow, and pink.

"Oh my God! This is for me? It's so... it's perfect! You really didn't have to!" I protested, mouth agape.

"It's a pleasure, my dear," said Millie, crinkles forming around her eyes, as her expression beamed with pride.

"Thank you so much!" I squealed as I smelled my flowers.

It was quite the bouquet; I already knew exactly where I was going to put them.

I fought like hell to convince Millie to let me pay for the flowers but there was no winning that fight. An hour had passed by the time we started the drive back to Chicago. I was carefully holding my flowers, refusing to put them in the trunk or anywhere I couldn't protect them from the ride, a smile plastered on my face, my cheeks feeling flushed with excitement.

"You really didn't have to, Jake. Not that I'm complaining, but you didn't have to stop by just to get me flowers," I reminded him.

"It was nothing really. As I am sure you can tell, my mother probably had a lot more fun than you did."

"That might be true," I admitted with a chuckle. "And your mom is lovely, and charming. Could never tell she's your mother."

Jake laughed that deep, honest laugh that made me warm up from the inside out and be more present.

The drive to my home was fast and sweet as there was no traffic at the time. I was almost sad when the car pulled in front of my house, as Jake and I were having a fun discussion about our favorite books.

Jake accompanied me up the stairs and to my front door. I was dying to invite him in, but felt a bit gauche, as I also didn't want to be rejected again.

"Well, this was fun," I said, looking at him once I opened the door, my flowers back in my arms.

"Yes, yes it was." He smiled.

"Thank you again. These flowers are just perfect."

"My pleasure." His jaw tensed a little.

I decided to be brave and got just a little closer to him. Perhaps my parents' presence was the problem earlier. Maybe now that it was just the two of us, he would give me what I really wanted.

Jake was looking down at me, his teeth clenched fully.

His eyes almost looked gray in the darkness, almost half shut as he looked down at me, making my blood rush through my veins.

"Would you, um, would you... like to... come... inside?" I suggested, barely able to breathe once I managed to utter the words.

Jake looked almost disturbed. "I, uh, I have a long day tomorrow."

"Okay, no problem," I quickly said, trying to save face. "I guess this is goodnight then."

Jake looked like he was in agony, which deepened my confusion even more. He got closer to me, his deep eyes staring into mine.

I closed my eyes just a bit, bending my head a little more towards him, making one last attempt to entice him, to make what I wanted very clear. Reason was no longer in charge, as my right hand lifted and posed itself on his chest.

Jake cupped my right cheek with his hand. I held my breath as he got closer, my lips parted and ready to feel his, but instead, he changed course and kissed my forehead for a few long seconds and shook his head.

"Goodnight," he rasped.

Before I could react, he was down the stairs and inside of his car.

I just stood there for a minute, letting the cold air reduce the heat burning my cheeks. The car hadn't moved. I was staring at it, trying to see the man inside, trying to understand what twisted game he was playing with me.

I let him do it again somehow. Get me thinking he wanted me, only to do absolutely nothing, even when I so clearly offered myself to him. Twice.

I swung the door open and slammed it, fighting the urge to throw the flowers in my hand to the ground. But they weren't responsible for my rage. Even if they reminded me of the exasperating man that just denied me... again.

Instead, I stalked to the kitchen and found a beautiful white vase, filled it up with water, and added some of the food powder. Millie had already cut the stems sideways, so I just placed the flowers in the vase. I took the flower pot and myself to my roof, currently semi-retracted.

It was perfect there, the cold breeze bringing my body temperature down. I sat down, hands on my head, trying not to scream.

I called Keisha. She would help me sort this out.

"Chloe?" she answered on the fourth ring.

"Sorry, Keish, are you sleeping?"

"Noooooo," she teased in between yarns. "What's up?"

I ranted for as long as Keisha let me. Iris and Amelia were somehow awake so they joined the call I didn't tell them that he went down on me. I was too embarrassed.

What was wrong with me? I went from hating the man for taking my job to hating the man because he clearly thought I wasn't good enough for him. In the span of just a few weeks!

How did I go from being distrustful of him to wanting to feel his lips on mine, his arms around me? It had felt like a date. It wasn't, clearly, but it felt like one and he must have known it. He took me to see his mother for crying out loud, who does that? I felt something, and he must have as well, I couldn't be making it up, could I? But then if he felt something, why would he reject me? Was I going crazy?

Keisha's solution was for me to either confront him or find someone else to date immediately. I refused to be humiliated by Jake ever again, so I decided to go with the second plan and find a decent guy urgently.

As I was starting to change my clothes to get ready for bed, I realized I was still wearing the necklace! How could I have forgotten?! Why did no one say anything?! The necklace was not light, but I wore necklaces often enough that I didn't realize this one wasn't mine.

I removed it from my neck immediately. Who knew how much it cost, and it was from the "not for sale" display and clearly gold and antique!

I was mortified and planned to return it the following day. I typed a few emails and then a few text messages to Jake that I never sent. Of course, now that I was livid and had decided to ignore him, I had stolen his mother's necklace and felt the need to apologize.

I didn't want to reach out like a panicked person, but I was exactly that. Do you text someone at 1 a.m. to apologize for stealing, or do you wait for a more decent hour on Sunday, or even better Monday when you see them? I couldn't call him that late.

Who knew where he was? Perhaps even in Lauren's bed, just the thought twisting a knot in my stomach.

I decided to fight my anxiety and try to fall asleep instead. I would be able to make a better decision in the morning. Or so I hoped.

CHAPTER 13

I QUICKLY DROPPED MY tan YSL bag and my jacket on the shelf behind my office chair and rushed to Jake's on Monday morning with the intent to sneak in and drop the necklace before he made it in. I had intended to be there earlier, but picking my outfit of the day had somehow derailed me and put me behind schedule.

I didn't have that much work to do, and if it wasn't because I wanted to return the necklace currently burning a hole in the box I was squeezing in my hand, I probably wouldn't have made it downtown at all.

I knocked, and as I heard nothing, I entered his space cautiously.

I rushed to the desk and placed the box in front of Jake's chair. I headed to the door, but went back, deciding I needed to leave a note, kicking myself for not thinking of that sooner.

Had I thought of it, I would have written the note in my office as opposed to spending more time in Jake's, but it was too late for that.

I quickly found a notepad on the desk. I stopped as my eyes had caught my name on the page I had opened the notepad to, written in cursive.

My blood suddenly started to boil, as my brain took over and I proceeded to read what was clearly not meant for me to. It looked like a list of all the deals I had worked on since at Motor Holmes, with some of the entries having checkmarks next to them. I was confused and was having a hard time understanding why Jake would track my work with such details.

I proceeded to flip through previous pages, trying to understand if I was the only target of such scrutiny or if he was paying that close attention to other people at the company.

"What do you think you are doing?" I heard shouted in my direction, as a door I didn't hear open closed violently.

I jumped and dropped the notepad on the floor. I swirled around to find Jake towering over me, the most brutal intense look in his eyes, his lips pinched, his nostrils flaring, and a deep frown on his forehead. He had the stubble of a beard he sometimes bore, making him look a bit rugged and somehow more threatening.

My eyes widened as I was having difficulty breathing. My mouth was agape, but I was struggling to find my words.

I felt like I had been caught doing something really bad, even if technically I came in there to do something good and had no intention to go through his things. Instead of saying anything, I pivoted back around and bent down to grab the notepad, grasping to just a few seconds to compose myself, only slightly concerned I would tear my black Tahari dress.

I could explain this. I desperately felt the need to. "It's not what you think," I started.

"You mean you weren't going through my personal items?" he scolded, fire in his eyes.

"No, I mean yes, but not intentionally..." I objected with a sigh, deciding that complete honestly was really all I had time to think about and deliver.

"I came here to drop off the necklace," I explained.

I swiveled again, bending a bit to grab the box. I slightly grazed Jake as I turned back around, meeting his eyes like a deer caught by headlights.

I really needed to get it together. "I'm sorry," I uttered impulsively.

He took a slight step back, putting his hands in the pockets of his black suit pants. If he was trying to look even more intimidating, he had succeeded.

"I was looking for a piece of paper to leave you a note. I opened your notepad, but then I saw my name and I couldn't help but read," I explained, a slight tremor in my voice I couldn't shake, hoping he wouldn't follow up after that.

"And?" he snarled.

"Um, well," I said after taking a large breath, my courage slowly coming back, coupled with irritation. "Why do you have all these notes and details regarding the deals I'm working on? I won't lie, it really has me on edge. And once I saw this my reflexes kicked in and yes, I kept looking. I can't imagine that you would have done any differently. It's important here to focus on the fact that I didn't mean to snoop," I tried to plead.

"I don't owe you any explanation, Chloe," he snapped, gritting his teeth.

I felt anger invade every inch of my body. It wasn't about the fact that he was currently treating me like a criminal. It was about the fact that I desperately wanted his approval, his lips, and I was feeling like a thirteen-year-old with a crush, and I couldn't stand it.

"You seem to forget that this is my father's company, I own stock in this business and to a certain extent, this is my inheritance. I am the one who doesn't owe you an explanation, Jake, not the other way around," I fumed. "I am sorry I went through your things," I uttered, trying to calm myself, "but I do need to understand what your problem with me is. You are tracking my every move, and frankly I have never seen anyone that interested in every single task I do, not even my father."

I held his gaze as I could feel my back stiff with tension.

"I am both a board member and the chief operating officer, Chloe, and it's part of my job to keep a close eye on any M&A or IP type activities in this company," he hissed. "I won't apologize for being diligent in doing my job, not to you or anyone." He paused. "Assuming you have been conducting yourself as expected, you shouldn't have any concerns with me being thorough." He raised an eyebrow.

"Fine," I sighed, realizing the snide comments were the best I was going to get from him, feeling defeated, but still too prideful to voice my real issue. "That's not what I came here for. I didn't mean to be here in your space like this," I hesitated. "I just wanted to drop this off, that's all, Jake. I, uh, also wanted to, um... whatever, never mind, I'm just going to leave now," I blurted as I set the box down on the desk and passed next to him.

I quickly exited, feeling weak in my knees, concerned I wouldn't be able to leave if I didn't make it to the elevator in the next few seconds. My brain was attempting to process what had just happened before nine am.

I couldn't help but feel guilty for snooping, but I was only human. Once I saw my name on paper, that was it; I didn't think, I got in fight or flight mode, and flight wasn't my style.

I finally got into my office and buried myself in my chair to try to compose myself, my hands quivering. My throat was burning, and I felt tears pricking in my eyes and I was fighting them with the little strength I had left, after that embarrassing confrontation.

Attempting to control myself, I brusquely stood, shoved some documents I needed in my bag, in a sudden rush to leave and just hide home.

As I wrapped up, I heard a knock at my door.

"Come in," I cautiously said.

Jake popped in, closing the door behind him. He just stood there, observing me, making feel naked once more.

I wondered if my eyes were red; the last thing I needed was for him to catch me in a moment of weakness. Avoiding his gaze, I turned around. I focused on fiddling with a pile of papers on my desk, pretending to organize them, just to have something to do with my hands.

"I'm sorry for the way I just handled that," I heard behind me.

I closed my eyes, taking a breath, knowing that I had to turn around to face him eventually. "All good."

"You seem upset," he queried.

"I'm not," I spouted out too quickly, turning to face him.

He was standing at the end of my desk. There was enough distance between us for me to gain enough strength to talk, and I was thankful for that.

"Just have a lot to do here."

"But you're packing," he noticed calmly.

"I only came in to drop off the necklace and apologize for forgetting to give it back before leaving your mother's store," I attempted to explain again. "I'm working from home today."

"I see. Well, it's yours, Chloe, so keep it," he said as he put the box down on my desk.

"I don't want it," I lied.

"I want you to have it," he insisted.

"Why?" I snapped.

"Because it suits you perfectly," he continued in that calm, deep voice that warmed up my stomach.

"At least let me pay for it," I pleaded. "It's quite obviously a unique and precious piece and—"

"No, that's not how gifts work," he interrupted, his hand up.

"I don't want anything for free," I explained, growing impatient. He raised his eyebrows. "Just please, let me pay you for it. I would feel much more comfortable if I am to keep it," I stated, hoping he saw my point of view.

"Are you trying to insult me?" he probed, bending his head, seeming honestly offended.

"No." I was quite baffled by his reaction. I hesitated but then went for it. I took a deep breath. I didn't have much to lose.

"I'm not the woman you should be gifting anything to. It should be my cousin. Especially after what happened this weekend," I exclaimed, impatiently running my hand through my hair, lips pursed, eyes wide.

Jake just stood there, staring at me. I expected him to have some sort of response, but nothing came.

I needed him to kill my fantasies, reveal himself as being just like every other successful man I had dated, weak and insecure, rejecting me for having what apparently were "men-like ambitions," daring to want a career, earning my own income, and refusing to depend on others.

I wanted him to explain to me that I should be attracted to men who equated their value to how many free drinks they bought for a person they were interested in. I needed him to tell me what I needed to hear so I could put an end to that stupid fantasy that was taking over my sanity.

I needed the strength to push him away so the attraction I felt towards him didn't grow into something more.

He kept the uncomfortable silence for so long, I felt as if I was starting to have an out-of-body experience, wanting to flee from the room.

"Okay. Fair comment," he admitted. I braced for the worst. "I could do that, or I could tell you the truth. Lauren and I had fun in the past but that's all we ever were. We are just friends now, and it's been like this for a while," he explained, volunteering more than I would have expected. "We are just social friends now."

I avoided his gaze, not wanting to show the unjustified relief I felt, even if he had ignored my other point.

"That's not my impression," I pressed.

"I'm aware that now she might want more than friendship, Chloe, I won't lie, but I made myself clear back then and I did now; there is nothing serious between us. She is just a friend."

"I actually don't care either way," I quickly lied, feeling defensive mostly due to feeling my chest go up and down much faster than normal. "Anyways," I said, dying to change the topic, "I'm not going to lie and say I don't want this necklace. Because I just love it too much not to have it."

Jake smiled. I couldn't help but reciprocate.

"I really have no problem paying for it or simply returning it as I understood it wasn't on sale, even if I admit the first option is a lot more appealing to me." I grinned. "I just didn't want this accident to, uh, make me seem like someone I am not," I volunteered, relying on truthfulness as the easiest path.

Jake seemed to appreciate my honesty I thought, hoping that the worst of that convoluted morning was behind us.

"Understood." Jake took a step closer. "But it's yours, and I won't take no for an answer," he taunted. "And I am sorry for my tone this morning."

I blushed, confused, searching his eyes, desperately trying to understand if that was him flirting, expressing interest, or just playing with me as he had done over the weekend.

I didn't dare to hope or make any moves that time around, even if I desperately wanted to sift my fingers through his thick curls, that cologne of his making me want to renege all my morning resolutions of keeping our relationship professional. What did he want?

Was I reading too much in his gift?

He proceeded to open the box, taking the delicate necklace out.

"Turn around," he instructed.

My feet moved before I could stop them. And before I knew what I was doing, my hands were holding up my hair so he could move in closer.

My body tensed at the anticipated feeling of the tip of his fingers on my bare skin. I closed my eyes, begging my body to simmer down.

He tied the necklace around my neck just like the last time. I slightly fluttered, just like the last time. I let go of my hair, turning around to face him, unable to resist being pulled to him.

"There," he whispered, "perfect."

"Thank you," I murmured softly, feeling shy and flirty.

"Chloe, about this weekend..."

I jumped slightly at the sound of my ringtone. The unwelcome noise was coming from my cellphone, posed on the table next to us. I turned my head to grab my phone, but before I could press ignore to Kyle's call, Jake was backing away.

I knew he had seen the call come in and couldn't help feeling like I also needed to explain my status with Kyle; I wanted to hear what he was about to say.

"I'll let you take this," said Jake, a coldness in his gaze.

He bolted to the door and out of the room, too late for me to say anything without making things weird.

I sighed but hit ignore on the call. I focused on finishing packing and leaving my office as soon as I considered it safe that I wouldn't run into Jake in the elevator banks.

Once in the Uber, I took a deep breath, my fingers grazing the necklace, my lips slightly bitten, as I recalled how close Jake was to me just a few minutes ago. Kyle probably saved me; what would have happened if he had kissed me in the office? And was it really true that he wasn't into Lauren?

What did he want? What did I want? I sighed, deciding to pay attention to the beautiful Chicago skyline, coming alive with everyone who works downtown making their way to their office for the day.

I needed a distraction to keep me from overanalyzing everything. There was an intensity about him, something not visible but yet palpable. I saw something behind the stoic face, the diplomacy and calmness he presented to the world. A lion, hidden in the shadows, but always there, right under the surface.

But I could see him, and every time Jake looked in my direction, I felt like the lion saw me, too. Deep under my skin.

CHAPTER 14

I SPENT THE FIRST half of the week working from home. My father had inquired whether I was feeling sick, since he knew I generally loved going to work in the office. We had a very flexible work from home policy for the executive office, as we didn't have to manage the day-to-day manufacturing operations, and our team usually took advantage of it. But I felt safer at home.

I needed some distance to process what I felt, and since I had no meetings that week, there was no need to be there anyways. Limiting my interactions with Jake to group calls or emails was great, even if I refused to admit I missed seeing him.

But every time I thought I was doing better, I would remember his face, his presence in a room, his smell, his fingers on my neck, the feeling of his tongue on my clit, and my heart rate would accelerate.

If it wasn't for that necklace that I still hadn't taken off, I would have thought that Jake was not interested in me. But that couldn't be; why would he take me to the flower shop? Why would he bury himself between my legs?

I couldn't figure him out, whether he wanted me or not. I reminded myself countless times that perhaps it was for the best. That he was right.

A relationship with a director of the company was a horrible idea. I shouldn't get involved with someone at work again, especially someone who was so close to my father.

I even went on a dinner date on Tuesday, with a man I had met online. Mike was 5'10" with short black hair and glasses framing a trustful gaze. An adorable dimple drew on his left cheek when he smiled. He was coming off a breakup, and I sympathized, as the pain I saw in his eyes reminded me closely of mine.

The date went well enough that Mike and I had joined Keisha and some other friends for thirsty Tuesdays afterwards. Everyone had a blast, including me, but after a few drinks, all I wanted to do was call Jake.

Keisha ended up taking my phone away from me. It was for the best.

After we left the club, we had taken an Uber to my house, and he even kissed me goodbye. But when I felt his lips on mine, I found myself wishing Jake had done the same when he dropped me off last week. When I fell asleep, my vivid dreams had him in almost every scene, close but distant and inaccessible to me.

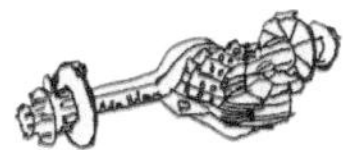

I had decided to extend my work hiatus. If my tasks were done well and on time, it didn't matter where I was. I worked a lot more without getting ready for a commute, using the time to be productive instead, and when free, to write. It worked out perfectly, as I was able to be home and have people come over to start the decorations. I was hosting the surprise birthday party for my father at my place.

My mother had chosen my house because it would be nearly impossible to hide a surprise party for my father in his own home, so I had joyfully agreed. It was supposed to be a small and chic Sunday style but Saturday brunch.

I had opted for Saturday because I had heard coworkers complain about Sunday events before (that I didn't organize) and I wanted to include as many people as I possibly could.

My father loved his team, so I knew it would be important to him to have them at the party.

I had invited Keisha but made sure to warn her that Eric was flying in for the event.

Kyle would be attending since he was a family friend at this point. The guest list was otherwise composed of a few close friends of my father as well as my uncle and his wife. I had not invited Lauren and was praying that she wouldn't make a surprise appearance, but I knew I had to be ready for the worst.

When Saturday morning came, I moved Penny to the covered part of the rooftop, where most of her stuff was, so she wouldn't get bored and cause chaos. I gave her a kiss and locked the door so she would stay safe and unbothered.

Keisha joined me first, in the cutest light green linen/cotton dress, her bouncy curls perfectly surrounding her angelic face.

"You look divine!" I said as I pulled her in my arms at the door and grabbed some packages from her to help. She had brought a birthday gift for my father and a few bottles of wine.

"You, too! Glad to see it suits you so perfectly!" Keisha was referring to the light pink fun and flirty dress she had convinced me to buy. The length stopped right below the knee, with an off-shoulder style, smocked back detail, and ruffle sleeves.

"We look so in sync!" I squealed.

We headed to the kitchen to continue setting up. I had hired my usual chef for the day, and she had prepared all sorts of delicious French pastries and croissants from scratch.

I was able to help with some chicken liver mousse—something I knew we had to have for a Holmes party. It was one of the very few things I learned to cook after I moved away from home. It brought me comfort in the times I was missing my family.

I had set up shop in my backyard, where two long, beautiful eucalyptus wood tables sat. They were large enough to fit my seventeen confirmed guests and family members.

The catering crew I always hired for events were there setting up. I was thankful for the help because there was no way I'd have the time to do all of the event planning and preparation by myself.

My initial idea was to have the party on the rooftop, but the weather was too variable this time of year—one day warm, one day a bit chillier, so I wasn't sure what to expect. I wanted all the guests to be comfortable throughout the evening.

Plus, that setting was much more conducive to the flow I had created. I used signs by the door that instructed the guests to simply proceed to the back.

It was the perfect scene, as my hydrangeas and peonies were in full bloom as they came alive from the Chicago winter. The outdoor sofa underneath the pergola had been cleaned and dusted for the occasion. There was of course a full bar with a grill. Some self-serve water dispensers with lime and oranges were scattered around.

I had six standing coolers, so people could help themselves to their own champagne as they walked around. The bar and the table were otherwise equipped with pineapple juice, orange juice, strawberry and peach puree, everything that was needed for mimosas, French 75s and bellinis.

A few people from the catering team were going to stick around to assist with the event, but I also wanted to make it a self-serve experience so people could roam around in a more organic fashion.

It was 11 a.m. when the first guests arrived, and within thirty minutes, I had a full house. Everything was perfect. Eric has just showed up, all in white. He gave me a bear hug.

"Nice party! Everything looks great" he complimented.

I lifted the box he brought to add it to the table I had set up in the kitchen for gifts.

Eric seemed a bit nervous. I knew my brother well enough to infer that he was searching for Keisha in the crowd. He stopped and smiled when he saw her pouring some champagne by the bar.

"Leave her be," I warned.

"She is not a child, Chloe, and neither am I."

"I don't care," I retorted, unaffected by that commanding and egotistical presence he seemed to maintain with everyone around him. "If you hurt her again, I will make you regret it," I threatened with a hint of a smile.

Eric half-smiled, cognizant that his usual captivating gaze didn't faze me. "I would never hurt her, Chloe."

"You have before," I pointed out.

He shook his head. "How did I possibly hurt her?" he asked, his piercing stare darkening.

"Ugh, not going to do this right now," I declared, rolling my eyes.

"Good," he acquiesced, kissing me on the forehead. "Don't know how of all the big brothers out there, I ended up with the little sister who thinks she is my parent."

"I can't help that I'm smarter than you," I joked.

"You probably are," he sighed. "Now, can I please go get a drink?"

"Yes, yes," I replied with a smile.

As I spun around to head back outside, there was Jake waltzing towards me, taking his sunglasses off, with the most gorgeous bouquet of peonies I had ever seen.

My heart skipped a beat, my hands suddenly sweaty.

"What are you doing here?" I inquired, perhaps a little too aggressively.

"Nice to see you too?" he teased with a smirk.

"Sorry," I corrected rapidly. "I didn't know you were coming?"

"I take it Yasmin didn't tell you?"

"Um, no," I sighed.

"I hope I am not a bother." He raised a brow at me.

"No, of course not!" I uttered at a higher pitch than intended, causing a few heads to turn in our direction.

I should have known that this was a possibility, but I figured if my mother was extending the guest list, she would have at least given me a heads up.

"Just you?" I probed, bracing myself to have to cater to my cousin in my own home and with the man I was drooling over.

"Just me," confirmed Jake with a smirk.

I was having a hard time hiding my relief as I smiled back.

"Let me help you with those!" said Keisha from behind Jake, swiftly coming to the rescue.

She picked the gorgeous bouquet from Jake while one of the party planning crew members helped her fill a vase with water.

"They are pre-cut" added Jake, completely comfortable with the attention his bouquet was getting him.

"You did a great job outside," he complimented, taking a step closer to me, as he folded his Burberry sunglasses and laid them down on the kitchen island.

"Thank you," I answered, a light tightness in my chest, wishing I had either the flowers or a glass of champagne to keep my hands occupied.

Jake was wearing an unconstructed Italian light gray wool blazer, a white t-shirt and navy kakis, with a pair of dark brown shoes. No scruff. He looked so good. Better than good.

And I had to resist the urge to reach out and run my hand along his muscular arms. He was being nice, but I wasn't going to fall for him, or his games, again.

"Where's Penny?" he asked, looking for her.

Was he serious? My cat was my weakness, and him caring for her, remembering her name, it did something to me.

"Safe upstairs."

"Fair. I guess I'll have to go up and say hi."

He had no mercy.

"I guess."

"I see you are still wearing your necklace," he whispered by my ear as he edged closer to me, his voice an octave deeper. I held the kitchen island for support. "I can't think of a better place for it than around your neck" he murmured in a guttural tone, sending shivers through my body.

Why was it that I felt heat rising? Where was Keisha? Why wasn't she grabbing my arm, shaking some sense into me?

Was Jake flirting with me again?

"How was your week?" he asked.

"Good. Busy," I forced out.

"I haven't seen you in the office much," he said with a frown.

"I've been busy," I repeated, voice tight.

What else did he want me to say here?

"I see." His jaw tensed.

He looked like he had more to say but didn't know how.

"The date go well?" he asked.

My eyes grew wide.

"What? How do you know that?"

"Your mother. Social media. Take your pick."

"You're not on social media," I pointed out.

It was the best I could come up with, while my brain tried to process this sudden conversation.

"That's not the point, Chloe," he added with a tick to his jaw.

I reminded myself to breathe.

"It went well," I answered, challenging him. "We will be seeing each other again this weekend."

"Oh, I don't think so," he announced.

I looked up, searching for answers in the subtle streaks of gold around the iris of his eyes, as he took another step, the tips of his shoes touching mine, but I could find no smirk, no mockery.

All I saw in his darkened stare was a reflection of my own desire, coupled with what looked like frustration or anger. My breath got shallow.

"Hey there!"

Kyle walked in, in his light pink pants and white shirt.

"Nice of you to join us!" he said to Jake, with too much excitement.

Jake shook the hand Kyle was offering, his face tightened with tension. The men stared at each other as I grew more and more uncomfortable.

Jake and I were standing quite close to each other, and he had no intentions of moving away from my side, it seemed. And I was paralyzed.

"Kyle, want to get me a drink?" Keisha asked as she joined us and wrapped her arm around Kyle's.

"Huh sure." Kyle had a confused frown on his face. He knew he wasn't Keisha's favorite person.

"Actually, I'll go with." She grinned as she pulled him away with her. I needed to remind Keisha that leaving me alone with Jake wasn't the idea here.

"I don't think he likes you very much," I joked, trying to bring us to a more palpable topic. Jake didn't bite.

I cleared my throat.

"Please thank your mom for the flowers," I said.

I headed to the bouquet, focusing on the beautiful round buds instead of the electricity I felt coursing through me. "I wish my peonies in the back grew like this. They are pretty, but nothing like these."

Jake drew closer, stopping right behind me.

"It's all about the soil," he explained softly.

"What do you know about planting?" I asked in surprise.

"I always helped my mother with her gardening, just so she wouldn't hurt herself. But I learned a thing or two in the process." He shrugged.

I tensed as I felt his warm breath traveling down my neck, causing a chill to run down my back. I froze, my heart rate accelerating, and I had to clench my thighs because I was instantly aroused by just his presence. It was pure torture.

I wanted to swirl around, grab him, kiss him, let him lift me on my kitchen counter and take me there, with the same desperate animalistic basic need that was making me burn in place.

But I wasn't going to get rejected again. I refused.

He ran his left hand down my arm, his lips now grazing my temple. His hand travelled up and down the side of my body to my hips, pulling me even closer to him, my back flush against his chest while my hands palmed the countertop in front of me.

I could even feel him, all of him, clearly strongly aroused.

"I made a big mistake," he breathed out. "I should have let you come for me that night."

"Jake..."

"Cutting it short when you wanted it so bad," his voice rumbled, "that wasn't very gentlemanly of me now, was it?"

A soft whimper escaped my lips, his now obvious desire for me pressed hard against my back.

"I think we should finish what we started," he hummed.

Fear and anticipation were driving me mad. People could see us if they walked in or simply leaned a little to look inside, and that terrified me, as some of our coworkers were outside.

But my body didn't care, responding to every stroke of his hand caressing me, coming dangerously close to between my thighs. I gripped the edge of the counter with all my strength, closed my eyes, slightly panting, trying to calm myself down, as I felt my slick arousal slide in my panties.

"They're coming!" we heard come from outside.

Jake growled but immediately removed his hand and backed off. Desperate to save face, I launched forward and out of the kitchen without looking back.

Everyone cheered "Happy birthday!" in unison when my parents showed through the back gate. My father seemed a bit flushed, which meant that he was both surprised and touched.

"You and your mother!" he tenderly complained as he wrapped me in his arms.

My mother was wearing a gorgeous long apricot linen dress that gave her that light vacation look one rarely achieves outside of the Caribbean. My dad was sporting a light blue suit.

He had been told they were going to go to a restaurant, so his attire perfectly fit the event. I knew my mother probably imposed his outfit on him anyways, and that was usually for the best.

"Happy birthday, Dad." I held him tightly.

"Thank you, sweetheart, this is amazing!"

He shook Jake's hand and added, "Glad you are here."

"Me, too. Happy birthday, Philip," wished Jake.

My mother hugged Jake, as well, a suspicious smile on her lips. "I am glad I could convince you!" she laughed.

I bent my head a little, trying to understand what the dynamic was. I would have rolled my eyes at my mother's wink at me if I hadn't just let Jake touch me like he did just a few minutes earlier.

I ran to Keisha as soon as I could. I had noticed that she had gone inside after she wished my dad a happy birthday. Keisha was sitting in the living room, her fingers scrolling on her phone.

"Okay, so why on earth would you leave me with him?!" I hissed as I sat next to her.

"Weren't you saying just an hour ago that you had gotten him out of your system with this working from home situation?" teased Keisha.

"Ugh," I said, putting my head in my hands.

Keisha placed her phone down, realizing I was more troubled than she thought. "What's wrong?"

"Jake cornered me in the kitchen... and we had a moment."

"What!?" shrieked Keisha.

"He got behind me and... he... he put his hands on my hips, and I almost lost it," I sighed, getting aroused just remembering how his palm felt on my skin. "When we were at my parents' house, he... he went down on me," I confessed, covering my face.

It sounded even worse when I said it out loud.

"What the hell!?" asked Keisha again.

"I know. He kissed me and then got down on his knees. But before I could finish, my parents called, and he pushed back like I had bit him or something. He said it was a mistake because we worked together.

"We never talked about it. I've been avoiding him but today, today he clearly was trying to touch me again."

"Oh my God." Her eyes widened in shock.

"So no, I'm not over him, Keisha. He is all I can think about. I want him so bad I don't know what to do with myself. And I am so ashamed," I confessed.

"Oh, sweetie! But that's a good thing! Means he *is* into you! He's just fighting it as much as you are!" cheered Keisha a little too loud.

"Who knows. What changed? He's been sending me mixed signals I just... I just don't know what to do. I don't know what he wants. What fucking game is he playing?"

My hands flew in the air with exasperation.

"And say he really was into me... I don't want this; I don't want to want this. But he's right, you know. We are coworkers, and he is technically the enemy, isn't he? I'm giving this situation too much control over me, and I fucking hate it."

I nervously ran my fingers through my hair and chugged the glass of champagne the server, Jeremy, set down in front of me on the coffee table.

"I know you do." Keisha laid a hand on my back. "But I mean, workplace romances happen all the time."

"I know, but I don't want that again, I just need to get it together," I decided as I sat back straight. "I just need to... I will sleep with Mike today if I have to. We are supposed to grab dinner tonight. I am done letting Jake mess with me like this," I declared.

I chugged a second glass of champagne Keisha just handed me after I pointed to it.

"Anyways, how are you?" I inquired, trying to focus on her.

"Oh, you know, it's still awkward," sighed Keisha, looking at the floor. I completely understood, too familiar with the pain in her eyes.

"You know if he wasn't my brother, he would be at the bottom of the ocean right now, right?"

"Yes," laughed Keisha, "I know."

"I'm still tempted."

Keisha let out a chuckle, the sound settling me a bit.

I knew she was a woman of few words, and the fewer the words the more pain she was in. I was suspicious that she hadn't fully moved on from Eric, even if she didn't seem to know it.

Sometimes I wished I could play cupid and perhaps even help them get back together, but I wasn't sure that was the answer. I was missing too much information to even be helpful. Eric, considering how tense he got anytime he saw a man talk to Keisha, was clearly still smitten.

But if I even dared to broach the topic further again, it would have to be at a different time.

We finally found courage to join the rest of the party and confront our own demons, after Keisha caught up with my champagne glass count.

CHAPTER 15

I SAT ON MY father's right side, my mother was across from me, joined by my uncle George and his wife Lisa next to him.

When the food was ready, Kyle immediately installed himself at my side. Keisha was seated next to him, with Eric daring to take the seat to her right, ignoring the death stare I gave him.

"Oh, Jake, come next to me!" shrieked Lisa, grabbing his hand, "I saved you a seat."

Of course they knew him. Lauren must have introduced Jake to her parents at some point, I realized, the seed of jealousy growing inside me.

The brunch was going quite well. And I found myself engaging in the small talk around me. My father looked pleased with how the party turned out, which made me happy.

I also found myself chatting with Kyle more than usual. He was acting flirty, which I didn't mind because it kept my mind off Jake.

But I couldn't help myself from eavesdropping on the conversation across from me. Jake and Lisa were talking about something, and Jake mentioned something about how nice my house was.

In true Lisa fashion, she had to turn the attention back to Lauren and made sure to highlight the fact that Lauren was modeling in Spain. I felt thankful that my cousin's career kept her away for the day. The idea of Lauren sitting next to Jake only drove me mad.

A short time later, the brunch was served. It consisted of four styles of eggs, three types of toast, the avocado, arugula and tomato salad, and the fluffy pancakes on the menu. It was finally time for dessert. The mini cakes of all flavors that my team had brought to the table after removing the food plates was the perfect ending to the meal portion.

"So, Jake, when are you stopping by the house? It's been too long since you've come over," inquired Lisa. "You know," she continued, specifically looking at me, "Jake and Lauren, they just adore each other!"

"Great," I said, unable to fake more than a half-smile.

"Lauren has been traveling so much," continued Lisa, not letting anyone else say a word. "Even I barely see her! But I am so proud of my gorgeous girl!"

"As you should be," said my dad, avoiding his wife's troubled gaze.

"We can double date when she comes back," offered Kyle.

"Kyle, no," I called as low as I could to not call attention. He was playing games with me.

That was never going to happen. I was never going to date Kyle again. But what got under my skin more was the idea of having to see Jake with Lauren. Spite coursed through me, causing me to shift in my seat to hide my anger.

My eyes met my mother's, as I ignored the intense stare I could feel from Jake's side of the table. My mother's eyes were filled with anger, and mine likely with a sadness I just couldn't hide.

My mother knew, I realized. I don't know if it was that dinner, but she knew I had feelings for Jake. And that was probably why she had been playing matchmaker a bit more intensely since.

Now she was realizing, horrified, that all she had done was hurt me. I wiped my palms on my dress, looking for a distraction so I could ignore the lump forming in my throat. Jealousy was consuming me from the inside out and it was choking me.

"Excuse me, everyone, but I'm going to get another drink. Dad, what do you say I bring you your favorite port?" I suggested.

"That would be great," he answered, with a hint of a frown on his forehead.

"I can go get it," offered Kyle.

"No," I fired off, swiftly getting up before him, I was looking for an escape. Alone. "It's in a secret stash, so you wouldn't know where to find it, as you don't live here," I explained.

I had snapped at him, but I couldn't take it back. I went straight into the house almost sprinting up the stairs, as I rushed all the way to my rooftop, panting. I had never felt the need to run away from my own home before, but there was a first time for everything. I made it to the glass living room, but that wasn't far enough.

I swung open the roof door and stepped further outside. I stopped by the edge, next to the small outdoor bar, eyes closed, praying for the slightly colder air to cool my burning cheeks.

That was all I could take. All I needed to hear to finally stop dreaming of a man who was spoken for. By my cousin no less, someone I had no respect for and strongly disliked. She was even easier to hate now than before. Lisa was speaking to me on behalf of her daughter, I knew it.

She was a conniving bitch, as much as her daughter. She figured somehow that I was into Jake, or at least suspected something. Who knows, maybe she had seen us in the kitchen I thought, blinking back the tears threatening to take over.

And she specifically kept bringing us back to the conversation of the happy couple, to send a message to me. Well, the message had been received.

How could I have been so stupid? How could I have allowed myself to be so emotionally involved in a non-relationship with a man I had met just three months ago?

"Chloe."

I turned immediately. Jake was walking towards me at a fast pace. I didn't care anymore. I didn't have the courage to hide or lie or play any games.

"Oh God, now what? What do you want?" I snapped.

"Chloe, you can't believe—"

"I can't believe what, Jake?" I screamed "What I already knew? That you are dating my cousin?" I inhaled a shaky breath.

"I didn't lie to you, Chloe, I am not dating her," he retorted, his voice hoarse.

"Oh really?" I mocked in a dry tone. "Is that why you didn't correct her poor 'so in love with her future son-in-law' mother down there?"

The words were rushing out of me with all the fury and pain I was feeling, and there was nothing I could do to stop it.

"It's all over Lauren's social media, Jake!" I shouted. "I'm not stupid! It doesn't even matter."

"I didn't want to make a scene back there, Chloe, that's all. I can't control what Lauren does on her social media page, and I have confronted her about that. I could also say the same about you and Kyle, couldn't I?" He got closer to me, jaw clenched. "Unless you tell me that there is still something going on there. Is there?" he asked through gritted teeth.

"I don't owe you an explanation!" I screamed.

"Neither do I!" he grunted in a louder but deep voice. "And yet here I am, Chloe," he added, his voice lower, deeper, "running after you to make sure you know."

"What, Jake? What? To make sure I know what? Just, ugh, what do you want from me!? I don't understand, I'm… I'm anxious…" I hesitated "I'm… confused, I just, I don't, I, I can't handle whatever this is anymore, I can't, I won't, be played with like, like—"

Jake closed the distance between us in a second. He wrapped his hand around my waist and brusquely pulled me towards him, shutting me up with his lips crashing on top of mine, hungry, aggressive, pushing his way in as my body woke up and vibrated under his touch.

My arms were on his chest, pushing him to put some distance even if every inch of my body protested at my decision.

I looked up to see a face I had never seen on him before, perturbed, almost in pain, his eyes burning.

"I want you, Chloe," he mumbled.

That guttural sound that came from deep within him sent me on a frenzy, as I removed my hands, there was no longer a barricade between us, allowing for him to pull me close again, lost in his embrace, enjoying his warm hard but soft lips, opening my walls with each stroke of his tongue in my mouth.

He tasted like the best thing I'd ever had. My hands found their way to his hair. He gripped my hips to pull me closer, his other hand still cupping my face, holding my head in place as he continued to unveil each and every single one of my resolves.

I moaned, my knees growing weak, overwhelmed with the rush of feelings causing ecstatic currents to run through me.

What was happening? He moved to kissing my jaw, then burying his face in my neck, kissing and sucking on every inch. I opened my eyes to make sure this was real as he devoured me. I closed them back, feeling every vein he sucked throttle with rushing blood. He kissed my naked shoulder and came back up to continue ravaging my lips.

"Fuck!" he grunted.

He suddenly lifted me up the bar, nesting his body between my legs. I could feel him, my inner thighs, open and wet, begging for him, for his throbbing cock to be buried inside of me.

He groaned in my ears as he bit them. I moaned back, at a complete loss.

"You are driving me fucking crazy, mein liebling."

The depth in his voice vibrated through me even if I didn't quite catch the last couple of words he muttered.

There was no time to ask, as his hand trailed up my legs, going up my thighs, cupping my ass cheeks, pulling me even closer. I called to God, but no one could save me.

He kissed the top of my breasts, lowering my dress so he could get better access to my bare skin, and my nipples were oh so ready for him.

"Jesus," he gasped.

I tilted my head backwards and moaned in blissful pain, seeing black and red as he twirled his tongue around my hard, tiny nipple, sending surges of current from my breast to my clit.

"Oh God, Jake," I breathed as my panties got even more wet.

"Yes, baby. Oh fuck. I need to feel you."

I nodded my head in consent as he moved a hand under my dress and caressed me through the soaked material.

"Fuck me, you're so fucking wet."

I yelped.

"I need to touch you, baby."

He moved the silky piece to the side and caressed my pussy from top to bottom.

"Oh," I moaned, I couldn't recall the last time something felt so agonizingly delicious.

My delicious escape got rudely interrupted by some incessant music. Jake eventually caught up, as he straightened himself, realizing the melody was coming from his pocket.

He made a frustrated sound but pulled his phone out. I was attempting to regain control of my senses, and I got down from the bar, holding it for dear life, my limbs numb, my body electrified.

Jake hit the side to silence it and put it in his pocket, a bit winded, breathing from his mouth.

"You don't have to reject it," I said.

"It can wait," he deadpanned.

I was starting to feel a bit of shame, coming back to reality, attempting to straighten my dress. I felt like my skin was burning, and I needed a minute to gather my wits.

"I'm sorry," I heard myself say stupidly.

He came closer, also catching his breath.

"You don't have to be sorry," he said, a confused frown on his face as he caressed my cheek, seeming to still be catching his breath. "After all, I am the one who put you in a... I dare say... delicate position. Twice now."

We both laughed, and I relaxed a bit.

"I'm the one who should be sorry," he continued. "But I want to be clear," he added as he searched my eyes.

"You mean you don't usually lift a girl up like that on a rooftop bar?" I joked.

Jake chuckled. "Not exactly, no," he answered. He took my lips in his once again; I moaned but put a bit of distance between us.

We both stared each other down as he helped me with my hair, gently placing it behind my ears. I tried to fix it the best I could.

"Now what?" I asked with a sigh.

"We join the party," he slowly concluded as his fingers traced his present around my neck, "with the port you promised," he held his breath, seemingly in an attempt to exert self-control, "and we talk about this when your guests have departed."

He was still looking at me, caressing my face with his eyes as if he was seeing me for the first time, making me want to take him to my bedroom, guests be dammed.

"You want to stay over after the party?" I offered.

"If you'll have me, yes, I'd very much like to."

His lips lifted with that sensual yet demanding smile that made my knees grow weak all over again. I closed my eyes, enjoying the feel of his warm hand on my face.

"Okay," I sighed, pushing him away slightly. "If you keep doing this, I don't think we'll make it downstairs."

"You're right," he conceded, taking a step back and placing his hands in his pockets. "So where is this port?"

"Downstairs," I giggled.

We went back to the covered part of the roof. Penny came out of nowhere to say hi to Jake. He leaned down to carefully scoop her up. She looked up to him with her adorable green eyes. My cat was in love.

After a few minutes, we headed to the first floor, to my wine fridge.

"This house really is amazing, Chloe," he said. "I never pictured you in a house this modern. But you've done a great job making it feel warm and like a home."

"Thank you. I'll take that as a compliment," I answered with a flirty smile.

I took a step back as he got closer.

"Careful," I warned, in a playful tone, in complete contrast to the burning ice in his gaze. "People are still outside."

"I don't care."

My breathing accelerated again, but I shook my head and pursed my lips as I scooted past him.

We headed back out with two bottles of port and a tray of small glasses. Jake helped me place the drinks on the table, under the curious and confused gaze of my family. A good number of the guests had left or scattered, since the actual meal portion of the day was over.

Keisha's eyes squinted, I avoided her gaze, as I knew if we made eye contact then there was no hiding the joy I felt or how horny I was. Some of the guests were sitting on the sofa area, while a smaller group was standing by the bar.

"Are you going to have some?" Jake offered to pour me a glass after he served my parents, completely ignoring my aunt who was clearly trying to catch his attention. "I didn't picture you as a port drinker," he confirmed after I shook my head. "Let me pour you another mimosa."

"Thank you." I grinned, unable to hide the way he made me smile.

I caught sight of my mother's victorious expression. I frowned a little at her, hoping she could compose herself, otherwise she would make me blush.

As the rest of the people got up from the table, Keisha took advantage to join me.

"Okay, what happened in there? You are positively glowing."

"Hm, if I tell you right now, I might explode," I admitted, unable to control my grin, electricity still coursing through me.

Keisha squeezed my hand, understanding that I was getting what I oh-so-needed even if I didn't quite want it.

I went to the bar to join Jake. He gave me a drink and poured one for him. We were just standing there, staring at each other. I was feeling as shy as I had ever felt. I bit my lips, and he let out a husky sound.

"If you keep looking at me like this," he breathed between gritted teeth as he took a step closer, "I can't be held responsible for my actions."

I sucked in a breath. Jake seemed unfazed that people were staring, as he slowly moved my hair behind my ears again, making me shudder as his fingers grazed my ears.

I swallowed hard and looked at the floor, feeling Lisa's gaze burning a hole through my skull. I peeked back up at Jake, finally starting to believe that we could be something.

And I didn't know what to do with that information. Jake's phone buzzed again. He bared his teeth as he took a breath. Something was clearly bothering him. He stared at the phone for a second, hesitating.

He finally decided and answered, "Yes."

I observed as his jaw tightened further, his eyes darkened, his posture becoming so familiar and cold, I shivered. He shook his head as he shut his eyes.

"How?" He listened as he opened them and stared at me for a whole minute. I felt debilitated, unable to process the coldness and sadness I could feel emanating from him.

I felt like I was in a room that was shrinking at alarming speed. He frowned, and I did the same at the concerned and curious look in his eyes.

"And you're sure?" He chugged the rest of his drink.

He hung up the phone, with not so much as a goodbye. He sent a few text messages. I felt like the earth was opening under me as the air around us dried out, and I didn't know why, and I couldn't move.

Something had shifted; it felt like a storm was coming, my heartbeat accelerating as goosebumps spread on my arms.

"Everything okay?" I asked, getting a little closer.

"Yes, all good," he dryly answered, shoving the phone back in his pocket.

I could feel him pulling away as he poured the both of us another drink. Once he was done pouring, he excused himself and he went to join my father, George, and Lisa.

I found courage to follow him. They had started talking about business already, so thankfully, I could slide seamlessly in the conversation.

It became clear that Jake was avoiding me when he found a reason to walk away after Lisa and George finally excused themselves.

Jake headed back to the bar and served himself a whisky. I was at a loss. I had no idea what that call was about, but Jake couldn't stand being next to me for long before he found a reason to move away.

I resisted the urge to follow him again, my pride taking over. I felt a short-lived relief when he came back.

"Well, I do have to go," he explained, looking at my father "I have plans that I can't cancel. Happy birthday again, Philip," he said as he shook his hand.

With that, Jake saluted everyone and proceeded to back out.

"I'll walk you out," I offered, wanting to catch up. We had a plan that he clearly had unilaterally changed without telling me.

"No need," he interrupted with the coldest smile as he turned around and just left.

"Everything okay, sweetie?" asked my mother who had just joined us, when my dad got sidetracked by Eric.

"Yes," I lied, looking at Jake leaving my backyard.

"Do you want to talk?"

"No, Mom, please, no."

"Okay," she answered, thankfully completely in sync with me.

My mom knew I needed to be alone, so she rushed Eric to the gate as my dad and her were on their way out as well. Before they left, she hugged me.

"I don't understand what is going on, sweetie, but I am here for you," she whispered in my ear.

All I could do was nod my head in the affirmative. If I opened my mouth, I would break down in tears. Even my dad seemed concerned, but I wasn't sure he understood that my heart had just been trampled upon.

Keisha and I headed inside when all the guests had left and sat in front of the TV. She just held me while I let the tears roll down my face.

CHAPTER 16

THE REST OF MY weekend wasn't as bad as it could have been. Keisha had basically forced me out of the house on Saturday night so I could go on my second date with Mike. We made it a double date—Keisha and this new man she was seeing, Mike and me. After the check came, he invited me over to his place.

The idea of being alone in my house with memories of how Jake—how he touched me...

At that point, anything was better than being alone, so I agreed. We went to his condo in the west loop. Mike had a nice open-floor concept two-bedroom two-bathroom apartment that I found quite inviting. My phone rang as he was showing me his small book collection by the window facing the street.

I stopped moving for a second, unsure of what to do when I saw Jake's number on the screen. My heart protested, but I silenced it. I didn't want to hear anything from him. We heard a loud and long honk coming from somewhere down the street.

We peeked out but it was too dark to see much, there was no one on the street and all the cars looked parked. The noise eventually stopped, so we moved on.

Mike and I watched television, wine in hand, until I fell asleep on his shoulder. When I woke up seven hours later, I was all wrapped up in a cozy blanket on his very comfortable gray couch.

I was lost for a bit but then relieved to see that I was still fully clothed and could recall the whole night. The awakening whiff of a fresh pot of coffee lured me to the kitchen, filled with shame.

"I am so sorry," I began with, unsure of what else to say.

"You have nothing to be sorry about," he said with the warmest smile, setting a very welcome hot cup of coffee in front of me. "I didn't have the heart to wake you up."

"I'm very happy you didn't," I confessed.

"And you get to try my new drip method." He grinned. I felt warm and safe in his company.

We had breakfast together. He made us the fluffiest pancakes and was proud to share his 'real maple syrup' with someone who could appreciate it.

After a while, we fell into comfortable conversation. I admitted that I was having a hard time connecting with anyone, and that discouraged me from letting anyone in.

He confessed that I was the first girl who had slept in his apartment since his breakup. Jane, his ex, had incredible taste, as seen throughout the place. It turned out they had lived together for six months until she moved out. Her family didn't want Mike for her, and that had taken a toll on their relationship.

Mike was still in pain, which to me meant he was still in love with her.

He asked me if we could take things slow, and I hugged him, letting him know that I would love nothing more than that.

Ultimately, we decided we weren't suited for anything more than a friendship. There were no hard feelings between us as we decided to just stay friends, give each other courage, and see where things would go when our hearts were a little less perturbed.

It was already 11 a.m. when I got home, but I was a bit more at peace. Still confused, but ready to make a good faith effort to confront Jake and try to move on afterwards. I couldn't shake a bad feeling, even if I was also hurt that he had just left, as if nothing had happened between us. If we could call him sucking me nothing.

To think that I would have let him take me right there, in the open air on my rooftop, if his phone didn't ring... I avoided going to the rooftop all day, not sure I could look at that bar the same way ever again.

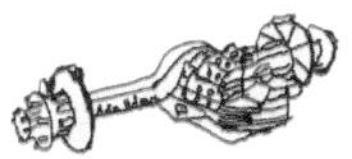

There was no avoiding going to work today, as my Monday was filled with in-person meetings, some of which I was anxious about, as I knew Jake would attend.

That morning, I chose to wear a black jumpsuit with a matching jacket. I switched to my black and gold YSL purse and completed my outfit with my shiny black Stella's. My spirit was not up for colors. I tried to take the necklace from Jake off a few times but eventually gave up trying because it had become one of my favorite pieces. By the time I got to work, I just hid it under my clothes.

If I could just disassociate Jake from it, I could keep it, but I didn't see that happening anytime soon, as every time I touched it, I trembled at the memory of his fingers branding me. I was running behind for my first meeting, so to make it on time, I headed straight to the conference room.

Jake was of course already there, in his black suit, with a dark blue tie, that brought out the blue depth of his eyes. He was standing by the coffee station, talking to another one of the directors. I was so mad at him I had a hard time breathing.

But I wanted—no, desperately needed—an explanation from him. And I was going to get it at some point. I also wasn't going to allow him to lead to me changing my behavior at work.

It was my father's company, after all. I swallowed and proceeded in their direction, exuding my most professional stance.

They excused me, as I poured myself a cup. I imposed myself in the conversation and felt a bit of satisfaction as I could tell Jake was either annoyed or upset. It was about time I took back control.

I fed off his discomfort and got even more comfortable and assertive during the meeting, going head-to-head with him on how to strategically approach some new client outreach, with my full-of-myself smile, I hoped, unnerving him even more. I tried to catch him all day, but by the time my meetings were over, he had already left the premises.

By Wednesday evening, I was growing impatient, and I was a nervous wreck as it became clear to me that he had managed to keep busy when I wasn't and vice versa all week. I wasn't sure if it was a coincidence or if he was avoiding me, my gut told me it was the latter.

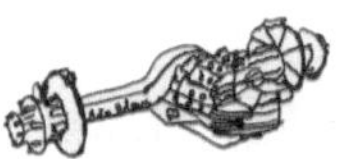

By Thursday, I had bribed Jake's secretary with Dunkin donuts. I also made sure to emphasize the fact that it was my father's company, so I would appreciate a nudge when Jake was free, right before she left for the day.

I rushed to his office once his secretary shared; he was back in there with no calls on his calendar. The executive floor was empty, which was not surprising for a Thursday evening during the summer. His door was closed but his light was still on.

I almost changed my mind now that I was so close, but I armed myself with the sliver of courage I could find and knocked.

"It's open."

I marched in and closed the door behind me. He was sitting on the corner of his desk, one foot up on his guest chair. He lowered his feet and dropped the document he was reading down on the table.

He silently stared at me with that intense, intimidating look that made me regret my decision profusely.

But it was too late to back down, so I charged forward.

"How have you been?" I asked casually.

"Good."

"It's been quite hard to catch you lately," I pointed out.

"I've been very busy. What can I help you with?"

I gritted my teeth, frustrated, and shook my head. My eyes widened, and I could feel them dry out as I spoke, fury taking over.

"Very adult of you, Jake. Who do you think you are? Don't you think you at least owe me an explanation for this change in behavior?"

He stayed silent for a moment, but I held his gaze. I wasn't going to yield.

"Okay."

He got up and slowly drew closer to me. I held my breath a little too long, trying to control my racing heart. It's not that I feared him. But when this man walked towards you, the slow current of power and control that emanated from him was commanding, paralyzing.

He stopped right in front of me, his teeth clenched, his now light blue eyes cold as ice. I wanted to run.

"What happened between us was nothing. Just a spur of the moment mistake between coworkers who probably shouldn't have drank so much in the first place."

I couldn't believe what I was hearing. My stomach felt like it had parted in half.

"Really? That's it?" I asked in astonishment.

"Chloe," he muttered as he closed his eyes and shook his head. He pinched the arch of his nose, looking exasperated. "We work together, for

Christ's sake. This would be a stupid idea. You can't keep finding your relationships at work; it's not a good look for you."

My blood boiled instantly. It felt like he had stabbed me, using my past against me. I curled my fingers, digging my nails in my palms. I could fucking slap him.

"Right." My jaw clenched; my body chilled. "Next time you want to remain '*principled*' and '*professional*', try avoiding putting your hands, or your face, under skirts, even out of the office," I irritably answered, "as that can also give the wrong impression." I took a step in his direction. "And while I am most certainly *not* your employee, most of the other women here actually are, and we wouldn't want a sexual harassment lawsuit in our hands because you simply '*changed your mind.*'"

His lips turned into a straight line, and I could hear him breathing, his nostrils flaring. He frowned as he seemed distracted by my neck and looked back at me. Confused, I touched my chest, realizing he was staring at the necklace he had given me.

"I forgot," I said as I proceeded to hastily unhook the necklace with slightly trembling fingers.

"Chloe, you don't have to." He looked a bit alarmed.

"Of course I do, Mr. Cunningham, I don't see how you taking me to your mother's flower shop at 11 p.m. and touching my neck, gifting me a one-of-a-kind necklace is professional behavior either," I blurted as I snapped the necklace off. "So here you go."

I threw the necklace at his chest, the piece hitting him before dropping to the floor.

"Of course, I hope you are not stupid enough to gift it to someone else in the office," I added. "That would be of very poor taste."

Before I could do anything, he was right in front of me, grabbing me by my arm.

"Chloe! Just…"

"Fuck you!" I bellowed, giving him a strong push back, letting him know it was not the time to put his hands on me.

We were both out of breath, as he took a step back. He seemed hurt, but I was seeing red with anger and could not care less about his guilt.

"Do not fucking follow me. Do not follow me again, ever," I ordered, pointing my index finger to him, before I stormed out of his office.

I almost ran to the elevator bank, my vision a bit blurred. I opted for the stairs, needing the pain of running in heels to make me focus on something else. My heart stopped when I heard the stairwell door open and close brusquely behind me.

I felt his grip on my arm before he even touched me, every single nerve ending in my body fully in sync with the surge of electricity emanating from him as he accelerated behind me.

He spun me around brusquely, grabbed my face between his hands and ravaged my lips as he groaned inside my mouth, getting a moaning whimper out of me.

I pushed against his chest, breaking the kiss. He let me but brought his forehead to mine, both panting, mouth agape, and eyes half closed.

"Where were you?" he demanded.

"What?" I sputtered.

"This weekend, where did you go?" He made an annoyed sound. "I stopped by, and you weren't home. Who were you with?"

I felt a cold sweat drip down my back at his icy tone, feeling the chill all the way insides my bones. My body shuddered, as his tone sounded almost like a threat. But I was too hurt to bow down.

"You can't keep doing this Jake, you have no right." My voice cracked, tears threatening to show my pain. "You keep pulling and pushing. I deserve more, damn it."

I saw a shadow cross his face as he stepped back. He shook his head, almost to himself. I took his silence as my dismissal, so I walked away, and he didn't follow me this time.

I managed to make it to my desk, my eyes burning.

I snatched my purse and ran out the building as if the devil was on my heels. I headed straight home. It was a wonder I didn't cry in the Uber, and by the time I got home, I felt resolved. I knew I could just numb what I felt with a glass of wine, it wouldn't be the first time. I was never going to let him play with me the way he did, ever again.

I worked from home the rest of the week and spent a quiet weekend for the most part. I took the days to write, finding the distraction quite soothing.

There was a silver lining in this situation, I realized. All the pain I was feeling was torture, but also great inspiration so I could work on my novel and hate the male character a little bit. Maybe the villain's name would be Jake.

I finished one and started on the synopsis for three more. I let out all my outrage and sexual frustration on the keyboard, relieving my pain through my characters, but also finding a fantasy resolution to my problem. After all, I could write happy endings, even if I didn't see one in my future.

It was midnight on Saturday night/Sunday morning when my cell rang. I almost dropped my wine glass when I saw Jake's name pop on the screen. I let it ring as I just couldn't bring myself to swipe and answer.

When the sound stopped, I kept staring at his name on my phone, desperately wanting to call him back. But I resisted. If I answered, I feared I would willingly put myself at his mercy again, for whatever he wanted from me, and I couldn't allow that to happen, not again.

CHAPTER 17

MONDAY WAS A BUSY day for me. The team was kicking off a medium-size acquisition of an e-drive producer in Korea. That meant I had to be on calls all day with Motor Holmes' outside counsel, which was the firm I used to work for.

I enjoyed catching up with my previous coworkers. I knew we had a great team and that I was in good hands. I missed them sometimes, especially now that I felt so confused when I saw Jake daily.

I ignored him and did all I could to remain professional. I had gotten so good at faking it that I almost believed it myself.

I had seen his pictures with Lauren on social media. Clearly, they were back together, if it was even true that they hadn't been a couple in the first instance. I had been pleasant when Jake and I were with others and had avoided ever being alone with him otherwise.

I couldn't help still being in awe of him when he got passionate during meetings, or clever on negotiation calls. My heart skipped a beat every now and then, when I caught him looking at me, but I managed to remain occupied. I worked out in the mornings, worked all day, and wrote until I fell asleep.

When I needed human company outside of work, I grabbed a drink with Keisha or Mike.

But my thoughts continuously went back to him, especially during all the hours I wrote. He became my muse, but in a passive manner, one in which he didn't control my emotions.

He was the inspiration for my current main male characters, there was a little bit of him in each man I invented for my heroines, and there was a little bit of me in each of those women.

My dreams had simmered down, or rather, my brain being too exhausted for me to be able to remember them in the first place.

"Coffee?" asked Jake behind me as I was daydreaming by the coffee station on a Friday morning, my body a bit sore from the aggressive bike ride I had done that morning.

I was going to decline as I already had stopped at Dunkin in the morning, but he already had a cup of coffee in hand that he was offering to me. I grabbed it, making sure I in no way touched his hand by accident.

There was no steam coming out of it. I gave him a quizzical look.

"I had it cooled down for you. I know you don't like it very hot."

I swallowed hard. I usually waited a good twenty minutes before I took a sip of my coffee to avoid burning my tongue. And he had noticed.

"Thank you," was all I could muster.

"I'm glad to see you more in the office lately."

"Well, I tend to be around when we are very busy," I explained.

We stayed silent for a few seconds.

"Chloe, I've been meaning to, uh, apologize for how we left things."

"Already forgotten," I quickly answered, doing my best to have an honest-looking expression. "Water under the bridge. You were completely right."

"I was still an asshole about it," he continued.

"True," I acknowledged. "But it all turned out fine, so all good. Led to me giving a chance to a guy I was seeing and, well, I am enjoying myself, so no harm no foul."

Mike would have completely approved of my usage of our friendship in that way, I thought, and although Jake looked like he wanted to ask more, we were in public that time around.

"I see," he paused. "Great then."

I could have sworn his nostrils flared, but he kept his gaze cold and distant.

"Yep. Well, see you around."

I walked away feeling like I deserved an award. Of course, I had been hanging out with Mike a lot but at that point we were more akin to emotional support animals to each other rather than anything else. It had become clear to me that he was so eager to post pictures of his "new friend" to make his ex-jealous, and I was all for it. If I could help Mike move on, maybe I could on my end. I already felt like it was working.

Having Jake believe that I was over everything would also help greatly. I had to keep the conversations short, because pretending wasn't my forte. And I had managed to get back to as close of a professional relationship as I could have with a man I still dreamed about, against my better judgment, and it was all I could ask for under the circumstances.

I was very excited when the weekend came. My dad and I were going to San Francisco from Wednesday to Monday for an electric car component convention, where I was hoping to network and get more business for Motor Holmes. The idea of not being in Chicago for a little bit was of course quite welcome.

While the summer had transformed into the perfect weather, the idea of not being in town and not having to see Jake provided me some comfort. I used the weekend to pack and book some nice restaurants for when we had open nights.

I had also scheduled a walking food and booze tour of some of the most eclectic spots in town, hoping my dad would be down, but knowing there was a slight chance I might have to go alone.

I was most excited for the Friday night private charity gala I had gotten tickets to. Ana, one of my friends from college and a party and event planner, organized that event every year, in different cities. The funds were going to a pro bono organization that provided free legal services to veterans.

The gala was an excuse to party while donating the proceeds to a good cause. My father had already kindly declined my offer to join. I didn't push him at the time I had booked it, as it was a bit of a younger party crowd, and I understood that the event would turn from gala to club type event at some point.

I grabbed a boozy brunch with Keisha on Sunday, Facetiming with Iris and Amelia, before joining Mike to a friend's house party. The event was a great time and certainly distracted me from thoughts of the man who still haunted my thoughts.

After seeing Mike and his ex-torture each other all night, I had decided to step in. I forced them in a room together at the house, and before the end of the night, Jane, Mike's no longer ex, and I were the best of friends. Jane had admitted that she had overreacted to their fight by leaving, and they had decided to take things slow but to try to work on their issues, mostly related to her parents opposing the relationship. At least one couple would get their happy ending.

CHAPTER 18

I ROLLED MY CARRYON to the office on Wednesday, wearing light blue jeans with holes, a light puffy white shirt, sand flat nude moccasin shoes, with my curls loose. I had no meetings for the day and was only going to be in the office for a couple hours, as I nervously bided time to head to the airport. When 1 p.m. rolled in, I called a car and waited for my dad outside, who I had pinged a few times to no avail.

He finally called me back. I put my sunglasses on to free up my hand and answered.

"Hey, Dad, I'm downstairs. Where are you?"

"Hey, honey. Ugh, don't hate me, but I can't make it. I'm still at home."

"What? Why? Is everything okay?" I exclaimed.

"Yes, I'm fine. I just have a sharp pain in my abdomen and the doctor thinks I might have some kidney stones."

"Again!?" I spluttered.

"Yes. But he doesn't think I will need surgery this time. Will try to pass them through."

"Okay. Sorry, Dad. I know those suck. Do you need anything? I don't have to go; I can come to the house."

"No, sweetie, I'm fine, and I already have your mom obsessing over this, I don't need more than one of you. I'm the one who's sorry, honey," he explained, "but don't worry, I already got someone to go with you, so you don't have to work those gigantic events alone."

My suspicion was confirmed before I could even ask. Jake waltzed out of the building, wearing a light blue sharkskin suit, his biceps well delineated, his sunglasses on. He sauntered towards me, a smirk on his face, phone in hand.

He stopped in front of me, looking way too smug and satisfied. I wished I had opted for much darker sunglasses as opposed to the light brown ones I was wearing.

"Hello?"

"Yes, Dad. I take it Jake is the chosen one?" I asked with obviously false cheerfulness.

"Yes, he immediately volunteered when he heard I couldn't go, as he didn't want you to go alone. I also thought of Kyle but honestly, we both know Jake is a much better choice for this."

"Of course," I added in a dry tone. "Well, get better soon, okay? I'll call you when we get there."

"Thank you, sweetie, have a safe trip!"

"Thanks, Dad," I said before hanging up. "Well," I crossly said to Jake, trying hard to stay composed, "ready for the airport?"

"Not quite," he responded. "I had my secretary change our flights for a little later. As you can guess this was last-minute, and I need to go home and get clothes."

"I see. Um, well, my ride is here." But as I turned around, the Uber driver had left, rightfully tired of waiting on me. I rolled my eyes. "Never mind."

"My car is right there," Jake said, pointing to the one a bit behind me. "You could just come with me, I won't take very long, and then we can head to the airport together. Would be good for you to also catch me up a bit, as I wasn't prepared for this convention."

I had a hard time making an excuse to bail out of this, so I accepted my fate. As the driver pulled closer to us, Jake opened the back door for me to get in as the driver placed my luggage in the trunk.

I was doing my best to stay cool. I was texting all my anger and panic to the group chat with Keisha, Iris, and Amelia, while avoiding pressing on the phone too hard, feeling Jake's gaze on me like podium lights. How was I supposed to be next to the man for almost a whole week when I was barely managing to be in a conference room full of people with him!?

I dared a glance in his direction. He was now busy on his phone and barely paying any attention to me. Great, if he tired of staring at me, and that was going to be his behavior going forward, then perhaps I didn't have much to be concerned about.

After about fifteen pleasantly quiet minutes on Lake Shore Drive, we arrived at his building. The driver entered the parking structure until we came to a full stop in front of a set of elevators.

"Want to come up? Would be more comfortable to wait there than in the car," he offered.

"Um, I'll come up." I wanted to see that view again.

I grabbed my work bag and Jake and I rode the elevator to his floor. I recognized the halls I had quickly run though back in early April. It seemed like ages ago.

The condo was as impressive as I recalled, with that breathtaking view of the lake.

"It's beautiful, isn't it?" he asked when I went straight to the window.

"It really is the most perfect view," I admitted. "I love staring at water. Love seeing all the boats."

"Same here. Anything to drink?" he offered as he walked to the bar.

I hesitated but realized alcohol could help me calm my nerves in the right amount. "Wine?" I requested.

"Is Italian okay?" he asked as he put a Coravin through a bottle.

"Yes," I confirmed as I drew closer. That was most certainly not a cheap bottle of wine. He poured me a glass and then himself one. "Hm, this is exquisite," I exclaimed after I took a small sip.

"It's from a small vineyard in Puglia," he explained.

"It's perfect." I smiled.

He grinned back. "Glad you like it."

We stared at each other in silence as I felt the wine warm up my cheeks. I turned around.

"Okay, let me go pack," announced Jake, "Make yourself at home."

"Thanks." I nodded.

I watched him leave, unable to stop myself from admiring his figure.

I proceeded back to the couch by the window, so I could leisurely savor that beautiful wine, while enjoying the amazing view, dreaming of an Italian vacation. A real break would do me good, I thought. I could drink wine in the south of Italy and have an adventure with an attractive stranger who could help me forget the adonis God I was forced to work with every day.

My imagination activated, I pulled out my laptop and started writing a scene, inspired by the tingly feeling I was getting from the wine.

I got startled a bit when I heard footsteps behind me, and I quickly closed my laptop. I didn't want Jake's prying eyes on my book. He would know I was lying if I said I was marking up a purchase agreement; he would ask which one and it would derail from there.

Jake was ready to go. Quicker than I expected since we had only been there for fifteen minutes.

We got on our way to the airport. Security was easy enough as we both had Global Entry. The flight wasn't delayed, so it was a smooth process to the plane. I purposely lost him in the line, not wanting to be close to him for longer than I needed to be.

It hadn't occurred to me where he would sit, but I was strongly hoping he hadn't just taken my father's seat, as that one would be next to mine. I boarded first and found my now two-seater in first class.

I relaxed when I saw him pass by me without stopping. I breathed a sigh of relief in knowing that he was not going to be anywhere near me.

I put my headphones on and started drifting into sleep, as I tended to do before a flight, the glass of wine helping tremendously. I hated flying, planes scared me, no matter how many times I was told that on average planes were safer than cars.

When I had to fly, I generally ordered wine immediately and chugged it as soon as possible to calm my nerves.

Once the flight took off and we were in safe altitude, I opened the tray in front of me and pulled my personal laptop out to continue writing my scene. I wasn't concerned because my privacy screen made it so people around me would have a hard time reading what I was typing.

I had been lost in my story for an hour without realizing, when a turbulence hit. I tried to keep calm, hoping they would stop. I let out a small squeal on the next one and dug my nails into the armrest. I shut my laptop halfway; there went my inspiration. I couldn't type while I feared for my life.

Another round of turbulence hit, and I closed my eyes, biting my lips, almost tasting blood, to stop myself from screaming. I opened my eyes when I felt movement in the empty seat next to me. It was Jake, with a concerned look on his face.

"Working?" he asked, pointing to my laptop.

"Yep," I said as I quickly closed my screen completely. "What are you doing here?" I inquired defensively.

"You seemed a little anxious, so I figured you could use the company." He smiled.

"What do you mean?"

He looked in the direction of my fingers still clutching the hand rest for dear life, my knuckles white.

"My seat is across and behind you, so I can tell." He shrugged.

"Of course. I guess you are doing the snooping now," I said, only half joking. How had I missed that he ended up seating around me still!?

Before I could say more, we hit another patch. Jake put his seatbelt on, moved my laptop to my bag without asking, and closed my tray. I was frozen with pure white fear.

He gently removed my clutched hand from the hand rest, pushed it up, and held my hand in his.

I couldn't complain. As much as I wanted to remove my hand, there was no force on earth that would make me do so. My fear far outweighed my pride at this point.

Another turbulence rolled in. I swirled my head and buried it in his shoulder, trying to hide my face. He grabbed my arm with his other hand and wrapped his arms around me.

I was focusing on his steady heartbeat, trying to bring mine down to his. Fuck decorum, I needed this, otherwise I would literally scream.

"It's okay," he whispered, kissing my forehead.

I knew he couldn't do anything if something was wrong with the plane, but he was managing to calm me down anyways, his smell, reassuring, his strong chest, comforting.

After five minutes of no turbulence, and when the seatbelt sign was turned off, I managed to compose myself and sit straight, clearing my throat to save face.

"Thank you," I uttered, avoiding his gaze.

"Of course." After another minute, he started unbuckling his seatbelt and getting up.

"You can, um, you can stay for longer and I can brief you further on the conference?" I quickly suggested, holding on to his arm.

I wasn't ready to be alone. As it tends to happen, there would certainly be more rough air.

"That works," he replied with a smile.

We spent the next few hours of flight time discussing the various companies who would be in attendance and strategizing on how to explain what differentiated us from competitors like Green Mile.

My secretary and I had put together small vellum binders with background information on the event, the attendees, and the various products that would be provided.

I shared the itinerary of the conference with Jake as well.

"You are always so meticulously organized," he commented.

"I try," I said, accepting the compliment. "Checklists are my favorite kind of drug."

"I get it." He grinned.

The rest of the flight was quite enjoyable, as we discussed strategy for the next few days. I had also benefited from Jake's presence as the flight attendants could not get enough of him.

I rolled my eyes a few times as they swooned all over him, but at least that meant I had plenty of bubbly to drink without even having to ask.

I can't say I blamed them at all. The want to satisfy and please Jake Cunningham was harder to stray from than one would think.

We checked in at the hotel in the afternoon. It was a big establishment, and a lot of the seminars were taking place directly in the many conference rooms, thus why my dad had chosen to stay at there every time he attended this convention.

It was my first time participating in the event. The space was beautiful, currently full, buzzing with guests probably all attending the function.

"So," started Jake as we took the elevator to the 20th floor to both of our rooms, "I'll stop by your room at 6:30 so we can head to the restaurant?"

"Yes, that works," I answered as we got off the elevator and headed in opposite directions. Jake had simply taken the suite that was reserved for my father. I was glad I had decided to book my own suite when I made the reservation.

My room was quite spacious, with a full living room featuring velvet green sofas and a nice kitchenette. I had chosen it also for the beautiful view it had of the city, planning to enjoy some alone writing time in my room to decompress when possible.

I quickly unpacked, hanging my clothes, arranging some in one of the drawers and lining up my makeup and care bags on the bathroom vanity. I always took the time to place my things in easy to find places. I immediately called the desk to have some of my clothing picked up for ironing.

After taking a long shower and straightening my hair, I was ready for game time; I just had to try to ignore the way my heartbeat accelerated every time Jake was around. Easier said than done.

It was 6:30 sharp when I heard a knock on my door. I hastily stepped in my beige stiletto's and added my button-size gold earrings and a delicate gold chain to complement my knee-length, boat neckline, black Blouson wrap dress with a sash belt at the waist and a wrap skirt with a slit at the hem.

I always went a bit more conservative when attending work events like these, not really wanting to call too much attention to myself. Jake was standing in the hall, wearing a dark black suit with a dark green tie that brought out the subtle flecks of amber in his eyes. I tried to hide my admiration.

Jake in a suit was *everything*. I grabbed my small gold purse and closed the door behind me. Jake was staring, I noticed, my cheeks slightly blushed as we rode down the elevator together. We both remained quiet.

We grabbed a cab and headed to the upscale steakhouse. The conference organizers had rented the whole place for the event. We both found our name tags on the table at the entrance, as we were guided to the happy hour room. The restaurant was quite impressive, with high ceilings and the most chandeliers I had ever seen in one place. The light gave the place an air of grandeur and luxury that I really admired. Jake grabbed two glasses of champagne from one of the servers and handed me one.

"Thank you," I said as we continued to look around.

The night was going quite well, with Jake and I working the room like we had planned. We had a few targeted individuals on our list that we spotted and made sure to chat with.

When we were separated, the other would come to the rescue if we exchanged a look long enough. We made the perfect team.

About an hour later, all the guests were invited to take our assigned seats in the dining room. Each table seated about ten people. I had used my contacts prior to the event to get us a seat at the Emporium table, as Motor Holmes desperately wanted to bring them on as a customer.

Both Jake and I had upped our charm on as we shook the hands of the table guests and introduced ourselves.

Immediately after we sat down, the servers started their rounds, adding beautiful salad plates in front of each guest, while others offered the guest our choice of red or white California wines. I stuck to champagne while Jake transitioned to red wine. The event presented various speeches by their CEO and president, as well as presentations by a few nationally recognized guests.

By the time dessert was served, the speeches had ended, and the performers of the night were shining and adding much needed ambiance to the festivities, as we continued to build connections.

One of the guests, Catherine, had seemed quite taken by Jake. After it became clear that we were only coworkers, Catherine had made sure to monopolize Jake's attention for a good part of the evening. I had ignored the two of them to the best of my capacities, doing all I could to focus on the task at hand; subtly sell Motor Holmes as a potential supplier to Emporium.

I was quite annoyed when I saw Jake take Catherine to the dance floor after dessert was over. She worked for one of Motor Holmes competitors for Christ's sake. But I took the time to strategically network a bit more.

Throughout the evening, I had managed to mask my annoyance at the pair. But I struggled when he offered that Catherine get a ride with us in our cab. It turns out she was also staying at our hotel and didn't want to ride back by herself. Most of the guests of the event were staying there, but of course, why not crowd a cab with the three of us instead of leaving with someone else.

It was 1 a.m. by the time we made it back to the hotel. Catherine was a beautiful tall blonde, much like Lauren. She was wearing a skin-tight white dress that put her features on display.

I certainly admired her confidence and how she didn't seem to mind all the looks she was getting. Mr. Cunningham sure had a type, I thought, a sour taste in my mouth.

"Want to join me for a night cap at the bar?" flirtatiously asked Catherine, putting her hand on Jake's arm. "And of course you can join me as well," she said quickly as she barely looked at me.

I did a slight eye roll.

"Chloe?" asked Jake.

"I'm good," I quickly answered.

I had no intent to be the third wheel when all I wanted to do was break Catherine's arm for touching Jake too much for my taste.

"I am exhausted, but I will see the both of you tomorrow. Have a great night." I walked away before anyone could insist.

Not that I expected Catherine to do so. I didn't realize how much I was clenching my teeth until I started feeling some pain in my jaw. The elevator was taking its sweet time, as Jake and Catherine, arm in arm, passed by and headed to the bar.

I was boiling by the time I got to my room. I had no right to be jealous, I reminded myself. Jake could not have made it more painfully known that he didn't want anything to do with me, even if he was attracted to me.

He wasn't mine to possess; he was a free man.

I hated him regardless.

I took a long hot shower, trying to steady my nerves in the hope of falling asleep faster. When sleep became challenging to find, I got a book on my Kindle and read until my body surrendered.

CHAPTER 19

I EXCITED MY ROOM early the next morning, not wanting to run into Jake under any circumstance. When I reached the conference room, I served myself some eggs and bacon and found a table. Unfortunately, Jake and Catherine had just come down together.

I pretended not to see them, distracted by the conversation I was having with Bob, another one of the attendees that were at my table. To my exasperation, Jake and Catherine had soon joined us.

I plastered on the best fake smile I could muster as I welcomed them, without interrupting Rob's story about his last skiing trip.

Thankfully, breakfast was over soon, and I could focus on the first seminar of the day. This was the heaviest day, with three two-hour panels back-to-back. Jake was back in beast mode, as he finally separated from his new friend and joined me for the lunch we had arranged with Emporium. I almost wished he was bad at his job, too distracted, but no.

Once again, we were the perfect team. Working in tandem to convince the company that we were the right fit.

The lunch ended with the Emporium CEO asking that we send him further information via email, so we could work on future plans together. I was over the moon, and by the time we got back to the next seminar, I managed to not care that Catherine had found her way back to Jake. This time, I was smart enough to not sit with them and find Bob again, for more stories I didn't really care for.

The seminars finally stopped at 5 p.m. I really wanted to be away from Jake, but we had already made plans to take an existing client out to dinner tonight, and short of faking an illness, there was no avoiding it.

"Congratulations," said Jake behind me as I was serving myself a cup of coffee to wake up after all the lectures.

"Thanks. Appreciate the help from you as well," I retorted.

"My pleasure, but really it was all you. That was your pitch."

I smiled, accepting the compliment. I could call Jake whatever name I wanted, but he wasn't one to take credit when he didn't have it, and he seemed to really respect or I dared think, admire me as an equal.

"We make a great team," I admitted.

"I agree. But you were excellent in there. The electricity and passion coming from you when you put your sales hat on; it's invigorating."

My heart softened a bit, while my cheeks reddened and my center tingled. This wasn't the reaction I wanted to have to what really was a professional compliment, but Jake's gaze confused me, and my body reacted to such confusion in a frustrating way.

"Want to grab a celebratory drink with me?" Jake suggested.

I hesitated for a second as I looked into his deep blue eyes. I needed distance from him, yet that invitation was tempting. But I couldn't let him get close again only for me to want more than he was willing to give.

"I can't; I have a lot to do before dinner," I explained. "I'm sure Catherine would love to join you, though," I added with an evil look, unable to help my knowingly petty comment.

"I'm sure she would," he acknowledged as he lifted his head a bit, eyebrow raised. "But I would much prefer your company."

I focused on my coffee as my stomach warmed up, while he observed every little facial expression.

"I find that hard to believe," I said defiantly, daring him to contradict me.

His eyes squinted. "And why is that?"

"You seem to have a type, and she fits it perfectly. Although, she probably has a semi working brain as compared to your usual, so I guess that's an upgrade from my dear cousin."

I knew I shouldn't have said that, but I felt my blood boil and could not stop the words as they made their way out of my mouth. My heart was taking control, my brain in panic mode. I always had difficulty hiding how I really felt.

I got even more upset when I heard Jake's guttural laugh, perhaps because he understood that I was hurting, but I smiled at him as I slowly took another gulp of coffee. Glad I could entertain him, I supposed.

"Chloe, I have no interest in her or in Lauren for that matter. I am trying to remain professional and cordial so as not to offend her."

"But you are usually quite clever, and we both know how, hm, how do I put it, direct you can be when you have no interest in a woman." I swallowed. "Yet I didn't see you working too hard to get yourself out of this specific situation," I added.

If only I listened to Iris and toned down my attitude, I thought, I would be able to sound less sour, but alas, I was always told I was passionate, at times, to a fault.

"Are you upset?" he countered, getting a bit closer to me.

"I couldn't care less," I abruptly answered, "but I can't say that I enjoy seeing my coworker fraternizing with the competition."

"Hm, is that really what bothers you?" he pressed, in a softer voice.

My heart skipped a beat, and my stomach tightened, as I could smell that intoxicating cologne he wore. But I found strength in my pain.

"What else could it be?" I asked innocently, bending my head to the side. "I'll see you at dinner," I added, finding the strength to provide a hint of a grin and walk away.

I resisted the urge to run, because I was coming out of my skin being too close to Jake. Once I made it back to my room, I shut the door and immediately laid back against it, my eyes closed, taking deep breaths to sooth my anxiety.

Yes, jealously was crawling inside of me like a parasite. I wanted him, desperately. I wanted those hands on me, I wanted to taste those lips again, but he rejected me, and now he wanted for us to what, be friends?

Yes, it was the professional thing to do, and the mature thing to do, I knew that. But seeing other women flirt with him or touch him drove me mad, my anger taking over, with my instinctual need to attack him for making me feel this way in the first place.

My conflicting emotions were all his fault after all, I decided, but I could do better at controlling myself.

Work was my best armor, so I distracted my mind with it, calling my father as well as my legal assistant to finalize the package I had already prepared in advance of meeting with Emporium, in case they said yes.

I wanted the documents to go out the next day, to not seem too desperate, but to also seem prepared and engaged. My father was thrilled to hear that we could potentially add a multi-million-dollar deal under our belt.

Jake had texted, saying he would meet me in the lobby so we could head to dinner. I had opted for a black wrap blazer with a folded collar and a chic pant suit. As always, I had my customary black heels and a gold purse. I let my hair down, enjoying the bouncy waves to waist.

I met Jake by the bar in the lobby. He handed me a glass of champagne. The ambiance was dark but still luxurious, with smaller chandelier providing a soft light. I admired the black shiny bar countertop, balanced with black and gold bar stools.

"Thank you." I nodded.

Jake was wearing a dark blue suit with a white shirt and no tie, one button open. I was unraveling in his presence, as was every other woman at the bar. Jake wouldn't stop staring at me, with a slight smirk on his face. I held his look for as long as I could, conflicted between desire and annoyance.

Between needing to move on and wanting him to be mine, my stomach was in knots again, so I chugged my glass and asked for a refill.

Once we were done with our drinks, we headed to the sushi restaurant.

The evening was going on smoothly; I enjoyed meeting some of my favorite suppliers face to face for the first time. I had a great relationship with the general counsel of one of our customers, Luke, and was genuinely enjoying his company.

Jake wouldn't stop staring at the two of us, but he was his usual pleasant self. We all enjoyed sushi, sake, and plenty of laughs.

By the time we finally made it back to the hotel, my feet were on fire. I grunted when we got to the lobby as Catherine, shrieking, was almost sprinting to us.

"Hi, there!" she squealed, hugging Jake like she hadn't seen him for a year. "I was looking for you! Oh, hi, Chloe" she said, barely looking at me. Why bother, I wondered.

"And goodnight," I said, as I had no patience for this.

I simply walked away to the elevator, without looking back. What they did or didn't do wasn't my business. I soon made it to my room, glad I could finally kick my shoes off, and change into my silk negligée. I then proceeded to remove my makeup, trying to ignore the bubble of envy in my stomach.

Envy for what? He would only be trouble, I tried to convince myself, so it was better to let him be someone else's problem.

I jumped when I heard a knock. I hesitated but still headed to the door. I hadn't ordered room service. I looked through the peephole to see Jake standing there. My heart raced as I inhaled sharply before opening the door.

There he was, silently intense, just looking at me attentively. I realized I was basically wearing very short shorts and a silk t-shirt, under which I was sure part of my dentelle bra was visible, but it was too late to cover up, and he was devouring every inch of my body with his gaze.

And why not let him see what could have been?

I was desperately searching his eyes, trying to understand what he was doing there, at my door, late at night.

"You left your cell in the cab," he explained as he got closer, handing me my phone, his jaw tense, looking down at me through hooded dark eyes.

"Oh, wow, um, thank you. That would have been annoying to say the least." I frowned.

"No problem," he said simply.

I couldn't shake the feeling that he had more to say.

"How did you find it?" I asked.

"I called you, and the driver answered. Since he was still by the hotel entrance, I just went out to grab it."

"Thank you."

"You're welcome."

He Just stood there, darkened eyes staring at me and not saying a word. He looked down my chest and slowly back up, taking his time over my lip before he met my gaze.

"And, um, why did you call me? Did you need something?" I pressed.

"No," he quickly answered. "Just, uh, wanted to coordinate for tomorrow. Want to meet for an early breakfast before we head to the conference room?"

"That works," I agreed, a bit confused. "No night cap for you tonight?" I dared to ask.

He impatiently shook his head.

"Let me be very clear, Chloe, I'm not interested in Catherine. I was strictly trying to keep her distracted so that you could have a moment with Emporium without the competition breathing down your neck. From what I've gleaned, Catherine is a fierce competitor, so I used my charm to lure her away. That's it."

I was intrigued by his quick explanation, and he didn't pretend to not understand what I really was asking. I had tried to be a bit more diplomatic, but he was suddenly the one who was quite direct. He made I sound like this was just a strategy, he was clearing out the way for me.

I observed the tick in his jawline, his thinned lips, and the frown lines darkening his forehead. Oh, how much I wanted to touch his face, and kiss him. But I could still hear him reject me in his office.

"Okay, well, good night. And thank you again," I concluded, trying to stay strong.

He stared at me for what felt like the longest second before answering in a deeper tone, "Good night, Chloe."

I quickly shut the door before I changed my mind.

He had played the role of a sidekick for me on purpose. When I put that lens on and replayed the event in my head, it seemed quite possible.

I felt relieved, I couldn't help it, and I desperately wanted to kiss him. But I had to be strong, I reminded myself. I was working on moving on from something that had barely started, and I wasn't going to get derailed just because every fiber of my body wanted the feel of him on top of me.

I put a playlist on, the notes of a Celine Dion song pulling on my heart strings as I continued my nighttime routine to get ready for bed. The song seemed perfect for how I felt, heeding a warning to my stubborn heart.

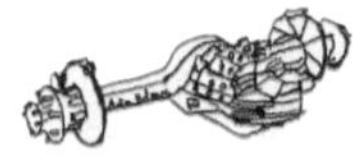

Friday was a casual day at the convention, so that meant jeans were acceptable. I was happy to dress down a little bit for a change, opting for a pair of well-fitted light blue jeans, with a white blouse. The shirt was made with comfortable light weight poplin with a bit of stretch, adorned with tiered sleeves and a removable sash. The V-neck was the right amount of flattering without being indecent.

I went with my small hoops. I completed my outfit with my Fetish du Desert heel, my current favorite Louboutins. The foulard-style nylon ankle tie and the pin-up print brought a splash of color to my outfit. Those were statement shoes, but I had just bought them and was itching to give them a run.

I grabbed my Dolce bag and headed to breakfast. Jake was waiting for me by the elevator.

"Good morning."

"Good morning," he answered, clearly admiring my outfit. I raised an eyebrow.

He smirked with one side of his face and shook his head to himself as we slipped into the elevator.

To my slight disappointment, and to Jake's clear displeasure, our breakfast had been highjacked by other attendees, and we couldn't be rude and ask them to leave. The point of the conference was to network after all.

The day went by fast thankfully, when the last seminar of the event ended at 4 p.m. We were able to find an empty high-top table at the hotel bar.

"I booked us a dinner with Copolliard," said Jake as we nursed on our sodas.

My back immediately went stiff. "Oh. And who is attending?"

"They sent Paul, I believe. He had reached out to us before coming here to meet, but he just confirmed. It's at eight at Cornish. I couldn't get an earlier time but figured it's fine since we don't have to wake up early tomorrow."

"I see. Um, I can't make it," I said, growing uncomfortable.

"You have plans?" Jake asked, appearing disappointed.

"Yeah, I do," I added defensively. "I'm going to a fun party tonight. I got tickets, and I really don't want to miss it."

"Your dad told me about the gala you are going to, but it's at nine, no? I made the dinner with that event in mind, assuming you don't really need to be there until much later."

"Thank you," I said, growing increasingly annoyed, "but I'd like to nap and do my hair before, and I just won't have time for both."

I was trying my best to remain composed, as the last thing I wanted was to be in a room with Paul Copolliard.

"Chloe," said Jake with a frown, seemingly exasperated, "you realize we are on a business trip. Copolliard could be a big customer for us. I would think you would take that seriously."

"I don't need you to tell me how to do my job, Jake," I snapped, "but it's a no. I don't like those guys very much, okay? So, I am not interested in pretending to enjoy their stupidity for a whole dinner."

I realized my voice was raised just a little, but I couldn't help it.

Jake squinted, clearly confused and concerned. "What am I missing here, Chloe? This is not like you."

"Paul is an asshole," I mumbled.

I was having a hard time maintaining professionalism, and I also didn't want to have to explain everything to Jake.

"Ah, I see," scoffed Jake, shaking his head. "I should have guessed," he said with a mocking expression that I wanted to wipe off his face. This no longer felt sympathetic.

"What are you implying exactly?" I demanded.

I knew exactly what he was assuming, and it unsettled me to the core.

"Do I really need to tell you? Seems like something happened between you two and now..."

I bit my lip very hard to resist the urge to make a scene.

"So, you just decided that I slept with him or something and now I'm upset? You know what, you are as much of a fucking jerk as he is."

I violently put my glass down on the table and rushed out of the bar to the elevator, fuming.

How dare he? Who the fuck did he think he was? Just because I had let him touch me, he now thought he could just talk to me as he damn well pleased!? I was aggressively pacing in my hotel room, desperately wanting to break something. Add that episode to why I always thought it was a bad idea to date coworkers.

I hated Jake almost as much as I hated Paul right this moment. If Jake hadn't been so quick to judge, I would have considered explaining to him that I did meet Paul, three months into my position at Motor Holmes. I had heard that the Copolliards where in town and had managed to arrange a meeting with Paul in Chicago.

He had insisted that we meet at a bar for drinks, as opposed to the lunch I wanted to arrange. I figured it was fine, as perhaps he wanted a less formal setting. The night had started well, and I thought I was closing the deal and signing up Copolliard for a contract with Motor Holmes. But as Paul continued to drink, he started to get inappropriate.

I brushed it off, tried to diplomatically reject him and change the topic. But later that night, after quite the awkward dinner, I was leaving the bathroom, and he was waiting for me in front of the door. Once I got out, he tried to kiss me, ignoring the clear rejection I was giving him when I told him no.

When I finally managed to get out from his forced embrace, he had launched at me again, restraining me, trying to force me to kiss him. His coworker had seen everything and had pulled Paul from on top of me, profusely apologizing for Paul's behavior. Still in shock, I ran out of the restaurant. I never told anyone other than my friends.

I knew I could never tell my father, as the last thing I wanted was to cause him worry. I just told him that while the pitch had gone well, Paul wanted to go with someone else for his business.

The idea that I'd be expected to dine with that man and pretend that he hadn't tried to force himself on me was revolting.

I had been so relieved to find out he had not rsvp-ed but here he was, sneaking his way in, with Jake asking questions I didn't want to answer. It was one of those unfortunate situations, as part of me thought I should say something, take the hit, to avoid him ever doing something like that to another peer. But then what? I could see how it would play out.

My dad would be outraged; he would reach out to Copolliard, maybe convince me to file a complaint against Paul. Then it would be a torturous "he said, she said."

I didn't trust his friend would be on my side and I didn't know anyone else who had seen what Paul had done. Even if I did win, even if there were actual consequences for him, I knew there would be backlash for me. Some men, too stupid to understand how to behave and not harass women would get cold with me, would avoid working with me, being at a bar with me, being in a room alone with me, afraid that they too might be accused of something like that.

Even if Paul wasn't a coworker, I expected that some idiots at Motor Holmes, and some idiots in the profession generally, would have that selfish irrational reaction. And I didn't want to give Paul the power to not only harass me but also impact my career in what would eventually just be a gray area that wouldn't really be actionable in the future.

What would I say exactly if I felt like someone was reticent to work with me for something like this? How would I prove it?

And the pain I would put my father through, having Motor Holmes involved in a scandal on my behalf, it just wasn't worth it. I could only hope that this was just an accident, as opposed to a permanent behavior on the part of Paul.

I wiped away my tears, deciding I wouldn't waste them on that poor excuse of a man. Instead, I went to the spa of the hotel, choosing to enjoy the amenities to their fullest, pamper myself a bit, take my mind off my troubles.

CHAPTER 20

I ALWAYS ENJOYED DRESSING up to go dancing. Because the gala wasn't part of the work conference, I didn't feel the constraint to dress in a professional manner.

I opted for a mesh fabric bronze peach dress, embellished with reflective sequins, crystals, and beads, with a cowl neckline and crisscross straps in the back. After doing my makeup and my hair, I added my gold pumps, grabbed my small gold wristlet, and headed out for the town.

The gala started with a silent auction. I bet on a few wine subscriptions, chatted with people, and eventually made my way to the party portion of the event.

It was everything I wanted, except that my friends weren't there. I had hoped to see Amelia and Iris considering I was in their town, but they were in Mexico again.

As I walked into the gala, the glitz and glamour were abundant all around. The upscale hotel was adorned with lights everywhere. The party was on two floors, with multiple bars and food stations in the corners.

I felt at ease as I enjoyed my cocktail.

It was the perfect place to forget all about Jake.

I quickly got into the groove, talking and dancing with strangers, making new friends, and letting the music take control of me. I had met a nice girl group of friends through Ana, who was frantically attending to the event, making sure everything ran smoothly.

The night was mine to dance all my worries away. I needed that moment to just have fun.

I had completely lost track of time when I noticed a man staring at me by the bar, slowly sipping on his drink. I stared at him, instantly knowing who it was. I would recognize Jake's silhouette in any crowd, even in the darkness. I didn't know if I was happy or mad at seeing him, so I decided to ignore him.

But I couldn't for long. I felt his gaze on me, caressing me, arousing me from afar. Short of breath and frustrated, I decided there was no avoiding him in any event, and at that point I was too bothered by his presence to keep dancing. I strutted to the bar furthest from him to grab some water, as it was the one away from the music speakers, in a quieter room. I could still feel him, going through the crowd, decisively making his way to me.

I was already tense, anticipating his warm breath behind my neck sending shivers down my spine and a slight throbbing between my legs.

He stopped next to me, ignoring me, and ordered himself another scotch. Once he got his drink, he turned to face me. I couldn't help but meet his gaze.

"Nice dinner?" I asked, trying to keep it casual.

He sighed. "No, not exactly, Chloe. I left early," he explained with hesitation. I frowned but focused on my water. "Chloe, I uh, I don't know how to say this..."

I was puzzled as he sounded lost for words, angry, tortured. I had an immediate urge to comfort him, erase whatever it was that was troubling him so much.

"I am so sorry for what I said earlier. I was stupid, and I didn't mean to offend you. I got carried away."

I silently nodded, somehow feeling embarrassed, looking down.

"And I feel like a fucking idiot."

I remained silent, then heard his aggravated sigh.

"I know what happened," he murmured.

My eyes widened. I felt guilty. I wanted to get away even if I had done nothing wrong. Jake caught my wrist before I could pass by him and escape.

"Chloe, please, don't run. It's okay, it's not your fault. Please, look at me," he pleaded.

I dared to turn, afraid of what I would see in his eyes. But there was no blame, no judgement, just concern and a lot of rage, his usual blue eyes almost looked dark, the intensity almost unbearable. I still felt off about this.

Confiding in Jake wasn't something I wanted to do, but it also seemed to come so naturally, so I relaxed just a bit.

"After we talked, I knew something was wrong. I did my research," explained Jake. "You are not the first one. I made his coworker tell me everything... I am so sorry."

My throat was slowly closing. The tears I was holding back were burning my eyes, threatening to roll down my face.

"Did you meet him?" I asked, my voice trembling, my head down, attempting to avoid his gaze.

"I did." I titled a bit, looking at his profile. I was taken aback by all the fury and tension contorting his face, his jaw enflamed, his forehead creased. "He needed to be taught a lesson. I couldn't just do nothing, Chloe."

I rotated fully to face him, panicked. I hadn't noticed the slight bruises on his face and his knuckles until just now, the darkness in the room making them seem more like shadows.

"Jake, I didn't ask you to," I whispered in horror.

"I know. But I wasn't just going to stand by. That man is a danger to society. The idea that he touched you, scared you, forced himself on you," Jake paused, his hands in fists, his knuckles white from the pressure. "There was nothing that could have stopped me from burying my fists in his fucking face."

I just leaned my head against his chest, unable to contain my tears any longer. He immediately folded his arm around my waist, holding me firm. I didn't quiver, I didn't sob, I just felt tears of relief wet his suit.

He held my head and kissed my temple. His protective hold made me believe everything was going to be alright. I didn't feel ashamed any longer, accepting his words.

I let out a breath of relief and finally acknowledged the fact that had been the victim—a victim who had been made silent in order to keep the peace. I felt myself ease up under the warmth of the hand he was tenderly caressing my back with.

"It's not your fault. It's never the fault of the person who is forced like this," he whispered, emotion thickening his tone. "He tried to take advantage of the situation. That makes him weak, not you, never you. I am sorry I acted like such a jackass earlier. If I'm being honest, I was just jealous."

I nodded my head, letting him know that I agreed with everything he had to say, and the tightness around my heart loosened a bit, his caress of my back melting my body stroke by stroke.

As I felt myself getting too comfortable, I quickly took a step back, putting some distance between us. The last thing I needed was for him to reject me yet again.

"Thank you," I managed to whisper as I dried my face. He seemed to reluctantly let me go. "Don't tell my dad; I don't want him to worry," I begged.

"I won't," he promised.

"I am sorry I, um, I didn't explain before..."

"You have nothing to apologize for, and you don't owe me or anyone an explanation. It's not something easy to talk about. I shouldn't have jumped to conclusions like this; I am the one who is sorry, Chloe."

"It still sucks, you know. You work so hard for something, and then it gets... murky because some dude can't help himself."

"I can't imagine how hard it can be for women in the workplace."

I sighed. "It's not always easy" I admitted. "All the things we have to juggle or account for on top of our jobs. All the rules we understand we have to follow or make for ourselves as we go, how to dress, how to talk, so men take us seriously and stop just seeing breasts or something they want to sleep with. The extra steps to be listened to. To avoid being sexualized.

"We should be appreciated for what we actually want to bring to the table, our work, our skills, our intelligence. But every now and then, a superior gets handsy. Then we aren't taken seriously, and men are able to repeat their behaviors because nobody hears us, it's just... exhausting."

"It's disgusting. We have to be able to do better." Jake nodded.

"I agree. And you know, the worst part is, when things like that happen to me, I... I sometimes somehow blame myself, I feel bad... like I did something wrong, like it's my fault... I felt so guilty about this Paul thing, like I cost my dad's business a relation with a company that could be valuable to us."

"Fuck that, Chloe, there is no scenario where any of this is your fault. Look at me." Jake lifted my chin towards him. "Some men just need to do fucking better. We all do. That's it. You shouldn't have to do anything, they do. Your dad would never want his company associated with degenerates like Paul anyways. And trust me, Paul is done for, it's just a question of time."

"Well, more importantly, since you punched him, I think I can forgive you," I said as a joke to change the subject.

"Oh, I am doing a lot more than that."

I swallowed hard. There was a dark side to this man, and I couldn't help but be intrigued. I felt the intensity coming out of him. I didn't know what he did, or how he did it considering how powerful I knew the Coppoliard family was, but I believed him.

"But I am not ready to go back to the hotel," I added.

"Of course," he said with a smirk, "the night is still young."

I finally relaxed more fully and smiled back.

"Want to dance?" I dared to ask. "Or is this not your style?"

"I'm not leaving your side," he said simply.

Content, I guided us to the main ballroom, and to the dance floor to join my friends. I picked up right where I left off, forgetting about Paul and allowing myself to feel to music and dance.

I had given him and his unwanted touching a lot of control over me through the years. I carried his act with me like a badge of guilt, as if I had been responsible for it. But tonight, it felt like a weight was lifted off me. Knowing that I had Jake's support untied the restraint that memory had on my psyche somehow.

The music coursed through me slowly, cutting the thread of discomfort Paul had wrapped around my core for so long. It felt like I was breathing a bit more freely.

And there was Jake, standing close to me, in his sexy suit.

I kept my distance from him, unwilling to risk another rejection, but Jake slowly got behind me.

"You're so fucking sexy when you dance," he whispered in my ear. "When you run your hands on your body like this."

Lord, I begged for mercy. I could feel his body pressing against mine. I shut my eyes, enjoying his firm presence, as I moved my body against his, to the rhythm of the music. He didn't back up; instead, he pulled me closer. I felt his hands gripping my waist, holding me oh so tight to his body, every curve of mine molded against him perfectly.

I opened my legs a bit more, allowing me to move my hips to the Latin song invading my senses. I heard him groan against my ear, as my breathing accelerated. I was starting to lose control, desperately wanting to feel his hand between my thighs, my silk underwear already wet in anticipation.

Not again, I reminded myself, not again, he would just reject me again. I forced myself to slow my movements and calm my racing heart, I needed to think rationally.

"I think I need more water," I declared.

He stopped, and I felt him tense behind me, but he never wavered. Instead, he guided me to the bar. I chugged a bottle of water under his watchful eye, praying for the cool water to tame my treacherous desires.

I was surprised to see that it was already 1 a.m. when I checked my phone. My feet were starting to kill me, my dress starting to feel more like a restraint.

"Okay, I think I'd like to go to sleep now," I confessed.

"I have a car waiting outside," he announced, anticipating my needs.

We rode in silence for ten minutes before we finally made it to the hotel. I could barely think straight when we got to the elevator, every inch of my body desperately wanting to be close to him, my skin tingling at the memory of his strong thighs around mine, at the need for *more*.

The elevator felt like the smallest room on the planet, stuffed, as if there was barely any air. Once he pressed our floor, he turned around to face me.

I took steps back until I felt the cold rail on my back. The temperature startled me, but I couldn't take my eyes off him as he menacingly walked towards me, his intentions incontestable.

My breathing was accelerated, my lips parted, my body completely hypnotized. Jake stopped right in front of me, his face distorted as he frowned, his jaw completely locked.

He looked like a beautiful beast as he took my face with his right hand, brought my lips to his, hot and hungry. I moaned, feeling electricity rush from my head to between my thighs. I kissed him back, lost in the primal need I had for him.

But as the elevator came to a stop, I snapped back to reality and attempted to put some distance between us.

"No," I said loudly, "not again. You made it clear that you didn't want me, you don't want this. I'm not putting myself in that position again."

I rushed out of the elevator, unable to look behind me, desperate to get away. I needed the safety of my room; I knew I wouldn't have the strength to push him away again.

I finally got to my door, fumbling to get my key card to work, but I was too slow, as he was now right behind me. He grabbed my left arm, whirled me around, forcing me to face him.

"No!" I gasped, struggling to breathe. He stopped, but he didn't move, his lips almost touching mine.

"Fuck, Chloe," he muttered between tight lips, his chest heaving. "Tell me you don't crave this as much as I do, tell me you are not dying for me to fuck you right now, and I promise I'll leave, and I'll never bother you again."

My legs shuttered as my lips quivered, unable to do anything but tell the truth.

"I can't tell you that."

Jake muttered something under his breath, grabbed the card from my hand, and shoved it in the hole with astute precision as his lips ravaged mine.

His arm lifted me slightly from the ground as I wrapped my arms around his neck for support.

He led me to the room and straight to my bed. With my arms still securely fastened around his neck, he set me down on my feet. He stopped kissing me for a second, but I wouldn't have it, so I grabbed his face with both hands.

"So eager, baby," he crooned.

He groaned, kissing me again, as he slid his suit jacket off. I held on to him for dear life, while his hands caressed my legs and went under my dress, stealing a moan out of me.

He was insatiable, hungrily kissing my neck, removing my thin straps out of the way.

I felt his hard, naked chest under his crisp white shirt, enjoying how his muscle contracted as his hands and arms travelled all over my burning body. I moaned, my head bending backwards to give him access, my fingers lost in his hair as he latched onto my nipples between his lips.

With his arms, he lifted me off the floor again, this time, my legs wrapped around his waist. I could feel the bulge of his desire against my wet pussy. I trembled in anticipation, so thirsty, as I would have given the world in that moment for him to be inside of me. He put me on the bed and proceeded to remove his pants.

My eyes timidly but hungrily admired all of him, throbbing and rising for me. I swallowed at the size of him. He pulled my dress over my head and lowered my panties down.

"You are so fucking beautiful," he murmured as he leaned on me and between my legs, drawing a finger between my folds. He growled. "Fuck, you are so wet for me, mein liebling."

I moaned as I felt him rub me to frustration.

"Please," I whispered, desperate for him to take me, but instead, he pulled me up more on the bed and grabbed my breast between his lips again.

I moaned in pleasure and frustration and grabbed on the pillows as he sucked. He continued to caress my ribcage and my belly, making circles with his mouth.

I felt like I was about to explode as he proceeded to open my hot and trembling labia with his tongue. I screamed his name and grabbed his hair as I felt his soft wet tongue on my clitoris, circling and sucking, quickly driving me to madness.

"Jake!" I gasped in euphoria.

He grunted and intensified his licks. I had never felt something so painfully delicious.

I felt a rush so intense, I had lost complete control of my body. All I could do was scream with all my being, surrendering to the most intense orgasm I had ever experienced, my body no longer subject to gravity.

I heard a wrapper open in the background, only vaguely aware of my surroundings. I saw him come up towards me, his eyes burning, a satisfied smirk on his face, stealing yet another scream as he slid inside of me with no warning, hot, hard, and fast.

I grabbed his back for support, wanting my body flush completely against his, desperate to merge with him even more, as he went in and out of me easier now, filling me fully.

"Fuck, I needed this." Jake knew how to drive me wild just with his words.

I could feel his desire, his desperate need for me, and I basked in it, my need rising again, enjoying him losing control of his senses inside of me, because of me.

He grunted as I smiled in sweet torture. I responded to his grunt, desire building in my stomach, my thighs tensing as I moved with him in perfect symphony.

I closed my eyes, feeling my peek coming as he slammed into me, deeper, faster, sloppier. I moaned louder and louder as I exploded, and as he groaned more aggressively, deepening his thrust further with a few more intense strokes I didn't think possible.

He slowly came to a full stop as he rested on top of me. I held onto him for dear life, feeling like I would die if he separated from me in that moment.

He didn't seem to be in a hurry either. He slowly caressed my body with his thumb, his head buried in my neck, not letting go of me.

"That was..." he said as he pulled me closer to him.

"I know." I sighed, feeling satisfied and sleepy.

Jake pulled out and proceeded to the bathroom. He brought me a damp towel.

I expected him to leave but instead, he got under the sheets and pulled me in his arms. We both fell asleep, with Jake holding me so close to him, my head resting on his chest.

I woke up in the middle of the night. I found my silk pajamas, and slipped them on before I got up to drink some water. As I came back to bed, I found Jake was also awake, gazing at me between sleepy eyes. Silently, I tiptoed to his side of the bed as he reached out for me.

Jake lifted me, sitting me right on top of him. I was instantly aroused, responding to his thirst as if we had never stopped touching each other. He started kissing and sucking on my neck as my hands travelled to his hair. He removed my straps, pulling my gown down so he could suck on my breast. I moaned, feeling myself quickly losing it again.

I couldn't remember the last time I had been so hungry for someone. My hand traveled down, grabbing his already hard penis. I sighed when I touched him, big, long and hard for me.

I positioned him between me as he pushed up gently, his girth filling me up oh so perfectly.

We both moaned as I started moving up and down, coating him with my wetness. Jake grabbed my hips, pulling me closer, thrusting deeper, and I could swear I saw stars.

His hands travelled along my back to my hair, his palm directing my head to his, as he grabbed my lips with a kiss. Impatient, he pulled my gown over my head, admiring my skin shining under the slight moonlight that beamed through the window.

"Fuck, baby," he whispered against my ear, making me moan further. "I don't know how I thought I could stay away from you."

"Is that an apology?" I teased.

"Fuck yes," he growled. "You look so perfect with my dick inside of you, baby."

I smiled, bending down to kiss him. With Jake buried deep in me, I felt complete.

We rode together with no inhibitions, completely dominated by the rise of fire inside, until we took each other to oblivion.

Saturday morning to the smell of coffee brought me back to my senses. I opened my eyes to find Jake in bed, a cup in his hands, looking at me. I let out a sigh, suddenly feeling a little shy.

"Good morning."

"Good morning." I pursed my lips.

He leaned down as I met him for a kiss. I was relieved as I wondered if he would have escaped to his room and sent me a note about how we'd made a mistake and needed to stop, after the fact.

I was afraid to find regret in his eyes, but he seemed completely comfortable, as he turned around to grab a cup of coffee that he handed me.

I sat up, keeping the bed sheets on me, as I welcomed the warm liquid in my throat. It already had milk and no sugar, just as I liked it. I was still touched that he clearly learned how I liked my coffee.

"I got us a reservation for brunch," he explained. "Figured we could play tourist today since the conference is over. There's a lot to see in this city, and I want to see it with you."

"Sounds good," I said, still surprised by the turn of events.

He pulled my body to his, tenderly kissing me. I felt my desire slowly rise as my hand grabbed his face. He set his coffee down and turned to grab mine, before he laid me down on my back, taking me to paradise once again.

CHAPTER 21

Jake finally left to go to his room and get ready for brunch. When he was gone, I attended to work emails, but couldn't help the nagging concern eating at my insides. I needed to understand why Jake seemed to have changed his mind. I knew I'd be unable to fully enjoy his new stance, afraid that he would change his mind again, and by then it would be too late for me.

My concerns weakened when he knocked and grabbed me into a kiss the second I swung the door open. I had opted for a simple flowy emerald dress, with gold jewelry, platform sandals, my hair tied to the side with a yellow ribbon.

Jake looked more relaxed than usual, dressed in a pair of dark blue jeans and a black polo. I didn't know how to handle the fact that he was treating me completely different, putting a hand on my back as we stopped at the desk to ask for laundry service. It felt intimate, like I was seeing another side of him he reserved for friends and family. And I enjoyed every bit of it.

"Hi!" I almost jumped at the screeching high-pitched voice coming from behind me. I turned to see Catherine had basically attacked Jake, holding him in a tight hug. He pulled back from her and planted himself next to me. "I was so afraid I would miss you before my flight! When do you leave?"

"We leave tomorrow evening," answered Jake, as he placed his hand back behind my waist. I froze, my eyes wide, as Catherine gave me a hateful stare, a look of confusion in her eyes.

"Chloe and I are going to try to enjoy today, visit some sites, brunch, food tour," he explained, staring at me. I cautiously smiled back, feeling Catherine growing more unsettled.

"I see," said Catherine with a flat tone.

"It was great to meet you, Catherine. Have a safe flight," said Jake, cutting the conversation short as he gently pushed me to walk with him towards the exit.

I did peek behind me just a bit, seeing Catherine fume in place.

"What was that about?" I asked as we got in a cab.

"Setting boundaries," he explained, intensely looking at me.

I blushed a bit, turning my head straight to face the road, doing my best not to react, but unable to control the corner of my lips.

We got to a wonderful restaurant, most of which was a beautiful large outside patio, decorated with a plethora of flowers all over the walls. The place was beautiful, effortlessly blending rustic charm with modern sophistication, and a romantic twist.

"You like it?" asked Jake, looking at my enlarged eyes.

"It's perfect!" I squealed as the hostess took us to our seats.

I was happy to see that we got one of the tables that provided a bit of privacy, removed from the rest. I loved that it gave us a view of the whole place, allowing me to admire the decor.

I scanned the menu filled with some of the most intriguing options. Once the server came back around, we placed our orders.

It was hard for me to let go and enjoy myself. I kept waiting for Jake to tell me he regretted spending the night with me, but that never came. Our brunch felt like a date, with Jake seducing me with every word, every smile.

After a few mimosas, we strolled around and sauntered through museums and art shows. We then joined the food and booze walking tour that I had booked. Jake grabbed my hand, and I was starting to allow myself to enjoy the butterflies I felt every time he pulled me to him and kissed me, or the joy I felt at hearing him laugh.

I had never seen Jake like this, so open with me, his relaxed demeanor making him even seem younger than usual. And I was enjoying every second of it.

We floated back to the hotel around six. I had a work call to reluctantly attend, and we needed to change for dinner, so we parted ways for a couple hours.

"You look stunning," he said, voice deep, when he came to get me.

I was wearing a halter neck, high-low silk black dress with adjustable straps. The dress had a low back cut, allowing him to caress my bare skin, sending electricity down my spine.

"I have something that would go perfectly with this," he said as he pulled a necklace from his pocket.

I was overwhelmed by emotions as he spun me around to set the necklace he had gifted me around my neck, lightly kissing my back when he was done. I was simply out of words because the man continued to surprise me with his actions.

Jake was breaking through my walls one by one and at fast speed, with every gesture, the night clearly being planned to please me. The necklace was a reminder, and it looked so good back on my neck—where it belonged.

"I can't believe you brought it with you."

"I really needed to see it back around your neck."

I swallowed hard, the possessive tone in his voice triggering a desire to feel him inside of me again. I sighed, and he laughed.

We walked from the elevator to a black car waiting for us outside.

Jake had really outdone himself, somehow managing to find a reservation at a restaurant I had tried to reserve a spot for two months before the conference, with no success. We got escorted to the back, to a separate glass room perfectly decorated for privacy and romance. We had two servers with champagne glasses for us. Jake walked me to my seat, pulling my chair for me to sit.

We were served a delicious seven course meal, the most scrumptious wine pairings accompanying every meal. The chef came a few times to make sure everything was going smoothly.

I was almost on edge when Jake got up and asked for my hand to dance to the wonderful saxophone music that was being played in the speakers. He took me to the middle of the room, splaying his palm on my back, holding my other hand in his. I felt myself warm up to his touch. I looked up, overwhelmed by what I thought I saw in his eyes.

"Jake," I started, hesitating, not wanting to ruin the moment but unable to stop myself, "last night, well this morning was… well, you were there," I said, staring at his suit. "I'm just, confused? Last time you were quite… clear and… I just want to know what you are thinking."

I stopped talking, realizing I was starting to nervously sound like a teenager.

"I know," he admitted in a deep voice. "And I'm sorry."

I looked up, searching his gaze, making sure I caught everything he was saying and not saying.

"I was only trying to push you away. I just… I really wanted to try to keep our relationship professional. Your dad hired me, and I don't think this was part of his plan. He's a great friend; I didn't want to put that in jeopardy. But the thing is, Chloe, there was no way I could look at you every day and not make you mine. I fought this; you know I did. This wasn't a choice. I didn't have any other option but to be with you."

I felt my blood pressure rise as I observed his troubled face, his frown, his tightened jaw, those eyes that felt like they were looking right into my soul.

My lips parted as I felt his come to mine. I welcomed him, my concerns appeased, allowing myself to cautiously enjoy this potential new relationship with my competitor.

"You hurt me, you know," I admitted timidly.

"I know, mein liebling. I'm sorry, I just," he sighed, "I try to keep my work life and my personal life separate. I didn't want to change that."

"I can understand that. I regretted dating Kyle for that reason, even if we parted ways amicably." I shrugged.

He winced ever so slightly.

"I tried to avoid this, but even I am not strong enough. It was killing me to have to stay away from you."

My heart swelled, and I kissed his neck.

"What does mein liebling mean?" I repeated the words as best I could.

"My darling, in German."

"I like it," I said shyly. "From your mother's side, I assume?"

"Yeah." He nodded. "She grew up in Berlin, moved to the States with her parents when she was a teenager."

"And your dad?" I felt him stiffen a bit at the question. I knew he had an absentee father, but he hadnt said much before otherwise.

"A deadbeat my mother met in college. They got married, had two children, and when life got too difficult, he just packed up and left us." His jaw grew tighter, a muscle twitching.

"How old were you when he left?"

"I was ten, and Rick was eight."

I was outraged on his behalf. I could see that even after twenty-six years, that abandonment still affected him. How could someone do something like that, walk away from a family, from their children?

"Are you... still in touch with him?" I asked.

"No," he answered, almost with disgust. "He's reached out a few times over the years, but no, it's not worth my time."

He shook his head. I could feel him tense and regretted asking him all these questions. He fell silent after that, a bit lost in his thoughts. I kissed his neck again and nested my head there. He held me tighter against him as we continued to sway to the rhythm of the song.

When we got back to the hotel, we went straight to his room. Jake had ordered a bottle of champagne to the room, but we never got to it, since as soon as we made it in, Jake stopped behind me, kissing my neck as he moved my hair on the other side.

I leaned my head back on his shoulder. He slowly unzipped my dress, kissing my back. The dress slipped from my body as he gently spun me around to see me.

"You don't know how long I've wanted this," he began, as he trailed his palm down my back to my waist. "You have no idea how hard it's been, being so close to you at the office and not being able to touch you."

He sucked on my neck, and I whimpered.

"I was always so hard for you. I was so fucking frustrated that I couldn't lay my claim to you. Especially when that bastard was around," he added while traveling to my already hardened nipple.

With every kiss, every caress, I melted into his arms further, his words resonating through me.

That bastard, I assumed, was Kyle. I loved knowing how much he wanted STÉ; how much he suffered. It felt good to know that the attraction, that feeling, wasn't one-sided.

"It was hard for me too, Jake," I admitted. "You were confusing me so much."

"I know. But I wasn't playing you. I was fighting this, fighting you. And I failed miserably."

He grabbed my other nipple.

"Oh, Jake."

He grunted and sucked harder.

"I'm so fucked," he said gruffly.

His grip on my back tightened as he guided me to the bed and got on top of me. He was going a lot slower this time. My skin heated everywhere he looked.

He forced himself to slow down, teasing me, gazing into my eyes, kissing my pupils, my face, caressing every single inch of my body tenderly. I was hypnotized, observing his every move, enjoying the desire and passion I saw rising in him.

I also trailed my lips on his skin, nudging my head in his neck, kissing his shoulders, his chest, my hands all over his body.

I moaned as he slowly pushed inside of me, his eyes never losing sight of mine, enjoying the fire he saw rising in me with every thrust.

"Jake!" I whispered, overcome by the feelings coursing through me.

He continued to thrust deep within me, slowly, deeply, the connection between us so overwhelming. I never wanted this moment to end.

"I can't get enough of you, baby." He exhaled a deep, ragged breath that I felt vibrate in my core.

He tightened his grip on my waist, limiting my movements. My heart rumbled. My body arched further, desperately wanting to be even closer to him.

He intensified his rhythm, as if suddenly possessed. He thrusted inside of me, faster and faster, stealing sobs and whimpers out of me. I clung to him like my life depended on it, leaving no space between us.

I grew ravenous, almost aggressive, and he matched me move for move.

"Jake, fuck!" I exclaimed in ecstasy.

"Yes, come for me, mein liebling, come with me," he ordered in my ears as I obeyed and came, holding on to him as tight as I could.

———————

Keisha

How was the party?

Alot of fun.

Keisha

Did Mr. Proper join?

He did…

Amelia

Spill it, Chloe. Whenever you barely text, it's because you're hiding something.

Oh, please.

Iris

And now she's defensive… What happened!?

He showed up. I caved. I was weak. We had sex. There, happy?

Keisha

Finally!

Amelia

Omg how was it???

Iris

Amelia! We don't need to invade her privacy like that. Only if she wants to share….;)

I don't want to share.

Iris

I didn't mean it. I was pretending to be respectful. Spill. Some of us need to live vicariously. Oliver has been buried under work for ten days now. Don't be selfish

Hahaha. Okay, fine. The man is gifted, and all I want to do is take off work to ride him all day. He's perfect, every darn inch of the man's body is perfection. And he knows just how to get me to melt and shake with pleasure. That enough for you?

Keisha

It's way too early in the day for this kind of heat [say more].

Iris

Oof!

Amelia

Nice :) nothing better than a man who knows what he's doing ;)

:) :) :) It's time for round 300. TTYL

Jake reluctantly let me slip out of his arms so I could go to my room and get ready for the day. I was floating on cloud nine, whispering songs as I started my morning routine.

I couldn't stop thinking about my conversation of the morning with Jake.

"What do we tell people?" I had asked, as he caressed my face. "Do we even tell people?"

"I think we should. We don't have anything to hide, do we?"

"No, we don't," I agreed, relieved further.

It meant that Jake wasn't just playing with me, as telling everyone included people at work and having to go through the awkward process of formally disclosing our relationship to HR.

"I do think," I added, "that we should maybe just keep it to ourselves for a few weeks."

Jake frowned, and I hurried to fill the silence.

"Only to play it safe," I explained. "I just want to enjoy this as between you and me for a little longer, before the rest of the world starts meddling."

"I understand," said Jake. "Whenever you're ready is fine."

He seemed a bit disappointed, but I tried to reassure him by pulling him closer for a kiss.

I just had been there before with Kyle, and I wanted to be a bit more cautious this time, make sure what we had was real before rocking the boat.

I did feel like I needed to perhaps explain more later on, I just didn't want Jake thinking something was wrong. I was starting to feel like perhaps a relationship was worth the possibility of disappointment, that at least with him, the risk of trusting him to have that kind of power over me would be worth it.

Jake had told me that he would be on a long call, so to pass the time, I got ready and started packing, leaving out only what I needed for the night and the morning.

I wasn't looking forward to going back home. I was afraid that this little love oasis we were in would end once we went back to reality, one I had to give real consideration, decide whether it was worth it to tell my coworkers to tell my family.

Once done, I proceeded to go meet Jake in his room. I came to a halt and hid behind a wall when I saw Jake just outside his room, talking to someone. I instantly recognized the profile.

Lauren's.

I couldn't hear them very well, but the conversation sounded heated. My heart dropped when I saw Lauren put her hands around his neck, press her body against his, and kiss him as she started pushing him back in the room.

He grabbed her arms and held her at a distance, but he pulled her in and closed the door behind them.

I held in my gasp and forced my shaky legs to guide me back to my room and away from this nightmare. I leaned against the door for support, shutting my eyes, blind with anger and pain. Tears I wanted to stop rolled down my face.

I didn't know if I should go back and confront them or hide in my room. No, that would only be embarrassing.

Why was she there? Did he invite her and somehow forgot?

She wouldn't be there if Jake hadn't shared his whereabouts with her. How did he think he would manage two women at once? It didn't make sense. Maybe he didn't plan to sleep with me. Maybe it was an accident and now he had to deal with both of us at the same time.

I decided to check Lauren's Instagram, and lo and behold, she was posting selfies of herself in Jake's room with the caption *"finally reunited with my love."* Her mother was the first comment.

Jake wasn't in the picture, but of course he had let her in, and she was sitting on his bed, on the bed he was holding me so tight on just an hour before. Perhaps she was just surprising him as she was coming back from Europe. But again, he must have told her where he was. And she probably knew that I was there as well.

Enraged, I decided I couldn't stay in the hotel any longer, every place being a reminder of the lie I had allowed myself to believe.

I wouldn't be able to fake this. Eyes blurry, I finalized packing. I frantically removed the necklace and dropped it to the floor, as it felt like it was burning a hole in my skin.

I carefully got out of my room and to the elevator, making sure they weren't around to see me. I jumped in a cab and headed straight to the airport, then booked myself the next flight out to Chicago.

It was 4 p.m. CT when I opened my front door, feeling broken and defeated. I had a couple glasses of champagne on the plane to help keep me calm and hopefully help me sleep, but all it did was intensify my headache.

I carried my luggage to my room and proceeded to unpack blindly, doing everything I could to distract myself from the heavy weight on my heart. As I caught a glimpse of my face in the mirror, I stopped and allowed myself to cry. The dark circles couldn't get worse than they already were.

Once I composed myself, after I showered, I went to grab my phone from my purse. I almost panicked when I saw all the calls and text messages I had received from Jake.

> Chloe, where are you? I stopped by your room but heard no answer

> Did you leave? The front desk told me you checked out

> Chloe? Where the hell are you? Are you okay?

> What the fuck is going on? Just tell me you're okay, Goddamn it, I am losing it.

> Great. You left.

> You got on a plane and left. Why on earth would you do that?

Answer me, damn it!

You left without a word. What is going on?

I am on the next flight.

I'm coming over. We need to talk.

I closed my eyes and stopped reading. He had the audacity to be the one angry. What was wrong with him?

I realized that both Keisha and Kyle had also texted. I decided to deal with Kyle first, as he would be a welcome distraction.

He was pleased to hear that I cut my trip short and wanted to stop by. I decanted some wine before he got to my house, wanting to do my best to hide my pain. I couldn't entertain any questions or conversations about Jake. Kyle was perfect for that.

While I waited, I had an hour-long call with my father in the evening, sitting on my front sofa, watching the sun set and the beautiful hues of blue and orange I had the pleasure to enjoy in the late evenings. He wanted to know how the conference went. He was quite impressed by the contacts Jake and I made, having also touched base with Jake earlier in the day.

It was clear that Jake had kept his account of events professional and hadn't told my dad about Paul or about us, and I can't say I wasn't thankful. My dad also reminded me that we were all going to Jake's New Buffalo vacation home on Thursday, for the upcoming fourth of July celebration.

Some business folks might also join, and so he expected his daughter to also attend. I protested, but he wasn't going to take no for an answer. It was a great chance to spend family time, he explained, and for me to continue to reduce tension with Jake. Not to mention that it had been on the calendar for a few weeks already.

I rolled my eyes and bit my lips but didn't know what to say. If only he knew, I thought. Perhaps I needed to tell him so that he could understand why the thought of being in Jake's house for days wasn't appealing to me.

Kyle got here at eight, wearing a pair of jeans and a blue shirt. He looked quite tan, as he had spent a few days in Hawaii. He brought me roses. We went and sat down in the living room in the back of the house.

He wanted me to know that he had broken up with his supposedly now ex-girlfriend. I told him how sorry I was to hear that, and perhaps he would enjoy being single as much as I was, preempting the part where he would ask me again if I would consider getting back together with him.

As I was getting ready to tell Kyle to go home, we heard the doorbell ring.

"Did you order something?"

"No, I didn't." I frowned.

"Let me go check."

As Kyle opened the front door, my throat tightened. I recognized Jake's aggravated tone. I couldn't make up much of what was being said between the men. I sighed when I heard the door close.

But my relief was short-lived. I could hear stomping by two pairs of feet heading in my direction. I sprang up and met them halfway in the living room.

"What the fuck, man? Why the fuck would he stop by so late?" said Kyle, seemingly exasperated, standing between me and Jake. Shit.

"What are you doing here?" I asked, feeling the blood drain from my face.

"Tell him to leave," Jake ordered, his eyes laser focused on mine. I heard Kyle scoff.

"You've got to be kidding me."

"Can't this wait for the office tomorrow?" I pleaded.

"No."

That was all he said. But the tone of his voice, the clench of his jaw, told me he wasn't going to leave. He never looked in Kyle's direction.

I swallowed. Hard.

"Chloe," hissed Kyle.

I kept a straight face, not wanting any of my feelings evident.

"We do have a bunch of meetings tomorrow, Kyle. We need to plan them beforehand."

Jake slowly turned his menacing gaze towards Kyle. He looked like he wanted to snap his neck in two.

"I'll talk to you tomorrow," I said, hoping he would take the bait and leave. I was about to kick him out anyways.

"Fine. Call me if you need me," he offered as he approached me to say goodbye.

I turned my head to avoid his lips touching mine. I heart a grunt from Jake. I couldn't understand why Kyle felt the need to try every now and then. I wanted to shove him out but felt a bit bad for him as he clearly had not moved on. And I didn't want to embarrass him too much. I walked him to the door and shut it behind him.

CHAPTER 22

AFTER KYLE LEFT, I held onto the doorknob a few seconds more than warranted. I heard his steps; I knew Jake stood just a few feet behind me. I gulped.

I wasn't ready for a confrontation this late at night. I was wearing my loungewear for crying out loud and getting ready to sit and watch TV while writing my book. And yet, trouble was standing right there in my living room, wrapped in a black suit and adorned with a purple tie, and my heart could not ignore it.

"Turn around, baby."

My idiot heart skipped a beat. I couldn't delay the inevitable any longer. I slowly pivoted on my heels to face him.

"You have some nerve. Showing up to my door at this time of night, unannounced and uninvited," I snapped.

Jake remained silent. But I noticed his tense shoulders, a shadow on his face. He was standing there, phone in one hand, looking as if he were torn about what to do or say.

I knew he wasn't going anywhere until he got his answer, so I stepped away from the door and walked back to the dining room.

A knot formed in my stomach and continued to tighten the closer he got. The silence was torture, as he put a hand in his pocket and stared at me, a look of frustration haunting his face. I wanted to melt into the floor and disappear.

"So, I take it you are avoiding me."

"Not quite," I lied, looking at the floor, feeling my cheeks warm up. "I just decided to work from home."

"Is that so?"

"Yes," I answered too fast, staring at him, feeling defensive. "I'm very busy and didn't want to fly late tonight."

He didn't budge, giving me that superior look I both loved and hated so much. I got even more defensive.

He shook his head.

"Why did you leave like this? No explanation, nothing."

I wanted to scream at him but held it in when I saw the intense look in his eyes. Frown lines marred his gorgeous face, and I could see he was clenching his jaw.

I wasn't sure whether I wanted to push him out the door or tell him exactly how he had fucked up this whole situation.

"I wanted to leave early." I didn't owe him an explanation, so I opted to leave it at that.

"Stop playing games with me, Chloe," he interrupted. Is this revenge for how I treated you before? We talked about this." He paused and took a step in my direction. "You must know that after what happened, you are mine, right?"

I closed my eyes, resisting the urge to tell the truth, his words reverberating in my ribcage, threatening to melt away my resolve. I instead proceeded to walking, heading to my kitchen, with Jake right behind me.

My trembling hand reached out for the decanter, and I poured us some wine to buy some time. He ignored the glass I put in front of him on the kitchen island as I chugged mine.

"What is it?" he insisted, now standing right in front of me, his eyes searching for mine, observing my every wince.

"I can't be yours if you still belong to her."

"Who?" he sputtered.

"Lauren."

"Lauren? God. I told you I want nothing to do with her. Look at me. Look at me, Chloe."

His guttural tone made every fiber of my soul vibrate. I knew if I looked up at him, I was done. I felt my eyes get wet and my lips get dry. I stepped back.

"I don't really want to talk about this," I said, feeling my cheeks burning. "There isn't much to say. We had fun in California, but I don't want this. This is never going to work, so please, don't make this harder," I begged as he took a step towards me.

"I'm not," he sighed, "you are."

He paused.

"And you're lying to me," he declared.

The pressure got to me, and I bravely lifted my head in his direction and gazed into his eyes, hoping he would take pity on me. Yes, I had lied like a teenager, but there was no way I could utter the truth without tears.

"The way you trembled under my touch just this morning, the way you screamed for me, you can't tell me I'm not the one you want."

My next lie got stuck in my throat, I knew if I said one more word I would cry, so I just looked at him, almost recognizing my sorrow in his intense blue-gray pupils. I forced myself to remember what was stopping me from going in to feel his arms around me: it was that just this morning, he probably did the same with Lauren.

"You were right," I doubled down. "We should have never gotten involved."

"No, we shouldn't have, but we did, and there is no going back." He took a step closer.

"Stop."

"We did because we had no other choice, because I wanted you... above reason, above all else, and you wanted me, too. And I know you still do."

He suddenly grabbed me by my left arm and pulled me to him. "You are mine, Chloe."

Before I could push him away, he grabbed my arms and flushed my body to his chest. I felt his lips violently opening mine. I tried to keep my lips closed, but I could feel him pressing further, his teeth hurting my lips, until the pain was too much, and I let him in, every stroke of his tongue demanding my submission.

A current ran through me from my toes to my head, as he kept taking from me, engulfing my every sense in his urgent need for me.

I felt tears roll down my face as my heart wanted to take control and just give into the wonderful relief of just feeling him against me. But I gathered my strength and pushed him back, my eyes wide, unable to stop my tears. He looked alarmed, realizing I was hurting.

"No! No!" I took a step back, nervously running my hands through my hair as I tried to compose myself. "You need to leave. I don't want you here."

I quickly passed next to him, heading towards the front door, my vision blurred, my body trembling.

He didn't follow immediately, but he finally got there as I could hear him striding behind me. I didn't turn around but instead remained on my path towards the door.

"You saw her, didn't you?" he guessed as I grabbed the doorknob.

I stayed in place, unable to speak. I heard him sigh, my silence being my admission.

Rage fueled me yet again. I straightened my back and turned to face him, my pain making space for a sudden need for violence. Feeling as if he had stabbed me, I got even more upset when he seemed a bit relieved as he shook his head.

"She just showed up. I didn't invite her; I didn't even tell her where I was," he explained as he took a couple steps in my direction.

"I don't care."

"Do you really think that, even if I was fucking stupid enough to put us in jeopardy for her, that I would invite her while on a trip with you? Think about it, Chloe."

I just stared at him, searching his eyes, reason slowly helping me see things through slightly different lenses. I wanted to ask more questions, but my pride was strongly in the way.

"She got the information from my secretary, a mistake she will never make again."

I remained silent.

"Lauren knows and has known that nothing can happen between her and I," he continued. "She keeps trying, as it's a bit... hard for her apparently to take no for an answer."

She had always had problems with that, I remembered. My cousin didn't take to rejection well at all. She considered it inconceivable that someone wouldn't want her above all other women. Granted, it didn't happen often from what I recalled.

"She wouldn't just show up, all the way from Europe, if you didn't keep the door open for her," I managed to utter. "Oh, and I saw you kiss her, my favorite part of the trip."

"Chloe, she kissed me. She did, not the other way around, and if you had seen it all you would have seen me push her away."

"It doesn't matter—"

"I couldn't have been clearer," he interrupted. "And the only reason I haven't told her about us is because you asked me for discretion. She asked, as she is suspicious, and I guess this was her last attempt at convincing me, but I explained that there was someone else. I told her that all I wanted was you, Chloe, that other women she is dying to find out more about."

"She was in your room."

I felt my hands turn cold and almost forgot to breathe. I wondered if he could hear my heart hitting my ribcage. He was in front of me now, searching my eyes.

"She didn't stay for more than five minutes," he continued to explain, his voice lower. "I booked her a flight to her friends in Cabo, and she left. I then went straight to your room, but you weren't there. I looked for you all over the place. I called you, I called everyone."

He stopped, his jaw clenching, seeming to have difficulty continuing.

"You just left. You left me there without a word. I fucking panicked, Chloe, I thought something happened to you."

He paused again, his tone wavering, the frustrated lines in his forehead growing deeper.

"Once I landed, I came straight here, only to find Kyle in your home, opening your door like he fucking lives here."

I let go of the doorknob, but still distrustful, I crossed my arms.

"Perhaps it's simpler if we stop this before it's too late. Be with Lauren and just let me be." I wasn't lying. I was exhausted.

"I don't settle, Chloe, and that would be settling. I need you to believe me."

"Why let her in your room? Why let her kiss you?"

"I pushed her away, Chloe. I went back to my room to call her a car so she would leave. I was just focused on getting her out of there frankly. I didn't think you'd react well to seeing her on my doorstep," he said, with the first smirk of the night on his face.

I remained silent.

"I was hoping to get her out of there before you came back. Not because I had anything to hide, but because I didn't want to upset you; I knew it didn't look good. I didn't want you to see any of it. I wanted her gone before you got there, because I didn't want to mess with what we had, I didn't want to ruin our trip. But that clearly didn't work."

"And you didn't invite her there? Before you and I got together?"

"No. There is nothing between us, Chloe, nothing. You were right there, in my arms, just an hour before she showed up. How could you even think I'd be wanting another woman?"

He cupped my face, lifting my head to force me to look him in the eyes.

"When you gave your body to me, I didn't take that lightly. You letting me in, confiding in me, meant something to you. And it meant something to me. I want to give us a chance, Chloe."

My heart melted when I saw him strong but also weak, questioning, his eyes a bit larger, searching my face to confirm his words, to erase the sliver of doubt he possibly still had, even as he sounded so sure of his control over my being.

He smiled, apparently having found what he needed. Jake proceeded to pull my body on his, his tongue parting my lips open and passionately seeking mine.

My brain had lost the battle and could no longer restrain my body from responding to his traveling hands and demanding grasp, my fingers desperately finding their way to his thick waves, my heart heavy with an emotion I had tried to ignore with every fiber of my being.

Every touch challenged my still skeptical thoughts, as he pushed me back against the front door.

I helped him quickly rip his jacket off; I needed to feel as much of him as I could. He brought my panties down as we frantically unbuckled his belt.

He lifted my legs, wrapping them around his waist, and placed his arms under my ass. He immediately pushed himself into me, slamming my back against the door, hot, passionate, throbbing more and more with every thrust. We were both short of breath, as I fed off the urgency I felt emanating from him.

He was relentless, pushing inside of me aggressively, making me see stars.

"Don't ever leave like this again," he ordered in between thrusts. All I could do was moan louder.

He wrapped his right hand around my throat and used his thumb to make me face him.

"I need to hear you say it, Chloe," he growled as he slammed into me again, with such force I felt the wood trims push against my shoulders.

If this was my punishment, I needed more of it. He pushed violently into me again.

"Ugh!"

"Say it."

"I won't... ugh!" He slammed into me again. "I won't do it again," I breathed out.

"That's my girl."

He was so deep within me; I felt full and wanted.

He moaned and grunted as he picked up the pace. We wrestled, looking into each other's eyes, feeding off each other's arousal and frustration, a delicious, coiled loop of electricity between us.

"Oh God."

"That's it, baby," he encouraged as he continued pumping himself inside me. My eyes rolled in the back of my head.

"Jake, I'm going to come!"

"Oh fuuck!"

I buried my face in his shoulder, feeling the most explosive and intense release I'd ever experienced. He groaned and shuddered inside me, holding on tight as I had lost any strength I had.

Our mouths met as we slowly kissed, still enjoying the current that invaded our bodies. I didn't want to let him out of me, wanting absolutely nothing to change.

He slowly placed me back on my feet. I was unable to hide my smile of satisfaction. We just stood there in silence for a minute, catching our breath, my head buried in his chest, breathing him all in. Finally, we both silently headed to my room, where he continued to make me feel like I was floating in the air.

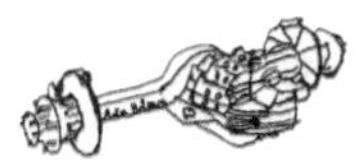

I woke up to a melody of sounds outside my window: birds singing, the sound of rain, and the feeling of warm kisses trailing down my spine, sending small electric currents through my body. It would seem like Jake had put my necklace around my neck while I was sleeping. The man was so possessive, I loved it. I could not think of a better way to come out of my slumber.

Jake pulled me closer to him, his strong hand around my stomach, his breath warming up my neck. Our Monday felt like the most perfect Sunday, as an orgasm eventually woke me up completely and then led to a much-needed nap.

We stayed in bed until noon, cuddled with my treacherous cat sleeping on top of Jake. We talked about everything under the sun as we both lazily petted her. This was what it felt like to date someone who accepted me as I was. It was refreshing, and every time we talked, all I wanted was for him to get on top of me again.

Penny's cushy, furry little paws were gently padding my cheeks. My little cotton ball was sitting on top of my chest.

"Penny…"

"Meow?"

"Yes, yes, I'm awake."

I couldn't stay annoyed for more than a second because of how adorable she was. I also needed some unconditional love, so I took her in my arms and held her there as I lazily rubbed her belly.

"Even I have to admit this is adorable," said Jake as he wrapped his arm around my waist and petted her.

I snuggled against him, feeling so content I was almost overwhelmed. It was the most perfect morning.

After we addressed some work emails in bed, we eventually made it to the kitchen for avocado toast and coffee. Jake couldn't keep his hands off my hips as I sliced a fresh avocado open, waiting for the bread he had set to grill. I felt like we were on top of a cloud, far from the rest of society, and if I had my way, we would never come down. It was a slow or rather close to non-existent workday, and it hadn't stopped raining.

Jake eventually sat on one of the bar stools, watching me pour myself a cup of coffee, as I was cooking the fried eggs to add on top of the toasts. I could feel the fabric of my silk pink dress robe set caress my body. I felt so sensual this morning, and all I wanted was to go back to bed with him. But we had to start our day.

When the open-faced avocado toast was ready, I strolled to Jake, setting the plate down as he pulled me closer for a kiss.

"I enjoy seeing you like this."

"If you refer to me in the kitchen," I teasingly warned, "don't get used to it. I know how to cook two things and that is it." I smiled.

He laughed. "Hm, I think your skills are better used elsewhere; I mean you barely clothed like *this* around me."

He sucked on my bottom lip.

"It feels weird to be having a lazy Sunday morning on a Monday," I admitted as I put my coffee down to wrap my hands around his neck.

"Meh, it's a holiday week. And I think we could both use a break, and that would be even better spent together."

He buried his face in my neck and sighed as I closed my eyes, holding onto his shoulders for dear life as he proceeded to remove my negligée.

CHAPTER 23

I BIT MY LIPS, while sitting at my desk, as I daydreamed a bit, remembering the peaceful Monday Jake and I spent at my house, filled with snacks, mimosas, cat cuddles, and passionate moments. The rain had created a cozy little bubble for us. Jake had taken me on my kitchen island. How was I supposed to eat there now without fantasizing about him?

I had spent a day in paradise with a man that made me feel so much happiness I was afraid it would burst out of me, and I'd realize it was all a dream. The trip to Michigan no longer felt like torture, I was looking forward to it.

While I wondered how we would manage everyone around for a few days, the idea of sneaking around made the whole event more appealing.

Early this morning Jake went home, and I headed to the office. I wanted to get ahead on work in anticipation of the Michigan trip and figured it would be easier to focus away from the bedsheets that now smelled like Jake, like heaven itself.

The day passed by in a flurry of calls and meetings. As the sun set so did the rush, and the office quieted. Thankfully, we had a work happy hour scheduled for the evening for one of the director's birthdays, the perfect way to end a hectic workday.

As I was sending my last email, Kyle stopped by my office so we could go a few floors up to the office lounge. We walked into a transformed space changed to host the birthday gathering. The room we sometimes used as a lounge had been morphed and the sofas removed to make place for a few high tops, and a long buffet-style serving in the middle.

There was a bar in the far-left corner with a good selection of beer, wine, and liquors, the usual bartender making cocktails upon request. The right side of the room remained the same, with a wet bar island and a few sofas.

My heart swelled when I spotted Jake by my dad, in his sharkskin blue suit. That man, in formal attire, was the greatest gift to the universe. And he was *mine*.

His eyes were locked on me as his gaze perused my body, admiring the way my off-white sheath sleeveless dress accentuated my curves. I couldn't stare in his eyes. I was afraid that if I did, everyone in the room would know that just a few hours ago, he was making me come. And I was craving more.

He quickly glared at Kyle next to me. I got the message and headed to the bar, I needed my dear bubbles to distract me from the overwhelming urge I had to go to him, grab his face, and beg that he take me right here on the table.

I spent the hour chatting away with everyone but Jake. Every time we managed to be in the same group, I didn't last more than two minutes before I needed space. I was losing my grip on my usual stoic behavior, his presence unsettling me more than usual.

When his eyes met mine, I felt like a fire was consuming me. It was like after having a taste, I had gotten even more addicted to him, and my desire for him was out of control.

I sensed him behind me before he positioned the palm of his hand on the small of my back. My body stiffened as I held my breath. He removed his hand and shoved it in his pocket as he laughed at a joke someone in the group had made. I had missed it. I felt like I was burning in place.

That man was going to be the end of me.

I finally got tired of socializing, so I excused myself, hugged my father, and headed to my office to pack my belongings and head home. Jake and

I hadn't talked about whether we were going to spend the night together again.

I startled when I heard the door I had left ajar slam behind me. Jake locked it and closed the distance between us in just a few strides, his tie loosened. I observed him with rounded eyes and parted lips.

"What are you doing?" I asked, my breath already shallow.

"Reminding you who you belong to."

In one swift motion, Jake lifted me up on my desk, pushing some files out of the way.

"We can't…"

My words got caught in my throat as he proceeded to aggressively take my lips in his, his pent-up anger deepening the kiss.

He cupped my breast with his right hand as his left held me closer to him, with him positioned firmly between my legs. I let out a whimper when I felt his hard cock against my panties, already soaked for him.

"Jake!" I whispered, trying to sound stern, my decorum fleeting through my fingers.

"Unbutton your dress or I will rip it off of you."

I gulped but proceeded to do as I was told, my hands lightly shaking, my breathing heavy. "Are you angry?"

I could see the darkness turning those blue eyes slightly gray. I knew something was bothering him.

He grunted but refused to give me an answer.

Was I going to let him take me right here, at work, in my office, with our coworkers just a couple floors away?

Jake was relentless. With one hand he unclasped my bra, his gaze heated as he freed out my breast. He grabbed my panties by both hands, pulled them down my legs, and shoved them in his pocket. He pulled me closer to him again and slid his fingers between my legs as his mouth devoured my nipple.

I held back my moan, afraid someone would hear us. He pumped his fingers inside of me until I whimpered.

He hummed in satisfaction finding me so ready for him.

"I've been wanting to fuck you all night, baby, and you, you've been ignoring me."

"I wasn't ignoring you, I...."

Suddenly, he lifted me off the desk and spun me around. He laid his hand on my back, bending me over.

"You were. Walking away from me, indulging that asshole's fucking jokes, his hand on your arm." I heard him unbutton his pants.

"Jake...I..." I lost my train of thought as he pounded deep into me.

I couldn't hold in my moan that time as Jake ravaged me from behind, every thrust feeling deeper and more aggressive than the last.

My eyes closed as his grip on my waist intensified. He was pounding into me with no pity as his hands held me firmly in place.

"Hold on to the table, mein liebling."

I brought my hands to each side of the table, wrapping my fingers around the edges as he slammed into me even harder.

"Oh, Jake!"

"Do. Not. Come," he ordered.

How was that fair when I already felt so wet, his dick deliciously stretching me out, energy pulling in the bottom of my stomach?

"I can't... I can't hold it."

"You will only come when I tell you to come. Is that understood?"

He dived into me so hard I felt the table move under me.

"Y-yes."

"Good girl."

He grunted as his rhythm quickened. He was close; I could feel it.

"Please," I begged, feeling my release starting to invade my senses, I didn't know how many more seconds I could endure this sweet torture. "Jake, please let me come, let me come for you."

"Fuck!" He slid out of me with no warning.

I cried in protest, but he grabbed me, swirled me around, and repositioned me on the desk facing him.

He slid back inside me with a groan, as he held my hips and cupped my face. His fingers wrapped in my hair, bringing our foreheads together, our heavy breaths mixing as our chests rose and fell.

"You are mine, mein leibling, make sure you remember that," he grunted, slamming inside of me some more. "Now, come for me."

Eyes half closed, I exploded around him at his command as he buried himself uncontrollably inside of me, causing me to travel up though dark skies and shooting stars, only aware of the feeling of him all around me, engulfing me in overwhelming satiation and need at the same time.

CHAPTER 24

"Okay, since I'm done packing" I announced as we cuddled on my couch, with the fireplace on, "do we need to stop by your place?"

"No, I have everything I need there already."

We had decided to drive up to New Buffalo Wednesday evening after work, to avoid the Fourth of July traffic, but to also have the place to ourselves before the guests started showing up for dinner in the evening the next day. I had arranged for Keisha to come over and make sure Penny was taken care of while I was gone.

"How long have you had that vacation home for?" I asked as I ran my hand on his chest.

"Four years or so for the main one. I didn't buy the whole thing at once. I needed a place to escape the city, unwind a bit," he explained as he turned to face me, his right ankle up on top of his other knee.

"Your penthouse didn't quite cut it?" I teased, my eyebrows raised.

He laughed, a relaxed sound complimenting the smile that warmed my heart.

"You'll see. It's almost like being by the ocean there. You'll love it."

"Quite generous of you to invite my whole family," I added, as he proceeded to caress my thighs. "Although, not sure you anticipated... us, when you planned this trip."

"I didn't," he paused. "Does it make you uncomfortable?"

"Hm, I don't know, a little," I admitted, nervously running my fingers through my hair. "Who was invited?"

"Your parents, Carl, Jeremy and Linda, with their partners. George and Lisa. It was an open invitation to the board for whoever wanted to attend. It was meant to be a small, relaxing, bonding time."

"I see," I absently answered, lost in rushed thoughts of how awkward the vacation could get.

"Kyle was also invited," he paused. "Is that an issue?" he asked as he observed my slight frown.

"No, not at all," I clarified as I got closer to him. "I'm just not sure I want people all up in our business quite yet."

"I get it," he said, his hand automatically going around my waist, his gaze surveilling my face.

I let him pull me on top of him, feeling his hard cock pressed in between my thighs. I moaned. The man was insatiable.

"It will be quite difficult to be sneaking around for the next six days," he muttered in a deep voice as he kissed my neck. I felt my blood rush through my veins.

"Might be fun," I whispered as I moved against him.

"Fuck," he grunted, eyes half closed as he got even harder.

He grabbed my waist, pulling me closer. With trembling hands, I undid his pants, helping him pull them down, unable to wait another second to feel him. He aggressively removed my panties, then positioned himself and slid his dick in me.

I held a moan as I grinded on top of him. He let me take the reins, his lips parted, his breath shortened, his eyes burning as he watched me unravel with every thrust. I let my head fall back as he trapped my nipple between his lips. I lost all control, riding him faster and faster as his tongue circled my nipples, driving me mad.

"Yes, baby, use me." The primal deep sound he let out made me want to intensify my rhythm. Oh, and I did. He buried himself deeper and deeper, his words my undoing, until I lifted us both in exquisite release.

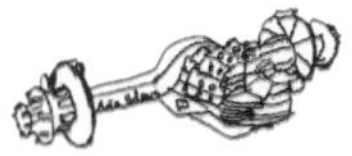

We got on the road to Michigan after sunset. Thankfully, the drive was only an hour and a half long as it was no longer raining. I kept my window down, enjoying the slightly chilly wind caressing my skin, and the smell of wet grass. I felt relaxed and comforted by all the green trees that came alive for spring, Jake's hand safely intertwined.

Driving to Michigan was so peaceful. The air was different here, cleaner somehow. Time slowed down, as compared to the busy Chicago city life I led.

I was having a hard time keeping my eyes off Jake, half expecting to wake up from a fantasy. I admired his strong jaw, traced by his light beard, his hair all shuffled by the wind. I bit my lip slightly, fantasizing sitting on top of him again, but in his car, riding him to infinity. It would have to wait.

He bent his head and glanced my way, almost as if he could read my thoughts, and I shyly smiled, too guilty to be able to pretend I wasn't having nasty thoughts.

The weather was now perfect, the earlier rain leaving space to a semi clouded yet suddenly sunny evening. It was great weather at 75 degrees.

We finally got to Jake's neighborhood. I was speechless at the size of the beach houses we drove by. I had been to New Buffalo before, as many of my father's coworkers had vacation homes here, but I hadn't visited any neighborhoods quite like this one. Jake finally turned right as a gate I hadn't noticed opened.

I couldn't believe my eyes. Most of the houses I had seen in New Buffalo were right off the street, but this one seemed to have what felt like a minute long drive before we stopped in front of a two-story mansion, heavily surrounded by trees. I was speechless.

"Here we are."

I turned toward Jake's amused face.

"*This* is what you call a vacation home!?" I spluttered.

"Well, it is." He smiled, quite aware that he had undersold it. "I never said it wasn't nice," he joked as we got out of the car.

"Nice is an understatement, Jake, big time."

He laughed.

"I do have a company rent it out when I'm not using it; it really just pays for itself with the rental income, and then some, when you consider that it can be rented all together or into two or three separate rentals with the coach houses."

"Oh good, I am judging you just a little less now," I teased.

This man continued to amaze me. He had to be one of the smartest men I knew—and continued to impress me with all his accomplishments—a major turn-on for me.

A man in his fifties, strong built, with kind eyes, opened the double oakwood doors and ran down the brick stairs to help us with our bags.

"Welcome home, sir. Good evening, miss."

"Good evening," I answered, still in disbelief at the size of this old English-style house, perfectly lit under the moonlight. I held in a gasp when I looked up, enamored by the stars.

"It's nice, isn't it?" Jake stood next to me, wrapping an arm around my waist. "You should go take a look at the stars from the deck. It's perfect." Jake grabbed my hand as we walked up the stairs. "Christoff, you can put those bags in the room next to mine, and you can put mine in my room."

"Got it." The man nodded.

Jake proceeded to giving me a tour of his two-story home with five bedrooms, six bathrooms, three living rooms, office, library, and game room, with a proper man cave, as he called it, despite the fact that it looked nothing like one.

Jake had bought the properties he called "coach houses" to his left and right for privacy, and for his guests when they visited, as if his place wasn't big enough. It was. He also explained that he owned some random farmland in the area as well.

I smiled, as we seemed to have the need to occupy space the same way. After all, I had bought the lot across from me to protect my view.

The last stop of the first floor was his office. It was simple, a desk with a few bookshelves behind it, with two other chairs and a sofa all facing bay windows looking over the lake. The color tone was somehow muted and warm at the same time.

I knew I would try to sneak in there and write a book from this amazing view later when I could have some alone time.

"What's the distribution of rooms for the next few days?" I inquired as we stopped by the thick caramel brown wooden desk.

"I figured I'd let the guests pick if they want to be in the main house or the coach houses," he calmly explained as he watched me park myself by the bay windows, staring at the dark sky and the stars I could never see in Chicago.

I sighed. Jake walked to me, turning me around a bit to face him.

"What's wrong?" he asked.

"Nothing really, but we probably want to think about this a bit?" I suggested.

"Okay. What do you have in mind?"

"Well, I think Carl, Jeremy, and Linda should probably go to the coach houses. Although, I wouldn't call them '*coach*' houses because they could literally fit a whole family in them."

"Fair." he grinned. "They each have three bedrooms and three bathrooms."

"Okay, so Carl and Jeremy and their wives can be in one, since they are great friends. Linda and her husband can be in the other. George and Lisa are buddies with Linda, so they can also stay there. So now it's my parents and, well, Kyle."

"Yes," he said patiently, as he tenderly moved my hair out of my face.

"I will take the room in the main house you told me about, which sounds like it's next to yours?"

"Yes, it is," he said holding a smirk, "and there is a private door in between them," he explained slowly, in that deep tone always filled with the unspoken words I always somehow understood.

"Ah, I see." I stared at the floor, suddenly feeling a little shy.

"There are two rooms on the other side of the hall. We could have your parents there. There are also beautiful rooms on the first floor, and one can go to Kyle since I can't un-invite him."

"Okay." I ignored the comment concerning Kyle even if I still shook my head a little. "And, um, with George and Lisa here, you don't think their wonderful daughter will show up?"

"She wasn't invited," he clarified as he gently lifted my chin to see my eyes. "And even if she came, it doesn't concern me, and it shouldn't concern you. Chloe, look at me, please."

I didn't want to let him see the sudden jealousy that was taking over my sanity like a virus. I generally considered those emotions beneath me, but then again, no one had made me feel like Jake had in a long time.

"I invited them because your dad asked me to. I am committed to us. If you want us to tell everyone, I am happy to do it. I would prefer it frankly."

I toyed with the idea for a second, but I wasn't ready.

"I know, but no, it's too soon for that. I just don't know that I will be able to stand still as she flirts with you," I admitted as I crossed my arms, distancing myself from him, but Jake wasn't having it.

"I won't let her bother you or make you uncomfortable, not again, I promise."

I was still feeling a bit defensive, ashamed of my emotions, conflicted between what I felt and what I wanted to feel. Jake had become this drug I needed at all costs in what I considered too short of a period. The fact that I wanted to disfigure my cousin just at the thought of her standing next to Jake scared and sickened me. I was putting myself in danger, at Jake's mercy.

The more I allowed myself to get attached him, the easier it would be for him to break me in a million pieces if he so chose, and I wasn't sure I could survive something like that again.

I didn't know if I could withstand a heartbreak from Jake. My walls were caving, my heart skipping beats at the sight of him, his smell intoxicating my senses, his eyes hypnotizing me. I was overwhelmed by him, day and night, it didn't matter if I was asleep or awake.

The reality of how much power he had over me was sinking in, as I stood in front of him, in his house, with seemingly nowhere to hide. I realized the problem wasn't really Lauren, it was me and how I felt.

I hugged Jake, both to hide my emotions and avoid his concerned gaze. He kissed my head, holding me close in his arms.

"Let's go on the deck," he said as he grabbed my hand and opened the sliding door.

We stepped out into the cool, dark night, on a big deck with a big U-shaped sofa and two eight-people dining tables. He led us to the sofa. We sat together, my head on his shoulders, as we both just reveled in the overwhelmingly beautiful sea of stars in silence.

Around 8 p.m., a young lady showed up and set dinner for us outside. I was starving and swallowed my steak and broccoli in record time, to Jake's amusement.

"What?" I said as he stared at me ripping the rest of the ribeye from the bone. "Not used to real women eating?" I teased, slightly offended.

"Not really," he admitted. "It's quite refreshing, and such an enjoyable sight." I blushed.

We both got distracted by my ringtone. We peeked at my phone on the table. It was Kyle. I didn't answer and focused back on my meal. He called again and then sent a text message. I could see Jake's jaw tighten at every beep of my phone.

"Someone desperately needs you, it seems," he remarked in an icy tone.

I wiped my lips with a wet napkin. Then I got up, violently grabbed my phone, and texted Kyle back. He was asking if we could drive to Jake's together. I simply explained I had other plans.

I turned to face Jake's cold stare. I went to him and sat on his lap, feeling the hard worked muscle under my thighs.

"You asked me to trust you, even if that... person was in your room and even if I saw her kiss you. I am asking you to do the same with me and Kyle. I think I've made my choice pretty clear."

Without warning, I kissed him. I felt him resisting me a bit, but I insisted until his arm wrapped around my waist, his other hand grabbing my face. He got us both up and sat me on the edge of the table.

I opened my legs so he could get closer. His lips soon got more demanding, his hand lifting my head so he could devour my neck. I moaned. He lowered my thin straps to get better access to my right shoulder.

I pushed him back a little, as I could hear the maid coming back for the plates while bringing him the port he had requested, and possibly with the chocolate fudge ice cream I was promised. He understood and took a step back, breathing heavily.

I jumped down from the table, quickly fixing myself, and headed to my seat as the maid made her entrance.

"Thank you, Lorna. This is Chloe. Chloe, Lorna."

"Nice to meet you, miss," said Lorna with a knowing curve on her lips. I could relate.

"Nice to meet you." I nodded.

Lorna was a short woman in her fifties, with gentle eyes and a smile as bright as the sun. I felt instantly comfortable with her.

Jake brought a deck of cards so we could play a few games. We shared my ice cream while he savored his port. Once we put the empty bottle of Rioja Jake had grabbed from the wine cellar in the trash, and after a couple rounds of poker, we proceeded to the bedrooms.

I was in awe, my room looking like it was taken straight from a place like Villa Igea, one of my favorite hotels in Palermo, Italy. This place took me back to when I blew through my Chase Sapphire points on a long weekend stay at that beautiful hotel with my friends. I smiled silently, admiring every detail of the furniture and the king-size bed.

Jake was standing in the doorway to his room, arms crossed, one foot resting on the door frame, looking at me caress and admire the woodwork.

"This is so enchanting, Jake; I feel like I left the U.S. and went to Europe."

"Thank you, that was the idea. Although, I can't take all the credit, as most of the furniture here came with the house; the owners didn't want to move their things, and they were moving back to Italy, so I guess they saw no need."

"I love this house! So much character mixed with simplicity, class, and luxury."

I swayed to him, my mind starting to let go of my concerns, feeling like we were no longer in America, and there was thus no danger to feeling as I did. This was just a moment in time, and I was going to be present damn it.

"Now, where are we sleeping?" I inquired, my face pointing toward the door to his room, a teasing quirk to my lips.

Jake bit his mouth a little and opened the door to let me in. His room was a more masculine version of mine. The ambience was similar and displayed the same exquisite furniture but had darker wood and less curvy furniture.

Jake lifted me off the ground suddenly, as I squealed then laughed. I stopped my chuckles when I noticed how intensely he was staring at me.

He turned to lay me down on the bed. I remained there, speechless, watching him undress, the moonlight from the bay windows making his muscles look dangerously traced and fit, arousing me further.

I admired the beauty of his body—strong, wide chest… his delicious abdominals that made my mouth water. Those arms that looked as if they could protect me from anything and everything.

Once he was naked and lying beside me, I expected him to proceed directly to ravaging my body. Instead, he gave me one simple command.

"Take your dress off," he ordered in a guttural sound that sent shivers of anticipation down my spine.

I had no choice. I got off the bed and undressed under his burning gaze and saw the admiration he had for my body. His stare lingered on my hips, my breasts, my ribcage.

After I finished peeling the last piece of clothing off, I returned to the bed and leaned back down slowly next to him, waiting for him.

He tenderly removed my hair from my face with his right hand. I was lost in the depths of his gaze, his eyes seeming more grey than blue in that moment. It seemed like he wanted to say something, frown lines appearing on his forehead. I started to grow concerned, as this romantic moment was starting to feel like something else.

"What's the matter?" I asked.

He tightened his jaw. My eyes widened, as I was starting to be very self-aware, and very vulnerable, laying down naked on his bed. His intense gaze alarmed me, reminding me of the skepticism and coldness from when I had met him again in my parent's home, or when he rejected me.

He sighed, his eyes softening. "I just don't think I'll be able to pretend there is nothing between us tomorrow."

Relieved, I chuckled, my hands drifting to his face, grabbing him and leading him closer to mine.

"We don't have to decide just yet," I whispered. "You have about twenty hours to convince me, though."

There was the full smile I desperately wanted to see again. I caressed his face, wanting to ease his worry. I was nervous about our relationship, but I also wanted it with all my heart.

Jake leaned down and kissed me, slowly calming me. I could feel him so hard for me. I was already wet. Frankly I had been since dinner.

He smoothly inserted his tongue between my lips, taking his time, arousing me with every sweet caress.

He trailed his fingers down my body, until he reached my center. He slid his middle finger in my pussy as he observed my every move.

"You are soaked, baby, all for me."

"Ugh, yes," I moaned, as he added a second finger, curving them to rub my g-spot. It felt so good.

I framed his face with my hands, trying to hold onto something as I enjoyed his fingers pounding into me, my eyes rolling to the back of my head.

"That's it, mein leibling."

I was already so, so close.

As if he knew I was about to come, he removed his fingers and got on top of me. He positioned himself and slowly slid his dick in me.

I was learning there was no better experience in the world than the fullness I felt when he filled me up, his weight on me. I loved the feeling of Jake doing something to me, taking what he needed from me. To see that usually stoic face wince as his eyes bore into mine was inebriating.

I didn't know what to do with myself, as this slow but deep rhythm was driving me even more mad than before. I desperately wanted more of him.

I dug my nails in his shoulders as I raised my hips to meet his. He groaned, feeding off my desperation for him.

His cadence intensified, his parted lips never more than less than an inch away from mine. He grabbed my face almost violently as we lost ourselves in each other.

He grunted again and came to a stop as his come shot into me. My orgasm quickly followed as I tightened my thighs around his waist further, never wanting to let go.

CHAPTER 25

THE SUNLIGHT AND THE sound of birds made it impossible for me to ignore that I had probably overslept. I rolled over, but Jake wasn't there. I turned back around to look for my phone, but it wasn't there either. I had probably left it in my room.

I took a second to once again admire the space around me; it was truly impeccable. I finally got out of bed when it was clear Jake wasn't coming back as I had hoped. I went straight to my room.

Someone had arranged my clothes for me. I opened one of the other two doors I hadn't explored to find a gorgeous bathroom with a jacuzzi. I opened the next door and found my empty luggage sitting in a perfectly full-sized walk-in closet lined with walnut wood.

Closing the door, I headed back toward the bed and noticed a piece of paper on the side table.

"*I suggest a bathing suit and proper beach attire for today.*
- Jake."

I smirked. Apparently, there was going to be some water activity in my day.

After taking a long shower, I found one of the two-piece suits I had packed. It was a white Italian set with black trim around the cups of the top. Sexy yet not too revealing. But then again, I had hopes that it wouldn't be on too long, because I wanted nothing more than for Jake to remove it and ravish me.

I added my portable charger, phone, sunscreen, sunglasses, white jumper, and flats to my bag, then went to search for Jake.

The house was even more beautiful than during the night, with a burst of light coming from the many windows and French doors that rendered the place classy and romantic. I was in awe.

"Hello, miss!" squeaked Lorna, quite excited to see me.

"Good morning, Lorna." I smiled, her good attitude contagious.

"I took the liberty of arranging your clothes for you. I hope that's okay?"

"Yes, of course, thank you." I was afraid I was being judged for not sleeping in my assigned bedroom, but it didn't seem like it. The woman looked genuinely happy to see me.

"I would offer you breakfast, but I was instructed not to," she added with a smile. "As Mr. Cunningham has other plans. You will love it!"

"Thanks," I said, getting contaminated by her jovial attitude.

She led me to the back of the house and swirled left once we reached the kitchen. She guided me through the patio and to the left of the property. We strolled on the shore.

It was so beautiful, I stopped a moment to admire the perfectly beige fluffy sand, with Lake Michigan waves gently coming and going. It looked just like the ocean, but I could see a bit of Chicago as there were barely any clouds.

"Beautiful!"

"Right? It's the most perfect day!" We stopped at a dock that had a large yacht anchored at the end.

There he was, wearing beige kakis and a blue shirt, hair flowing, with his Ray Bans on, sporting that light rugged stubble I had grown so fond of. He landed me his hand as I stepped on the deck and got to the boat, him giving me a boost as I struggled to find some balance.

"There you go," he said when I made it on board.

"Wow," I exclaimed as I looked around the yacht. "Of course you have a yacht. I should have known."

"Are you judging your captain?" he teased.

"I wouldn't dare," I retorted as he pulled me closer for a kiss. "You left early," I slightly complained.

"You looked so peaceful; I didn't want to wake you. More importantly, I wanted to surprise you."

He took me by the hand and led me to the second floor of the yacht, where a living room and table with two seats were waiting for us. We were next to the captain station. My mouth fell open when I saw him proceed to the open cabin and get the boat moving.

He stood there silently as I sat down, unable to take my eyes off his biceps contracting with every move. Yes, I was getting aroused.

A second man joined him in the galley. When we reached calmer and deeper waters, Jake left his second mate in charge, pulled back the sails, and lowered the anchor.

Jake then joined me at the table, uncovered the meals, and sat next to me. "Bon appetit," he said. "Lorna insisted on feeding us a proper breakfast."

Jake was acting as if him piloting one of the most luxurious three-story yachts I had ever been on was just ordinary course. But it was definitely not ordinary for me.

Jake was one of those men who didn't do flashy anything. He dressed well, he smelled divine, he wore a beautiful watch. He was clearly very well off, but he didn't flaunt it. He just enjoyed what made him happy, and I loved that about him.

"Jake! This boat is amazing! It's a work of art! You certainly downplayed this trip!"

"I didn't mean to," he said honestly. "I just couldn't resist taking you out here and having you all to myself before everyone else gets here."

My heart warmed up at the idea that Jake just wanted to share his wonderful life and priceless experiences with me.

"Thank you," I said softly.

I attacked the fruit plate and eggs in front of me as I gazed at the beautiful skies, the blue water of Lake Michigan scintillating under the shining sun, and enjoyed the wind on my skin, as we were blessed with a proper warm summer day.

The mate took care of cleaning up the table when we were done. Jake then dismissed him, and he headed to the third floor. Jake took me for a tour of the downstairs. It was impressive how spacious it was, with two bedrooms, two bathrooms, a living room, and another kitchen. I had never seen anything quite like it.

"How often do you get to enjoy this?" I asked.

"Not nearly enough," he confessed. "But I generally come here a few times a year and sometimes I spend a whole month here, so I get more use of this place than most people in our corporate jobs generally allow themselves to."

"I need to save more and buy myself one of those. I think something about a third of this size would be just fine for me," I joked. "But I think I'll start with the vacation home first, of course. I love my house, it's a dream, but there is nothing like being next to water."

He handed me a mimosa. I realized that I was cornered by the kitchen island right behind me, as he placed himself in front of me.

"Jake..." I tried to sound stern but failed miserably. "We are not alone."

He took a few sips of his drink, his eyes burning a hole through me. I also savored my drink, enjoying the bubbles in my throat, feeling myself getting more aroused without him even touching me.

Anticipation rose within me as I felt his leg graze mine. I opened my legs wider, inviting him in as I set my glass down next to me. He did the same and lifted me onto the countertop. I moaned, grabbing his face as he almost violently pressed his lips to mine. He quickly removed my bikini bottom.

I started unbuttoning his pants, but he held my hands.

"Not yet, mein liebling, I want to taste you. I want your thighs around my face. I want to feel you come while I eat that sweet little cunt of yours."

The greed in his gaze, those sharp turquoise green eyes looking at me as if he was about to consume me, made my body shake in eagerness. I was already wet by the time he got down on his knees and pulled me closer to the edge of the island.

I couldn't take my eyes off him. The idea that this force of a man was at my mercy was exhilarating. He parted my folds with his index fingers and took a good look at me. I could feel the heat rise up in my cheeks, suddenly feeling a little self-conscious. Thankfully, I was bare down there.

"I'm obsessed with your pussy, baby. So fucking soft, so ready for me." I moaned at his words. Jake talking dirty was my favorite thing in the whole world.

He licked my clit, slowly at first, with the tip of his tongue, his eyes observing me.

"Hm," he growled. I moaned, resisting the urge to bend my head backwards. No, I wanted to see him as he savored me. He licked again, this time circling me with the tip of his tongue.

My eyes rolled back as I fought to keep moaning to a minimum. I didn't know how much more of this torture I could endure.

"Please, Jake," I begged.

I felt the vibration on his laugh between my legs. He ran his tongue bottom to top, bringing my wetness all the way up to my clit, as he proceeded to alternate between licking and sucking.

I grabbed his hair between my fingers as he moved me deeper into his mouth. How did he know exactly how to suck me like this?! He soon became hungrier, his hands traveling under my butt and lifting me off the table so I could be closer to him.

He was relentless and so in sync with my body. He could read every move, every jerky movement, intensifying his licks and twirls as my body started to shake.

"Oh God, oh God, Jake. Jake, I'm coming!"

I let out a high-pitched scream as I trembled uncontrollably in his hands, his tongue continuing to make the current run through my body, explosions coursing through me like a sock of electricity. It was the most intense feeling I had ever felt.

I leaned back completely on the countertop, unable to sustain my own weight. Between dazed eyes, I saw him get up, a smirk of satisfaction on his face. I smiled back at him, feeling myself very slowly drift back down to earth.

I watched him unbutton his pants, the flex of his forearm awakening a new thirst in me. My orgasm wouldn't be complete until he came.

I lifted myself back up, and opened my legs wide, ready for him. He penetrated me, hot and thick, making me gasp. He let out a sigh of relief. I hurried my fingers in his hair as he throbbed inside me, his desire for me coming out of every pore of his body.

"You feel so good, baby," he grunted as he thrusted his dick deeper inside me. "I could spend all fucking day inside you, fucking you over and over again."

Desire pooled around my clit again, every strategic thrust of his also rubbing me there. He pulled me up, so I straddled him. I gripped his ass with my nails, wanting him as deep as possible. His thrusts intensified, a frown on his face.

"Look at me when you come," he ordered. "I want to see what I do to you."

I lifted half open eyes, meeting his burning gaze, recognizing my own loss of control in his eyes.

"Fuck!" he uttered.

I felt him shudder inside of me, as my own orgasm made me grab on to him, my entire body tensing around his, my pussy pulsing around his dick, Jake never letting go of me.

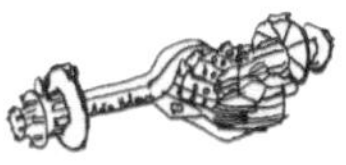

We rested on the long couch in the front of the boat, enjoying the great view of the houses on the lake.

"Why a sailing yacht? I love it, but I didn't even know it was a thing."

"I enjoy the process" he explained as he poured us more mimosas. "But if in a bind, it still has a full-blown motor."

"I love it, as I find sails quite romantic. My ex took me on an actual sailboat on a date and..." I stopped myself, realizing I was bringing up an ex.

I had sworn to never recall any of the good times I had had with Danny, but in some ways, being there, moving on, gave me a peaceful feeling. I had no ill thoughts left against Danny.

"What happened?" encouraged Jake, my silence indicative.

"Sorry."

"Don't apologize."

"Ugh. Well, I told you about the guy I dated in law school before, Danny. He was probably the first guy I was really... into, so to speak. Someone I saw a future with. Long story short, he um, broke my heart, cheated, etc. What really hurt, though, is that he eventually admitted I wasn't wife material. In his eyes, anyways."

"Because?" asked Jake, raising a brow.

"I was overqualified for the position."

"That's ridiculous," he scoffed.

"I'm not joking," I explained at Jake's confused look. "The whole alpha thing, that was the point. He didn't like that I was going to have a career. He didn't like that I was also going to be a lawyer," I sighed.

Saying it out loud now that I didn't love him anymore almost seemed comical every time I did.

"He told me he wanted a woman with less options, so he could dictate their life better, as the bread winner." I exploded in laughter.

Jake didn't say much, he just looked at me. I stopped laughing.

"What a fucking idiot. I'm sorry that happened to you, Chloe."

"It's fine. Well, it's fine now. Really."

"Some men are cowards. Some men can't handle a woman with a career."

"I know. The weirdest part is, he claimed that he didn't want kids, just like me, so it never really made sense, you know. It's not like the conversation came up as part of what we would do if we had a child. He literally had an issue with the fact that I would have a career, equal to his.

"He even mentioned that someone would need to stay at home, would need to be flexible, and that wasn't going to be him. And I never got it since neither of us wanted children."

"It's likely because he had an inferiority complex. It had nothing to do with you. Well, it did, you were just too good for him." Jake leaned in my direction. "It's funny," he added in a deeper tone, removing some unruly curls from my face. "Everything you are, your wit, your independence, your ambition, your temper, your sense of humor, your intelligence, the way you spark when you get what you want..." he grunted, "I wouldn't have it any other way."

I swallowed hard, leaning in his direction.

"Including the no children thing?" I whispered.

"Including the no children thing," he repeated, somehow making it sound sexy as he grabbed my face. "I've never wanted one," he admitted.

I didn't know why, but relief susurrated through me. I was happy to hear that me not wanting kids wouldn't be a dealbreaker for him. I was realizing how much more I wanted from Jake.

He paused, lips almost touching mine. I gasped in anticipation, lost in the depth of his ocean-blue gaze looking down into my eyes, a hint of a frown on his face.

With his face so close to mine under the sun, I could see the slight lines making that beautiful skin look strong, stable, and eternal. It was sweet, sweet torture, I didn't know what I wanted more, the moment to freeze forever, or his lips ravaging mine.

"I think you were made for me, Chloe."

My breathing was accelerating. With a serious look on his face, Jake kissed me, deeply, slowly, intensely.

I wrapped my hands around his neck, bringing us both back down on the long cushions.

We spent a lovely day on the boat, as we laid back in the outdoor lounge area still, enjoying the view. I just realized a few more boats were around us, all keeping a very good distance, offering each boat much appreciated privacy.

We had napped, eaten a little more, and I had pretended to have learned a lot more than I did about sailing, as this god in swimwear decided to teach me.

His muscles contracting under his suntanned skin distracted me and irritated my senses. Jake walked over to me and lifted me for a kiss as I laughed.

"I don't think you'll be in a position to sail us back to shore," he teased as he kissed my neck.

I set my hands around his neck, unable to stop my laughter, feeling caught in his devious looks.

"No, captain, I'll have to put myself in your capable hands once again."

I kissed him fully, honestly, letting my desire take control. I was starting to trust a man again, with my heart. And it felt amazing.

He gently stopped me, as it was getting quite late, and he needed to help his mate get the sails up to take us back to shore.

It was 5 p.m. by the time we got to his house, only an hour and a half before guests were set to arrive, so I rushed to my room to get ready.

I showered and straightened my hair. I chose a blood orange knee-length cocktail dress, flattering my curves. Then I slid on my beige Louboutins and headed to Jake's office, where we had decided to meet. The plan was that we would admit to driving together, as my car was of course nowhere to be seen. The story we had invented was that we got to his place just a couple hours before the first guest.

I was floating in the air, replaying our outing in my head repeatedly. He liked me just as I was. My career, my success, was a turn-on for him. This adonis, this man I couldn't be around for more than a few minutes without wanting to be in his arms, was apparently turned on by all of what I was.

I knew some men had to be like this, but I had lost hope. I had closed out my heart, refusing to put myself at a man's mercy ever again. It would seem I had found someone who respected and admired who I was, while I could feel the same towards him.

Danny had confused me quite a lot, and for a long time. I was having a hard time letting go of my reservations, my fears, my reticence to ever let myself be vulnerable again, but Jake knew how to peel my layers away one by one. He made me feel wanted, he made me feel safe. And I was starting to no longer want to run away. Maybe Jake was made for me too.

But I had to try to behave for the next few days; it was my idea to keep whatever we were a secret, but I was quietly exploding with joy, excited at the prospect of letting go, and I wasn't sure I could contain it.

I opened the door to Jake's office and immediately regretted not knocking as I now had three pairs of eyes on me. Jake was sitting in his office living room with George and Lisa.

George was wearing a light gray suit with one of his famous 'summer" purple shirts that I hated so much. His wife, thankfully, for however displeasing the woman was, had opted for a long grey jumper that I couldn't help but admire. My cousin most certainly got her style from her mother.

"Apologies for barging in like this." I stepped in, shutting the door behind me. "I didn't realize the rest of the crew had already arrived."

I tried to hide my surprise as I hugged my uncle and accepted the cold shoulder Lisa had given me.

"George and Lisa just arrived," explained Jake as he stood up, a glass of scotch in his right hand, his left hand in the pocket of his gray suit.

He was wearing a white shirt, un-buttoned on top, and no tie. He portrayed that smirk I did my best to ignore, as I would be unable to remain as casual as I was trying to feel if I looked at him for long.

"Anything to drink?" he offered as I sat down across from him.

"A glass of red would be great." I dared to look up.

He was intensely staring at me, with that sizzling smile that made me want those skilled fingers between my thighs. My lips pursed, as I was unable to resist him. How did I think I'd be able to hide how he made me feel again?

He went to the back of the room to pour me a glass as I admired the view.

"So, you guys drove together?" inquired Lisa, giving me one of those obnoxious looks she had when she thought she was the smartest person in the room. She wasn't.

An illusion her daughter had also inherited from her.

"We did," I answered, crossing my legs, resting my right arm on the chair, holding Lisa's clearly accusatory gaze. This was going to be fun.

"Wish I had known; we could have carpooled!"

"Maybe next time," I added with my best stoic face. "Thank you," I said when Jake handed me a glass of the Rioja we had enjoyed the night before, his fingers caressing mine in the process, making my blood rush.

I blushed, the wine reminding me of the rest of the night. He went back to his seat, still observing me.

Jake focused on his phone for a few seconds. Mine vibrated shortly thereafter.

> Ready to come clean, mein liebling?

> Should we tell them how my face was buried in your pussy just a few hours ago? How you screamed my name?

I choked on my wine.

"Everything okay?" asked Jake with the most innocent concern on his face.

He was taunting me, daring me, and I knew it, ravaging me from a distance. I felt like a puppet, and he was deliciously pulling my strings, but I had to be strong. It was too soon.

"I'm fine," I answered between coughs.

Lisa seemed flustered. I was, after all, a threat to her daughter's relationship with Jake. She made that very clear. Jake was enjoying my visible annoyance as my aunt continued to ask me questions about what we did for the two hours I had supposedly spent alone with Jake.

I was the one who asked for more time before telling anyone. He was now amused as he could likely tell how tempted I was to march to him and kiss him to shut my aunt up once and for all.

CHAPTER 26

EVENTUALLY, THE REST OF the guests, including my parents, arrived and were guided to the main living room. We joined them there.

Jake has insisted that I stand by his side, and we received invitees under Lisa's disapproving scowl.

My mother was dressed in a gorgeous yellow cocktail dress, and my father was in a light green pastel suit that complimented her dress perfectly. I hugged them, happy to have a reprieve from the Lisa inquisition.

Now that every guest had made it, it was a full house. Save Kyle, who had not arrived yet.

Jake had left the room a minute to go see how the patio dinner setup was going.

I was hiding by the entrance of the living room, tempted to disappear in the kitchen under the guise of helping, when I felt a hand around my waist. I panicked a little bit and turned around, but thankfully it was Kyle.

"Kyle!"

"Hello, beautiful" he said as he hugged me and kissed my cheeks. He pulled me in close. A bit too close for my comfort.

Just as I was about to ask him to release me, Jake's deep voice resounded behind me, startling me. I turned around to see he had returned to the room. Thank goodness.

"Kyle, welcome."

Kyle reluctantly let go of me to shake Jake's hand, as I took a step back to extricate myself from his other arm.

"Thank you for having me, man. This place is gorgeous," complimented Kyle.

"Make yourself at home," added Jake as he positioned himself right next to me, his hand placed possessively on the small of my back.

Shit.

Kyle gave us both a weird look, his eyes bouncing back and forth between us. I played innocent and had to resist the urge to hold my breath. Kyle reluctantly walked to the bar, unable to say anything to Jake.

I looked up to Jake, but he was avoiding my gaze. His jaw clenched, and then he simply walked away.

I wanted to reach out and grab his hand, but didn't know what to say. How could I make him see that there was no competition here? Kyle was simply my friend. Sometimes a bit too handsy of a friend, but I had no feelings for him anymore.

I sighed and joined the group again.

Dinner was finally served on the patio. Both tables had been put together, and a gorgeous hand-sewed nap covered them. My father sat on Jake's right; my mother next to him.

And as soon as Jake sat, Lisa scurried over to claim her seat to his left. George was next to her. I avoided that side of the table and chose to sit at the opposing end, where I stared directly at Jake. I wanted him to look at me, to see me and understand that I wanted no one else but him.

He was still avoiding me, being his charming self to my family. I closed my fists, trying to calm down. I knew he wanted to lay claim to me, and as flattering as that was, I still had my reservations about making this an actual official relationship.

Kyle sat to my right, with Carl and his wife to my left. I found myself obliged to carry the conversation at my end of the table, but we soon fell into a comfortable chatter, so I took the moment to sit back and enjoy it all.

Some couldn't help themselves and chose to engage in business talk, at the expense of the spouses who had to once again hear their partners talk all about work. Who was I to judge them, though? I loved my job just as much as they did.

I found myself discussing future plans and noticed that Jake seemed a bit more relaxed as the evening went on.

At one point the topic of doing business with Copolliard came up, and Jake had to disclose that he thought they were a bad match. I appreciated it greatly because I know he did it for me.

Once we had finished dinner, we were told to enjoy the patio area. The smell of the water on the lake brought about a calmness, and we all seemed to just want to soak it in.

Fireworks began, and the crowd gathered to watch them. I took advantage of the fact that Jake had been left alone. I approached but took a minute to really look at him—he had a glass of port in hand and stared up at the moon—gosh, he was so handsome.

I stopped next to him, my arm grazing his, my hand next to his on the wooden rail.

"I will tell him about us tomorrow," I finally got the courage to say.

"I am not asking you to do anything you don't want to do, Chloe, but if he puts his hand on you one more time, I will break it," he warned as he turned his head sideways to face me.

I swallowed hard. I always felt like Jake had a force not to be reckoned with right under the surface, a dangerous power which now was focused on wanting to take title to me. And I reveled in the feeling.

"He needs to know," I insisted as I timidly put my hand on his.

I saw him look behind me to see if anyone was watching us. I no longer cared, as the idea of him thinking even for a second that I might want to be with Kyle was unacceptable.

"He needs to move on. I just want to tell my parents first. And I also need to be able to kiss you whenever I feel like it."

He looked behind me again and then leaned down and stole a kiss. I wanted more, but I wanted to talk to my father first, but I frankly didn't expect any pushback, even if technically I was now dating my father's friend, quite the opposite.

"I can talk to him, if you prefer," he offered.

"No, let me go first. I am sure he will then talk to you."

He sweetly removed my flowing hair from my face. That simple gesture filled me with warmth, making my knees weak and my heart rate accelerate. I could no longer deny my feelings as fireworks lit up the skies. I just stared at him, horrified.

"Everything okay?" he asked as he held me, concerned as my face likely looked like I was about to pass out.

"I'm fine," I answered quickly, shivering. "Just a bit chilly."

He immediately removed his jacket and covered me with it.

I didn't want to but felt instantly warm when I smelled his scent around me. I peeked at him again. I was undeniably falling for him. Could I possibly be in love with Jake already? The thought paralyzed me for a bit.

All I wanted to do was run away as fast as humanly possible.

But I feared it was already too late.

As the night festivities came to an end, guests started to proceed to their temporary abode within the hour, guided but the regular staff of three Jake always had in the house. I walked my parents to their room.

"You seem to know where everything is here already," observed my mother in a low voice as she held my arm up the stairs.

I smirked, unable to resist her. My mother and her instincts were something for scientists to study closely. She somehow knew that something was going on between Jake and I, and I never said a word. That was a superpower.

"I don't think anything would make your dad happier than you and Jake together," she whispered as my dad was joining us by the room.

"I'll tell him tomorrow," I admitted, my cheeks turning pink.

My mom held me in her arms under the curious gaze of my father. I could no longer hold back what I felt, and being able to tell my mother made it all feel even better.

I stayed with my parents a little bit and eventually headed to my room. I wanted desperately to open the door to Jake's room, but I held back.

I was terrified that I would utter those words, those words I had said before but never really meant, and hadn't gotten to the one time I would have meant them, if he looked at me for more than one second. I let go of the doorknob.

Perhaps it was better if I slept alone tonight. I changed into one of my linen white sleeping gowns, as the evening was a bit warmer than usual. I opened the French doors to a lovely balcony, wanting the night air to lull me to sleep. I just stood there leaning on the balustrade, admiring the moon and the stars on this warm summer night.

I closed my eyes when I heard the door to my left open and close. I could already smell him, and my blood quickened as I heard him slowly walk towards me.

He slid his hand around my waist and turned me to face him in one swoop. My resolve vanished as his lips went straight for the vein in my neck, making my blood quicken.

He detached my gown from behind my neck and let it fall to the ground, leaving me naked, outside in the middle of the night. I felt the light wind harden my nipples. He lifted me in his arms and carried me to the bed where he made passionate love to me.

There was no going back. I was undeniably, inevitably falling in love with Jake Cunningham.

CHAPTER 27

JAKE AGAIN WASN'T IN my bed when I flipped to his side early in the morning. I tried not to take that personally as I knew he had guests to attend to.

Instead, I strolled out to the balcony, instantly smelling the aroma of the Lavazza Keurig coffee I was preparing. I grabbed the warm mug and sat in the coziest chair out there. The grass was a tad wet, and I could see some droplets shining under the bright sun. Not a cloud in sight again.

Closing my eyes, I enjoyed the light breeze and hearing nature come alive. Summer was so short in the Midwest; it gave one a lot more appreciation from crisp, sunny days like these.

I allowed myself to fantasize about Jake and I coming here to be alone next time. I would love to swim with him at night in that pool I could see from my room. I could only imagine what we would do, how he would grab me, kiss me, drive me...

I interrupted my reverie, aware that it was too early in the day to be so aroused.

Before too long, I was quite impatient to see him, to tell my father about us, to stop hiding, so I decided it was time to leave the confines of my room and face reality. My doubts hadn't gone away completely, but I had called my friends early that morning, and they had convinced me to fully take a leap of faith.

The truth was I wanted Jake more than any other man I had ever dated, body and soul, for me and me only. There was no going back from how I felt. And I was starting to accept that, even enjoyed it.

To start my day right, I knew a workout needed to happen. I opened my Peloton app for forty minutes, then proceeded to take a quick, steamy shower and re-straighten my hair.

I decided on a simple detailed knee-high white dress with thin shoulder straps. It was flattering without showing too much. I added my opal earrings as they went perfectly with the necklace Jake had gifted me. Looking into the mirror, I couldn't help but smile; the necklace I was wearing was a reminder that everything was going to work out.

I had a man who not only supported me but wanted to be with me, for exactly who I was. I'd found someone I wanted to try a real serious relationship with. And while part of me was still a little apprehensive, I was ready to take the risk.

I waltzed straight to Jake's smaller windowless library office, where we had agreed to meet. That was where he kept his collection of rare books he had explained, and he wanted to show some of his most prized possessions to me.

"It's open," I heard after I knocked.

I pushed the door and walked straight to the man who was standing by the desk. I put my arms around his neck, letting some of my weight lean on him and kissed him.

"Good morning, baby," I whispered.

Jake grabbed both my arms and removed them from around his neck, brusquely backing away.

Confused, I took a step back.

"What's wrong?" I asked, feeling my skin crawl as I searched his cold eyes, his frown, and the disgust I saw in his flared nostrils and the twitch of his lips.

"Did I do something wrong?" He didn't answer. "What's wrong, Jake?"

He lifted his head, looking at me as if I was beneath him. As I was about to get closer to him, I heard the door behind me open. I pivoted swiftly, only to see Lauren breezed in wearing a skin-tight bright pink short dress, sending a chill down my spine.

Lauren headed straight past me, as if I was invisible. I took a few steps back as my cousin almost bumped into me in her haste to get to Jake. She wrapped her arms around his neck and kissed him. Jake just stood there, kissing her back.

"Good morning, sweety," she said. "I've been looking for you all around!"

"Well, you found me now," he added, a half-smile on his face.

I held on to the chair on my left for support, my mind unable to register what was going on fast enough.

"Hello, cuz!" screamed Lauren as she quickly pivoted in her high heels and hugged me. I wanted to peel my skin off. Better yet, hers. "So good to spend a few days together!" added Lauren. "It's been way too long!"

"It has," I uttered, searching Jake's cold, hard face for answers, but he was ignoring me.

"Lauren," he called as she turned back to him, "do you mind leaving us alone for a bit? Chloe and I have a few work issues to finish discussing."

It didn't quite sound like a question.

"Ugh, fine," she answered, her arms around his neck again. "But don't take too long! I got new bikinis I'd love for you to see on me by the pool." She kissed him again, running her bright red nails down his shirt.

Tears filled my eyes. I couldn't believe that was happening.

"See you around, cuzo!" she bellowed in my direction, a look of sheer satisfaction in her eyes as she left the room and closed the door behind her.

I twisted towards Jake, who was leaning back on his desk, both hands in his pockets. A frown was plastered on his forehead. I couldn't believe my eyes; my body felt suddenly very frail and cold, my breathing uneven, nerves stabbing the back of my neck and shoulder.

Something felt different. Jake wasn't explaining himself or trying to convince me that nothing happened this time. He was standing there, arrogant, cold eyes staring at me sternly, his lips twitching with what I could only still describe as disdain.

"What is this, some kind of a fucking joke?"

"Not quite." He slowly proceeded to put the folder he had next to his hands in one of his desk drawers, locking it and putting the keys in his pocket. "What do you want?" he asked.

I felt like I was in an alternate universe, tempted to run out and open the door again to see if she would still be in the same situation.

"What do you mean what do I want? What... what is going on, Jake!?"

"Nothing is going on, Chloe. Simply, you were right. You and I, it was a stupid mistake," he explained as he shoved his hands back his pockets, the thick desk in between us looking like it was getting larger by the second.

"A mistake? A mistake that you did three times last night and this fucking morning?" I exclaimed.

My voice and body were shaking.

"What, now she shows up and your true fucking nature comes out?"

I found the courage to walk all the way to him.

"Answer me!" I screamed as I took a few steps more, stopping right under his nose. "Explain it to me!" I almost begged, my voice breaking.

His jaw clenched as two ice cold, dark eyes stared at me, seemingly unfazed by my distress.

"I simply changed my mind, Chloe. Lauren is what I need, what I want."

"Really? Since when? Because you told me she meant nothing to you, you told me I was—"

"I know what I said," he interrupted abruptly, "but I was wrong. So fucking wrong. I am sorry if I hurt you, but come on, it's barely been a week between us; it couldn't have meant too much, could it?"

He almost seemed aggressive, his patience thinning.

I gawked at him in disbelief, seeing the cold, calculated asshole he used to be, his previous warmth absent. All that was left was a wall, and a cold, distant man who as it seemed never cared about me.

A tear finally rolled down my face. Embarrassed, I took a few steps back, looking at the ground, hoping it would open from under me and get me out of this nightmare.

"Well, if Lauren is the kind of woman you want standing next to you, building a life with you, you and I would have never worked," I said, finding strength in my pain. "I am no one's accessory, nor do I need one. So, it's good we stopped it on time," I lied, a defiant look in my eyes.

"I'm glad you agree," he retorted as he slowly took a few steps in my direction.

I immediately stepped backwards as I aggressively wiped the tear that had escaped.

I had so many questions, so much I wanted to understand, but my pride wouldn't let me crumble.

"You are, unsurprisingly the same type of trash as my ex." He flinched, but he stayed silent. "Is she staying here?"

"She is." Of course.

"Great," I concluded in defeat. "Well, I'll see you at lunch."

I didn't wait for answer and, resisting the urge to run, I magically made it through the door without falling apart.

When I was out of the room, I rested my back against the door for a moment, attempting to catch my breath and hold back the tears that were threatening to erupt.

Scanning around anxiously, I saw that the hall was clear, so I quickly made my way to my room and locked both doors.

Behind the safety of those walls, I broke down and fell to the ground, my body shuddering with every tear. I covered my face with my hands to try to muffle the sound, unable to control myself, the pit in my stomach growing at an alarming rate.

I didn't understand what had just happened. What was going on? What was Jake doing? What had he done to me?

Nothing made sense; this wasn't the man I had gone to bed with just the night before. This was the man I hated and feared a few months ago, but worse, because now he had my heart and had stepped on it with no pity. He looked at me like I was shit under his fucking shoes. After making love to me all night.

What had changed? Was something different? Or was he messing with me this whole time? No, someone couldn't just fake all that, could they? Yes, they could, I reminded myself.

People lie and some are just quite good at it.

It seemed like Jake fit right in with those who lied and had trampled all over me for the thrill of the chase. At the end, he was back with the person he truly wanted.

Lauren, of all people. I closed my fists in anger and called to God for help. I thought Jake liked me because we were so alike, but instead, he preferred her.

Why waste my time then? Why break my barriers? Why not stop it after we had slept together in California? Why convince me to be official only to leave me behind like a used towel? Nothing made sense, but the pain in my heart was the only thing I knew to be real. And it was agony.

CHAPTER 28

AFTER AN HOUR OR SO, I had composed myself a bit. I was trying to focus on how to hide the pain that inundated me. I knew though that I wasn't ready for confrontation. I texted my mother to explain that I didn't feel well and that I would skip the lunch by the pool. I would try to join for dinner I lied.

Someone knocked on my door. I wiped my puffy tired eyes immediately, got up from the bed where I had taken refuge and went to the door.

"Who is it?" I rasped behind the door.

"It's Lorna, bringing you your lunch? Your mom said you weren't feeling well."

"Oh, thank you, Lorna, but I am good. I am not hungry."

"Are you sure? I brought you some soup and crackers to calm your upset stomach."

"I'm good, Lorna, thank you. I will let you know if I need anything."

"Okay, miss, you can dial the number next to the phone for the kitchen if you need anything."

"Thank you, Lorna," I said, attempting to control my now quivering voice.

I shuffled to the bay windows. I caught a good amount of noise now that they were open. I peeked a bit, as I knew everyone would be sitting on the pool patio eating.

And there they were, all happy and chatty. Lauren was sitting right next to Jake, touching him every second she could. Her parents were also there, with Lisa probably reveling in her daughter's victory. My mother on the other end seemed angry.

My heart sank because I knew she was as confused as I was, and I would have a lot to explain to her even though I didn't have any answers of my own.

I held my breath as I saw Jake glance up in my direction, as if he could see me.

Fuck him.

I took a few steps back and closed both the bay windows and the blinds. I didn't need the light anyways. I went back to the bed, covering myself with the thick comforter, closing my eyes to try and sleep the pain away.

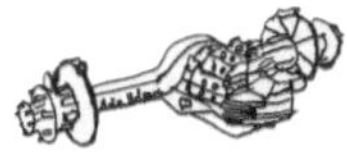

It was early evening when I finally got out of bed. There had been a few knocks on the door—which I didn't answer—and sporadic calls and text messages—that I ignored, but everyone seemed to be off in their own little worlds, so I had time to get myself together as best as I could.

I feared I could no longer hide in my bedroom as my father was threatening to make Jake open my door if I kept ignoring them.

My mother had texted me to ask what had happened with Jake. I answered that it was over, and I wasn't ready to discuss it. My mother respected my silence and promised to try to keep my dad off my back.

I proceeded to the bathroom, where I observed my puffy eyes, my red cheeks, and my chapped lips. Great. I looked as bad as I felt.

Letting my anger control my pain, I was resolved to make it to dinner and then simply call a taxi or private service car if I could leave this place and never look back. But I was going to leave with a bang.

I removed the necklace he had given me and set it on the marble countertop. I would just leave it here in his house where it belonged, not around my neck.

I shaved and exfoliated. I rubbed on my luscious Coco Mademoiselle body cream and sprayed the perfume. I added some curls and dimension to my hair as I parted it to the right side of my face. I took my time with my makeup, lining my straight nose and jaw to perfection. I chose my most audacious dress—a sleeveless black cocktail dress with a sweetheart neckline. It was both classic and sensual, the tight fit hugging my curves.

The square back was quite low, revealing my golden skin tone and shaping my buttocks to perfection. The dress finished with a side slit that showcased my fit legs. I paired it with my So Me Spike Red Sole Sandals and a small black Yves Saint Laurent clutch.

Satisfied, I took a deep breath and proceeded to the formal dining room.

All the guests were standing in the back of the room, enjoying their drinks, the chatter loud enough to be heard in the hallway. I hesitated, feeling my hand lightly shake. I jumped when I felt fingers on my naked back.

"Stunning," whispered Kyle.

"Thank you," I said.

I accepted the arm he was offering me, thankful for the support he didn't know I needed, and we walked in the room together. I ignored all the eyes turned in my direction, afraid that if I saw Jake's I would lose my balance.

I instead focused on Kyle's flirts, smiling as well as I could. Kyle had opted for a light brown suit that fit him well, his hair pulled back. He took us to the bar, where we stopped to chat with Linda and her husband. I ignored the burn I felt when Jake came into view.

Drinks in hand, Kyle and I joined my parents, who were unfortunately standing with Jake and Lauren. I held on to Kyle for dear life. For all intents and purposes, tonight, he was mine. Tomorrow, I would have to apologize and remind him that no matter what happened, we were never getting back together. The feelings just weren't there anymore.

But tonight, I was letting my inhibitions fly because my enemy was now the man standing across from me with the intense blue eyes boring straight into Kyle. I was going to use Kyle just as he used me.

Just as Jake used me. Turns out they were one in the same, the difference is that the latter instance was slowly destroying my soul. But neither would know that. I was in control now.

We engaged in casual conversion as Linda joined us. My mother observed me with a preoccupied look on her face. I did my best to whisper in her ear and assure her that Jake and I ended things amicably. My mother could see the pain in my eyes, but she didn't push, understanding that I was holding on by a thread.

I found it in me to be as charming as I'd ever been, laughing, smiling, accepting the compliments that came my way, ignoring the pull to stare at the enigmatic presence Jake exerted in his black tuxedo hybrid suit, coupled with a white shirt and a black tie.

God, I could still smell him, but I resisted and barely looked at him, especially as Lauren, in her quite short sparkly white dress, was almost rubbing herself on him. After three glasses of champagne, I numbed the throbbing in my chest and almost convinced myself I wasn't in agony.

We finally proceeded to the dining room. Just a few more hours I thought, before I was out of this place forever.

I picked the seat the furthest from Jake and Lauren, with Kyle next to me. He was enjoying himself. He couldn't let go of me and clearly understood how to source from my current state of vulnerability, and I let him.

My eyes did cross Jake's a few times during dinner; it was much harder to avoid, especially when he spoke, as he naturally commanded the whole table in his direction. I could have sworn Lauren was tantalizing me, as she gave me that perverse smile she was so good at.

"Don't let her get under your skin," whispered my mother to me. I loved that woman to death, her grip bringing my strength back.

"I won't."

Dinner was finally over. I could not bring myself to eat, but I toyed with my salad and my salmon enough that I hoped to not call attention.

After what was for everyone else a pleasant dinner, we all proceeded to the terrace outside, where the house staff served a few aperitifs and desserts. It was a beautiful night, with the moon half full and the stars shining. I stared, wishing they could take me away.

A noise distracted my reverie, and I looked around. Jake was nowhere to be seen, and neither was my father. This was my chance to escape, almost unseen.

"Mom," I said as I joined her. "I have to go. I can't... be here anymore."

"I am so sorry sweetheart; I still don't understand what happened."

"We, um, changed our minds. Well, he did," I painfully admitted. "And I wasn't warned."

I couldn't say more without crying, feeling my eyes get wet. I lost my words.

My mother hugged me. "I understand, my darling."

"Dad..."

"I will handle him. Just leave, don't worry. I hate Jake for doing this to you, I just don't understand, I could have sworn he—"

"It's okay, Mom," I softly interrupted. "It's fine. I am going to my room now; I will try to call a car."

"If you can't find one, I will drive you."

"No, Mom, you've also had your fair share of bubbles," I teased. "I can call a company car if it comes to that."

I exited the party, relieved at the idea of leaving the house. Maybe once home, I could burn my sheets and pretend this was all a bad dream.

But as I passed by the small library, I heard a few voices, and they sounded agitated. I reduced my pace and silently got closer as I recognized Jake's frustrated tone.

"They will never be able to run their business again," he said, "I can assure you that much. It's just a question of time. Be it by legal means, or otherwise."

"But we need to find the fucking spy first," I heard my dad add.

"Very close, Philip, very close. We have a way to trace the transferred IP back to the computer who sent it, and we know which passwords were used to access the information from your servers; it's only a question of time."

"I am relieved Kyle got cleared," added my father.

"I was and still am surprised," said Jake, sounding cautious.

Afraid that I had been caught as both men fell silent for what felt like forever, I trusted my gut and swung the office door open. They both seemed a bit disconcerted by my presence.

I probably hadn't gotten exposed I realized, but it was too late to back down. I just stared at them for a second. For once, they both seemed at a loss for words.

"What are you talking about?" I asked bluntly. Jake was staring at me, standing behind his desk, my father across from him, turning around a bit to face me. He also got up.

"How long have you been standing there?" asked Jake.

"Long enough" I disclosed defiantly, ignoring Jake. I didn't come in for him after all. "Dad, what's going on?"

"It's time we tell her." He sighed, looking in Jake's direction.

"I would advise against it," warned Jake sternly, his eyes locked on me.

"It's time," repeated my father. He fully turned to face me. "You might want to sit down for this," he cautioned.

"I'm good," I answered as I noticed Jake's outrage.

I liked being by the door, especially as Jake was moving to the bookshelf, and thus closer to me. My father rested his right hand on the desk.

"A few months ago," he started, "I became worried that someone was funneling trade secrets and potential patent filings to Green Mile."

"Why?"

"There were... rumors... that they had developed technology similar to ours for the e-axles we are launching this winter. The CEO was even bragging that they would be able to go to market by fall of this year."

"Fall? But they just started diving into the e-axle business. We have the patents..."

"Yes but, with the way he described it, I became suspicious, I asked around."

"We did wonder how they could have come up with a competitive product to us that quickly," I recalled from earlier conversations a few months back.

"Yes. The way one of his people described the gear later on, the bearings, the development process, that smug look he always has when he talks about our company, I was sure something was off."

I was getting quite agitated with Jake intensely gawking at me from the corner, leaning against his shelf, arms and legs crossed, arrogance emanating from every inch of his body.

"Did you find who did it?"

"No," added Jake, "but we are very close."

"We?" I stared back at my dad.

"Yes, hun, that is the reason I hired Jake, sweetie. I needed an outsider for this, someone I could trust. Jake's specialty is corporate espionage investigations, specifically around a potential leak of proprietary information. I needed someone who I could trust to handle the process smoothly, efficiently, while not raising any suspicions.

"He has been at the forefront of strategically joining companies, in the background mostly, to uncover such betrayals. He runs a private top-secret company for that. He rarely if ever does the work personally, but I begged him to make an exception this time. I needed someone I knew was competent and that I could trust with everything I have."

A laugh burst out of me.

"Him? You trust him!? Oh, come on," I said, trying to compose myself.

"Chloe," my dad warned.

"No, Dad, really? And why am I just finding about this now!? Why didn't you involve me in this?"

"Sweetheart, please don't look at me like this. I trust you with my life, you know I do. I just didn't want to involve you. I didn't know how dirty this could get, hell I still don't. I wanted to protect you."

"I don't need you to protect me, Dad! I need you to let me get involved. I am your GC, for crying out loud!"

"Part of my rules is that once I am involved, no one else gets informed," interjected Jake. "I don't want anyone compromising the investigation, and I don't want the culprit to be accidentally warned."

"So, you convinced my dad to leave his own daughter out of this?" I screamed in his direction, my body warm.

"It is my job to keep things unbiased, so yes," he retorted. "I don't know you; I don't know anyone at your company, which is part of the point. Every single person there *is* a suspect. Including the owner's daughter." I felt his words to the depths of my bones.

I wanted to jump on him and slap that fucking smirk off his lips. He was really getting under my skin. The amount of anger and hatred emanating from him making me feel like I did something wrong. He eyes, they were lethal.

"Do the other shareholders know? The rest of the board?"

"No, no, I am keeping this under wraps for now. Everyone is a suspect."

"You still should have told me, Dad," I pushed back, attempting to concentrate on my father instead. "I could have helped."

"I know, but I didn't want to put you at any risk or get you involved in any mess. You have a license to protect, a legal career. I didn't want any potential negative press or negative outcome to impact you," he explained as he got close to me and grabbed my hands in his.

I softened, seeing my father's anxious gaze, but I was still deeply insulted. Being kept out of the conversation meant to me that I was or still was a suspect.

The idea that my dad could even for a second think me capable of something like this was the last straw of what turned out to be one of the worst days of my life.

"Honey, why do you look so hurt?" asked my dad, "I know it wasn't the fatherliest act, but what would you do in my position? What has you so upset? I know you understand what I did; you would have done the same to protect someone you care about, including me."

I remained silent as I looked at the cause of my dismay, standing behind my father, stoic, hands in his pockets, with that calm cold look that made me want to scream. I resisted the urge to curse both out.

I didn't think my father thought me guilty, but he did allow Jake to put me in the box. Jake, the hero in my father's eyes, the one who treated me like I didn't matter. He was the one my father had trusted essentially with the future of the company he created the company he was still a major owner of.

Not me.

"I want to help."

"I don't want you involved," answered Jake.

My father gave Jake a look pleading for reasonability.

"You work for my dad," I reminded him.

"I run my own process, Chloe, and I don't take orders from anyone, even your father. And he understands that. Those were the terms of my engagement."

"Chloe, let's just please trust Jake," begged my father, trying to clear the air.

Seeing desperation in his eyes was my weakness; I felt defeated. I had lost the battle months ago the minute that man had stepped foot in the company. I just didn't know there was a fight to be fought then.

"Fine, Dad. I was excluded from this already anyways. Please, don't ever keep me in the dark on something like this ever again. Or I will just leave and go work for a company that understands the value I bring to the table."

"Chloe, please," he pleaded.

I ignored my father's apologetic gaze and stomped towards the door. I stared at Jake with all the anger and the hatred I felt towards him in that moment.

"I hope you solve this as soon as possible so I never have to see your fucking face again," I cursed calmly, coldly, as we heard the first thunder split the sky in two, the light reflecting in the window.

For a moment, it was just me and Jake in the room, tears in my eyes, fury coming out of every pore, both of us frozen in a moment in time, staring, unable to look away.

I would destroy him.

"And I'm going home tonight. I no longer have to make a fucking excuse for that anymore," I added as I turned towards my dad. "I love you, Dad," I said before leaving, "but I am very disappointed and very hurt that you still treat me like a child."

I hurried out of the room to avoid more tears and slammed the door behind me. I sprinted as fast as my heels and my shaken body allowed.

I ran upstairs, pulled my luggage from the closet, and angrily started to throw my clothes in, my sight blinded with hot angry tears, my brain doing its best to process while I was still in shock.

I heard heavy steps in the hallway, but by the time I could shut the bedroom door closed, Jake was inside my room, lips parted, looking like he could murder someone. I tried to get away, but Jake slammed the door behind him, grabbed me by the arm, and forced me to face him.

"That little scene you pulled in there, bravo!" he growled, nose flaring, anger and loathing coming out his stare, his lips turned into stern lines.

"How dare you?" I screamed, feeling stupid, used and manipulated, "How dare you put my dad against me!?"

"You did that all by yourself!" he barked back.

"I did no such thing! You're the one who told him to keep me uninformed in this whole charade, weren't you, as if I'd ever do anything that would harm my own family!"

"Stop lying to me!" he yelled as he aggressively grabbed my other arm to stop me from moving away as I was attempting to do.

"You're the liar! You're the one who slept with me, used me, and for what? To have a little fun while on your secret mission! You played me!" I fumed, my throat closing, my eyes burning. "God, you made *me* your mistress for fucks sakes, *me!* And you call me a liar!? What did I lie about huh, tell me, what is it that I did to deserve any of this?"

My lips quivered, tears pouring down my face, but I didn't care. All the hurt, all the sorrow, it was all coming out, and I couldn't stop it, I was exhausted and felt like I had nothing else to lose.

"That's not true, Chloe, it's not... I didn't plan any of this!" He hesitated, his voice deep, his eyes dark, searching mine, looking confused, almost hurt, but he let go of me brusquely, and as I struggled to regain my balance. He took a step back, as if I had burned him. He started pacing, running his hand quickly through his hair.

"I know that you provided Motor Holmes IP to Green Mile, and got I assume substantial compensation for it to support this lavish life you claim you don't want your father to help with. Fucking bullshit. You are exactly who I thought you were, a spoiled fucking brat who was bought by the highest bidder."

I stood there, feeling my blood turn to ice in my veins, my cheeks and fingers suddenly cold. This must have been what feeling stabbed felt like. Was he saying that I was the culprit in all this!?

"That's impossible!" I muttered, trying to remind myself that staying silent could incriminate me further. "I didn't do anything, I would never! Why would I destroy what would ultimately be half mine in the future!?"

"Don't," he said putting his hand up between us as I took a step toward him. "You disgust me, and frankly I don't know why I haven't told your father about this yet. I really wanted to be wrong, you have *no* idea how much, but I'm not, and that little innocent face of yours is not going to convince me otherwise. As of this morning, I have all the evidence I need. And it wouldn't be the first time you steal from your own family."

"What? Oh God, what is happening? What are you talking about!? I swear, Jake, I didn't do anything! You have to believe me," I implored.

But he just stayed put, staring at me in anger and contempt. I hated the man but the idea that he could be disappointed or repealed by me was torture. And imagining him making my father think I had betrayed him was agony.

"You have to tell me what you think you know," I begged, trying to reason with him, "otherwise how can I fairly defend myself? I don't know what you have, but whatever it is it's not true, it's just not. Someone must be setting me up. Jake, please," I pleaded as I finally got to him and grabbed his front arm with my right hand.

His breathing quickened; he hesitated but took a step back. I closed my eyes, trying to control the lightheadedness.

"You are one of the ten people at this company who have full access to this information. Even the employees who actually make the products only have partial and limited access."

"It doesn't mean I did it, Jake. How could you even think that?"

"Because I have proof, Chloe, it's over! Over!"

"What proof? What's the proof!? It wasn't me, Jake!"

"For fucks sakes Chloe, STOP LYING! Stop fucking lying! You used me enough, don't you think? My team looked at your laptop; I got the results this morning, the emails you sent and deleted, they are all there. Your computer is one of the few high-level privileged ones that don't generate a notice to the compliance team when you send confidential information to non-Motor Holmes email addresses. Even Kyle doesn't have one. I really thought it was him, but he checked out, Chloe. Everyone else did. Except for you!"

"You think I am stupid enough to use my work email to commit fraud!?" I sputtered.

"Why not? You knew your dad would never suspect you."

I walked away, turning my back to him. I cradled my head in my hands, trying to stop the room from moving, but it didn't work. I took a few steps towards the desk in my room, holding onto the chair to try to stop myself from passing out.

Jake hurried to my side, holding me by my arms.

"Don't fucking touch me!" I shouted as I quickly pulled away. "I don't need you to pretend that you care."

"Chloe..."

"Fuck. OFF!" I yelled as he tried to get close again.

"Fine," he grunted, "but I need you to sit down."

I turned around and sat on the edge of the bed. It was the only way I could try to not fall on the ground, and I couldn't stay up.

We stayed silent for a few seemingly eternal minutes. How could so much have changed in so little time? I was face to face with a stranger. Someone I used to know. Or rather, someone I thought I knew. How could I have been so stupid?

"I need you to give me time," I said a bit more composed. "I need time to prove you wrong. You claim not to want to spook who is doing this. If you accuse me, you will accomplish just that, because I swear on my life, it wasn't me."

Jake silently sat next to me, his hands between his legs, staring at the floor, as if calculating his next move.

I felt like I was finally getting to him, as I recognized that distant look he got when his mind was going a thousand miles an hour, his face, contracted.

"I believe I have all the proof I need, Chloe. I hope for your sake that you aren't trying to play games with me. It won't work," he warned, still staring in front of him.

"Noted," I simply answered.

"And don't even think of fleeing... not from this house before Wednesday and definitely not from the country. I will have you watched; I can promise you that."

"You can't tell me what to do. I am not leaving the country, but I am sure as hell not staying here another second!"

I quickly rose, with Jake matching my tempo. The idea that I would have to stay here and watch Lauren call him *"sweetie"* one more time made me want to throw up. Prison might be better than that.

"You are *not* leaving. I don't want to have to find you. You asked for time, and I am giving you up until Wednesday. Until then, you don't leave my sight. Is that understood?"

I was panicked at the idea of having to be in this house for four more days. All the guests were set to leave on Sunday, so the group would get smaller, and I'd have less buffer between me and Jake.

And Lauren.

That would destroy me.

I couldn't explain that thought without admitting that as of less than a day ago, I was in love with him.

"If you leave," he warned, "I will tell your father everything."

"You'd break his heart, and for no reason!" I screamed, going closer to the desk again, as the weakness I felt hadn't subsided.

"It would be your own doing," he added as he took some steps towards me.

"How do you want me to investigate who is setting me up from here exactly?"

"I don't see how different it would be in Chicago."

"That's because you believe it's me, but it's not."

"Those are my terms, Chloe. You are not going to change my mind. And you're not going anywhere."

I couldn't stand the hatred in his piercing gaze. Less than twenty-four hours before, he was gazing at me with what I thought was love in his eyes... Caressing me in this very room.

I couldn't stay here until Wednesday. Not only because I needed to find out the truth of who was behind this betrayal, but I also couldn't fathom the idea of seeing him with another woman any longer. I believed my dad would not buy that I stole from him, he just couldn't.

Jake probably knew that, thus why he hadn't said anything yet, and likely why he was pretending to give me a chance so there would be no doubts when he revealed me as the criminal, but I wouldn't give him that satisfaction. And I had just come up with a plan on where to start with the task of proving my innocence.

There was no winning tonight though, and it was passed the time I could even get a car anyways. Not to mention the rain was now in full force.

"Please leave," I said as I walked to the bathroom. "I'd prefer that your girlfriend not come get you here, and I need to get ready for bed. And if you're going to hold me hostage here, I need another bedroom."

"That's fine."

"Oh, and Jake?" I added, giving him one last look. "I'm never going to forgive you for this." I glared at him with the most hatred I had felt towards a human being in a long time.

"I'm counting on it."

I violently closed the bathroom door, waiting until I heard the room door open and close before starting to undress. I jumped in the shower, hoping that the dripping hot water would steady me, but all I could do was cry.

CHAPTER 29

Eventually I was out of tears. I forced myself to get a grip and poured all my energy into the task at hand, I had to prove my innocence. The sooner I did this, the sooner I could get Jake out of my life, forever. I put my white pajama set on, grabbed my laptop and sat at the desk, with the cup of coffee I had just prepared.

Hands nervously running through my hair every minute, I looked everywhere I could for any weird emails or emails I couldn't recall. Two hours later, nothing. I knew there was a way to access deleted emails. I called IT and they tried to help me but to no avail.

I knew who the perfect person would be to help me, so I texted Mike. Thankfully he was awake even if it was already 1 a.m. Unfortunately, he wasn't sleeping for the wrong reasons since he had broken up again with his girlfriend.

I couldn't do anything else but be honest with him. I was unable to hold back the searing pain coursing through my body like poison. So I told him exactly what had transpired in the last few hours.

I was momentarily distracted by the noise I thought I heard coming from the other room.

I wondered if Lauren was in there, if Jake was alone. Why would he be pacing around his room? Or was I just imagining the sound?

Then my thoughts turned dark, and I considered the idea that they could be in Lauren's room... making love. And I was instantly sick to my stomach.

Regardless, it didn't really matter. I couldn't think of that at this moment because the man I thought I was in love with was now trying to prove I was guilty of espionage. My sole focus needed to be on proving my innocence. I couldn't stay in that hell. I knew how to build a defense, and that's what I was going to do.

"Oh, stop it, Jake!" Lauren squealed loudly, followed by her irritating laughter. I retracted, grabbed my phone and my laptop, and ran out of the bedroom like a fire was behind me.

I asked Mike to hold while I found a place that would offer me silence.

I went straight to the first floor and walked around for a bit until I got into the reading room. There was a couch that I recalled was comfortable and would be perfect for me to sleep on.

I pushed the wooden door slowly. The light was off, thankfully, so I knew no one was in there. I decided to keep it dark and use the light from my phone to guide me to the light green couch.

Relieved, I sat down and got back to my conversation with Mike. He was kind enough to agree to drive all the way to me the next day to search my laptop and help me not feel alone in this house. With that in mind, I was finally able to close my eyes at 4 a.m.

Four hours later, I woke up suddenly, startled by my ring tone. I jumped, confused, not recognizing my surroundings, or the thick furry blanket I was wrapped in. I remembered where I was, anxiety quickly pouring back into my body as I recalled the day before, Lauren's awful laughter being the last disturbing memory.

It was Mike on the phone; he was letting me know he was a few hours away. When we hung up, I realized the blanket was the Pottery Barn furry throw from Jake's room. He had been in his office apparently, I just didn't think he would do anything to give me comfort or warmth at this point.

I sprang to my feet, realizing I had to sneak back up before anyone saw me. Just my luck, as I was reaching for the door handle, someone pulled it in the opposite direction. I stayed put as Jake entered the room, closing the door behind him. He just stood there in front of me, too close for comfort. He was wearing a dark blue polo with white pants and tan moccasins with no socks. I had to remind myself to breathe.

I was still frozen, my eyes unable to leave his. I searched for words, but I didn't make a sound, and neither did he. You don't just accuse a girl of corporate espionage and then stand in front of her like this and cause this kind of visceral reaction.

The memory of Lauren's laugh made me shiver, common sense making its way back. I broke the eye contact, hurried past him, almost hitting him in my rush to leave. I sprinted to my room, thankful that no one saw me. No one other than Jake.

I ignored the pinch in my heart and instead focused on getting ready. I had chosen my light blue ripped jeans and a fluffy white shirt, coupled with my Follies Strass stilettos, putting my hair in a ponytail. There was no time to waste. The plan for the guests was to go sailing after breakfast but I intended to skip it to work with Mike.

I headed down, but instead of meeting the team at breakfast on the patio, I went straight outside. Mike's BMW was just pulling in. The valet got his car, a bit confused as I hadn't announced a visitor. I ran into Mike's arms when I saw him, feeling a little more reassured now that someone outside of the company and fully on my side was joining us.

"You're going to be okay," he whispered in my ears as he rubbed my back.

Feeling uneasy as Mike stopped his comforting touch, I turned around. Jake was standing on top of the stairs, his hands in his jeans, the wind blowing his white shirt and his thick blonde hair. I held my breath, feeling as if I had gotten caught. There was nothing to be ashamed of, I reminded myself, as Mike and I walked up the stairs.

"Mike, Jake. Jake, meet Mike," I said, trying to pretend I didn't feel Jake's coldness in my bones. Jake just stared at Mike and remained silent.

"If you're going to hold an innocent woman in your house, I hope you don't mind if I stay with her."

Mike took me by surprise, and I smiled. Jake didn't flinch.

"I hope I am allowed to have a guest?" I asked with an innocent smirk.

"You do whatever you want, Chloe, as long as it's here," he declared with disdain before he stormed in, never acknowledging Mike.

We stepped inside but went straight to my bedroom. I locked the door, relieved to be in my safe space with a friend.

I felt it necessary to have Mike sign an NDA, and we also signed an engagement letter for the services he was about to provide. Considering the situation, I was appropriate, and Mike wasn't offended.

Mike connected his laptop with mine and requested for a bit of time alone to get everything set up. I spent an hour on my phone on the balcony, anxiously pacing. Lorna had brought us food that I had barely touched, but Mike was enjoying his BLT as he typed.

It was three hours later when Mike was finally ready for me to join him. He found exactly what he was looking for. Unfortunately, it wasn't good news.

"All the proof he says he has... it's true..." explained Mike.

I felt my heart sink a I let myself fall on the bed next to Mike.

"Someone is setting me up..."

"Or using you, big time," added Mike. "Look, there are four emails here to a Gmail account. I spotted them because they were encrypted and large. But they are here. Four emails were sent with what looks like confidential information of your company in the last year or so. The emails are from you on four distinct dates," he explained.

I blindly grabbed the notebook he handed me, where he annotated all the email exchanges dates, times and subjects. It was all there. I skimmed the document but couldn't process much. Someone had taken my laptop, in multiple occasions, to steal from my father.

I frowned as I read some more. September 20th and September 21st. The latter date was familiar. It was when the first file with some IP information was sent. I quickly grabbed my cellphone to look at my calendar for the year before.

The first red herring, I explained to Mike, was that on that date I was traveling to Mexico for Amelia's book party. My computer was with the IT department getting rebooted because it had crashed the day before, while I was in the middle of a very important call. Frustrated, I had walked down to the IT center and been a little rude.

I had apologized within a few minutes, and they had offered me a loaner laptop so I wouldn't have to be without one the entire day. They assured me my laptop would be ready within a couple days.

The day I left for Mexico, I stopped by the IT office to check on my laptop, but it wasn't ready, or so I was told. I had gone back to my office but had left almost right after, having to catch my flight.

Close to ten months later, even if I did get my laptop back, the loaner was still in my possession, in a drawer in my office, as I never returned it when I came back.

"That is great news," said Mike, after I explained.

"How do I use it?"

"Let me track the IP address of the computer on that day. That helps at least show that the computer wasn't in Mexico with you. Your phone's IP address would easily show that you weren't in Chicago yourself when the emails were sent out. I can try to breach in the security system for more information. They might even have a gps or wifi tracking. And you have proof of your trip?"

"Yes, I have my ticket. I have restaurant receipts, I have pictures...."

"So, if I can show the laptop never left the States, then it can't be you! Frankly, even just not being in the office at that time helps. Did you take an Uber?"

"Yes."

"Even better."

"What if someone says I logged in on the VPN?"

"The IP address of the computer wouldn't change. The VPN login would be from another device, right?"

"Right..." I answered, having a hard time believing I did find proof of my innocence so fast.

"All I did was check emails on my phone in Mexico. I replied to some."

"So, we have full proof that you weren't here. And from what you tell me, someone at your IT department had your laptop. There must also be proof of that."

"So, someone in the IT department could have done this. But that still doesn't explain how they got access to the files themselves to send."

"I mean, someone in the IT department must have your logins. Or enough of them to be dangerous. I was able to access some of this information here that someone clearly tried to keep away from you. It wasn't easy but it wasn't hard either. Your security systems could use some improvements. Can't say that someone in your team couldn't break privileges, get the documents using your information, and email them through your email."

"Can you track the email it went to?"

At this, he frowned. "No. It's all encrypted."

I looked at the third date of information. It was December 31st of last year. I checked my calendar again. I had people over to celebrate the new year. There were around forty people in attendance. But who was there that would want to frame me for this?

The fourth date was just a few months before, in March. My calendar reminded me that I was at my parents for brunch that day. That email was sent right when I was at my parents' house, and yes, my laptop was with me. That was a couple weeks before I met Jake. There had been about twenty people at that particular gathering brunch.

Last, but certainly not least, was the last email with no attachments that Mike showed me straight on the screen. On my father's fucking birthday, so it had been sent from my house. That email was even more incriminating.

———

This might have to be my last email to you. My father hired someone to investigate, and I fear he is close. I am seducing the new guy to see what I can find and discover exactly what he knows. I don't know If I can get him to flip sides. But as long as he's under my feet, if he thinks I am into him, I can do what I want with him. The idiot has no idea. I hope you appreciate the sacrifices I am making for us here. I can't stand him, but I have to play the game. And I play it perfectly. Hope you're not jealous ;) I can't wait to be with you. I miss you.

 All the very best,
 Chloe

———

What the hell? I was pacing now, my brain unable to slow down.

I then grabbed the laptop from Mike. I was one of the most obnoxious people when it came to organization. And it was going to pay off. I had the list of the guests to the brunch (that I basically organized), the new year's party at my house, as well as my father's birthday.

I had gone the extra mile and sent invites. I required that people respond with an acceptance or denial of attendance. I also had pictures of the nights in question on my phone. Using both pictures and the list of attendees, I could easily know exactly who was there.

"It pays to be a bit anal, huh?" teased Mike.

"Oh yes, yes it does," I answered, a smile of vindication on my face.

I took the time to painstakingly type all invitees to events in an Excel table on my personal laptop, flag everyone who had declined in a column, and everyone who had accepted in another. All I had to do now was use pictures and my recollection to track actual attendees in the last column of each of the tables I had created. Any guests who attended all events would then go on the suspect list.

I also needed to track the staff who served food and provided valet services at each event. Thankfully I had thought to retain those lists as well. It was important to know exactly who was going to be at my house and my parents' house. There was going to be some overlap with the staff there as well I reminded myself, because I always hired the same team for things like this, for consistency but also for convenience. But none of those folks had access to my work building so I focused on guests who also had access to my office.

"You also can try to get the list of anyone who swiped their card in your building. Anyone from your company who came to work those days in September."

"You read my mind," I said to Mike with a smile. "And it will reduce the list since many folks stay at home. But I don't know how to do that."

"I can help," added Mike with pride. "But I'd need access to the building computers. Which I assume you don't have."

"No, but let me think about this. I don't, but that fucking asshole does."

Someone knocked and interrupted us. Mike got up to open the door. It was Lorna, informing us dinner would be served a bit late at 9 p.m.

"So," asked Mike teasingly as he sat back next to me, "are we going to dinner?"

"How can you think of food right now?"

"Well, I am hungry," he admitted, "and I could use a break. Let it serve as a distraction for both of us. Get our minds off everything for a bit and enjoy a meal."

I was really looking at him for the first time since he got there. I had been so focused on myself that I completely forgot that Mike, behind that warm and shy smile, was also suffering. After all, his girlfriend told him they were over, again. I noticed the slightly dark shadows under his eyes, remembering he had told me he hadn't slept for days.

"I am so sorry, Mike," I said softly, putting my hand on his arm. "I am such a bad friend..."

"No, no," he interrupted, his cheeks turning pink. "Fraud takes precedence over heartbreak."

I laughed. Even as he was in pain, he kept his lovely sense of humor.

"Okay," I decided, resolved to pay more attention to his needs. "This is what we are going to do. At this point, I don't know who basically committed corporate espionage, but I at least know how to prove my innocence. Thanks to you.

"The September date being my salvation. I know we have work to do to determine who had access to my laptop on each date. But even without that, we have proof."

"Correct. Are you going to tell Jake?"

I stayed silent, thinking about it for a second. I wanted to tell him, no, scream it at him. Call him an idiot and tell him to go fuck himself, but I didn't want to make a scene. I also wanted the satisfaction of finding the culprit myself, to not only prove Jake wrong, but to also show him that he couldn't even do his job, that I could do it better than him. That my father never needed him in the first place.

If I gave him proof of my innocence, he would just continue doing his job. He had more resources than me; he would connect the dots, use the information I provide and find the culprit before I could.

He would be victorious in my father's eyes after he accused me, used me, and treated me like a disposable toy.

No, I wanted revenge. I was out for blood. Jake was a proud man, proud of himself, proud of his intelligence, and the worst thing I could do to him was attack his job, his skills, his professional worth.

And I had what I needed to do just that. I had the list of potential traitors, I just needed to narrow it down. I had an advantage he didn't. I knew these people; I wasn't an outsider. And clearly, someone thought they had gotten away with it.

If they continued to think I had no idea, they might even try to use my laptop again!

Jake wanted me to be a villain.

Well, I would give him exactly what he asked for.

"I don't think I will tell him. Let's take the evening off. Thanks to you, I have my hail Mary pass, so we can relax a bit. Thank you so much for coming here so fast," I said as I hugged Mike.

I had a plan, but first I was going to shower again, change, and take Mike for a drink and to dinner. It was the least I could do. And there was no way I was attending dinner with all those people.

I was tempted, enjoying the idea of being now so calm in front of Jake, having him wonder how I was keeping such a poker face. But no, there was no need to put Mike in an awkward situation. Plus, Lauren was there, and despite all the hatred I felt towards Jake currently, seeing him with Lauren would tear me apart.

CHAPTER 30

MIKE HAD GONE BACK to his car for his duffel bag. From what he texted me, Lorna was waiting for him and took him to another guest bedroom a couple of doors down from my room. She was surely following orders. Who did Jake think he was? But then again, it wasn't like I wanted Mike to sleep in my room, but the idea of pretending sounded great to me.

I wanted us to leave before 9 p.m. My mother had texted me to tell me Jake, my parents, and the other guests were still sailing but on their way to the house. I wanted to be out before they got back. I also packed and hid my luggage in Mike's car.

I was still considering leaving, trying to convince myself that I was no longer afraid of what Jake could do. The more I thought about it, the more I was convinced he wouldn't tell my father. He claimed to have known for a day now and didn't say anything.

What was he waiting for, more proof? Perhaps he did have doubts that it was me? No, I thought, he was clear that he believed me capable of betraying my family like this. I assumed he had also seen the email where I supposedly knew who he was and was using him. Which was ridiculous.

I opted for a simple emerald-green French Connection short dress with long sleeves. I added some waves to my hair and did my makeup. I chose my beige heels and my beige Yves Saint Laurent small purse to complete my ensemble.

"You look stunning," said Mike as he greeted me by the car, looking at me with admiration.

Mike had kept his same khaki pants and simply changed his black polo for a blue shirt with thin stripes. He had added some gel to his hair and smelled of vanilla and patchouli.

He opened the door for me and then got in the driver's seat. I had managed to find a table at one of the most coveted restaurants of New Buffalo and was quite impressed with myself when we managed to get seated on the huge deck overlooking Lake Michigan. I was glad I grabbed my light beige sweater as it was a little chilly by the water.

The night was perfect, the moon shining but allowing for some stars to provide a romantic flair to the slightly cool evening. Would have been a great night to be on the yacht with Jake, I thought, saddened by the memory and the absence of him.

No, there was no need to fantasize about a man who was out of reach, who had hurt me so deeply I hadn't quite processed the past few days yet. Besides, my focus for the night was Mike.

"You actually believe she meant it?" I asked after Mike explained that his girlfriend had left because she thought their relationship was getting too serious too fast.

"I don't know," he admitted, his right hand rubbing his face, as he did when he was confused.

"I think it's her parents," I added. "Last time you broke up, they were quite... involved in the problem."

"They've never thought I was good enough for her," he admitted.

"They are stupid if you ask me." I frowned.

How dare they think that about someone who drove all the way to New Buffalo to come to rescue his friend. If Mike was willing to go to these lengths for me, I could only imagine how loving he was with his girlfriend.

Mike grabbed his Coke Zero and chugged it. He didn't want to drink as he was going to drive himself (or us) back to Chicago tonight.

"Do you think it would help if we made her jealous? It worked last time."

"I mean, it can't hurt," he said, feeling a bit hopeful.

"Let's do it then."

I scooted my chair closer to his, put my arms around him, leaned myself in his arms a bit, as he wrapped his right hand around my shoulders.

When the waiter brought the steak and salmon we ordered, I asked him to take pictures of us. I picked the one that made us look the most as a couple in love and posted it on social media with the caption "Hot date @Captalar" and tagged him.

"There," I announced, "and I hope her stupid parents see this."

"Thank you." his shoulders got a bit more relaxed.

"I am sure she loves you, Mike. With the way she cried last time, she must. She's probably confused, I know it's been years, but the marriage conversation is so… finite… She probably just panicked a little."

"I hope you're right." He paused. "I think you are. Let's see what to-morrow brings."

I was satisfied as a more permanent smile was making its way back to Mike's lips. It was important to me that he was okay. I chugged what was left of my third glass of champagne, as I had already ordered a bottle before Mike kindly reminded me that drinking and driving was not recommend-ed. I would not let a good bottle go to waste.

I had almost forgotten about Jake and his accusations by the time we were devouring a slice of the most wonderful seven-layer chocolate cake for dessert. I asked for and took care of the bill, even under Mike's protests. Treating him to dinner was the least I could do after all he had done for me.

"So, what do we do next on this espionage situation?" inquired Mike as he shoved a big spoon of cake he claimed he didn't want into his mouth.

"I think you are enjoying my demise a little too much," I joked.

"Well," admitted Mike, attempting to chew at the same time, "now that we have proof of your innocence, it's a lot less concerning, no?"

"I guess. Still a pain, though. I don't really want people to know what I was in Mexico for."

"Not even me?"

"Nope. But it's better than prison, or my dad thinking I can do something like this to him I guess, and I can give a reason, but I don't want to necessarily explain why I lied about where I was. But perhaps if I find the culprit, I don't need to go into too many details to prove my innocence.

"All that should matter is that I wasn't in the office and thus wouldn't be able to do something like this. Whoever did this must have tracked me, sending the email on the 21st after I got to work, but they didn't realize that I barely stayed there that day. I don't know. For the next few days, I will focus all my efforts on finding out who did this.

"But I don't think I can do that from here. For example, I want to go to the office, talk to the tech folks, try to figure out who had my laptop and when on that day, who worked on it."

"Won't they be suspicious, though, if you ask questions?"

"That's the concern." I ran my fingers in my hair. "Although, for the days I technically had possession of my laptop, could they have sent those emails remotely but pretended I sent them from my laptop?"

"No, the emails were definitely sent from that laptop."

"I just need to figure out where it was that day then."

"But clearly the IT team didn't have access to it when you weren't in the office."

"But whoever did this managed to get to my computer while it was with the IT department, or it might be more than one person. Which would make sense if we thought someone broke the firewall and got my password information to gain access to those documents perhaps," I wondered, resting my elbows on the table, holding my hands tied together, resting my jaw on top of my knuckles.

"I also need that loaner. I worked on it; I created documents on the local drive but didn't delete them. It should show that I spent most of the September dates working on it."

"Yep, also very helpful."

"I will have my mother go to my office and send it to your house if that is okay?"

"Of course. But are you going to tell her?"

I pondered that for a few seconds. Did my mother know why Jake had been hired? How would my mother react to me telling her my father's investigator was accusing me of espionage?

I couldn't imagine my mother would just wait around for me to find a solution. This wasn't like when my cousin had let me take the blame for her thievery; my mom would certainly tell my father, and it was just too soon.

Jake's words came back to me in a rush. "*It wouldn't be the first time you steal from your own family.*"

I swallowed hard. I came to the realization that Lauren had likely told him about the incident all those years ago, of course telling the false story. The one where I steal money from my dad, as opposed to her. And he clearly had believed her. I wondered in what context that conversation come up. Had he told her about the investigation?

"Chloe?"

I closed my eyes to get rid of the thoughts and the sudden urge to break a vase on my cousin's head.

"No, I don't want to worry her. Maybe my secretary. She loves me to pieces and barely understands technology, so I can't really see her as a suspect anyways. But no, I will just get it when I get in."

"Anyone in IT you can trust to give you building security information?"

"No, I mean, I just don't know them. BUT I'd bet that Jake got all that information, including building swipes. He was provided with all access basically and he has a team, I'm sure of it. Hell, he could have already infiltrated the IT team with new strategically placed hires to get him the data."

"Would you ask him for it?" Mike inquired.

I paused. Would he be willing to help me prove my innocence when he was so convinced of my guilt?

"I don't know. I don't think he would give it to me. Also, I don't want him to know I have a way to prove my innocence. Not until I know who did this. I want to outshine him, teach that asshole a lesson."

Mike just gave me a look. He didn't seem as sure of my convictions as I was.

"What?" I asked, a bit defensive.

"I'm sorry." He hesitated. "I just recognize my pain in your eyes..."

I just glared at him. But my breathing quickened after his words, a lump growing in my stomach, my hands slightly sweating.

I looked down and my now white knuckles, my nails digging in my palm to distract me from the deep sorrow trying to consume me. I had been stronger than I thought about this.

After all, I had been burned before. But the look of sympathy in Mike's gaze shook me, made Jake's deception more real.

I had told Mike everything when I called him. More than I should have perhaps. After all, Jake's betrayal was not relevant to the process of proving my innocence.

But I told him because I couldn't quite separate the two. The investigation was how he got in my life. Then he seduced me, broke my walls down, and got close to my heart. Too close. And now he simply got rid of me like yesterday's trash, leaving me breathless, confused, and outraged, and my bed cold without him in it.

"I am not in pain, Mike." I swallowed to regain my composure. "I'll move on in any event. We barely had any time together."

Although I couldn't deny I felt him under my skin.

I added, "It's not the same as your situation. You guys have been dating forever. It's not. It's just not. All I want is to do his job better than him and never see him again. So yes, fine, I will ask him. I don't know what else to do. I am sure he has it, so I'll try not to give too much information as to why I need it.

"I guess I'll have to stay one more night in this nightmare so I can try to talk some sense into the man. But tomorrow, I'm leaving. I can't spend every night wondering what... they are doing in that room next to mine," I finished between my teeth, jealousy pouring through me like venom.

I nervously shuffled my right hand through my hair, my left grabbing the champagne glass and finishing its contents in one gulp. Mike wrapped his fingers around mine when I set my glass back on the table, trying to silently console me.

I grabbed his hand back but didn't say anything. It hurt too much.

"I'll be right back." I got up and headed to the bathroom.

I needed a breather. So, I lingered in front of the dimly lit mirror after I washed my hands, the lighting accentuating the slightly dark circles under my eyes and the hollow that was deepening in my cheeks. That was what I had wanted to avoid. The feeling of void, the tart taste in my mouth, the disappointment that inevitably came once one put oneself out there, the all-consuming need for another.

I straightened myself, retouched my makeup a bit, and inhaled deeply. I didn't have time to feel anything but cold and controlled anger right now. The type that thrived on focus and rationality, the kind that could take that man down.

I grabbed my purse with determination and exited the room.

I held a little scream as I exited the bathroom and slammed into a man who was in my way. Before I could even make out who it was, his scent wrapped me whole and gave him away.

The knot in my stomach tightened and caused a terrifying sense of dread to course through me at the sight of a man I thought I mattered to just yesterday.

I felt his hand around my waist as I tried to balance myself.

"Fun date?" he inquired, a cynical smirk on his face.

Those cold blue eyes tried to tear my soul into a thousand pieces. I pushed him away, removing myself from his embrace.

"Amazing I'd say, but you had to come here and ruin it," I answered, my jaw lifted in a defiant manner, quickly gaining back control of my movement and my words as I Ignored the chaos in my stomach, the cold of my hands.

"I told you not to leave the house," he said calmly as his jaw tightened, raising the hair on my arms.

I rolled my eyes.

"Whatever happened to innocent until proven guilty?" I asked, alcohol giving me courage to mock him.

"As far as I am concerned, you *are* guilty."

Anger took over, making me shake just a bit.

"And do not roll your eyes at me."

My eyes widened a bit, but I wasn't backing down.

"Well, why not have fun while I await my sentence?!" I scoffed.

"You weren't just having fun, you were leaving."

"No, I wasn't."

"Is that why you packed all your clothes?"

I looked up at those darkened furious eyes and swallowed hard, unable to understand my body temperature.

"I was considering it..." I admitted. "But I chan—"

"We are leaving," he interrupted, grabbing my arm and heading towards the exit.

"No!"

He spun towards me, an aggravated look on his face.

"Do you want to make a scene here?" he threatened, his head bent defiantly.

"Do *you?*"? I retorted. "You're the animal here."

"Enough," he grunted, shaking me.

I froze, my chest pounding as I looked in his eyes, feeling like time had stopped. There was nothing else but this man, those darkened cold sage eyes, this tempestuous look, stopping me in my tracks, and that hand burning through my wrist.

"Everything okay?" I heard Mike say behind me.

Jake ignored him and pulled me in his direction.

"Hey, dude, let her go!" snapped Mike as he tried to put himself between Jake and me.

The threatening look Jake gave Mike sobered me up a bit and woke me up from my stupor.

"It's fine, Mike," I said, trying to diffuse the situation. "Let's just all go outside."

Jake knew me too well. I wasn't one to make a scene, and I noticed the shocked eyes of some of the guests who were next to the bathroom; I wanted this public display to end.

I brusquely pulled my arm from Jake's hand, hurting myself a bit in the process. I winced in pain but held my ground and proceeded to the exit, taking deep breaths to try to slow my heartrate. As I went down the stairs, I felt Jake's possessive arm around my waist again.

I pushed him, but he wasn't budging. Perhaps it was the fact that I almost missed my step that tipped him off, but I didn't care; I didn't need his help.

Jake's car was outside, the driver's door open. Clearly, he had told the valet not to touch it. Mike's car was right behind as we had the valet go get it when we paid the bill. Jake, without hesitation, went straight to Mike's car and ordered that they open the truck. I turned to Mike and hugged him.

"I have to deal with this brute. I need those records. I will call you tomorrow," I whispered in his ears.

"Are you sure?" he insisted, looking suspiciously at Jake behind me, his usually soft eyes filled with concern.

"Yes, it's okay. My parents are also in his house, and they would freak out if I just left like this anyways," I reassured Mike.

"Okay, call me," insisted Mike as he let go of my hands.

I turned around, and without even a glance at Jake, found the courage to put one leg in front of the other and climbed into the passenger seat.

He closed my door and immediately got into the driver's seat. He slammed the gas pedal, and in a few seconds, we were out of the restaurant parking lot and speeding through the dark night and the empty road, on our way to his house.

"Put your seatbelt on," he hissed between his teeth. I rolled my eyes. "Don't make me put it for you," he warned.

I held back a retort and fastened my seatbelt, not looking at him. I needed his help to eventually destroy him, so for now, I needed to behave.

Plus, I was doing my best to keep a cool demeanor, but my chest was pounding, my belly still in knots. My hands were damp again, and I could feel a bit of humidity down my spine; I never sweat.

Was I having a panic attack?

I needed to get myself under control. I wouldn't give him the satisfaction.

We both stayed silent the whole way home, the tension between us building louder than words.

I rehearsed so many times what to say during this drive, how to ask for the data without explaining why I needed it, but I couldn't utter the words, I couldn't focus. The idea of even talking to him was painful.

I looked at him a few times on the side, all I saw was a wall made of contracted muscles and white knuckles. I could feel his anger boiling all the way to my seat. I tried my best to fuel my hatred, to turn my heart into stone, to see him as a tool, but I couldn't help but be aroused by his smell, memories of his hands over me warming me up, having my skin crawl again, for different reasons than earlier.

My heart was pumping so fast I was afraid he could hear it. I dived into our memories together, revisiting some of our memories, some of his body language through different lenses. His hesitation, his snarky remarks and at times cold behavior.

It all made sense now. Everything I didn't quite grasp the past few months, the uneasy feeling I had since the reception at my parents' house. My gut tried to warn me. but I missed it, or rather, I ignored it, lost in the depth of his ocean gaze instead. My alleged culpability was always in the back of his head, tainting our every interaction. He had never been honest, likely calculating our every exchange.

Jake came to a halt once we got in front of the house. He turned off the car and removed his seatbelt.

After a few seconds, when neither of us got out of the car, I leaned a bit to look at him. He just stayed there, silent, looking in front of him, his hands resting on the door and on the stick shift, as if unsure he wanted this to be our stop.

He looked troubled.

I resisted the urge to take his hand, to touch his neck, his hair, to try to soothe him, to convince him I was innocent; to convince him I didn't fool him.

But he didn't deserve it.

"I need your help," I finally managed to say, swallowing hard.

He crooked his head slightly in my direction. I tried to ignore those now almost gray eyes reminding me of a storm and stared at his hand clammed to the stick shift instead.

"I need to find the log information for any laptops sent to the IT department for the past three years."

"What for?" he asked.

"I want to know who else had access to my laptop."

I decided to be generic, to just ask for three years of information instead of specifying dates. I wasn't sure that was enough to not tip off Jake as to what I needed, but there was no other way to give him an explanation he would accept.

"That's your defense? Someone else used your laptop, every time?"

He let out a cruel laugh and shook his head.

I bit my lip to stop from telling him to go fuck himself. I lifted my gaze to meet his. His jaw tightened, and the gray in his blue eyes darkened further.

"Yes," I admitted.

He sighed and opened the door to step out of the car. I hesitated but followed. He was almost at the stairs by the time I caught up with him and grabbed his arm.

"Please," I begged, my voice slightly quivering. I cursed myself for it.

He stopped walking and focused on the part of his arm I was holding. His nose flared as he slowly turned to face me, removing my hand.

"You are not going to waste my time here, Chloe, it won't help you."

"I am not trying to buy time," I retorted, "I am trying to prove the truth. That I didn't do this. And the least you can do is give me a chance to defend myself before you ruin my life even further than you already have."

My voice wavered at the last sentence; I said too much, but it was too late. I could feel a tingle behind my eyes and could only pray he didn't see it. I opened them wider in a desperate attempt to hold back the tears I could feel prickling. It didn't matter if he knew I was hurting, but I didn't mean to admit it. I didn't want to show weakness.

"Also," I added quickly, to save face, "I assume you found a way to my laptop, didn't you? To get the 'incriminating evidence' you needed?" I pushed, putting air quotes around the words. "To find those emails I supposedly sent. When did you do it? In Chicago, in my house? Is that why you came to see me? Oh, better yet, our first night here? Is that why you slept with me in the first place? For access?"

Jake's gritted his teeth, his head shaking just a bit, his blue eyes still growing a darker gray. I kept waiting for him to answer, but he didn't.

He just stood stiffly, searching my now wet eyes. I could hear his accelerated breathing matching mine.

I worried he could hear the turmoil currently taking place inside of me. His silence said it all.

"That's what I thought," I paused. "Well, if you could do that to me, so could someone else."

"No."

He paused and swallowed hard.

"Not unless you shared your proprietary passcode, not just the one to access the laptop. No one else has that one, not even the IT team."

I sighed. I so wanted to convince him it wasn't me; to remove the accusations I saw in his gaze, to stop feeling like he was stabbing me every time he looked at me.

But if I convinced him, I reminded myself, I wouldn't be able to wave my victory in his face later. I had to focus on that hatred to fuel my fire, to ignore the pain and the pit in my stomach.

"Then if you are so sure it's me," I added, resigned, "there's no harm in giving me the information I'm asking for. It's not like I can go get it as you've instructed me to stay here and be your prisoner, and believe it or not, I don't want to jeopardize the chances of finding the real traitor. It's not in my best interest."

I held his gaze defiantly, even as I felt my eyes fill and my heart swell.

"Fuck. Chloe, I…"

Jake took a few steps in my direction. He was a lion getting too close to his prey, for the prey's sake. Jake stopped in front of me and shook his head, almost to himself.

"Fine," he conceded.

I wanted to reach out to him, one more time, touch his face, now so close to mine, kiss him, ask that he believe me, beg even, but that wasn't our only issue.

The other one was now standing on top of the stairs, wearing a short pink silk robe that was only appropriate for a bedroom date. Jake followed my gaze and turned around.

I used that moment of distraction to sprint past him and finish going up the stairs. I had gotten what I wanted; we had nothing else to talk about, all I could do now was go to bed and try desperately to sleep.

"He is all yours. You two deserve each other," I said as I passed by my cousin, looking straight ahead of me as I headed straight to my room.

CHAPTER 31

I COULDN'T SLEEP, I had a throbbing headache, the type I got when I was under a lot of stress. So instead, I sat at the desk and started analyzing the lists of all the people who had attended both my parties and my parents'.

Thankfully, the lists only had twenty people in common, including me. I then proceeded to eliminate anyone who didn't have access to my building. Someone internal was the only explanation I could muster, for how someone had managed to get my laptop from the IT department to send the first email. My list was now down to seven:

1. Me

2. Dad

3. Kyle

4. Gerard (the CTO)

5. Carl

6. Linda

7. Richard (the IP lawyer)

I opened my laptop to check meeting attendees for September 20th and September 21st. Unfortunately, there was a board meeting on the 20th, so as is custom, everyone had been in the office, so there was no way to reduce that list further, outside of the overlaps between the lists.

I had now five suspects, with Carl potentially eliminated since he hadn't been in the office that Friday. Kyle, even if I didn't believe him capable of betraying my father, had to remain on the list. I felt a bit guilty, feeling as if I was as bad as Jake accusing me of a minute, but it would be stupid to remove someone from the list just because I thought I knew them well. You never know.

I then started creating profiles on my personal laptop for each of my suspects, using everything I could find on them on the internet. I wanted to remind myself of previous jobs, hobbies, country clubs, sports, any information I could gather and any connections to Green Mile.

I also separately started a list of all directors and officers of that company. Using LinkedIn, I also tried to get other high-level employees who would be good target audience for someone to provide that type of confidential information to. It needed to be someone who could use the information and who could make the company use it in a way that wasn't too suspicious.

Perhaps someone who had an IP expertise to make it believable that they could have created the technical data, the compilation method, the drawings and the process they had used in the e-axles. The information that had been passed on was highly technical in nature. The idea was to see if any of the people on that list had any connections to anyone on the other list, if they went to the same country club, used to be coworkers or anything along those lines.

What I needed from Jake was a list of anyone who went into the IT offices on September 20th and September 21st, and anyone who called for IT services would be useful. Right after exiting the elevator to that floor, one needed to swipe their ID to get in.

Of course, if someone was in front of a person they would be nice enough to keep the door open for them, but if someone on my list had gone to the IT offices that day, that would be good circumstantial evidence.

I also created a new email on my private laptop using an encrypted messaging system Mike had made me install. He had made me change my passwords to all laptops, emails, confidential data access etc. I sent him an email with all the information I had gathered, explaining that I had a lot more work to do there.

It was three in the morning when I started feeling sleepy. I hadn't realized how much time I had spent working on my lists and profiles. I had been so busy thankfully, that if there had been any noise from Jake's room, I hadn't heard it. I undressed and got into bed, my body aching from sitting at the desk for so long, my mind plotting ways to torture Jake, my heart, silently bleeding.

That's the thing with love. It doesn't just dissolve because you have been harmed, because the one you trusted trampled on your heart. It gets meddled with sadness, misery, agony, all present due to such love.

You don't stop loving the one who hurt you; you just suffer more than someone who never loved.

You. Just. Suffer.

PART 2

CHAPTER 32

Jake

WOULD I LET THE fear of misunderstanding cripple me? Or would I straighten my back, take a deep breath, and stick to my guns?

"Thank you so much for having us," said Philip, bringing me back to reality.

"It's my pleasure."

I shook the hand George was offering. I wished that Lauren would leave with her parents, but she was still here, clutching at my arm as I stood by the front door, saying my goodbyes to the guests as they left. It had been a long weekend, but she didn't seem fazed.

"We had a great time," said Philip as he leaned for a pat on the back, his daughter and wife behind him.

I glanced at Chloe as she was hugging her mother goodbye. She had taken me by surprise this Sunday morning, when she showed up for brunch, her face radient, in this frustratingly flattering gold skirt and silky white t-shirt that were driving me crazy. I hated how my body reacted to hers whenever she was near, as if she was a magnet I couldn't help being pulled to.

"Are you sure you don't want to come with us?" inquired her mother one last time.

I couldn't help but notice the concern in Yasmin's voice, and the worried gaze Chloe gave me even if just for a second.

"Yes, Mom, I'm good. Jake and I have some work to do, and it's just easier if we finish it today. I'll call you when I'm back."

Yasmin hesitated but let go of Chloe's hands and thanked me for having them over, before grabbing her husband's arm. I wondered how much Yasmin knew. Philip hadn't told her anything, but I couldn't say the same for Chloe. She had been cold with me since Friday, so she must have known something.

"Well, that was fun!" exclaimed Lauren as I closed the door.

"I'll be in my room," quickly added Chloe as she stomped off towards the staircase.

I ignored the discomfort I felt every time she was away from me.

"Meet me in my office in twenty minutes," I ordered.

Chloe stopped in her tracks, her shoulders stiff. She inhaled sharply and continued her walk, never turning back.

"Do you really have to work?" pouted Lauren.

"Yes, thus why I asked you to leave earlier." I was growing a bit impatient.

"Don't be rude," she chided as she kissed my cheek.

I tried to be cordial, feeling some guilt over my tone. Lauren was undoubtedly one of the most attractive women I had been with, and there had been many, but she bored me to death.

We had been on and off for a few years now, breaking it off every time I felt like she was getting too attached to me. I had kept coming back though, falling for her advances every now and then. It was easy; she was beautiful, it wasn't exclusive, and I had needs.

But things had gotten a bit complicated when I made the mistake of letting Chloe crawl under my skin. Now I found myself encouraging Lauren just a bit, as her presence helped me restrain myself from going to Chloe's room, asking for forgiveness, and ravaging her until the ache she had unleashed in me was satiated. I needed all the help I could get in that department.

I hadn't pushed back when Lauren had called to invite herself to my house for the weekend, and now she was here, unwilling to leave even after I told her she should, and even after I reminded her that we weren't and would never be a couple.

"I'll see you for dinner, okay?"

Lauren perked up at my words and kissed me.

"I'd better get ready then!" she squealed as she ran to her bedroom to get ready.

It was only 2 p.m. I realized, but I knew Lauren would take all afternoon to get ready. That was the type of life she led, and while there was nothing wrong with that, I needed more from the person I would call a partner in my life.

I shoved my right hand in my pocket and pulled my phone out as I marched to my office and shut the door behind me. I headed straight to the display of scotch bottles I had spread on the bar next to my desk and poured myself a glass, neat. I chugged it, enjoying the distraction of the burn as the liquid went down my throat. I poured myself another one.

How had everything gotten so convoluted in the span of just a few months? When Philip had walked into my office earlier in the year, I had refused to do the job myself. After all, my private investigation company was successful enough that I rarely handled any of the work personally.

I had fell into the PI profession by accident. It all started early in my twenties, when I had decided to find my father. I looked for the man for months, honing computer skills I didn't know I had, until I found him all the way in Europe. I had flown to see him, only to discover that he had formed a new family, away from my brother and I. I flew back to Chicago and never looked back. I also never told my mother. I didn't need her to suffer more than she had. All I took from that mess was the realization that

I had a knack to find was was meant to be secrets, to stay hidden. And secrets were an invaluable currency.

My company got successful and was what had gotten me the capital I needed for creating my PE empire, and now I focused my time on running my private equity firm instead. I just ran the PI company as a side business. I managed it, but I didn't go on assignments myself anymore. That was the task of the team of highly skilled spies and investigators I had trained and put in place, after all.

But Philip had pulled at my heart strings, and I eventually accepted to roll my sleeves and oversee that one personally, as a favor to him, in honor of our years of friendship.

At the time, it seemed like a straightforward case of insider trading, a problem that normally wouldn't take more than a couple of months before we would discover the culprit, and based on my experience, it was usually a family member or a trusted employee.

How was I supposed to predict that Chloe would get in my way and cloud my judgement as she did? I had a reputation for being great at my job, efficient, to the point, and unwavering.

But Chloe had put those rules of practice in danger with every sensual smile, every infuriating eye roll, every lift of her defiant chin, every sexy lip bite, every step she took when she strutted away from me in those deviant red soles of hers.

I should have known she'd be trouble since that first night at the bar when we met, when I saw her in that revealing little black cloth she wore for a dress. It had been a coincidence, but I had recognized her the second I laid eyes on her.

After all, I ran a background check on every high-level employee at Motor Holmes as part of my diligence. Even then, I had noticed her beauty, but pictures were nothing compared to seeing her standing there that night.

I hadn't been able to stay away, especially after she had put herself in harm's way like that, getting drunk with her friends in that little fucking dress, unaware of the fucking predators in the room.

I smirked at the memory of her shocked expression at her father's house the next day, when she realized who I was. God, she was beautiful in that dress, sensual, regal almost, and I had felt the air leave my lungs when she waltzed in.

She had impressively kept her composure then, even if I saw the fire in her eyes as I enjoyed provoking her further with the dance. It had been an excuse to get my hands on her again, against my better judgement.

One had to be in control of their emotions to maneuver what she had pulled off. I combed my fingers through my hair aggressively, enrobed in the dark thoughts and the ire I felt but unable to control my body's reaction to thinking of her.

Even after she used me the way she did.

The woman had slowed my investigation down. She distracted me in the office on a daily basis, contradicting me every time she could, and those eyes, driving me to forget any decorum or reservation I had that night at her parents' house. And then in California. I knew I had taken a big risk going with her to that conference, aware I could barely control himself around her.

But I had convinced myself that I needed to go, gain her trust a bit more, try to see if she could provide any useful information to my still fruitless investigation. All my resolves, all my defense mechanisms, went away when I understood what Paul had done to her, after I had shamefully let my jealousy get the best of me and insulted her.

When I saw the fear in her eyes, her tears completely destroying my heart, there wasn't a force alive that would have been able to keep me away from her. Not even my job or my integrity.

I had even forgotten about my sore knuckles after the punches I had landed on Paul and his friend. When I got back to Chicago after that trip,

I had made sure to blacklist their company and the both of them on the market, so they'd never get hired in corporate America again.

Men who tried to abuse women, and those who were complicit, had no place in any industry, and with all the information I had gathered on them, they were doomed to fail in any business endeavor they tried to undertake.

Being in the PI world came with a few perks, especially after over ten years in the business. I had access to the most powerful people in the world. It didn't hurt that some of them owed me a few favors.

I had been enjoying Chloe's company more than I had any women before her, and I had to admit how disconcerting that was.

Her wit, her intelligence, the glimmer in her eyes, and the slight purse of the right side of her lips when she knew she was winning a negotiation, her sense of humor, the way she carried herself, all had plucked at my usual composure little by little until I caved.

It took me and my team longer than it should have to realize that she was behind the information leak. After all, I knew from experience that those closest to you were the most likely to abuse your trust. I had seen it time and time again. Siblings stabbing each other in the back, children robbing their parents of their money because they dared cut them off to teach them to be self-sufficient.

When someone came to my company for private investigation services, it was never a good thing. It generally meant that someone had betrayed someone else. It made me a witness to the worst people had to offer.

From an early age, I learned that people were unreliable and often would let you down. When my father walked out on our family, I finally understood how selfish people could truly be.

Yet, with Chloe, I couldn't discern between reality and the fantasy world that we created. She had muddled my process and distracted me from my mission.

Her sweet pussy was my undoing. It may have seemed like I was in control of the situation, but Chloe was the one holding the reins.

But by the time Chloe organized that brunch for her father, I had caved and couldn't avoid touching her in her home at the party. Then I felt like I had been sucker punched in the gut when I got the call, that Kyle, the one person I thought for sure was the culprit was innocent, I panicked. Because Chloe hadn't been cleared yet.

I didn't want to believe she was involved in this, but the facts told a whole other story.

So, that day I put my walls back up. I wanted to finish my investigation first, find the asshole so that I didn't fall for her too hard before knowing the whole truth.

I gave the order for my team to find a time to get her laptop and investigate further. But California had changed everything. I was weak, and I fell for her tricks.

Chloe hadn't grown up with a silver spoon, I knew that. But she had obviously grown accustomed to it and had decided that she needed to get more of it from an early age. According to Lauren, she had stolen from her parents before.

She had also acted very suspiciously a few times, including when we were going to California. She closed her laptop nervously every time I was around her, but I chose to ignore all the evidence that was clearly in front of me the whole time. That was until I got to see those emails on her laptop with my own eyes on Friday, after I finally allowed myself to betray her trust one more time, just to take her off the list of suspects.

The plan was to tell her the truth afterwards and pray to God she would forgive me.

It turned out, she was the one who needed to beg for forgiveness. Not only was she the culprit, but in those emails, she admitted to knowing who I was from the get-go and purposely manipulating me to get her way.

I rolled my fingers into fists at the thought, chugging another glass of scotch.

I fucking fell for it. I had fought battles, I had killed and been shot at in my line of work, but I was fooled but a 5'3" brunette in high heels.

I grunted, upset at myself for letting this go so far, letting her use me and cloud my judgement so easily.

I moved to my chair, sat down, and fired up my computer. I needed to do something. Anything to calm the rage that rose inside of me just thinking of her laughing behind my back with who knows who.

A few minutes later, I heard a knock and checked my watch. Right on time, of course.

"Come in."

Chloe marched in, her defiant chin already raised towards me, those dark brown eyes breathing fire in my direction.

I ignored the blade that twisted in my stomach at the look of hatred in her eyes, hatred I had put in there.

Hatred that I needed to feel towards her. Good, I thought, I could feed off it.

"You summoned me," she followed, looking irritated that I was wasting her time.

I clenched my jaw and slowly stood up, not taking my eyes off her. Hers looked red, as if she had been crying.

"I thought about your request from last night."

I noticed her holding her breath.

God, she was confusing. I needed her to act guilty, to stop inciting doubt when all the evidence pointed out to her for Christ's sake.

All the emails were from her computer. My team had checked everyone else's, lifted every rock we could think of. I had reserved her laptop for last, contrary to my better judgement, desperately wanting the facts to absolve her, but it was as transparent as water that her email, her laptop, and her passwords had been used multiple times to send confidential documents to their competitor.

To let them know she had me wrapped around her little finger. And even now, she fucking did.

"And?" I picked up on the slight shake of her voice.

"I will give you the information you asked for."

After going back and forth, I decided that I had nothing to lose letting her see it. She was adamant at proving her alleged innocence, and well, if there was even a sliver of a chance that she had been played as she claimed, I wouldn't stop her. I couldn't.

Because even if I didn't believe her, some very small part of me was having trouble reconciling the woman I had gotten to know with the type of person who would do something like that to their family. Even with all this evidence against her.

Plus, she was as stubborn as it got, and I didn't want her snooping and asking questions that would tip others of my investigation, especially if she was right that someone was setting her up.

Doubtful, considering the personal detail of the last communication, but my stupid self still hoped, still wanted the evidence to be wrong.

A pitiful part of me still wanted to think that she actually had felt something for me.

My gut had seriously failed me on this one. I was simply having a hard time admitting that to myself.

"Thank you," she breathed out. "Where are the files?"

I proceeded to the double doors on the right side of my desk and swung them open. She followed me inside. It was a small continuation of my library, with my most precious book collection. On the rectangular oak table in the middle were piles and piles of documents, along with a single laptop with a USB next to it.

Chloe was speechless for a few seconds, but as I expected, that didn't last long.

"Jesus, and here I thought you would make it easy."

"Welcome to my world, sweetheart."

She squeezed her eyes shut for a second, and I took pity on her.

"All the information is also on the USB," I added, trying to help.

"I assume I am not allowed to take any of those documents with me?"

"No. Or the laptop or the USB. You are limited to this room. You can take notes. And no, you can't have your phone with you in here either."

She flinched.

"Bastard," she whispered loud enough for me to hear.

I grabbed her arm and forced her to turn around and face me.

"You are lucky I am indulging your silly little task when we both know you did it, Chloe. Don't provoke me."

I was saying that more for my sake at this point. As a reminder that she was never mine. She fucking played me.

She was about to speak but held back. Her stare, her nose flare, were filled with disdain and disgust. It was torture to see so much darkness in her eyes, those eyes that just a few days before had longingly looked at me and asked that I took her and made her come all over me on my yacht.

My body ached for hers. I wanted to lift her up, pull that silky skirt up, and fuck her sweet little cunt until the pain in her eyes was flushed out by the waves of pleasure I knew I could give her. I scratched my throat, trying to control the ache I felt. I had to remind myself.

I didn't mean anything to her.

She was just playing me.

And boy, did she do it well.

"That's what I thought," I added at her silence.

I searched her eyes for a few more seconds before I exited the room, shutting the door behind me, unable to stand the cold stare she gave me any longer.

I paced aggressively in my office, raking my fingers through my hair incessantly, trying to calm down. Of course I had an erection, getting in the way of intelligent and effective thought process.

But I allowed myself to doubt. What if she wasn't lying, what if my first instinct was right? What if her only crime had been perhaps being careless enough to let someone steal her passcodes? What if she had been set up and the real culprit was roaming free in the enterprise? What if my team had left some stones unturned?

I felt like my objectivity had been compromised, unsure if my doubt were rational or due to bias, because deep down, I wanted her to be innocent. I wanted to believe that those eyes had been truthful to me.

I wanted to believe that she was really mine.

I proceeded to my basement. I had another more rustic office there. It's where I kept my surveillance and security tapes, but I had put another war room overnight there so I could review all the documents my team prepared, not with the approach of finding where the information had come from, but to find out who would have been able to set her up like this. Of course, I also had installed hidden cameras in the office spaces upstairs to surveil her as she went through the files.

I sighed, my anger leaving a little place for hope, hope that she was innocent, hope that this was a misunderstanding, hope that I had meant something to her. Even though, if I was wrong, if she was telling the truth, I didn't know if she would ever forgive me.

CHAPTER 33

Chloe

It had been over four hours since I sat on that chair in his office, searching through a painful number of reports and documents. It took me a while to get used to the formatting and come up with a more efficient system to go through the information. After three hours, I was able to go faster and rely on specific IT terms to search the logs more efficiently. But I needed a break, as the words were starting to blend in front of my eyes.

I couldn't believe he had caved and allowed me access to all the IT files as well as the building and floor swipes, considering how convinced he seemed that I was the criminal. Perhaps he was starting to realize that there was a chance I was in fact innocent.

Otherwise, why waste time instead of going directly to my dad?

What I needed was the information, as soon as possible, to be able to get out from the hell I was in.

I knew I at least had good circumstantial evidence of my innocence, thanks to Mike, but that wasn't enough. It was personal at this point, not just because Jake was accusing me but because someone had deliberately set me up, making me look naïve and stupid, two things I didn't tolerate.

Someone had accessed my laptop in my own home, under my nose. That person had found out Jake's identity somehow, and knew something was going on between us. That person knew I was a suspect and laid the groundwork to make sure there was no doubt that it was me. And I wouldn't feel at peace until I found out who from my short list of overlapping guests had done this.

I finally surrendered at 11 p.m. and slowly rose from the chair, taking only my tablet with me.

It was late Sunday night, and all I wanted to do was curl up in bed, let my brain get some rest while it also continued to process how my life got ruined in the blink of an eye.

I woke up at 6 a.m., spending an hour on the phone with Mike explaining what I had done so far and getting tips on efficiency. I then confirmed Keisha was still able to watch my little bundle of joy for me. I took a quick ten-minute shower, slid on a pair of black leggings and my most comfortable white crop top, coupled with black tennis shoes with no laces. I tied my hair in a comfortable loose ponytail and headed down.

Thankfully there was no one in the kitchen, so I stole myself a cup of coffee, black as I didn't want to waste time looking for milk or cream.

I headed straight to Jake's office, taking a deep breath, my shoulders more relaxed when I realized he wasn't there. It didn't mean he wasn't somewhere in the house, but at least he was leaving me in peace so I could gather data.

I picked up where I left off. I had tried to gather random information on other laptops and other days to see if there was a pattern but that had been pointless, so I focused on what I did know. I gathered the names of all

100 plus employees who had entered the building on September 20th and 21st.

I began adding the information on which floors the individuals from my more limited list, who also appeared on the list of employees that entered the building that day, had swiped. I flagged anyone whose name also appeared on the list of employees who entered the building that day who wouldn't normally have a reason to go on my floor.

I then used the employee roster to search if any of the IT employees had visited any executive floors that day, especially floors where the people on my limited list had offices.

Then, I proceeded to zoning in on laptop repairs lists, as every time an employee brought a laptop to the IT department, there was a log created. I couldn't find the entry to my laptop work, even if I did bring it to the IT department.

I knew Max had been the one to check it in for me, but I couldn't find that anywhere in the records, adding Max to my list of suspects, as someone who could potentially be helping one of the higher up executives from my roster.

The list of people who had brought their laptops for work or for which a log had been created wasn't particularly helpful.

I started seeing a light in the tunnel around 1 p.m. when I managed to find an entry for the loaner laptop I had received.

My head whipped up when I heard the main office door open and close. My spine tensed, as I heard steps come to a stop in front of the internal door. I watched the doorknob twist, and of course, without knocking, Jake walked in, wearing dark blue jeans, a black cardigan over a white shirt, his hair a bit disheveled.

Agitated, stressed, and tired, I just stared at him.

"What do you want?" I snapped.

"You need a break," he announced matter of factly.

"I will take one when I want to take one."

He let out an exasperated sigh, taking me by surprise. Why was he the one stressed out? After all, he wasn't the one falsely accused of stealing from his family. By someone he trusted, no less.

"Look," I said, standing up, "the sooner I can get through those stupid files, the sooner I can get out of this place, and you never have to see me again. So please let me be; I am a grown up. I don't need you to tell me when I need a fucking break."

I felt blood rush in all directions in my body, my legs suddenly feeling weak.

His jaw pulsed as he closed the small space between us, worry darkening his eyes for a second. My heart jolted at his sudden proximity, my hands holding on to the desk for support.

I had been glued to the chair for eight hours straight, and my body was catching on to that now that he distracted me. I felt debilitated, fueled by wrath and exasperation. My toes felt cold, my hands slightly shaking, nothing left to help create any of my usual composed filters.

"I need you to eat something."

I spun my head suddenly towards his, my eyes dilated with anger and stress. He clenched his jaw, his usual frown getting darker, his head shaking. I took a closer look, and I could have sown I saw worry torment his expression.

I sighed, reason peeking its way in. I had made good progress; I had good notes that I snapped shut so he couldn't take a look. A break would do me good so I could have the strength to continue for the rest of the day.

"Fine."

He let out a sigh of relief, seeming a bit disconcerted when I stared up at him again. I rolled my eyes, finding strength in my burning desire to get as far from him as I could. I grabbed my tablet and stomped aggressively passed him.

I came to stop when I reached his main office, grabbing the backpack I had left on the desk with my laptop and my phone in there.

I slid in my tablet and checked my phone. Nothing special had happened with work, and Mike had texted to ask how I was doing. Seeing his name made me smile, reminding me that I wasn't alone.

I lifted my head up when I heard a throat clear, darkened blue eyes staring at me, seemingly impatient or annoyed.

"Ready?" he asked.

"For?" I replied, one eyebrow up, prepared for war.

"We are going to a late lunch."

I laughed bitterly. "I'm not going anywhere with you."

"This isn't up for discussion. I gave the staff the day off, so there isn't anything to eat here."

"I'm sure we have leftovers." I shrugged.

"They took it with them. I am rarely here past the weekend," he explained at my confused gaze, "so I generally let them empty the fridge. Lorna can't stand it when food goes to waste."

I rolled my eyes. He grunted and took a step closer to me, standing right in front of me.

"I am going to need you to stop this," he said in what sounded like a threat.

"Or what?" I challenged, bending my head to the side.

He took one more step, his teeth clenched, and I could feel the heat radiating off him. My treacherous fingers itched to run through his wavy hair.

The standoff was officially making me wet, and I was beyond ready for him to take me right here.

I knew he was into punishment fucking. And I reveled when he punished me with rough sex. And when he praised me when he got what he wanted. But still, how could my body be so needy for him after all he had put me through?

My heartbeat accelerated and my lips parted as his gaze trailed down my face to them, his breathing matching mine. It was torture; I felt myself combust, but I couldn't move, my body wanting him to cave into me. But he grunted, took a step back, and marched to the door, a clear order for me to follow.

I wanted to fight him, torture him in the hope of inflicting on him a bit of the hurt I was feeling. I wanted to see if he cared, if all of this really did mean nothing to him. I wanted to understand if he found himself caught in an impossible situation, or if it had been just a game he set in motion to get close to me and get information, but there was no strength left in me.

I wiped the single frustrated tear that had found its way down my cheeks, took a deep breath, and followed.

We drove in silence as I spent most of the time on my phone, texting Mike, using anything I could to distract myself. Perhaps it was the lack of food from the day, but the smell of him was intoxicating, the bottom of my stomach in knots, wanting that hand which was currently tightly wrapped around the steering wheel to travel up my thighs instead.

I switched position as I felt a zing in my core. I noticed him flinch and turn his head towards me, but I ignored him, pretending to be consumed by my cell. We finally arrived at what looked like a seafood restaurant by the water.

I opened my door first, my backpack in hand, rushing to the entrance. I could hear him right behind me. He grabbed my arm to slow me down, his fingers feeling like hot metal against my skin. I jumped a bit but stayed in place as he gave his name to the host. He walked us to a table on their big deck, with the most gorgeous view of the lake.

If I wasn't so upset, I would have been able to enjoy the light breeze and the smell of water caressing my skin, working on appeasing my senses.

Perhaps that was why he took me here. We sat in front of each other. I dropped my bag on a chair and continued browsing my phone.

"Are you going to put that thing down?"

I slowly lifted my head, giving him a bored expression. I sighed, languidly setting my phone down on the table, and stared at him, hoping all my hostility was palpable, wanting to mask the pang in my heart, staring into the eyes of a man who had betrayed me.

He held my gaze as he ordered us some water, iced tea for me and two tuna and salmon entrees off the menu.

For as much as the waitress was trying to gain his attention, he didn't budge. I felt my insides heating up, but I wouldn't give him the satisfaction of breaking the silence first.

His gaze confused me in many ways, his blue eyes shadowed with more gray than usual, as if a cloud was looming over him.

No, it wasn't sadness I was detecting, it couldn't be, just pure coldness and evil, because that was who he was. The man who wanted to ruin everything I had worked so hard for with a vile rumor, but only after he had gotten inside of me, in more ways than one.

"Have you found anything useful so far?" Really? exasperated, I sighed deeply and shook my head.

"Not quite, but I am getting there."

"What does that mean?"

"It means I will find who did this, and when I do, I will destroy them, and I will ruin you for even thinking I could do this to my family, even if it's the last thing I do."

I hadn't meant to let those words out, but I had thrown decorum or diplomacy out of the window, choosing to nourish my resentment to mask the pain.

His jaw tightened but he laughed, a sparingly threatening sound that made my insides vibrate.

He wasn't a man who liked being challenged.

"And how do you plan on doing that?" he asked, with a smug expression I wished I could slice with my knife.

"It wouldn't be fun if I told you," I answered, a deviant smirk on my lips.

"Still. You *should* tell me," he challenged.

Thankfully, the waitress was back with some warm buns, butter, iced tea, and water. I took advantage of the interruption, sipping my drink out of the straw as calmly as I could without breaking eye contact.

I saw him shift in his seat a bit

I put my drink down and grabbed a bun, adding all the butter I could fit in, and biting into it. I wasn't sure what was going on, but I was clearly making him uncomfortable, his eyes darkening as he looked at me as a meal he was dying to taste.

I traced his gaze to my shirt. One strap was falling over one of my shoulders, showing a tad bit of cleavage. He might have used me, but his body wasn't indifferent to mine, that in itself was an asset.

I did not fix my shirt.

"I don't owe you any explanation, Jake. You didn't have any consideration towards me, so I don't see why I should have any towards you."

"Chloe," he added with a grunt, "if you let me help you..."

"I don't need you or your help. And while I appreciate you letting me use the files, you put me in that situation to begin with."

His face tensed as he straightened himself, putting his elbows on the table, his hands joined together in the middle. I shifted back and crossed my hands, not wanting our fingers to touch, suddenly aware of how small the table was.

"It's not personal. It was never meant to be personal."

He ran a frustrated hand through his hair.

"No? It feels pretty personal. And you're the one who made it so. You're the one who tried to play me in your little fucking plan. Tell me, did you come up with the story my dad gave me, about why he hired you? You did, right?"

"Yes," he admitted, "but you understand why my identity needed to be hidden. Otherwise, I can't do my job."

"Of course," I mocked. "And, let see, this event at your house this weekend, part of your conniving 'investigation' I assume? So you could spy on people, get what you want?"

He leaned back on his chair and crossed his arm.

"Yes."

"And it's still not personal, Jake?"

I heard the slight tremble in my voice, my broken heart trying not to cave in. I wouldn't let it.

"And I know you think I used you. I saw the email about us I supposedly sent, but I didn't send it. I didn't know who you were until I heard your conversation with my dad."

I paused, trying to control my emotions, but it was no use. I needed to be heard. I had nothing to lose.

"So, every single interaction I had with you had been honest. I am the one who got fooled. I am the one who got used, not you. And if there had been even a small chance to salvage this mess you made, any chance of me forgiving you for lying to me, with how you treated me during this trip, you ruined even that small sliver.

"I will never, ever forgive you for this. You made a mistake by not telling me who you were, but you made an even bigger mistake accusing me and treating me like a criminal. And if you ever even did have an ounce of feelings for me, when I do prove my innocence, you will regret what you did. And even then, I will never ever fucking forgive you."

His jaw flexed. His gaze was so intense I felt like it was burning right through me. But I ignored him. There was nothing left to say.

We continued the rest of the meal almost in silence, the awkwardness only interrupted by the excellent service. The waiter likely could feel the tension emanating from the table.

Once he paid the bill, we headed back to the house. In what was becoming our typical manner of parting, I bolted out of the car without a word and went straight back to his office, not losing sight of my task.

CHAPTER 34

Jake

I HIT THE STEERING wheel a few times, hoping the pain coursing through my hands would calm me down, trying to beat the urge I had to follow her up the stairs, pin her against the wall, and slam inside of her, releasing all the frustration and anger that had accumulated since my team confirmed where the emails had come from.

Her rejection, the way her nose pinched with disgust every time she looked at me, her words, it shouldn't hurt so much. I shouldn't feel like someone took a large knife and shoved it in my heart, I shouldn't feel this panic at losing someone I never really had.

But I did.

I felt every single one of her hate-filled glares or winces directed at me, and if she was innocent, I deserved every single one of them.

I had been honest earlier when I told her it wasn't meant to be personal. But she wasn't wrong; it had become so. I wouldn't be so fucking destroyed, I wouldn't be as livid as I was, I wouldn't feel as if someone had pulled my organs out with their bare hands if all I had found was the crime.

That would have been bad, but if I was honest with myself, if I dived deep down to my bare soul, what hurt like hell was the last email more than anything else. Where she admitted to having a relationship with whoever the fuck she was supplying the information to.

The words I had read *"Hope you're not jealous :) I can't wait to be with you. I miss you"* were seared into my memory.

If only I hadn't broken my own code of ethics and slept with one of the suspects, none of this would have gotten so complicated so fast.

I loved women, enjoyed their company more than most, but I had always managed to resist their charms.

But things were different with Chloe. She was gorgeous and sensual, with sexy curves that kept me awake more than once at night... but it was more than that.

It was that drive of hers I admired, her ambition, that innate thirst for success, the passion with which she undertook anything she spent her time on. It was the enjoyment I took in sitting back, captivated by how she worked a room, how I could see her brain going a thousand miles per hour, her words sometimes having trouble keeping up with her crazy brain.

She always seemed ahead in thought in any situation, her wit usually setting her apart from everyone else in the room. It was how she rolled her eyes and sighed when the world around her was going too slow for her. It was all those things that had brought me to my knees.

Now here I was, hitting on a fucking steering wheel to appease the torturous gut-ripping pain I felt at the fact that I had clearly hurt her, and she wanted nothing to do with me.

I finally left the car and headed to my other office, turning on my various screens. I had spent the day doing my best to work, fully aware that the little screen I used to spy on her was consuming most of my attention. Looking at her like this, focused, determined, searching for her salvation through pages and pages of data shook my convictions of her guilt even further.

Doubt—the enemy of success, crept its way inside of me deeper every time she sighed, ran her hand through her hair, or laid her head down on her arm on the table with a light scream.

I was the one doing that to her, to someone I had to admit whose existence had become an unhealthy and alarmingly concerning interest of mine. And she had barely eaten or drank anything, too absorbed by her task to care.

I had to step in and do something, thus the lunch. If that meant sitting across from her as I resisted the urge to take her into my arms and kiss her until she forgave me, to make sure that she ate something, so be it.

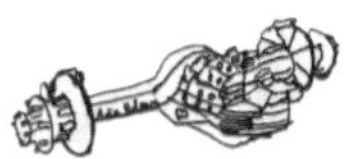

I managed to get a couple hours of work in until I heard a noise coming from my left screen. I stared at it, panicked at seeing her hold her face in both her hands, clearly crying, her shoulders vibrating with every sob.

I brought my hands into fists, my lips thinning unto a line, concern tearing my insides out. I got up to go to her, but as I got to the door, I hit it instead.

"Damn it!" What the fuck did I think I was going to do anyways? She fucking hated me.

I grabbed my phone and called Kushar, the second in command I had tasked to help me with this investigation.

"Hi, Chief," he answered on the second ring.

"I need you to see if you can find out if she had possession of her laptop every single time one of those emails were sent out."

"But Chief, clearly she did it, we discussed this just this morning. Some of those emails were sent when she wasn't even in the office, from her house."

"Look some more, Kushar. Something is off, I know it. Like I told you before, I need to be completely sure about those, no rocks left unturned. I need to know with absolute certainty that someone else is not setting her up."

"All her codes were used, codes no one else had access to..."

"I am asking you to do your job. Start giving me results, got it? Look. Again."

My cold tone could cut through stone. Kushar acquiesced immediately as I hung up the phone.

I couldn't shake the feeling that I was missing something, that although all the evidence pointed to her, her behavior wasn't consistent with her supposed guilt.

Kushar wasn't wrong. She seemed like the perfect candidate for this behavior based on my experience. She was very clearly living above her means, even though her father and her claimed he hadn't supported her financially since she got to college.

But even with her lawyer salary, and her now reduced in-house salary, she was either spending all she had, and potentially in debt, or she was relying on support in addition to her salary. Her wardrobe alone cost a small fortune. The woman rarely repeated an outfit.

Perhaps she grew desperate to maintain her lifestyle but keep her independence enough to steal from her own father. Kushar had showed me bank statements of hers, some of which showed hundreds of thousands of dollars transferred from an account he was working on tracing. How else could such transfers be explained if she didn't have another job?

Even with that, and the emails, I couldn't help but wonder if I had jumped the gun, telling her I knew she had done the deed, before I could double-check the work my employees had gathered. In my defense, I hadn't planned to.

Kushar had been working with me for years and had handled way more complicated and delicate tasks than this one, so I rarely had the need to double check his work or intervene in the past. He was my best employee after all.

But part of me felt like something was off. The woman I had gotten to know, the woman I had held in my arms, seen shine when she accomplished something, loving her parents without reserve, she couldn't betray her family like that, her own company, and to a certain extent, her inheritance.

I had been so angry and disappointed at both her and myself when Kushar broke into her laptop and found all the evidence, that when she eavesdropped on my conversation with Philip and I followed her to her room, I exploded on her and let it slip.

I had intended to keep cool and calm, and not say anything until I had no doubt whatsoever, but my personal interest in her clouded my judgment and I spoke too soon.

And there she was, spending two full days under my roof as I ordered, looking for ways to prove her innocence.

What if she was innocent?

What if she had been set up?

What if I was the fucking idiot who lost the best thing that ever happened to him?

"I will never ever fucking forgive you." Her words, they haunted me.

CHAPTER 35

Chloe

I spent the rest of Monday gathering more and more data. After I let myself have a breakdown, I felt a bit calmer and finally saw another light in the tunnel.

I searched more broadly for anyone who had brought anything to the IT department in the days around when I brought my laptop. That information brought some color to my data, including when such individuals swiped their cards back again on another floor or to exit the building.

I had a growing suspicion since creating my original list, based on overlapping parties, but I was not one to jump to conclusions. I wouldn't be any better than Jake if I did that. But my results were creating what I was starting to see as a clear picture.

It was 2 a.m. when I finally realized I had spent over eight hours sitting at the desk again. But considering the data I had gathered on my tablet, it was all worth it. Assuming Mike agreed with my analysis, I had a culprit, and I was going to destroy him, along with Jake.

I got up, grabbed my tablet, and stepped out to the main office while yawning. I placed my tablet in my backpack, held it by the handle, and turned off all the lights before I stepped out.

I held a scream as I almost ran into a dark figure that appeared in front of me. I looked up to see icy blue eyes staring at me, arms holding me to keep my balance. My body heated up, his touch sending shivers all the way down my spine as I instinctively held my breath, confused between my need for him and my desire to crush him, to get revenge.

He got closer and slowly ran his hands down my arm, accelerating my heartbeat, goosebump raising on my skin.

"Chloe…"

Alarmed at my body's still ridiculous reaction to him, I aggressively pulled my arms away and ran towards the stairs, all the way to my room.

As I closed and locked the door behind me, I started pacing, hands trembling, ordering myself to simmer down, and remember that no matter how much I yearned for him, he was the enemy, and I needed to show him no mercy, even if every fiber of my being vibrated with need when I was in his presence. Even if I missed him with everything I was.

While I felt a bit guilty for sleeping in the next morning, in the house of my nemesis, I thought, after my discoveries of the yesterday, I deserved a little rest.

I spent an hour on the phone with Mike before I finally made it downstairs, in the best of spirits. Mike agreed with my hypothesis. Knowing that I had my freedom in my hands was what I needed to leave this prison. I was still going to spend the day digging some more, looking for more proof in case I missed anything, trying to prove my conclusion in more ways than one if I could.

I had another plan in mind. I needed to steal the USB. While I had the useful information written, I wanted all the files with me so Mike could do his own deep dive.

I found a Dunkin Donuts caramel iced latte with a warm and toasted everything bagel at the desk. My heart skipped a beat, but I refused to let any emotions take over, not appeased simply because he brought me one of my cheat day meals. But after staring at the bagel for all of two minutes, my stomach was making me quite aware that I skipped dinner the night before.

I caved and devoured the bagel as I did my happy dance while sipping the deliciousness in my mouth. This nightmare was close to being over, and I felt so much lighter.

CHAPTER 36

Jake

A SMALL SMILE OF relief and satisfaction tugged at my lips as I watched her eat her bagel, making that little dance I had found so adorable the few times I caught her doing it in the office.

One of my favorite things about her was her excitement for food. I knew tempting her with her favorite coffee and bagel would force her to eat. I hesitated to leave it on the desk, but I knew she would likely refuse to take it from me if I brought it to her myself.

I was concerned because I knew she sometimes skipped meals—so absorbed in her research and trying to prove her innocence—and the bags under her eyes seemed to be getting darker by the day. She was stressed, nervous and so angry, all because of me. Even if she was guilty, it still tugged at me to see her like this.

She seemed to be in better spirits this morning, though, which led me to believe she had found something. I could ask her to share, but I had a feeling she wouldn't go down so easy.

I called my team, but they only had useless updates. If she found something, I was relying on them to also find it. And I knew they would. I just had to be patient—and watch her like a hawk in the meantime.

Around 1 p.m., I decided to bring her a burger, hoping to bribe her into feeding herself again. When I opened the door to the room she was in, I saw her back stiffen, her smile disappearing, as cold brown eyes stared at me with contempt.

It tugged at me, but there was nothing I could do about it.

"I brought you food."

She sighed and rolled her eyes, giving me one of those sarcastic lip twitches I knew so well. "Thanks."

She grabbed the bag I handed her and dropped it on the floor next to her. I clenched my teeth, annoyance starting to take over. I decided to leave her alone, avoiding a fight.

As I got back to my office, I noticed that she had left her station. I could still hear her laughter though, so I knew she was in one of the monitored rooms. I switched the view on the camera to the main office.

There she was, leaning on my desk, phone to her ear. She laughed out loud again, the sound of pure happiness I had so enjoyed in some of our more friendly chats.

"Mike, no! Come on, please don't do that!" she squealed, laughter making her lean her head back.

I tensed instantly, thick black jealously coursing through my veins. Of course, she was talking to Mike. I had investigated him once I realized he was in her life. But the timing of when they met saved him from also being a suspect. He had become her confidante during this whole investigation, and it wasn't fair, but I couldn't stand it.

She stayed on the phone for another twenty minutes with that fucking guy. I did my best to focus on my other work but was unable to take my eyes off the screen for more than a minute at a time.

It irritated me that they had grown so close. She had even tried to share a room with that man, in my fucking house. I would have cut Mike's arm before letting him lay a finger on her, under my roof, next to my room. Mike had been lucky Lorna stepped in and offered him one of the other rooms, because I was ready to tell him to sleep in his car.

I managed to focus again when she finally went back to the room. Unfortunately, almost every hour, she came back out to check her phone, smiling and giggling at whatever text messages she was so frantically responding to. It was clear that she was in the middle of a fun conversation, probably still with Mike.

I hated admitting how much it bothered me. When I saw them at the restaurant the other day, it took all the strength I had in me not to punch Mike's head into a wall for daring to ever touch her and trying to remove her from my house.

Rights be dammed, but even if she was a potential criminal, I would not allow another man to have her. I couldn't.

Around 7 p.m., I decided to go back to my office. She was finally done with all those phone charades but still hadn't touched the burger.

I was getting worried about her again; I couldn't help it. I entered the room as she was closing the laptop in front of her, her tablet safely tucked under her right arm.

"Done for the day?" I asked carefully.

"I am," she answered, a yawn coming from her lips.

She had opted for a more comfortable look instead of her usual style of high heels and top-end fashion. While she looked damn good in those outfits, that one hugged every curve just right, and I couldn't help but remember how my hands were tracing those curves just days ago.

"Do you need anything?" she asked, clearly growing impatient.

"You didn't eat. It's time for dinner."

"Christ! I had better things to do, Jake, like trying to free myself from this fucking prison you have me in."

"Yeah? Is that why you spent most of your time on the phone, laughing all day at God knows what?"

I didn't mean to say that, but I did, and now she was staring at me with rounded eyes, understanding the implications of my confession.

"Of course, of course you are spying on me. Are there cameras in my bedroom too? Do you fucking touch yourself watching me shower?" She took a step closer to me, her hands slightly shaking. I ignored the jab.

"You didn't think I'd leave you here alone without supervision, did you?"

"Oh, of course not, since you don't trust me. And this is your job, right? Spying? Tell me, did you have me surveilled?"

Her cheeks were red, her eyes dark with fury.

I stayed silent, my lips thin, raking frustrated fingers through my hair. My lack of a response was louder than words. There was no point in lying to her.

She was on the list. The team followed protocol. I didn't have to disclose that I personally stalked her social media. Or covered the shift the night she went to Mike's house. That I called her that night, willing to risk it all to keep her from him. That I knew she spent the night in his fucking house, that sleep didn't find me that night, as I imagined what they were doing.

"Ugh!" she screamed. "I can't believe this! you fucking had me followed?"

"You were a suspect, Chloe, like everyone else."

"Was Mike a suspect?" she demanded.

"Why? Because you fucked him?"

Chloe mouth dropped opened, but her shock didn't last long. She moved her hand back and slapped my right cheek with all her strength.

I can't say I didn't deserve it. It was a low blow, but I wasn't in my right mind. How could I when I was consumed with jealousy?

"Fuck you!" she hissed.

I grabbed her hand before she could slap me again, shaking her, and smacking her body against mine so she could stop moving, but all I accomplished was an unwanted reaction at her proximity. Feeling myself getting hard, I released her.

She stepped back to avoid falling, her cheeks burning, her eyes wide. I knew I had gone too far; I had no right.

Chloe's eyes started to fill. I hesitated but closed the distance between us, torn between kissing her and apologizing. But she retreated and stormed out of the room.

What the fuck was she doing to me?

I was always ten steps ahead in everything, but with Chloe I had no control over my emotions, and that terrified me to no end. Especially since she used my weaknesses against me. I decided to chase after her, making it all the way to her bedroom. Locked, of course.

I resisted the urge to break the door down, pulling back and focusing on breathing. This wasn't the way; she wouldn't open the door in any event and all I would create is yet another fight. Fed up, wanting the torturous situation to end, I sprinted back to my office.

If my fucking team couldn't do their job, I was going to do it myself, start over, with a different lens. If there was a sliver of chance that Chloe was innocent, I needed to know now, before it was too late, before I irreparably damaged what we had.

According to her, I already had, but Chloe had become a necessity for me. If I was going to have to try to go back to a life without her in it, I had to make sure no rocks were left unturned.

CHAPTER 37

Chloe

I TRIED TO HOLD back the tears, but my anger was too much for me to gain any control over the storm raging inside me. How fucking dare he have me followed? And have the audacity to seem upset at the idea of me sleeping with Mike? He had no right to act remotely jealous.

The night in question, when I slept over at Mike's, nothing happened. But that was none of his business.

We weren't together and frankly, treating me like a criminal negated any rights he might have had in the first place. My cousin was probably sucking his dick in his room every night while I was right next door. Held against my will.

But it was the end of this charade.

I made a split-second decision; I was getting out of here.

I had stormed out of the room with the USB in my pocket. I had spotted his car keys on the credenza outside the office on my way up the stairs. Resolved to end this hell, I grabbed them, praying Jake wouldn't notice.

A few seconds later I heard his hurried and angry steps stop at my door, but I was relieved when I heard him leave. There had been no commotion since, so I assumed he hadn't noticed his keys missing.

I knew my luck wouldn't last too long though, so I frantically packed my carry-on and my backpack for the second time. Whatever I forgot I could buy; all I had to make sure of was that I had my laptops, my tablet, and the USB I now hid in my bag.

Once I was satisfied, I took a few deeps breaths, trying to slow down my heart rate. My cold hands were slightly shivering. Fear almost caused me to back down, to stay put like I'd been told until this was all figured out.

But when I heard a female laughter in the hall that I recognized a little too well, I found my strength back and slowly opened the door once it sounded like the coast was clear. I silently made my way down the stairs, avoiding any creaks or sounds.

I opened the front door, and rushed down the front steps and veered left, where his car was parked. I opened the trunk, shoved my bags in, and climbed to the front. Even as I started the car, I tried to keep the lights as low as possible to not attract any attention.

I finally drove off and hit the road. The minute the car was out of sight from the house, I pressed the pedal to go as fast as I could.

CHAPTER 38

Jake

LAUREN HAD JUST OPENED my office door, without knocking, and slid in. She was wearing quite the revealing purple negligée, the thin lace contouring to her near-perfect body.

I sighed. I was sitting on my chair, enjoying the sound of the now pouring rain, the thunder silencing my internal struggles a little, sipping on a glass of scotch. Lauren trotted further into the room, making sure to pause in provocative ways so I could see her.

The sight of her, which would normally make me hard just a few months ago, was more just irritating now, when all I wanted was to wrap my hands around the curves of the woman upstairs.

"You like what you see?" she asked, her eyes glowing with confidence.

I sighed again.

"Lauren, I still have a lot of work to do."

"Awe, but you can take a break," she insisted as she waltzed towards me, until she got close enough to run her fingers through my hair.

I almost winced, angrier at myself for not even being tempted to oblige.

"No," I said, removing her hand.

She shoved me, frustrated.

"I don't understand you!" she screamed. "You used to find me irresistible, and now... now, what, you have the hots for my stupid cousin?"

There was no more use in denying. Lauren wasn't stupid.

"This whole fucking trip, all you did was stare at her, talk about her, look for her. What the fuck, Jake?!"

"I'm sorry, Lauren. I have always been clear with you about us."

"She still loves her ex, you know; you are wasting your time."

My lips thinned. She was trying to provoke me, play with my sanity. But all I could think of was punching Kyle so he could never look at Chloe ever again.

"With or without Chloe, Lauren, you and I will never work."

I felt a bit of guilt, but I knew Lauren didn't love me. She wanted the social status of being with me and that my wallet provided. She had always made that clear with her actions. She's never just slept with me for starters, and I didn't care.

"Fine," she said. "But you always come back. We will see if I take you back when that happens."

She lifted her head with whatever pride she had left and walked out of the room, violently closing the door behind her.

I ran my hand on my face in exasperation. How did I let things get so out of hand? How did I let a woman get so deep under my skin that even Lauren could tell how disturbed I was by her?

I also felt like a dick for how aggressive I had been with Chloe earlier. I had let my albeit unjustified jealousy get the best of me and had not only offended her but admitted to violating her privacy.

It was part of my job, yes, but the anger and disappointment on her face toyed at my insides in an unacceptable manner.

The rain was getting heavier by the minute, the wind making some tree branches hit the windows. The thunder was loud and crisp, reminding me of how startled Chloe became when the thunder got heavy when we were in her house.

Desperation filled me with a sense of doom. I needed to talk to her, iron things out. Whatever that meant.

She had to hear me out, and I had to make sure she was okay. Okay with the thunder, and okay with me, as much as someone I had accused of a crime could be. I went up the stairs two by two. I paused before knocking to make sure I wasn't too aggressive.

"Chloe?" I called when she didn't answer. "Chloe, we need to talk."

Silence continued to greet me.

"I... I didn't plan this. You and I, it was never supposed to happen. I was hired to do a job, that was supposed to be it. I didn't mean to get involved and I didn't mean to hurt you. I slept with you because I fucking wanted you, no, needed you to be mine... fuck. Open the door, mein liebling."

I refused to continue to talk behind a closed door. I needed to see her reaction to what I had to say. I turned the doorknob, pleased to find it unlocked. But she wasn't in the room.

Frowning, my gut told me something was off. I went to the bathroom and the closet to look for her. Not only was she not there, but neither were any of her clothes.

"Shit!" I shouted. "Chloe?"

I checked a few more places, the kitchen, the living room, nothing. She wasn't in my office, but the USB was gone.

And then it hit me like a brick.

My car keys had disappeared, and she was nowhere to be found.

Fuck! She was running.

I cursed again, panic invading my senses, as I looked at the terrible darkness outside. She was driving in this fucking rain, alone. Chloe barely drove in Chicago, relying on car services most of the time. Bile rose up my stomach at the idea of Chloe getting hurt.

I had to go after her.

I put my headphones on, grabbed a black leather jacket, my phone, and the keys to the motorcycle I kept in the shed. It was fucking reckless of her to do something like that, but I had no one else to blame but myself. I had pushed her to her limit, I knew it.

If something happened to her, I just didn't know what I would do.

As I sped to the shed, I activated my GPS tracker. I had one installed in the car thankfully, so I could see exactly where she was. My heartbeat accelerated as the app spotted the car. She wasn't very far, perhaps a ten-minute ride away, but of course she would continue to drive, so I had to be faster than her to catch up with her.

She was heading home, I was sure of it, but for some reason, it didn't seem like she was on the right road. Her location was a place I knew well since I owned farmland there. She was nowhere near the road she should have been on if she was on her way to Chicago.

I ran to the shed, put my helmet on, and started the bike. I let the roar of the motorcycle run through me, trying to distract myself from the white fear that was invading my body.

I couldn't panic; I just had to find her. The roads would be slippery, but I was used to driving my bike in dangerous conditions.

After a few minutes, my phone started beeping. I stopped to check it. The car had come to a stop for over five minutes. My jaw tensed; something was off. I checked the car app, and there it was.

It seemed like there had been an accident; the app was sending an emergency notification.

The airbag of the driver had been released.

I was already starting to lose signal, the weather having no mercy. I took a screenshot of her location. I tried to contact the emergency company I paid for situations like this, but I couldn't get through.

I tried to dial Chloe, but similarly, the call would hang up before it started. I put my phone in my pocket and focused on the road trying to calm the chaos boiling inside me.

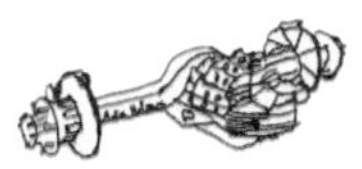

I finally swerved off the main road into the farm roads the GPS was taking me to before I lost signal. I was completely soaked, the light from the motorcycle barely showing the way, but then I saw it.

I saw red lights blinking on the right side of the road. I could hear my heartbeat quicken at the thought that she could be hurt, or worse. I tightened my grip of the handle as I approached.

The car was partly in the ditch. I could see smoke coming out of the completely destroyed front. She had hit a tree. I felt my hands shake, but this wasn't the time.

I stopped the bike abruptly and sprinted to the front driver door. It was a bit stuck, but I took a breath and yanked it open with all my strength.

Nothing was going to stop me from getting to her. I felt like someone had punched the air out of my lungs when I caught sight of her.

She was leaning back, her head tilted to the side, blood coming down the right side of her face.

"Fuck, baby, can you hear me?"

I brought shaking hands to her throat, looking for a heartbeat. Relief coursed through me when I heard her moan slightly.

"You're okay, you're okay, mein liebling, I am going to get you out of here."

I had to think quick. I knew you weren't supposed to move someone from the scene of an accident. Leave it to the professionals. But we were in the middle of a fucking thunderstorm, with no working phones and a smoking car.

I needed to get her out of there. So, I reached out to remove her seatbelt. She winced and moved her head straight.

"Shh, baby, don't move. Don't move; I am getting you out of here."

"What's happening?" she murmured.

My heart tumbled. She was talking. Besides her head, I didn't see any other signs of harm, or anything visibly broken. She was holding part of her stomach. I touched her arm delicately.

"Tell me where it hurts."

She rubbed her stomach and chest. The wheel or the airbag that was deflating must have hit her hard when she drove into the tree.

"Can you grab on to me? I am going to put your arm around my neck."

I slowly took her hands, seeing her wince at every movement. She obeyed and let me wrap her elbow around my neck, as I placed an arm behind her back and another one under her knees to lift her out.

"Ugh…"

"I'm sorry, baby, I'm sorry."

I held her as close to my body as I could without hurting her. She rested her head on my right shoulder. The only silver lining of this was that I owned a cabin about a seven-minute walk from where she crashed. Never more thankful for investing in the farmland in the area, I walked on the side of the street, to take her there.

There was no way I could drive her back to the house in her state on the motorcycle. Perhaps once in the cabin, I could get signal and call a helicopter.

"No," she whispered, I could barely hear her over the pouring rain.

"What's wrong?"

"My bags, I need my bags."

"That is not important right now."

"I need them." She started moving as if trying to get down.

"Chloe," I warned.

"At least the backpack," she insisted. "Please."

She winced again and tensed around me.

All I could do was oblige. I walked back to the car, strengthening my hold of her as I bent down to get the car keys, open the trunk, and grab the backpack from it.

I put it on my back and started my walk again towards the cabin. I understood why she wanted the bag, assuming all her research was in it, and the USB she stole.

Her innocence, that was all she could think about even in her current situation. Guilt and doubt were ripping through me like a wild tide. Perhaps I had accused her too soon, and now the consequences were her in pain in my arms.

Fuck me, this was all my fault.

After a few minutes, I finally got to the cabin. It was a simple wooden structure. I had renovated a few for some of the farmers to have a place to rest when needed.

I knew this one was currently empty. I unlocked the door and kicked it open. Chloe was shivering against me now, both of us soaking wet.

"Wake up, baby."

I called to her as I laid her down on the plush dark carpet in front of the fireplace. She grimaced but kept her eyes closed, teeth still chattering.

After I laid her down, I found a few thick blankets. I proceeded to remove her wet clothes and wrap her carefully in a few.

I checked both of our phones, but neither of them had signal, and hers was almost dead. The power was also out in the neighborhood. Thankfully the place had a generator.

I turned on the battery and blasted the heat. I didn't flip any lights on, as I didn't know how much charge was left and I didn't want to use it all, not knowing how long we would be stuck in the cabin.

I then proceeded to the small kitchen in the back, in search of some wooden logs. I brought a bunch and arranged them in the fireplace. I poured some lighter fluid and lit it on in no time.

I stripped my soaked clothes off and kept my boxers on. She was resting on her left side, facing the fire. She wasn't shivering as much now, the flames quickly warming up her damp body.

I slid a pillow under her head and sat next to her. She opened her eyes ever so slightly, looking at me through thick and still wet eyelashes, her brown curls splayed behind her

I gently bent her head towards me, making her swallow some pain medicine found in the bathroom cabinets. She protested but chugged the pills with water. I then used cotton balls and rubbing alcohol to clean the wound on her head. After I dipped a few times, she tried to remove my hand.

"I know, baby," I said as I blew some air on her wound, "but I have to clean it to avoid an infection."

She grunted, and I smiled. I'd never been so happy to hear her annoyed at me.

Once I was done with applying some pain cream and a bandage, I lifted the blanket and proceeded to inspect her body, making sure nothing was broken.

I had stripped her down to just her black silk lingerie.

Lord, help me.

She kept her gazed locked on me as I exerted light pressure on various parts of her arms, her legs, and her stomach in silence.

"Ugh."

She held my hand. I clenched my teeth. I had touched what looked like a tender spot on the right side of her stomach, which had already started to bruise. It didn't seem like she had broken a rib, as she would be hurting a lot more if she had, but she was very bruised. I hoped the pain meds I gave her would help.

"I'm still cold," she said as a shiver ran through her.

I moved myself behind her and laid under the blankets. I gently brought my body to her, spooning her, my arm wrapped around her waist.

She moaned, and I clenched my jaw. Her thick ass was lined up perfectly with my cock, and I had to think of something that would calm me down before I did something inappropriate, like slide in her hot...

Damn it.

I had to stop myself from thinking about her body.

I needed to focus on making sure she was safe.

I still held her close, running my hand tenderly on her thighs, her side, her arm, trying to warm her up further, never taking my eyes off her face. Her eyes were closed, and she seemed content as her breathing slowed.

She languidly turned around to face me. She let out a shaky sigh and moved ever so slightly in my direction. I held a breath, unable to resist wanting to run my fingers on her damp body, all the way under her bra and under those sexy panties she always wore.

Instead, I rested my head on top of hers, wrapped my hand around her hips, and tucked her feet under my legs to warm them up.

"Thank you," she breathed out, sending a zing directly to my reckless cock.

God, her body was firm and soft, slightly rubbing against my chest. I ran my hand up and down her back and shoulders, to continue warming her up.

I took her face in my hands and kissed the top of her head with a tenderness I never knew myself capable of. I was shaken, disturbed, unable to control the chaos raging war inside of me.

When I saw her in the car, seemingly unconscious, with blood pouring from her head, part of me had died. The white-hot blinding fear, the debilitating sadness and anger I felt had stricken me, and it had been all too revealing.

The fact that at that moment, I would have given anything to trade places with her was all too much for me to handle. But there was no denying what I felt anymore, no room for ambiguity.

Criminal or not, I was irrevocably, undeniably in love with Chloe Holmes.

I pulled myself a bit from her to search her eyes, my right hand still cupping her face.

"What happened?"

"I got lost. Um, then there was a deer, I think. I swerved, I didn't see the tree." She winced a little.

"Why did you do this, Chloe?" I asked, and she sighed. "You got hurt. You... you could have died and—"

I stopped my sentence abruptly when I heard the slight tremor in my voice. I swallowed hard, my jaw tightening, trying to hold back the feelings that threatened to invade my being.

Chloe shut her eyes.

"I guess I don't do well in captivity."

Her lips slightly tugged to the side.

I felt myself calm down. Of course, in the middle of almost dying, she was making jokes, because that was who she was, and she couldn't help her smart mouth. I shook my head, both in disbelief and enjoyment.

"I would have taken you home tomorrow," I admitted

"I'm not known for patience" she retorted, opening her eyes to look into mine.

Her playfulness had vanished. She looked sad and tired.

Where would we go from there?

She snuggled back into me, her head now buried in the left side of my neck. I slowly ran my hand up and down the left side of her body, in the hope of caressing her to sleep. But I felt my cock get hard in response, bulging against my boxers.

I abruptly stopped my movement. She grunted in the cutest way, sending a pulse through me again.

This was dangerous territory.

She might have been a traitor, she might be the type of person who would sell their family for money, but I also might have accused her unfairly, blamed her too soon. And right in this moment, she was curled up in my arms, the light of the flames dancing on her tan skin, a beautiful canvas, covering her with a dark golden hue, the smell of rain and burned wood lingering on her skin.

I gazed down at her head in the crook of my neck, looking at her shut eyes, her mouth slightly open. Her chest was rising and falling at a quick pace.

Doubt was tearing me apart.

Was she trying to manipulate me again? Had it started as a game for her, and turned into more?

I couldn't fathom that the small woman I was currently holding in my arms could be so manipulative.

No, she wanted me, she wanted this.

She wanted this as much as I did, despite all the hatred she felt towards me.

As if she could hear the chaos raging inside of me, she grabbed my arm, moving me closer to her, the blanket falling further down her body. God, I was dying to touch her, to make her feel good, to erase the pain, the hurt she was in all because of me and my brute behavior.

I grunted, and she let out a shaky breath against my neck.

What was I doing? I needed to stop. Stop this madness before it was too late.

"Chloe…" I sighed. "Did you use me?"

I wasn't a man known for being emotional. But my heart was shredded, and I needed to hear her say something.

"I didn't, Jake. I never faked any of this. God, how could I?"

I heard it. Fuck, I felt it. The tremor in her voice, the tears she was holding back, they stabbed me to my core.

If she was lying to me, all I could do in this moment was let her have her way.

The woman I loved was lying in my arms, barely clothed. I was already done for.

My body took over control of my brain, my hand resuming its trail up and down her shoulder and her arms. It then traveled down her thighs, coming back up to grab a fill of her ass. It next went up her back. She moaned, arching her body more towards me.

"You are making me lose my fucking mind," I whispered.

"Mmmm."

She moved her hand from my arm to my neck, playing with my hair. I backed up my face to look at her. She raised her head slightly; those brown now reddish eyes burning through me.

I would give her whatever she needed from me, and I knew just how. She was inviting me, need and desire pouring out of her every pore. I moved my hand on her stomach, slowly, torturously proceeding down between her thighs. When I caressed her through her wet panties with the tip of my middle finger, she moaned and buried her head back in my neck. My dick throbbed again.

I couldn't take her, for as much as I wanted to, she had just been in a car crash, but I could alleviate her ire, make her come hard and enjoy every second of it.

I brushed my hand up her stomach again, feeling her tense in anticipation, her pelvis moving towards me. My fingers traveled down, sliding under her panties and between her pussy.

"Ugh..."

Fuuuuck me.

She was so wet for me already.

I was doomed.

I could hear her breathing louder as I moved my middle finger up and down, spreading her wetness to her clit, where I knew she liked it most. I rubbed her there in circles, tenderly.

"Hmm," she whimpered against me, her body already shaking.

She leaned her head back on the pillow. I could see her pointy nipples hardened through the lace material. I didn't have time to remove her bra, so I lowered my mouth and grabbed her left nipple between my lips, through the lace of her bra. I felt her pulse under me as her head bent further back, and her hand grabbed my hair, holding me there. I went for the other nipple, eliciting a desperate cry out of her.

I continued to rub her now raw and bulky clit, her hips moving up and down against my hand.

My dick was throbbing, my underwear now wet with pre-cum. But this wasn't my moment, it was hers, and I felt like a god, making her tremble and whimper like this under my touch.

I didn't care what that fucking email said; she was enjoying how I made her feel. She was desperate for me to make her come, and I would gladly oblige.

"I love to see you like this, baby. Ugh, yes, that's it."

I felt her breath quicken with every raspy word of mine, a smile of satisfaction tugging at my lips.

"Ugh, Jake, please, ughhhhh!"

Her movements were getting more aggressive, I was afraid she would cause herself more pain, but she didn't seem to care, her orgasm rising quickly through her, until I felt her body completely tense into a standstill.

She broke around me, her body tense and then suddenly relaxing, limp, wanting more of my heaviness on her.

I brought her closer to me, enjoying her post-orgasm trembles and her chaotic breathing. This one had been a very intense one for her I thought, satisfied, even if my dick was pulsing, begging to be let out to join the fun.

Her breathing slowed down, but she was still holding me close, her legs wrapped around me

I knew she could feel my need against her; there was no hiding that.

Just when I thought she was falling asleep, she dragged her hand down my stomach and wrapped her fingers around my cock.

"Ugh," I moaned, tense, my dick responding to her touch. "No, baby, it's okay. You're hurt."

But she didn't listen and continued rubbing my cock. It was almost desperate in nature. The urgency just pushed me closer to my own orgasm. I was seconds away from exploding.

"Baby... ugh," I growled when she yanked my dick a bit.

I closed my eyes, trying to resist her. That was a fool's errand, really. She sneaked her hand inside my boxers. I jerked at the contact of her skin as she wrapped her hand around my dick, rubbing it up and down.

It felt so fucking good.

I opened my eyes. She was staring at me, mouth agape, her chest heaving. She was a thirsty little one, and thirsty for me.

"I need you inside of me, one last time. You owe me this much." Her words echoed in every chamber of my heart and left darkness in their trail.

There was no way this was our last time.

"Ugh, fuck, baby, we..."

"Please. I don't want this to end," she whispered in my ear.

Those words, her need, her sadness, her begging, confirmation that she did want me, they were my undoing.

I frantically helped her pull down my underwear. Before I could regain any self-control, she lifted her left leg above my hip, as we both guided my dick between her open thighs to that tight pussy, sliding myself inside of her, easily, deeply, softly.

We both moaned as I deeply went in and out of her.

"Fuck," I rasped, holding her face in front of mine, breathing her in, kissing her deeply, longingly.

This was torture, sweet, magnificent, unbearable misery. I was using the few fibers of control I had to fuck her slowly, not to come too fast, to make sure she could also get there before I let loose.

What I wanted to do was pound her to the ground savagely, frustration and need taking over, but she was hurt; I couldn't do more damage than I had already done.

She grabbed my ass, forcing me to lean more fully on top of her. I lay both my forearms around her head, caging her in, supporting my weight up to not crush her too much.

"Jake!" she whimpered.

"Baby, I can't hold it back any longer" I grunted. "You feel so fucking good, ugh, fuck, come with me baby, come with me."

She dug her perfectly manicured nails into my skin, forcing me even deeper in her sweet cunt, until it almost felt like my body was seeping inside of her.

I accelerated my thrust, deep, disorganized, lost in a feeling of blinding need and completeness I had never experienced before her.

"Ugh"

"Fuck!"

"Jake, oh God, Jake, oh oh, uhn, ahh, ahhh!"

"Ugh!"

I exploded inside of her, warm cum mixing with hers in the most intimate obliterating orgasm I had ever had.

As she held me close, seemingly desperate to have more of me, my heart pounding out of my chest, I admitted the truth to myself.

Criminal or not, there was no life, no place, no time in it, that I didn't want that woman to be mine, body and soul, only mine, now and forever.

Principles. Be. Damned.

I was so fucked.

CHAPTER 39

Chloe

I woke up in a haze, confused, unable to recognize my surroundings. Through tired eyes, I noticed that I was wrapped in a plush blanket in a bed, in what appeared to be a wooden cabin.

My body felt sore, and when I tried to turn, I felt a jab of pain in my side. I was slowly remembering.

The fight with Jake, the car, the accident.

I had gotten lost on my way to Chicago, when the GPS stopped working. It was pouring rain, with thunder making me jump every few minutes. I could barely see the street, and I eventually swerved to avoid hitting an animal, smashing into a tree I hadn't seen instead.

It all happened so fast. I had tried to call for help, but I'd lost signal. I had passed out in the car, unable to find the strength to leave and look for help.

Then, when I had lost all hope, I had heard a voice, his voice.

The process was murky, but I remembered how he had taken care of me, what we had done, what I had begged him to do.

"Shit!" I cursed, covering my face with my hands, regretting it instantly as I felt a throbbing pain on my forehead.

I couldn't help feeling a bit aroused again, remembering how his fingers had given me one of the best orgasms of my life, followed by that wonderful feeling of fullness, and the second explosion.

I shouldn't have, I knew I shouldn't have. He was the enemy, the person who used me and was accusing me of vile actions against my own family.

But he was also the man I couldn't stop thinking about, the man who had made me vibrate, who made me feel alive, challenged, accepted with all my flaws, my strengths, and my weaknesses.

Even if it was all fake.

All the anger, all the outrage, disappointment, sadness, and longing that I felt cumulated last night into an uncontrollable need to come, for him, by him, with him.

I really hoped that I got my fix, because what we did last night, we couldn't repeat it. It had been a mistake; my need for him had been stronger than my hatred in that moment. But that didn't make it right. If I let him come any closer to my heart, he would destroy it, irreparably so. If he hadn't already.

I made an effort to get out of the bed. I was desperate for a shower.

I found my phone. It was already 10 a.m. I cursed but was happy to find my luggage and backpack in the room. I got cleaned and dressed in fifteen minutes, eager to make my way back to Chicago.

I picked one of my favorite white dresses, repacked my bags, and left the room with them, not moving too fast as the side of my stomach still hurt.

The space was quaint, combining the rustic log cabin theme with black metals and simple but classy dark furniture. The technology had also been updated to include the conveniences of a modern house.

The best part? I could smell the coffee.

I turned left by the dining table, to head to what looked like a small kitchen. He was standing there, a cup of coffee in hand, wearing black sweatpants and a white t-shirt, looking at something on his phone, a frown on his face.

This was the most underdressed I had ever seen him and it hit me, hard. It somehow made him feel more real. He lifted his head when I walked in.

"Hi," I said, annoyed at the memories from last night.

"How do you feel?" he asked as he walked towards me and handed me a cup.

"Good, thank you."

"It's already cooled to a drinkable temperature, for you that is." He smiled.

I scratched my throat. If there was one thing I couldn't handle, it was charming Jake.

"Thank you."

"I, uh, I called for a car. It's outside for when we are ready. I am taking you to Northwestern to get checked up."

"I feel fine."

"It's just in case." He shrugged.

He moved a hair strand behind my ears.

"Fine," I agreed. I didn't have the energy to fight him.

"About last night…"

"Nothing to discuss," I quickly interrupted, wanting to hear no part of whatever he wanted to say.

This was going to be one of his "it meant nothing speeches", I was sure of it, and I didn't think I could handle another one. Besides, I was the one who was upset, I was the one who got hurt, not him.

"I need to know. I need to know what it meant to you," he pushed.

I peered down at my coffee. His eyes would read into me like an open book, so I had to avoid his gaze at all costs.

He cupped the right side of my face.

"Look at me," he grunted. I swallowed hard. "I need to know if it was real for you, as much as it was for me."

"It was a lapse in judgment, that's it. You didn't actually think, considering where we are, what you did to me, that it would mean anything else, did you? I told you it was the last time."

I casted my eyes up and caught a glimpse of him, the now darkened eyes, the tense expression, the closed nostrils. I refrained from reaching out, unsure if I was seeing pain in his expression or just a reflection of the confusion I was feeling.

He was searching for my eyes, looking for something. I held his gaze, my pain fueling my strength.

"Chloe, I know you think I calculated all of this, but that's not how it all happened."

"It doesn't matter how it happened. What matters is that I am innocent. And I am eager to go back to Chicago and prove it to you, or anyone else who dares to accuse me of betraying my own family. That is all I care about. And then you and I never have to see each other again. I go back to my life, and you go back to yours."

"I don't think that's what you want."

A dark semblance of laughter left my throat.

"What we did last night, Jake, was just a goodbye fuck. Closure. At least for me. That's all."

He took a step away from me, brusquely removing his hand from my face, as if it had burned him. I opened my lips to say something but realized I couldn't without him hearing the tears I was holding in the back of my throat. So I changed the topic.

"I am ready to leave when you are," I added, trying to end our exchange.

"Fine. The car is here. I will wait for you outside."

He stomped next to me and grabbed my luggage as he left the room. I held on to the countertop for support, trying to stop the tears from falling.

He had no right confusing me like this, making it seem like he was also suffering. He had no right to make me wonder if it was true, if his task and his involvement with me were separate.

It didn't matter, though, I reminded myself as I stabilized my breathing. He had proven himself to not be trustworthy, and I couldn't be with someone like that.

After I finished my coffee, I took ten minutes to address some emails, the ones from Mike I didn't need Jake looking at while in the car. My dad had called me, but I decided I would talk to him once in Chicago.

Once done, I packed up and went to join him. He was leaning against his black Audi, scrolling on his phone, that same preoccupied frown on his face.

He lifted his head as I approached, walking towards me and taking my backpack. I wanted to protest, but my body was already complaining under the weight, so I let him grab it.

He held the front door open for me, and I slid in. He walked around, secured my bag in the backseat, and sat next to me.

"Ready?" he asked as I buckled up.

"Ready," I answered, looking anywhere but him.

CHAPTER 40

Jake

HER WORDS WERE ECHOING in my head like a broken record, twitching a blade in my stomach every time. *"What we did last night, Jake, was just a goodbye fuck. Closure. At least for me. That's all."*

I could feel the anger emanating from her side of the car. She had been fidgeting with her phone the whole time, answered questions if I asked them, but otherwise ignored me completely. I couldn't blame her though; even after the night we had spent together, she saw me as the enemy, as a threat to her life, whether she was innocent or guilty.

When I carried her to the bed the night before, she had instinctively held my hand and sleepily asked me to stay with her. I had obliged, relieved that I could spend the night with her, take her temperature, make sure she was okay, while I counted the hours to be able to get her checked by a doctor.

I had spent the night arranging for a car, getting a doctor appointment with my physician, and reviewing the data Kushar claimed didn't show any other suspects, looking for a mistake, a misstep on the part of my team.

While I had been tempted to breach the poor security on her laptops, her tablets, and her phone, I couldn't bring himself to do it. I knew how betrayed she already felt that not only I had done that before, but I had her followed. The idea of adding one more lie, one more deceit, made me feel disgusted with myself.

If there was evidence that she had been framed, I would find it in no time. The stakes were now a lot higher based on the call I had with Philip in the morning.

"There has been a development with Green Mile," I mentioned.

"What happened?" Chloe asked.

"Your dad called earlier. It seems like they approached the board to make an offer of acquisition. When the board rejected them, they started to approach some of the shareholders to convince them to sell. They're trying to do a hostile takeover.

"They claim they can put their e-axle in business a few months before us. Some of the shareholders are concerned that we won't be able to stay competitive with a company like Green Mile having similar technology to Motor Holmes."

"Shit."

Chloe tensed. I didn't want to have to share bad news with her, but she needed to know. I had told Philip that she was sleeping but that I would tell her as soon as she woke up.

"You didn't tell him about... the accident, did you?"

"No, I figured you wouldn't want me to."

"Thank you. He has enough to worry about with this now. Did he discuss next steps?"

"He doesn't want this to get out. Once rumors start circulating in the market that we might get bought out, it might affect business. He wants to find the traitor, find evidence that Green Mile is behind it, and use that to our advantage."

"We won't sue them?"

"He'd prefer to avoid that."

"We need evidence to negotiate with them regardless."

"Correct."

"Too bad it's not me, I guess. You'd be done with your investigation by now."

There we go. Fuck, did she hate me?

"Do you know who did this then?"

I couldn't stop myself. At this point, assuming it wasn't her, she might be able to help me find who had done this. She took a few seconds to answer.

"I will find out who did this."

"Chloe, I don't want you to get involved. If you know anything, tell me so we can fix it. If you don't, don't do anything without talking to me first."

She let out a laugh.

"What changed? A few days ago, you were so sure it was me. And now you think I am going to work with you?"

I sighed. Of course she was right.

But what could I say exactly? I didn't know what to think; I didn't have the answers. I was confused as fuck.

My gut was telling me we had missed something. That the woman sitting next to me couldn't possibly have done this. I couldn't think she used me either after last night. But I needed the proof. Even if just to reconcile my principles with how I felt about her.

"Chloe, all I want is to get to the bottom of this. And if you didn't do this, if you have information on who really did, we should be helping each other. So, work with me here, please. We don't have a lot of time."

"No, we don't."

I could see the gears turning in her brain. She got that distant look that occupied her face when she was thinking. But I didn't think there was anything else I could say to get her on my side.

All I could hope for was that she stayed out of trouble while I tried to figure this out.

It was midafternoon when we walked through the hospital, straight to the side section where Dr. Jackson worked. Chloe looked confused, rightfully so. I wasn't a patient man, and because that, I always arranged the best and most efficient process for all my services. My health wasn't any different, and hers wouldn't be either.

Dr. Jackson was a fifty-five-year-old African American man who had been taking care of me for a good ten years now. He was already in front of the door to his office, waiting for us.

"Jake," said Andre, shaking my hand, "great to see you."

"Great to see you too, Doctor."

"Nice to meet you," Andre added to Chloe, using the charming behavior I knew he reserved for certain female patients as he shook her hand.

"Nice to meet you, too," said Chloe, slightly wincing.

"I heard you were in a car accident," he started, gently putting his hand behind Chloe's back and guiding her towards the exam room on the side of his office. "Jake, would you mind waiting in my office?" asked Dr. Jackson, when he noticed I was right behind them.

"I do," I answered, unfazed by the severe look he gave me.

Chloe rolled her eyes, but instead of complaining said, "It's okay, Doctor."

"Okay then," replied Dr. Jackson, with a slight smirk on his face.

I was the one to roll my eyes, knowing Dr. Jackson well enough to guess what he was thinking. And he wasn't wrong; I wasn't going to let Chloe out of my sight.

Chloe, as instructed, got into the hospital gown so Dr. Jackson could do his job. As much as I didn't enjoy seeing him press and prod her body, the bruise was even darker than before, and she was still in pain. Her forehead had also started to swell.

Thankfully, after a few scans, Dr. Jackson confirmed that no bones were broken, there was no internal bleeding and no concussion. Her muscles were obviously sore, but with some rest and pain relivers she would be fine.

I finally felt my shoulders relax, suddenly aware of how tense I had been for the past fifteen hours or so.

She was okay, she was going to be fine.

"Thank you very much, Doctor," Chloe said as Dr. Jackson wrote her a prescription and gave her some pills to take for inflammation and pain.

He smiled. "My pleasure, Chloe. We will let you get dressed."

"Thank you."

I stepped out with Dr. Jackson and waited behind the door for Chloe.

"She got very lucky," the doctor remarked.

"I know," I admitted, rubbing my face, letting out the fear I had kept in for the past hours. "She hit a tree, swerving away from some animal, likely a deer."

Dr. Jackson clapped a hand on my back. "She's fine. You can breathe now, son."

"If something had happened to her, I... I don't know how I would keep going. I don't think I would be able to handle it, her, not existing."

"I can see that...."

We both turned when we heard the door open. Chloe stepped out, still ignoring me, and shook the doctor's hand again.

I swallowed hard and sunk my hands in my jean pockets. All I wanted to do was take her into my arms and kiss her until she forgot the past few days. Instead, I had to stand there and watch her smile dampen every time she looked at me.

"Thank you for taking me, but I am going home now," she announced, walking around me, not waiting for a reply. "I need my stuff."

"I'm taking you home."

"No need. Mike is up front."

And there he was as we stepped out, shooting me an angry glare. I found myself hoping Mike would dare either touch Chloe or try to hit me; it would take just a slight movement for me to plow the fists I had next to my body into his face.

But instead, I retrained myself and obliged, not wanting to stress Chloe. I walked to my car, still parked outside with valet as I had instructed. I opened the trunk and got the two bags out. Mike was right behind me.

"How can you be so irresponsible and let her drive like that?" inquired Mike now that Chloe was out of earshot.

"She took my car. I didn't let her do anything; she just did it."

"All this is your fault," declared Mike. "A damn shame really, to lose a woman like Chloe over false accusations."

I took a step in Mike's direction. He flinched but didn't move.

"She is still mine," I sneered, a growl in my throat. "And if you dare touch her, or lay your fucking hands on her ever again, you can kiss your fucking fingers goodbye."

Mike eyes dilated a whole centimeter, but he didn't say anything. Instead, he took the luggage from me and went to Chloe. I remained by my car, watching Mike take care of her, dying to be the one she would allow close to her again, the one she would smile at and thank with her hand on his arm the way she did him.

Instead, all I could do was watch her walk away from me, with another man. That was fine, I thought, it would give me time. Time I needed to sort through the hurricane inside, time to prove her innocence, and then beg or crawl for a second chance.

CHAPTER 41

Chloe

ONCE WE ARRIVED AT my house, Mike stayed and helped me get everything inside. Four hours after his departure, I was cuddled on the couch and ready to sleep off the shit show that were the last few days.

All in all, putting aside the accident, I was in relatively good spirits. I still had a lot to take care of, but I was alive... and finally home. It was time to get everything squared away so I could reveal who the true culprit was.

Every time I thought of him, I wanted to scream... Kyle—my ex-boyfriend and the guy who was still trying to get me to get back together with him—was the insider. I was convinced and could prove it beyond a reasonable doubt.

Kyle Campbell was the person who had put the company in danger.

He had been at my home during the parties, he was in the office when I gave my computer to IT. He was in the IT room on September 20th. Max, the IT technician who was responsible for my laptop repairs had gone to his floor as well, for three hours, on September 21st.

His prints were all over this. No one else from the list of Motor Holmes employees suspects who had also attended my social events came close. None had been to the IT department or had any interactions with IT.

It was Kyle. But I didn't think he did it alone. My guess was that Max had a hand in it.

All I needed was proof that Kyle had been communicating with the competitors outside of my inbox. Max, I was sure, had just been paid for access to my codes and my laptop. I suspected Kyle took care of the rest afterwards.

Another dead giveaway I had missed was how he signed his emails, with "all the very best" before his name. He had used the same term before using my name in the emails that came from my laptop, but I always signed with "Regards."

He betrayed me. And I was going to play the game until the end.

Time was of the essence.

I spent the rest of the day catching up on work with hot compresses on my stomach, my darling Penny sleeping and purring next to me. Not much had happened in my absence since there were no current deals on the horizon.

Keisha had also stopped by and spent the rest of the evening with me, mouth agape, after I explained all that had happened in just a few days. We had called Amelia and Iris, with Amelia offering to talk to Alejandro to see if there was anything he could help with.

Days had come and gone. Jake had kept his distance, traveling according to my father.

I had been back to the office since I returned from New Buffalo and tried to act as if everything was normal, as if my universe hadn't shattered, engaging in my usual pleasantries, and turning up the flirt with Kyle a notch.

Even if my heart hadn't been torn into pieces.

But it was finally game time I had been waiting patiently for that day, literally counting the seconds. Kyle had asked me to co-host a cocktail hour at his house planned for tonight, like we used to do.

I had worked from home during the day, with the plan that Keisha would join me here so we would get ready.

I was thankful for Jake's absence, using it to rationalize with my heart, to remind myself that whatever I was feeling, no matter how much I missed him, missed those eyes, missed his mouth over mine, we would never work out. That didn't stop me from using social media to try to see where he was, to see if he was with Lauren still. He wasn't.

"We are going to out that bastard so bad," said Keisha as she aggressively put some mascara on.

"We'll see. I need his phone, his private laptop, anything I can find, so Mike can take a look. I have no doubt there are other communications; those emails can't be all there is. Once we know, once we have proof that he not only stole the information but sent it to Green Mile, we will have what we need to force them to the table, get to an understanding, or we out them to the world."

"Agreed. He just used you as a cover to send the actual information. Fucking asshole. You can take him to court, get an urgent TRO, get the rest of the information through discovery, crush their fucking neck there."

I smiled as I pulled up my black jumpsuit and secured the strap on my shoulders. Keisha was a force not to be reckoned with in the court room, and I was lucky to have her by my side. If there is one thing Keisha and Eric had in common, it was how they bent juries to their will.

"I know. I don't know if that evidence would be admissible in court. But I also don't think my dad would want to go there anyways."

"Jake, though, I mean, I think we have to, I don't know, think about that more."

I stopped and glared at Keisha in the mirror.

"I know, I know, but still. He was hired to do a job. You can't deny that it doesn't look good for you, sweetie. Plus, Kyle was clever, sending that last email, making it look like you were using Jake so that even if he was inclined to help you, he would resist because of that."

"I don't care. He didn't need to make me feel... things for him and then treat me like a criminal. I don't care how bad it looks."

I stopped as I heard my voice wobble.

"Do you love him?" asked Keisha tenderly.

My heart skipped a beat, but those weren't words I would ever let myself utter, not for that man. I silently proceeded to put my Jimmy Choos on and look for my purse, my eyes blurry.

Keisha gave me an understanding look and continued to get ready.

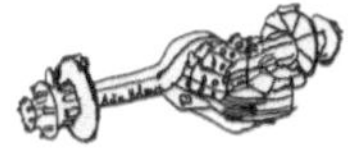

We got to Kyle's overpriced apartment in River North. We were on our best behavior, hugging Kyle pleasantly as he let us up and opened the door in his beige pants and blue shirt, unaware of what was to come.

His apartment was a small two-bedroom, one bathroom apartment, with floor-to-ceiling windows. It was a simple contemporary style, containing all the comfort one could ask for, while paying a premium for the location and amenities of the building.

"Thank you so much for helping," he said as he kissed my forehead.

I stopped myself from slapping the hell out of him, even if my hands itched to cause him pain.

He had used me and been a traitor to my family. He had put the company my father had built from the ground up in jeopardy for a quick buck. And then tried to pin the blame on me.

But I needed to play the game. Do whatever I had to do to convince him we were still on good terms. Because I was not leaving the apartment without the proof I needed.

The guests were starting to roll in. With the help of Keisha distracting me when she could tell I was about to snap, I kept my cool all night and was the perfect hostess. I even let Kyle parade me around in front of his guests, as he claimed that we were back together. I stood for pictures, held his hands, gave him my best charming smile.

I didn't correct him because I was fine with him thinking we were back together. That meant I would have free reign of his house.

Keisha and I also made sure his drink was always full, and water was never near him. When we considered him inebriated enough, I excused myself to use the restroom in his bedroom. I locked the door and looked around, in his dressers, his night tables, everywhere.

I was close to giving up when I saw a small safe in the back of the suits in his walk-in closet. I tried a few passwords, his birth year, birth days but those didn't work. I decided to try my birthday and was shocked when I heard the unlock noise. Of course, why not use my information? He was fucking me over in any event.

I opened the safe to find two watches, some money, and two burner phones.

Jackpot.

With trembling hands, I grabbed the phones with cloth, locked the safe, and pushed it back to where it was.

I slid each phone in one of my pockets and rejoined the party.

"Everything okay?" Kyle asked when I joined him and Keisha in the kitchen.

"Peachy," I said, accepting the glass of wine he was handing me. "Can't say the same for you on the other hand," I teased.

He chuckled, "I'm fine, sweetheart, you know I can handle my alcohol."

"Of course." I walked away from the spit coming out of his slurring mouth. "Keisha, should we bring another round of shots?" I suggested, pretending to also be a bit tipsy.

"That's what I'm talking about!" screamed Kyle before planting an overly wet kiss on my mouth on his way to the living room. Once he left, we snuck to the hallway.

"Here you go." I handed Keisha the phones. No other words were needed. We had Mike waiting in the parking lot.

"No laptop?" she asked.

"Nowhere to be found."

I regained my composure as Keisha sprinted to the exit. I poured about twenty shots of tequila, and a shot of water for me, and went back to the living room to entertain the guests.

I had been texting with Mike all night. The task was taking a while; he needed a few more hours.

Thankfully, it was already 11 p.m., and most of the guests had dispersed to the after-party. It was within walking distance of the apartment. We were supposed to join them, but I wanted to sneak the phones back safely in their place first.

I started to think maybe I had played the game too well and convinced Kyle that we were actually back in a relationship. He wouldn't stop touching me... and I honestly wanted to throw up, finding him repugnant.

So, when all the guests had left, Kyle asked Keisha to leave too because he wanted to be alone *with his girl*—unless she'd planned on having a threesome with us.

When she looked at me, concern etched on her face. I reassured her that I could handle Kyle alone. I knew Mike had to be getting close to finishing the job, and it was only a matter of time before I could get out of here myself.

Keisha reluctantly left but told me to call her if anything happened or I got uncomfortable.

As soon as the door slammed closed, Kyle stalked toward me. He grabbed my hand and pulled into his bedroom.

"Fiiiinally," he slurred, "alllll alone."

"I know."

"Take this, take this thing offff you."

"You need to drink some water, Kyle," I said. But he wasn't listening. He pushed me on the bed and clumsily climbed up on top of me.

"I knew you would come back to me, not to that ssstupid, ssstupid, fancy ssstupid man."

He started kissing my neck. I closed my eyes, my knuckles white from the tight fists I had them in. I could probably give him a good knee in his penis to get him off me, but I needed to buy time.

"Let me get you water," I insisted, trying to push him off.

"I don't need fuckin wather."

He pulled himself up a bit further, clumsily trying to remove his shirt. He then gave up and focused on kissing me instead. I wanted to cry, but I knew what was to come; I just needed to be strong for a few more minutes. I couldn't ruin it when we were so close to finishing this.

As predicted, his movements became sloppier and sloppier, until I heard deep snoring in my ear. I stayed there under him for another minute before I gently pushed him away from me. He remained on his side still, and I was finally able to get away.

I removed his shoes and managed to pull his belt out without waking him up. I covered him with a blanket, slid a pillow under his head, and tiptoed out of the room. While I was tempted to press the pillow on his face instead, I needed him to believe I was interested in him until the last darn minute.

I closed the door behind me and pulled my phone out. Keisha had texted. I let her know I was fine. Now, I just had to wait.

About fifteen minutes later, Mike was done, and Keisha was back at the door with the phones. I took them and quickly snuck back in the room. Kyle was still in the exact same position I had left him in, snoring to his heart's content. I tiptoed over to the closet, took my time to lay the phones exactly as I had found them, and slid the safe back in its spot.

I was relieved and couldn't believe how easy this had been. Having to stand this asshole for a few hours was a small price to pay for my freedom, for a chance to save the company.

We went to Mike's car, and all three of us drove to my house, exhausted but agitated by the adrenaline thrill and our victory.

"Mike, you are my hero," I said as I gave him the longest hug. "I can't believe this."

"I mean, he has no idea you are on to him. Great heist!"

We were sitting on my back patio; I was free and almost in the clear, but I was having a hard time accepting that this short nightmare was indeed over.

Mike had downloaded countless text messages, emails, and even photos from those burner phones. Kyle had been in touch with another person who, based on the conversation, seemed like either a high-level officer or someone with keen understanding of the e-axles business, for over a year now.

There were many communications with that person explaining what that person needed, and Kyle plotting to find the information wanted, letting them know when he had bribed the IT manager at Motor Holmes to get access to my laptop and send the information. The problem was that precautions had been taken by both Kyle and whoever he was talking to, using code names for everything they could.

I suspected the CTO and major shareholder of Green Mile, Chad Gorbel. He had attended the same college as Kyle, and while he was senior, they had definitively overlapped.

Unfortunately, Mike couldn't trace the other phone number, so we couldn't connect them that way.

There were also a few messages with a man who went by K, about how he'd make sure there was no evidence against him. It was unclear what K's role was, but he was helping clean the record further for Kyle, otherwise he wouldn't have needed to text K on burner phones.

I was savoring the moment, high on adrenaline. That was what victory tasted like.

"What are you going to do now?" asked Mike.

"I have no idea," I admitted truthfully. "Obviously, I need to tell my dad. But I can't do that on the phone, and he is traveling. There is no doubt that Kyle provided another company with proprietary information; there were even conversations around when we were reaching out to customers, who we were targeting in those text messages. He really fucked us over."

"Fucking asshole," said Keisha, her lips parted as they did when she was infuriated. "This is great information. But we need to tie Green Mile to this. We need to show they had access to the information, that they used it."

"I know. But really, we just need enough to scare the shit out of them. My dad doesn't want the scandal."

"You're not going to tell Jake?" asked Keisha, gazing in her drink like it was the most interesting thing in the world.

"No. I am going to enjoy being the one who did his job for him, showing my dad it was stupid to not let me handle this in the first place and hire this brute instead."

"Understandable," said Mike. "I, um, I really think that you two should talk though..."

He looked in the direction of Keisha. I saw the complicity between them. Clearly, they had been talking about me. I couldn't be mad at them, as they were looking out for me, but this was pointless.

"About what?" I shrugged. "No, he doesn't get to treat me as he did and get a chance. It's not like he is in love with me or anything. He used me, just like Kyle, just like Danny."

I swallowed my tears. Jake was the first man I felt like saw me as an equal and enjoyed that aspect of our relationship. To find out that the peace, the sense of self I had experienced in his company, was all fake wasn't something I could forget or get over.

"He threatened me, you know," continued Mike. "When I picked you up at the hospital? He said you were, uh, 'his' and I would lose my hands if I ever laid them on you again. I wanted to clarify I never did, but I didn't want to risk it."

Keisha exploded in laughter, bending her head backwards.

"Omg," she added, her hand on her chest.

I rolled my eyes at them, chugging the rest of my wine, trying to hide the way my stomach dipped, and I had to laugh because somehow, even through Mike, he could get to me.

None of his possessive bullshit mattered, I tried to remind myself. But I couldn't help the chill those words had caused to run through me.

About an hour later, I was finally alone with my thoughts. I took the longest bubble bath, with a bottle of coconut water and a shot of St. Germain. I needed to re-center myself. My tired body needed the heat to relax my tense and bruised muscles, each breath opening my lungs with the warm smell of rose and lavender.

I needed to shut my mind off, not to think of what could have driven Jake to make such a threat to Mike. He had no right to be jealous, but clearly, he was.

I didn't think he was pretending; he had no reason to. Part of me wished, part of me hoped, even if I didn't want to have anything to do with him.

I decided to focus on myself, on my innocence, and how I was going to present it all to my father on Monday when he was back and finally get rid of Jake, and all that he entailed. We could then zero in on destroying Green Mile. The thought should have brought me joy, relief, but all I felt was a deep emptiness, a sense of loss, and fear that I would never see Jake again.

CHAPTER 42

Jake

LUKE, ANOTHER ONE OF my employees, had looked at me like I had grown another head when I decided to start over, going through all the work and evidence we had gathered in the past few months. I didn't care. I had spent fifteen plus hours a day for the past two days going through all the dats summary and exhibits with a fine-tooth comb. When that proved to be fruitless, i bypassed K and went to Luke, focusing on the raw data, some of which Chloe had reviewed. The stakes were higher now that there was an actual threat that Philip might lose his company.

While I hadn't bothered with the grunt work in years—that was why I had a team after all—this was too delicate for me to just rely on K.'s conclusion that Chloe was guilty.

While all the evidence pointed to her, I couldn't shake my gut feeling. And after the night we spent in the cabin, despite her words the next morning, I had hope. I understood how different my diligence would be, since as opposed to looking for a guilty party, I was looking for proof of Chloe's innocence.

It had taken every ounce of self-control I could muster to stop myself from crashing Kyle's party to drag her out of there after I saw the pictures on social media. Why the fuck had she gone to him in the first place? But the task of potentially proving her innocence was more important.

I started seeing a light at the end of the tunnel on Saturday evening when I noticed that Chloe had checked out a laptop on one of the days. Yet according to the data, the email of the day had gone from her usual laptop. I double checked the IP addresses of all her emails for that day, and only emails related to the proprietary information sent out came from the IP address of her usual computer, showing it at the office when the emails were sent.

If she checked out a loaner that day, why would she then be using her other laptop in some instances at the same time as the other one? She wouldn't need to do both.

Even more interesting was that from checking the IP address and calendars at the time, Chloe was traveling to Mexico while her main laptop was sending emails from Chicago.

I had access to flight information, Uber rides, restaurant expenses on her credit card, a thousand miles away. Her social media posts showed her in Chicago, but after a few calls with my contacts at the social media company, I was able to confirm she posted those pictures while she was in Mexico. None of that had made it in the reports K sent to me.

It. Wasn't. Her.

IT WASN'T HER!

I started pacing my home office in my Chicago apartment, fingers raking through my already messy hair. I ran my hand on my unshaved face, closing my eyes, both relief and guilt invading my bones. I could feel the tension in my jaw.

"Fuck!"

I grabbed my phone to call her but put it down. I wasn't sure what to do. Call her? Text her? Go to her? It was late in the day, and if I had to bet, she was either going to dinner or at home.

How I wished I could turn back time, rewind to that day when she looked at me with hope and was starting to trust me. Just a few days later

I jumped the gun, allowed Lauren to humiliate her, accused her of vile actions, and ruined the best thing that had ever happened to me.

I messed up. I fucking messed up.

No. I stopped by my bar and poured myself some scotch and chugged it. I needed to find out who had done this first.

Whoever it was, they had no idea what was coming their way. This was personal. And I wasn't one to let my enemies have a chance to strike back. This person had decided to frame the woman I loved, harm her and her family.

There would be hell to pay.

I had just spent an hour on the phone with Luke, as I continued to pace a hole in the floor. Kyle, my original suspect, was strongly back on the list. I had found an unusual amount of back and forth between Kyle and one of the IT technicians the day it looked like Chloe was using two laptops at the same time.

I instructed my team to re-do the background search on Kyle, look again at his friend roster, his connections; there had to be one with someone at Green Mile.

Maybe K. had missed something, but I had an unnerving suspicion. While they had looked through his work cellphone, they hadn't found anything. Which means if it was Kyle, he was relying on burners. We needed to search his house.

Luke was going to follow Kyle, and another member of my team was going to dig in further into the investigation. I had opted to giving them their tasks separately and ordered that they send me updates every hour.

But, my mind was made up. I needed to see her.

I grabbed my keys and drove to Chloe's house. The knot in my chest felt like a searing pain at this point, shame and guilt combining with the sheer fear of having lost her teared through me.

A woman I considered my match, someone who could take my dry sense of humor and who challenged me to be the best version of myself and expected the same in return. Someone I couldn't get enough of, a heart I had broken in a million pieces, after she opened up to me about her trust issues, about never feeling like men saw her as qualified to be with.

I had to get to her. I wasn't above begging; I needed to do whatever it took.

My phone rang, and I frowned when I saw an unknown number pop up.

"Yes?"

"Hi, um, Jake?"

"Yes, who is this?"

"It's Keisha. We are at Chloe's house and... we can't find her. Something is wrong. We think... we think... she's missing."

"Five minutes."

I hung the phone and threw it on my lap, my knuckles turning white on the steering wheel as I slammed my foot on the pedal, piercing through the night on Lake Shore Drive.

I had barely parked the car before I was running up the stairs two at a time. Keisha was at the entrance, eyes puffy and red. She let me in, and I found Mike standing in the living room, eyes wide.

"What happened? Where is she?" I demanded, my blood boiling to a fever.

I had to remain calm; it was the only way I could find her. I couldn't let the fear of losing her take over; I couldn't afford to.

"We were supposed to have an early dinner tonight. She never showed. We called and called but nothing. We drove here to meet her but... we found the door slightly open, not locked, and one of her heels was just outside, at the bottom of the stairs."

Keisha pointed trembling finger to the floor, to those heels Chloe had worn the last day of the conference in California.

I felt like my blood was draining out of my body, fear and panic trying to paralyze me.

"Any idea who could have done this?" I pointed to Mike, who was twisting his fingers. "Kyle?"

They both looked at me in shock.

"You know?" asked Mike.

"And you know, which means she knows."

In just two strides I had closed the distance between me and Mike, and I was lifting him to his toes by his collar.

"What did you do?" I growled, my fist itching to plaster Mike's face in the wall.

"Stop it! Stop!" screamed Keisha. "We don't have time for this! We have to find her."

I dropped Mike back down and turned to Keisha.

She took a step back, my anger seemingly consuming all life in the room.

"Chloe found out. She investigated and realized he had access to her computer each of the times the emails were sent out. We organized a party yesterday to distract Kyle so we could search his house, grabbed burner phones that we found, get the information and then... Chloe put them back in his room..."

"We have burner phone text exchanged between him and someone we assume works at Green Mile about the IP," chimed in Mike.

"He must have found out somehow…" added Keisha wish fresh tears running down her face.

"Fuck!" I howled. "Of course he did. He has hidden cameras all over his place! Even a fucking amateur could have seen them!"

"I didn't get a chance to inspect his place," added Mike defensively.

I stopped listening and called Luke.

"Where is he?"

CHAPTER 43

Chloe

IT WAS THE THIRD time I was trying to open my eyes. My body felt heavy, my head was throbbing, and I could feel a bump forming on my forehead. My eyes were slowly getting used to the darkness of the space.

I could now see that I was in a poor lit room, the air was cold and heavy, and a bit dusty. I tried to move, only to find that my arms were tightly tied in front of me, and my legs were wrapped to the chair I was seated on.

"Well, hello there."

I sucked in a breath at the sound of Kyle's voice. He moved from wherever he was hidden to come to stand right in front of me. He crossed his arms, giving me that smug look he got when he thought he was doing something smart, which generally wasn't the case.

"What am I doing here? What happened?" I demanded.

I was starting to remember; someone had grabbed me as I was leaving my house to meet Keisha and Mike for dinner. Now I was sure it had been amateur Kyle, who hadn't expected me to fight back.

He had to carry a nasty bruise where I had bitten him, I was sure, but I had hit my head on the wall right before the liquid he had forced me to inhale though a cloth had started to take effect.

"You acted like a little cunt. You know what you did. Throwing me a party, only to spy on me, take my stuff, tsk, that was a mistake."

"Let me guess, you decided that the only way to get out of trouble was to kidnap me? That was well thought out."

He flinched, taking a step toward me.

"Shut up. I... I needed to show you what happens when you mess with me. I can be dangerous, Chloe. I can."

"You stole from me. You stole from my family. And you framed me for it!"

"Yeah... I did. I just, I knew your dad would never take me seriously."

"Kyle, what are you talking about?"

"I will always remain someone who he calls as needed, but I'm never appreciated, never promoted. I needed to take matters in my own hands. I have an expensive lifestyle, Chloe. I had to keep it up. Keep up appearances. I needed more money, and I wasn't willing to wait for it any longer, so I took it."

"Of course not. Why work hard if you can just take what is not yours?"

"Shut up!" He slapped me so hard my vision blurred, my right cheek burning, and I could taste blood in my mouth.

I decided to stop antagonizing him. I didn't know Kyle to be violent, but fear and panic could bring out the worst in people.

I knew he hadn't calculated the consequences of his actions. Kyle was never good under pressure; he usually panicked and made rash decisions, only this time, it led to me being in a random place, barefoot, and tied to a chair.

Kyle was interrupted by his ringtone. He glared at the phone screen, tensed, and stepped out of the room. I took the opportunity to scan my surroundings. I had no idea where I was. This looked like the basement of a house, with shelves filled with random items like plant holders and golf clubs. I also noticed some bikes.

There were no windows, so presumably this was a storage room. If I could get up, perhaps I could try to open the other door in the room and see where it took me. I tried to rise to my feet, but I was too tightly bound to the chair.

In my movements, I felt something in the inside pocket of my jacket. When Kyle took me, he clearly had made sure to keep my purse away from me, as I could see it on the floor at the other end of the room. But I had also taken my work phone with me, which was in my pocket.

Hope rushed through me. I bent my tied hands back just enough to grab the cell from my pocket. But when I tried to place an emergency call, I saw I had no signal. Great.

Before I could try again, I heard a noise by the door. I quickly turned on the video recording on the phone and dropped it back in my pocket. Kyle walked in, looking troubled and distracted.

I held in a scream when the door behind Kyle swayed opened aggressively. A man of average height, a bit buff, stormed in the room, a mask on his face.

I panicked and tried to lift myself again, but Kyle stopped me and violently slapped me, making me dizzy with pain, the copper taste of my own blood chilling my bones.

The man crossed the room and stopped in front of me. I glanced at him through half closed eyes, the pain made worse when I tried to focus on something. I was about to pass out. I shut my eyes and let my head fall back, unable to sustain its weight.

"Way to fuck this up, Kyle! Why the fuck would you take her to my home?!"

"I panicked, Chad, I..."

"Don't use my fucking name!"

"She is barely conscious," snarked Kyle.

I kept my head tilted to the side, and my eyes closed, hoping they believed I was still out cold. If they knew I was listening, depending on what they discussed, it could cost me my life.

"Don't use my name, you fucking idiot, unless your plan is to kill her. What are you going to do with her?"

"I don't know!"

"No one was supposed to get hurt in this. We were just supposed to steal the goddamn information, use it for our axles, and get them out of business. Taking a life wasn't part of the plan."

"I know, I know, I am thinking about it! She might be helpful to us; you could even offer her a position at Green Mile on top of mine..."

I heard a grunt but couldn't tell what was happening. I heard Kyle make a muffled scream.

"Okay, okay, you don't have to hit me, man, let me talk to her. Give me a chance. I messed up. I am going to fix it. Let me fix it."

"I can't imagine that she would want to work for me after all this shit you pulled, Kyle. It's one thing to steal from Motor Holmes, but now you fucked with her safety."

I heard the man sigh, holding my breath for what he had to say.

"You have an hour. I don't want to hurt anyone, but after this fucking mess you created, we might not have a choice but to get rid of her."

I tried to control my heart rate; I needed to remain calm. I couldn't let them see the fear coursing through me at the thought that they might kill me.

I heard steps, and then a door close.

"Shit," cursed Kyle. I heard him pacing, trying to decide what to do. "Chloe, Chloe, wake up! I'm sorry I hit you so hard," he said as he shook me, making my headache worse.

I pretended to slowly open my eyes, taking stock of my surroundings. Kyle was standing in front of me, a look of concern in his eyes.

"I didn't mean for any of this to happen. I didn't mean to bring you here."

"Where are we?" I rasped.

"I messed up so much. Why did you have to dig in my shit, hun?! Why? All was well, I got all the money I wanted from Green Mile, and they were going to give me a job on top of it, but you had to fucking ruin it all!"

"What is your plan here, Kyle?" I asked, anxiety making me a bit fidgety.

"Who else knows?" he asked, ignoring my question as he towered over me. He was attempting to intimidate me, but it wasn't working.

"Why would you think someone else knows?" I demanded.

"Because how would you have known otherwise? How would you know about what I was doing? How would you plan this whole thing in the first place, take my phones like that, trick me like that?"

"I didn't mean to hurt you," I lied, trying a different approach to avoid the topic.

He crossed his arms, having the audacity to look hurt.

"But I accidentally found some emails from my inbox that I knew I didn't send."

"And? That doesn't mean it was me."

"Well, I wasn't sure it was you. It could have been other people, too. But turns out it *was* you. You used me, Kyle, and you framed me. Yet you say you love me."

I shed a tear. But it wasn't for that bastard, it was from fear and fury.

But I needed to put all my energy in distracting Kyle, play with his emotions, get him to think of something else to not realize the holes in my story.

I didn't know what he was capable of in his irrational state, but clearly hurting me was on the table. And I wasn't going to put Jake, Keisha, or Mike in danger.

"I do love you!" he screamed, seemingly offended.

"I don't believe you!" I cried out, pretending to be hurt. "Why would you frame me then?"

"Because!" he explained as he lowered himself to his knees to face me directly. "I figured your father would just forgive you! He would understand that you made a mistake, if he ever found out, and hide it for you, forgive you. I considered telling you, but you're so 'principled'," he added with repulsion. "I wasn't sure you would participate in all of this. I figured I would come clean to you if it all exploded. I thought you would forgive me. I thought you loved me even if you didn't seem to think so."

"I... I don't know what to say."

"But he showed up and my plans started to wobble. You no longer gave me your attention. He took possession of you, Chloe, at every meeting, at every interaction."

I didn't pretend to not understand who he was talking about. Even Kyle had noticed the hold Jake had on me from the minute we met.

"That's not true, Kyle."

"Of course, it is!" He rose up suddenly, almost hitting me in the process. I flinched. I didn't know how many more slaps I could take.

"Now I don't feel like I could convince you to be by my side if things took a turn. And you snuck into my place, but you didn't confront me. You were gathering evidence, weren't you? Weren't you?!"

Spit was coming out from his mouth in alarming proportions. I was losing him again.

"No, no, I just wanted to be sure before confronting you, that is all. I didn't want to be embarrassed if it wasn't you. And how... how did you know?"

"How did I know what you did? I have cameras, Chloe, who do you take me for? Hidden very well, in my smoke alarms."

He was acting smug again, proud of himself. I did look around for cameras, but I never knew him to be paranoid, to the point of hiding them so cleverly. It didn't occur to me that he would have them in the damn smoke alarms, or why he would think of checking them in the first place.

"What made you suspicious, though?" I whispered.

"I saw that kiss," he admitted with a sneer. "I saw Jake kiss you in Michigan, and I saw how you responded to him. You have been drooling over that fucking guy since he stepped foot at that fucking party. He's also been gawking at you like a hawk, everywhere you go.

"I also know who he is. I know your dad hired him to spy on the company, find a rat. One of his employees works for me! And you know what I think? I think you are working with him; you are helping him."

My face paled, my palms suddenly sweaty and cold, and fear invading me even further. I thought I was manipulating him for information, but he already knew too much of what I was trying to hide.

"Did you tell him it was me, huh? K. made sure he destroyed some of my mistakes, gave him fake reports, but you, I didn't anticipate you finding out. Does he know? I will fucking have to kill him if he does! Tell me!"

Kyle started shaking me, increasing my headache and making me dizzy.

"No, no, I didn't tell him. He doesn't know anything, I swear! He thinks it's me! Please, Kyle, don't... don't hurt him."

"Why do you care if he lives or dies!?"

"I don't, I don't care, but I don't want another person to be in danger for no reason."

"Chloe, I am not an idiot. And your reaction at the thought of me killing him tells me everything."

"I swear, Kyle."

The idea that he could hurt Jake made every fiber of my being turn on high alert. I had to protect him at all costs.

"I don't believe you!"

"Why not? You and whoever was helping you did a damn good job at framing me! A bunch of emails from my laptop and access to confidential information with my password. Why wouldn't he believe the evidence right in front of his eyes?! And yes, I was into him, very much, but he dumped me as soon as he thought I was a criminal. He went back to Lauren, and he will tell my father that I did this.

"Because as far as he's concerned, I'm a liar who decided to steal from the people I loved the most, the people who gave me everything. He thinks me capable of going that low, just for money, for insatiable ambition. He thinks I used him, when in fact it was you, you!" My voice broke.

I let the tears flow. I didn't give a damn, and frankly I was terrified, cold, overwhelmed by the fact that these could be my last moments alive. He could see me like this, raw, broken. My pride was too damaged and weak in this moment to protect me.

He straightened up, crossing his arms again, a thin line on his lips. Honesty seemed to have worked to calm him down.

"Are you going to tell him? If I let you go, are you going to betray me?" he demanded.

How much of a psychopath was Kyle really, thinking he would be the one to be betrayed? But this was my chance to bargain for my survival, so I had to play it safe.

"Why would I help him? I hate him."

"Clear your name? You have proof it's me now, no?"

"I only needed the proof to bargain with you. To make sure you knew I had something over you. Now, if you kill me, this will never end. Jake will still tell my dad it was me, but then I would be dead, and that would be suspicious timing."

"I can make it look like an accident. Well, my partner can anyways."

I swallowed hard as bile rose to my throat.

"I serve you more alive, Kyle. We can come up with a deal. While I love my family, I am angry. I am angry my dad let the shareholders give that asshole my board seat. He voted for him! He humiliated me in front of the whole company, disrespected me, treated me like I didn't deserve it. You know that."

"But you love him. Why would you not just tell him the truth, huh? Why should I believe you?!"

I was losing him again. He returned to me, grabbed my face with his hand and aggressively bent my head upwards to kiss me. I repulsed immediately before I realized my body was making a huge mistake.

"You can't even stand me, Chloe. This is not like the kiss you gave him. You soiled yourself, didn't you? You let him touch you? You can't lie to me!"

"Kyle, leave him out of this, please, that is all I am asking. He doesn't need to get hurt. Do whatever you want to me, but please don't hurt him. I'm begging you."

He slapped me for the third time. I was starting to drift out of consciousness, my ears ringing, when we both got startled by a noise that seemed to come from outside.

Kyle turned, frozen for a second, looking at the door on the far left. I followed his gaze. I forced my vision back into focus; that was my chance. He was distracted. I gathered the small amount of strength I had left, stood with my knees bent turned to my side and slammed the side and back of the chair into him, making us both fall on the floor, the chair and I on top of him, before I tumbled to the side, my head hitting the floor. I screamed.

"Bitch!" he yelled.

Fear invaded my stomach as he stood back in front of me, rubbing his arm and shoulder.

I heard another noise; he pulled back the fist that he was going to use to punch me and ran out of the room.

I tried to stand, but my body didn't have the strength to follow my will, my eyes fighting to stay open, until they closed.

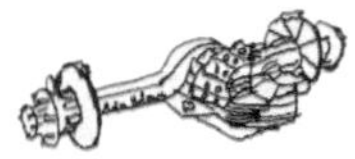

"Chloe, Chloe? God! Baby, please wake up."

How many times would those words, that voice, be the one to take me out of a slumber? My body wouldn't listen to me, but that voice, that was all it took for my consciousness to rush back to me, my pupils fluttering open, and trying to focus on the unshaved and distorted version of Jake's face, with those deep blue eyes sucking out and bringing in life into me at the same time.

He slowly lifted me from the chair. I screamed when I heard some gunshots, the shock forcing adrenaline through me.

Jake pulled out a gun from the back of his pants and pointed it at the door. When no one came through, he repositioned the gun in his jeans.

"We have to go. I'm getting you out of here."

He took me in his arms and rushed to the other side of the room, to a door I hadn't noticed until now. It looked like it was still dark out, which meant I had only spent a few hours in this hell.

Jake started running towards a car. He opened the door and dropped me in it. He immediately buckled my seat belt and lowered my chair.

"Do not move."

The savage glare he gave me, the tightened jaw, the intensity of his movement, there was no room for argument. And at this stage, I was going to be more obedient than I have ever been in my entire life. Jake looked like the lion that was always hidden behind those mesmerizing eyes had been set free.

He closed the door. I shut my eyes to stop the earth from moving but jumped up once I heard more bullets fired. I looked up to see Jake on the driver's side of the car, shooting at his opponent. It was still very dark and wherever we were was very poorly lit.

I heard a thump coming from the direction Jake was shooting at. Satisfied, Jake got in the car. He made a ridiculously precise U-turn, making the tires screech, and skidded off to the street at high speed.

I leaned back down, the rush of adrenaline wearing off, and my body ache taking over. I silently closed my eyes again, this time feeling safe and protected.

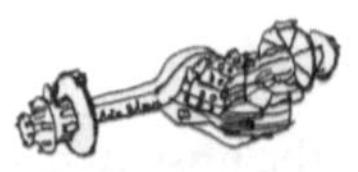

I felt when the car came to a full stop. I slowly opened my eyes and lifted my body into a seating position. We were in the three-car garage I seldom used; we were at my house.

Jake got out of his side, opened my door, removed my seatbelt, and lifted me in his arms.

"I can walk," I protested, but he ignored me as he opened the garage door and crossed my yard.

My backdoor was open, with Keisha in the doorframe, tears smudging her beautiful face, her praying hands in front of her lips. My eyes filled, as I fought Jake to let me down, and ran into the warm embrace of my friend.

CHAPTER 44

Jake

THERE WERE NO WORDS to describe how the past hours of my life had felt like. While I was no stranger to danger, I didn't think I could ever explain how it felt like to find out that Chloe had been abducted, all because of me.

But she was here, I reminded myself, safe. Bruised, but safe, currently cradled in the arms of Keisha and Mike.

Not mine.

All three of them sat on the couch by the kitchen with Penny, while I stood in front of them, hands in my pockets to stop the urge I had to reach out to her and hold her. I couldn't sit still.

She had rejected all my attempts to help her. She was barefoot, her skin pale, her face smudged, and her lips still bleeding.

The rage I felt was unmatched.

"We need to take you to the hospital," I repeated, looking at Keisha this time, begging her for support.

While Chloe no longer gave me death stares, she still ignored me as much as humanly possible.

"Like I said, twice already, I'm not going anywhere."

Chloe lifted her body up, trying to look like she had more strength than she did.

"No part of my body was really hurt, I promise."

I sighed, my head twisting in disapproval.

"You hit your head, Chloe," I explained again, sounding harsher than I intended.

She rolled her eyes but squinted from pain.

The lump in my throat grew bigger as I tried to swallow. She was going to the hospital one way or another.

I looked at Mike, the tightening in my chest increasing.

"Take her. Please."

Both Chloe and Keisha looked up at me. I ignored them both when they rolled their eyes. I then turned my gaze on Mike, one that told him not to contradict me.

Mike swallowed and turned to Chloe.

"He's right, you know. You have an open wound on your forehead."

Chloe sighed. She understood why she needed to go; she just didn't want to go with me.

"Fine," she added in defeat.

I felt like I was burning in place as I watched Mike help Chloe up. She was leaning on him for support, his arm around her waist.

I couldn't stand this any further. Fuck it.

Without warning, I closed the distance between us and lifted her into my arms.

"Hey!" she protested, but no one dared come to her rescue once they saw my face.

I wasn't going to let Mike or any other men put their hands on her, for that matter. I ignored her, as it was clear that she didn't have the energy to fight me.

That broke me more.

We all went to the garage. I gently sat her in the back, with Keisha sliding in next to her. I secured her seatbelt, under her stern gaze. But I felt her hold her breath as I put my hands around her waist, my face only a few inches from hers.

My eyes darted between her sensually parted plump lips, her dark eyes looking panicked. My jaw tensed, as I lingered a bit more, and scanned the honey brown of her eyes, traced her determined jaw, and went back to her eyes again.

I couldn't tell if she would let me kiss her or if she would slap me if I tried. Now was not the time to rattle her, I reminded myself. It was time to make sure that bastard hadn't damaged her more than I could tell.

Mike climbed in the front passenger seat, and we drove off. I had Chloe's purse, so I was able to open the garage with her remote as I had done earlier.

"So, what happened?" asked Mike.

"I'm not sure," answered Chloe.

I looked at her through the rearview mirror. Our eyes met, and I held her gaze a few seconds longer. I had almost lost her. I needed to remind myself that she was there with me, that the nightmare was over.

"How did you find me?" She held my gaze in the mirror.

"Mike and Keisha realized you were missing when you didn't show up for dinner last night. We were suspicious that it was Kyle. It wasn't hard to track his phone after that. I got my men and some people Alejandro sent me."

Luke had easily tracked him down. And with the help of Alejandro, who was the fiancée of one of Chloe's friends, they were able to figure out a way to get into the apartment.

When Alejandro offered to send reinforcements, even if I didn't need them, I agreed. Turned out his men were highly trained, and the two teams joined forces with no hiccup. We all agreed to meet in Chicago and drive to Wisconsin to find her.

"Where is he?" she whispered.

I held the steering wheel harder and clenched my teeth.

"He escaped."

"Where did he have me?"

"He drove you to Wisconsin."

Her eyes widened. "Wisconsin? Was I in a house?"

I pulled in front of University of Chicago Hospital, since it was just a few minutes away from her house. I turned around to face her.

"Yes, Chad Gorbel's house."

CHAPTER 45

Chloe

I WAS JUST GOING through the motions, answering the doctors' questions, letting myself be prodded for the second time in less than a week, lost in my thoughts. I was feeling quite shaken by what had happened just ten hours ago. It felt surreal that Kyle had thought to drug me and take me all the way to Wisconsin.

What was even more surreal was Jake coming in there, looking like some possessed warrior trained for situations like this, and pulling me out. He literally saved my life.

Would Kyle have killed me just like that? Would Chad? When did high-level executives in companies become criminals, or people who go through bullets to save my life?

I was trying to remain grounded, but considering it was now 6 a.m. and I had been sleep-deprived for most of the night, I wondered if I was about to wake up from what would have been a very realistic nightmare.

Both Jake and Keisha were in the exam room with me, observing my every move, refusing to leave my side.

The only one who had respected my privacy was Mike, who was seated in the waiting room. I came back to my current reality when the doctor suggested I spend the day under observation at the hospital because I had a mild concussion.

"No, no, no, no. I am not staying here."

I heard Jake sigh, but I ignored him.

"You don't have to," the doctor added, "but you shouldn't be alone in your house either if you decide not to stay."

"Sweetie, it's for your own good," added Keisha in an attempt to sway me.

I shot her a death stare, and she rolled her eyes, knowing my stubborn self wouldn't budge.

"I can stay with her," offered Jake.

I opened my eyes wide, pleading silently to Keisha.

"I have to go to court, but I can stop by in the evening?"

Was Keisha smirking at me? I closed my eyes for a moment, considering whether staying in the hospital would be a better option than being in a house with Jake for God only knew how long.

No, I needed my space, and I needed to help my father. It would be much more difficult to do from the hospital.

"Fine," I conceded, still managing to ignore Jake's burning gaze.

Keisha and Mike left the hospital to go back to work. Jake and I silently drove back to my house. It irritated me to no end that he looked so comfortable opening my garage and walking into my house, as if that was a habit we had already developed.

Okay, fine, he had saved my life, but still. I couldn't hide the fact that seeing him so overprotective, taking control of the situation, both turned me on and provided me some comfort.

When we walked into my house, we both sat in the living room in the back, with Jake sitting on the coffee table so he could be across from me. And way too close.

Penny wasn't a traitor today; I think she could tell something had happened to me, so she stayed on my lap, rubbing her sweet face against my chin.

"How do you feel?"

"Fine."

"Chloe, come on. Talk to me."

I bit my lip. I knew he could read me like a book, but admitting to weaknesses out loud wasn't my forte. I sighed and shook my head, wanting to stop the tingle I could feel in my throat.

"Do my parents know?"

Jake hesitated. "I called them when I drove you home earlier today. They are back in town and on their way here."

"Shit!" I cursed, putting my head in my hands.

"I had to, Chloe."

"I know. At least you saved them from having to wait for you to find me."

"They are livid that I didn't inform them sooner. But I had to act fast; I didn't have a lot of time, and I didn't want anything or anyone to put you in even more danger than you already were."

I raised my head, disturbed by the concerned raspy tone of his voice. His eyes were scanning me, searching mine. I could feel the tension emanating from him.

"Thank you. Thank you for saving me."

"You don't have to thank me, mein leibling. I... I just... this life, without you in it..."

"Jake... I am forever in your debt for saving me, but this changes nothing between us. I need to get cleaned up," I sighed as I quickly got up, afraid that my resolves might not be as strong as I made them sound. Penny ran away.

I felt the room move under my feet. Jake immediately wrapped strong arms around me, bringing me close to his chest. I just leaned on him, finding comfort in having him so close, feeling his heartbeat under my palm.

"Let me take you to your room."

Before I could protest, he lifted me off the ground. I grabbed onto him, eyes closed, trying to swallow the lump in my throat. He set me down gently in my bathroom.

"I will be right outside."

Part of me desperately wanted to tell him to stay with me, but what good would that do? I nodded and shut the bathroom door.

I started by washing my face, barely recognizing myself, the bony structure, the deep dark circles and the bruises reminding me exactly how real the situation was, how much danger I had been in.

I exploded in tears, trembling fingers covering my lips.

"Chloe? Are you okay?"

I couldn't take it. I leaned on the bathroom door, my body shaking.

"Chloe, please, open the door for me, baby, please."

I hated him.

I needed him.

But I didn't want to see him.

I didn't have the strength. So, I just cried holding to the door, knowing he was right behind it. I couldn't say a word, all I could do was cry, and cry some more.

Eventually I calmed down. My dad needed me, there wasn't much time for breaking down. And I had just the thing.

I quickly padded the pockets of my jacket, now remembering what I had managed to do right before he saved me. The phone was still there. I pulled it out with shaking hands. It had lost charge.

I brusquely swung the bathroom door open, Jake looking at me with a grave expression on his face.

"My phone."

I proceeded to my nightstand and plugged it in, heart racing. I knew I had to give it a few minutes to turn back on, but the wait was killing me. I gazed into Jake's red eyes for a few seconds, my eyes swelling again, and heart pounding on my ribcage.

"I turned the recording on when Kyle left the room" I explained. "He thought of taking my personal phone, but he didn't realize I had my work phone with me too."

"You think it recorded something useful?"

"That's my hope. I remember someone Kyle called Chad coming in the room; it can't be a coincidence."

We both impatiently waited as the phone finally turned on. I unlocked it and went straight to my videos. There it was. An hour-long dark video of the worst time of my life. I looked up at Jake and played it.

"This was such a fuckup, Kyle!"

I smiled for the first time since I had been back home.

"We got them."

CHAPTER 46

Jake

"You have been drooling over that fucking guy since he stepped foot at that fucking party. He's also been looking at you like a hawk, everywhere you go."

Chloe paused the video. Keeping her head low.

"That's sufficient," she announced.

It wasn't.

My breathing had accelerated while listening to the recording, vacillating between torment at hearing in how much danger she had been, and blind rage at what Kyle had put her through.

I wanted to find him, choke him until I saw the life leave his body. He had hurt her, physically and emotionally.

All of this was my fault.

And now, the woman I loved had been harmed. She was next to me, looking frail, bruised, and as strong as ever.

I wouldn't press her for the rest of the recording. As much as I wanted to hear what happened next, she didn't want me to, and for now, I would respect that. But there was no scenario in which I didn't hear the full tape. I had to in case there was any information on where Kyle could be hiding. And if he had hurt her further, I had to know.

He was already a dead man anyways.

"We have Green Mile where we want them."

I heard the doorbell ring. Chloe jumped a bit.

"It's your dad. How about you relax, take a shower? I will go downstairs and handle this. I also grabbed your purse, so I will also get that from the car. You meet us downstairs when you are ready."

"Okay." She set the phone down on her bed and went back to the bathroom, closing the door behind her.

I swallowed hard, the burning in my stomach intensifying. It killed me to see her like this. She was letting me take control, without even one retort, and that wasn't like her. But that was clearly what she needed now, a shoulder to lean on, someone to help her carry the weight off all of this, while she found her bearing. And I was going to give her whatever support she wanted from me.

I desperately wanted to tell her I loved her, to get on my knees and beg for her forgiveness, but that was not what she needed in the moment. She needed me strong, competent. She needed me to help her dad, help the company, and find Kyle and Chad, make sure nothing else could harm her.

There was also something else I had discovered through the messages from the burner phones. Something the recording further confirmed.

K. My most trusted employee had betrayed me.

That would probably explain why I hadn't been able to reach him since yesterday evening. I didn't yet understand why or how K was connected to Kyle, but that explained all the obstacles and the gaps in information I saw when I reviewed all the data we had compiled.

It explained why Kyle looked clean at first glance. It explained why K. had never reported any information that would have clearly exonerated Chloe, information he had surely easily found. It would explain the mystery around those random bank transfers K. had presented as evidence that Green Mile had paid her off.

Now I knew what they were; I knew about Chloe's secret.

If there was one thing I couldn't stand, it was when people made me look like a fool.

A quick call to Luke set it all in motion. K., along with Kyle and Chad, now had a target on their backs. It was only going to be a question of time. Once I found K., I would crush him like the bug that he was.

I proceeded downstairs and opened the door to horrified expressions on both Philip and Yasmin Holmes' faces. Eric, their son, was also with them, glaring at me as if I was the enemy.

"Where is she? Where is my daughter?" asked Yasmin, her eyes filled with tears.

"She's upstairs," I tried to reassure as I closed the door behind them. "She's showering, and she should be down here soon."

"How is she?" Philip made sure his wife sat down, but Philip, Eric and I remained on our feet.

"She's fine. A bit bruised. She has a concussion, but she will be okay. I am staying here with her, and I will take her to the doctor again in a couple of days."

"Did you find Kyle?" asked Eric, his body tense.

I recognized the rage in him; I felt the same way.

"Only a question of time."

"What happened exactly?" asked Eric. "How did she get involved in all this mess?"

My jaw muscle flinched instinctively. I knew I would have to explain myself at some point, explain how I had managed to put Chloe in harm's way during my investigation.

"Kyle framed Chloe. He used her computer and her passwords to send Green Mile Motor Holmes' proprietary information. I confronted her about it. She was adamant that it wasn't her. She asked for a chance to prove her innocence, so I gave her access to all the data my team had gathered. She didn't share her findings with me.

"Seems like she had found evidence that Kyle had framed her and took matters into her own hands. She went to his house and found some burner phones with information on them. Kyle realized what had happened, and he took her hostage."

"How dare you, Jake, how dare you accuse my daughter of something like this?" yelled Philip.

"I shouldn't have." I didn't know what else to say. "Even when all the evidence pointed to her, I should have trusted her."

"You fucking idiot!" grunted Eric as he grabbed me by my shirt. "She could have died!"

I drew a sharp breath and wrapped my hands into fists. Eric was playing with fire, but I understood where he was coming from, so I restrained myself and didn't react. His sister had been in danger. Because of me.

"Eric, calm down," ordered Philip, but Eric didn't budge.

I could only tolerate so much. I shoved Eric's hands away. Eric held my gaze though, and he didn't step back.

"I need everyone here to calm down," ordered Yasmin as she got up from the couch.

She walked to her husband and put her hand on his arms, her eyes, the same depth as Chloe's, on me.

"She won't admit it, but you broke her heart. I hope you know that." Her words tore me apart. "But you also did everything in your power to save her." She looked at her son. "Keisha told me he put his own life in danger to get her himself. He's the one who rescued her."

I noticed Eric's jaw tense at the mention of Keisha.

"Thank you, Jake," said Philip.

"I should have protected her," I admitted, my chest tightening further.

"My daughter is quite stubborn, Jake. There wasn't much, short of locking her in a room, that you would have been able to do to stop her from taking matters into her own hands. The minute she found out Motor Holmes was in danger, that was it," admitted Yasmin.

"What are you to her anyway? I assume you wouldn't put your life in danger like this just because she is my father's daughter."

I turned to face Eric.

"I'm in love with her. And I fucked up."

It was plain and simple, and I didn't care who knew. She was mine, and the world needed to know that. I would do whatever it took to earn her forgiveness.

"Okay, okay, we are all very tense. Let's sit," proposed Philip after clearing his throat. "There is a lot to talk about."

"Agreed. I will make some coffee," added Yasmin.

"I will need something stronger than that," I said.

"Couldn't agree more," added Eric.

Seemed like he was a bit calmer now. We all sat down while Yasmin went to the kitchen.

"We have to find that bastard," said Philip under his breath.

"I will not rest until we do. We have Max, though, the IT manager who helped him."

"What do you mean we have him?" Eric was frowning again.

"He is being interrogated." I didn't provide any more details.

"Legally, I assume? Actually, you know what, I don't want to know. They deserve whatever comes their way."

I ignored Eric and continued. The less they knew about my interrogation techniques, the better.

"Chloe recorded Chad talking to Kyle about everything. It's audio, but you can hear Chad's voice very clearly. We have what we need to bring him to the table."

"We need to do more than that. We need to force him to sell us his company. And we have to make sure he can never, ever pursue business in this industry again. Same for Kyle, and whoever else worked with them."

We all brusquely stood up when we heard Chloe's voice as she came down the stairs. She was wearing what looked to be silk pajamas. She was the most beautiful woman I'd ever seen.

I went to her, holding her hands as she met us. Both her father and her brother wrapped her in their arms. Yasmin was right behind them, putting the tray she had brought on the coffee table before going to her daughter.

They were all sobbing, making my eyes burn for the third time in the day

I tensed, frustrated that I couldn't take her in my arms as well, kiss her, caress her, hold her against my chest to make sure she was okay, protected, safe. And my desire for her was taking new forms, invading every single one of my senses.

I needed to feel her, to be inside of her, make her mine over and over until I no longer felt this blinding fear. Until she smiled.

I had almost lost her. I had had time to contemplate what a life without her would be. The terror that had engrained in me would take time before it could heal.

She had cleverly arranged her makeup to reduce the visibility of her bruises, still considerate of her parents in this situation. But I knew exactly where they were, so I could still see them, the location of each one of them imprinted in my psyche forever. Her damp curly hair was loosely falling down her back. She looked like an angel to me.

"I'm fine, I'm fine," she kept reassuring her family, slowly getting out of their embrace.

She took a seat in a solo chair and pointed us to the three-person sofa. Her family sat there. I remained standing not too far from her.

"Any updates on the whereabouts of Kyle or Chad?" she inquired, looking at me.

Her fierceness was back, her mind clearly ready for battle.

"No updates yet, but we will find them. They cannot hide forever."

"Dad, what do you think? Why don't we do our own hostile takeover? We have what we need to force him to sell for cheap. It's that or we sue them in court."

"Well, yes, it's the best way to make sure we have control over the IP they stole."

"Why not ruin them in court?" asked Eric.

"As fun as it would be to see that, I don't want a scandal. I don't want our brand associated with this mess. We are securing contracts, months away from launching our new e-axles. This would damage our brand, our clients' trust in us, and our business prospects down the line," explained Chloe.

I was bursting with pride. I shifted my position as I could feel myself get hard. This was my woman: thoughtful, cold, and ruthless when she needed to be.

"I agree," added Philip.

"I am so glad you are okay, honey," said Yasmin, her voice wobbly. I felt my own throat constrict.

"Me too, Mom."

Chloe sucked in a deeper breath.

"I have a recording with Chad on it. We can use that." The room fell silent, understanding that we would all be privy to the horror Chloe really was in with this audio.

"We will," I added. "Can you send it to us?"

"Um, yes."

I noticed she got a little uncomfortable at the idea, but she knew it had to be done.

The doorbell rang again. It was Keisha and Mike. I let them in, as I stepped outside to take Luke's call.

"Yes?" I answered.

"We've got a potential location for Chad."

"Send me the address."

CHAPTER 47

Chloe

I WOKE UP FEELING like I had slept for days, even if I had been woken up a couple of times per doctor's orders.

Keisha had spent the night with me. I figured Jake would disagree and want to stay himself, but he wound up leaving as soon as he accepted the call last night. I didn't know where he went, but he did it fast and didn't say much.

My family stayed for a while, which I enjoyed. I didn't realize how much I needed to just be in their presence, especially my brother. Eric having flown in on the first flight in once he heard what had happened. I loved that I had my family to lean on.

I wasn't ready to process how I felt yet, so I decided to focus on the business and what the next steps were. I needed the distraction I had to make sure Motor Holmes' future was no longer in jeopardy.

I had emailed the video recording to Jake. I wanted to cut part of it beforehand, but time was of the essence, and I refused to slow down anything just because I didn't want him hearing how desperately I tried to protect him. How scared I was. How I got hurt. But I asked him to give a shortened version to my dad as I knew he would push to get something.

I no longer had the energy to hide anything. What I felt for him, the need I had to feel his warmth around me, to bury my face in his neck, none of it mattered.

He had lied to me, betrayed me, hidden who he was and his intentions, and he had slept with me while he investigated me.

Even after getting to know me, he thought me capable of selling my dad's hard work to the highest bidder. He had paraded Lauren in my face, in his house, in front of family and coworkers. He had let her in his room, in the bed I had shared with him.

There was no coming back from that.

The plan was to use the video and all the other data we had gathered to coerce Chad into submission, acquire his company, and put this nightmare behind us.

This also brought up several other issues. We needed someone to revamp the IT department and the security measures we had in place. Clearly. There was no one better for the position in my mind.

Mike was still helping a great deal. He had proven to be a confidante and a true friend. To thank him, I offered him the position of head of IT in my father's company. Although I hadn't consulted with anyone prior to the offer, no one had protested, including when I made him a salary offer he couldn't refuse. Mike had instantly accepted.

"You're awake?" asked Keisha as she slowly opened the door.

She was wearing her own set of yellow silky pajamas, matching mine. Keisha walked to me and slid in the spot next to me on the bed.

"Thank you for staying with me," I said as I rubbed Penny's head.

"Of course. Plus, it was the only way to get the hulk to leave."

"The hulk?" I started laughing.

"I mean, I don't know what else to call him. The man would roll you in bubble wrap and put you on his shoulders if he could."

I laughed, my heart warming up when I remembered how Jake cradled me in his arms. The thought made me sad though, knowing that we could never be together.

"Chloe... I know you are upset. You have every right to be. But you didn't see that man when he found out you had been taken. I frankly had never seen anyone transform like this in a matter of seconds. He would have torn the world apart to find you."

I sighed, blinking back the tears that blurred my vision.

"That doesn't change anything. It's... it's too much."

"It's only too much because of how you feel about him."

"No. Also, like, who are you and what have you done with my 'I don't believe in marriage or everlasting love' best friend?"

"I never said it doesn't exist. I just think it's very rare and thus not worth the trouble to look for. And I also think I might be witnessing it with you."

I sat up, running my fingers through my curls, a tinge of annoyance I couldn't hide in my voice.

"That look he gave me when he accused me of selling the information, it's... I can't unsee it. And there is Lauren; they kissed right in my face, Keisha. I can't just... I won't just move on. All I want to do is break her face and punch him until my body can't keep doing it anymore."

Keisha sighed and sat up as well, taking my hand in hers to force me to look at her.

"I know he messed up. There is no denying that. He messed up real bad. But trust me, that man is in pain, and he is paying for it. And I don't care about his pain, but I know you are suffering, as well. I am just not sure that holding ónto his mistake and forgetting everything else you guys shared, including the fact that he put his neck on the line to save you, got shot at to save you, is worth it. I just want you to be happy."

I broke down in tears. Keisha also cried, as seeing me in that state affected her, too. I let Keisha take me in her arms, the feeling of my friend's unconditional love allowing me to let all the emotions flow out of me and on her silk clothes.

The day went by in a peaceful haze, with my parents and Eric visiting again. They couldn't stop fussing around me, and I let them.

I understood. The idea that my life could have ended, that my family would be left with the whole of my absence, teared my heart apart. I held them closer and let them reassure themselves that I was okay. It was 8 p.m. by the time everyone, including Keisha, finally left. I had an important client meeting the next day to get ready for.

I knew Keisha was a little bit shaken when Eric announced that he was going to stay in town a little longer, to make sure I was okay, and he wouldn't leave at least until they found Kyle, but I didn't press her for how she was going to cope. All I could do was be there for when Keisha was ready to talk.

I was surprised and startled when I heard my doorbell ring. I hadn't ordered anything and wasn't expecting anyone. I peered out of the bay windows to see if there was a car in the middle of the street, but they were all parked, and it was too dark to decipher the car stationed right in front on my house. I hesitated but after the second ring, I turned on my ringtone camera on my phone.

My heart pulsated when I caught sight of Jake in the camera. He stared straight in the lens, likely knowing I would be checking. I felt a sudden knot in my stomach.

"Open the door, Chloe," he instructed to the camera.

He of course knew I was home, so I inhaled slowly, telling my traitorous body to control itself.

I opened the door wide to let him in. Jake's face looked agitated; he clearly hadn't shaved and hadn't bothered to comb his hair.

He was wearing a dark gray suit with an off-white shirt, the first few buttons open, with no tie. Gone was his usual stoically perfect composure. He looked a bit rough in the best of ways.

I felt a shot of electricity between my thighs, my mouth suddenly dry at the sight of his perfectly traced muscles under the suit. Whoever his tailor was deserved a medal.

Apparently, a near-death experience just made me even more irrationally eager to have him. To feel alive.

"Any updates?" I asked as he stopped walking and turned around to face me.

"We had a tail for Chad, but he beat us to it."

I walked to the kitchen, with Jake right behind me.

I poured him a glass of scotch and served myself a glass of wine.

"What are you doing here, Jake?" I sighed.

"Keisha left, even though you told me she was also staying tonight. You are not spending the night alone."

"Seriously? Are you still spying on me?"

"I'm not spying on you. But you don't expect me to not have someone watching over you when you won't let me stay next to you, do you?"

"I've told you before, you are not my keeper, Jake. If I wanted some security detail, I would just gotten it myself."

Jake closed the distance between us, now standing right in front of me. I could almost feel his breath, the smell of him intoxicating my senses, those tight broad shoulders I wanted to run under my palms. I ached to feel his hands gliding on my skin. For him to lift me on the kitchen island like he had done before.

But that was not in the cards. I wasn't going to let my desire govern over my better judgment.

He sighed.

"Chloe, Kyle is still out there. He took you right here, right in front of your house. It would be fucking stupid to leave you here with no protection. And you've heard the doctor; you shouldn't be alone for at least the first forty-eight hours since the concussion."

"Then I can call Keisha back." I grabbed my phone from the kitchen table.

"No." Jake put his hand on mine. "I am not leaving your side, Chloe. I am staying right here," he announced in a low and controlled voice, leaving no room for argument.

"Why? There is no reason for you to be here. I don't want you here."

"I know you are only saying that to hurt me, baby, you don't mean that."

My breath was getting shallow, so I took a step back. This much closeness clouded my judgment, made me lose sight of all the pain he had caused me.

"Jake, you betrayed me."

He shut his eyes and shook his head.

"I know. Chloe, I am so sorry, I am so. Fucking. Sorry. I should have never accused you like this; I should have trusted you," he said in a raspy voice.

"You should have. But instead, you..." Tears threatened to choke me, but I managed to keep going. "You believed Lauren, instead of me, when she was the one who stole that money from my dad all those years ago. I tried to protect her when I saw her, but she framed me."

"I didn't know, Chloe."

"That's not the problem. The problem is that you didn't ask. You took her by her words. And you ignored mine. You used her lie to see what you wanted to see."

"Chloe—"

"Jake, I am begging you," I sobbed, "don't come any closer. That's not fair to me."

He looked like someone had punched him, but he came to a halt, his body noticeably stiff with tension.

"You brought her to your house, in front my family, in front of me," I cried, my voice shaking, a tear running down my face.

"I didn't bring her, she showed up. Nothing happened."

I let out a dry laugh.

"You expect me to believe that?"

"I know what it looked like—no, I know what I *let* it look like. But nothing happened."

"You still embarrassed me, humiliated me."

"Chloe, please, I am so fucking sorry, baby. Let me take you in my arms, let me show you how much I regret everything."

That look on his face, primal, raw, and unfiltered, was tearing at my resolve at alarming speed. I wanted him so badly to erase the pain of the past few days. I wanted our complicity, our jokes back. I wanted him thrusting inside of me, losing control at the very last minute.

God, I wanted every part of him. But I couldn't get past the hurt.

"I can't." I aggressively wiped the hot tears that had fallen down my face and let out a shaky breath. "How did you find out it wasn't me? Did Mike tell you?"

"No, for the past few days I reopened every single document my team had gathered in the past few months. I looked for every proof of your innocence, of someone framing you. And I found it, I found it too late, but I did. I realized you were not in Chicago when some of those emails were sent from your laptop. I also realized where those random transfers to your bank account came from."

My eyes widened. Of course he had access to all that information. Who knew the depth of his investigation company, but he likely had employees trained in cyber espionage, able to gather whatever information he wanted, even if supposedly protected by other institutions.

And now, he knew my secret.

"Did you tell anyone?"

"No. Clearly you don't want anyone else to know. But you could have told me."

"Why would I tell you?"

"We were dating, Chloe. That information also would have helped."

"Oh, now it's my fault you didn't trust me?"

"No, it's not. But you didn't trust me either."

"There is a difference between waiting for some time before confessing my other career to you, and you accusing me of corporate espionage," I said between greeted teeth. "You looked at me with so much disgust Jake, it just..." My voice broke.

He closed the distance between us, prying my mouth open with his lips, his tongue demanding to be let in, demanding my surrender.

I whimpered, and brought my hands behind his neck, my fingers lost in his hair. He moaned in my mouth, framing my face with his hands. I felt between my legs pulsing, my body pulled to his like a magnet. But the memory of his face, of those words "*You are exactly who I thought you were, a spoiled fucking brat who was bought by the highest bidder*" were stronger.

"No." I pushed against him and took a couple step back, trying to regulate my breathing. "No. We are not doing this. If you want to stay here, just stay, I don't care. I am going to bed."

I sped the other way around the kitchen island, knowing that if I passed by him, I wouldn't be able to take another step away from him.

I quickly went up the stairs and didn't stop until I made it to my room, shutting the door behind me. I went straight to bed, the pillow muffling my sobs as Penny bundled herself in the crook of my neck.

CHAPTER 48

Jake

I WAS SET UP in the guest room closest to Chloe's. The idea that she was likely naked in a room so close to me wasn't letting me concentrate, but I had managed to block it out for most of the evening, when I was working with my team to find Kyle.

The good news was that my team had caught another Chad accomplice that worked at Green Mile. And they were making him talk, by whatever means necessary. I needed to get my hands on the rest of that team.

Chad, of course, didn't really seem like the kind of man that would go to the lengths of murder for his business, but he had allowed Kyle to hide Chloe in his basement. And according to that tape I had listened to over a hundred times already, he was considering drastic options to deal with Kyle's fuckup.

I sat up on the side of the bed, grabbed my phone again from my nightstand and played the message, my body already tensed and wired.

"*Are you going to tell him? If I let you go, are you going to betray me?*"

"*Why would I help him? I hate him.*"

"*Clear your name? You have proof it's me now, no?*"

"*I only needed the proof to bargain with you. To make sure you knew I had something over you. Now, if you kill me, this will never end. Jake will still tell my dad it was me, but then I would be dead, and that would be suspicious timing.”*

“I can make it look like an accident. Well, my partner can anyways.”

“I serve you more alive, Kyle. We can come up with a deal. While I love my family, I am angry. I am angry my dad let the shareholders give that asshole my board seat. He voted for him! He humiliated me in front of the whole company, disrespected me, treated me like I didn’t deserve it. You know t hat.”

“But you love him. Why would you not just tell him the truth, huh? Why should I believe you?!”

I heard the swallowed scream that made my blood boil every time I played the video. He had dared put his fucking hands on her. And for that he was going to lose them, right before he died.

“You can’t even stand me, Chloe. This is not like the kiss you gave him. You soiled yourself, didn’t you? You let him touch you? You can’t lie to me!”

“Kyle, leave him out of this, please, that is all I am asking. He doesn’t need to get hurt. Do whatever you want to me, but please don’t hurt him. I’m begging you.”

I shut my eyes and flinched when I heard the slap, followed by Chloe’s scream, tension raking my body.

I held the phone with tightened white knuckles, not throwing it against the wall in the fear that I would wake up Chloe. I had broken a few already today.

That son of a bitch deserved to have each of his limbs cut off. He had dared to inflict fear in her, threatened her safety, her mental peace. He had forced himself on her and physically and emotionally harmed her.

I used extreme measures sometimes when I needed information from people in my line of work, but K., Kyle, and Chad were going to be approached more like Luke usually handled critical situations for me, with no regard for their humanity. They had lost that right the minute they fucked with what was mine.

CHAPTER 49

Chloe

I LAID IN BED with my eyes wide open. I had been trying to sleep for three long hours, twisting and turning in my bed instead.

Even Penny had gotten tired of me and was now sleeping on the opposite end of the bed. It didn't help that Jake had called me from the other room every hour, per "doctor's orders."

As much as I resented him, I couldn't help but want him in my bed. I wanted to feel wrapped in his arms, inhaling his smell, my fingers toying with his hair as they had been before the Michigan trip. Before I knew who he really was.

I was going to do everything in my power to forget him, even knowing that there was no forgetting Jake Cunningham.

I finally got some restless sleep around five in the morning.

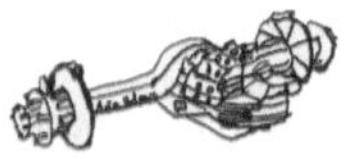

The smell of coffee slowly drifting under my bedroom door woke me up. The aroma brought me back to consciousness, my keen awareness of Jake's presence in my home rushing back to me at full speed.

I couldn't stay in this hell. I decided that I would make it back to work, the idea of being stuck in the house for one more day unbearable. I got ready for the day and headed downstairs

When I got to the kitchen, I found Jake sitting there, sipping on a cappuccino, reading something on his phone. I looked around and saw enough breakfast to feed a small army but couldn't find one dirty pan in sight. He was wearing a pair of light jeans and a black shirt, flattering his strong biceps and chest.

My throat dried up, my thirst for him more and more uncontrollable. I put my heels and my purse down. He got up when he heard me walk in.

"What is all this?"

"Breakfast," he simply answered.

"Did you make this?"

"I did." Of course, the man could both shoot to kill and cook breakfast apparently. "Sleep well?" he inquired as he handed me a cup of coffee he had clearly poured earlier so it would cool down for me.

He was towering over me, standing a little too close for comfort.

"I did."

I was not in the mood this morning, irritated, having slept for less than three hours according to my watch.

"I'm glad."

There was nothing glad about the tension in his jaw, the intensity behind those blue eyes.

I scratched my throat. I took a seat at the kitchen island, and Jake proceeded to serve me a plate with eggs, avocado, and a slide of bread.

I was starving, and thankful for having all this ready for me to devour. We ate in silence.

Once finished, I headed towards the living room.

"Thank you for breakfast. I am going to head to the office now."

I proceeded to putting my heels on and grabbing my phone to order myself a car. I startled when I heard his voice so close behind me so fast.

"You can't be serious."

I sighed and turned around, my eyes traveling straight to those lips I so desperately wanted to taste.

"I can't stay here, Jake. I'm going to go crazy... thinking. I can't."

"Chloe, you can work from here. I don't want that fucker anywhere near you, and we don't know where he is right now."

"I'm not staying here, Jake."

He sighed, tucking his hand in his pocket.

"Fine, but I'm taking you to work."

I knew there was no use in protesting. I finished putting my shoes on, shoved my phone in my purse, and followed him to the car. I almost screamed when I saw the tall built man standing in front of my door.

"Good morning," he said as if I should have known to expect him. I noticed the gun tucked in his waist.

I glared at Jake in silence as we got in his car. The man sat in the driver's seat. This car was bigger than the one he usually drove, with seats facing each other, the partition closed.

As we started driving, I noticed a second car trailing behind us.

"Seriously, Jake, don't you think this is a bit extreme? How many guards did you get?" I exclaimed.

"There is nothing extreme in making sure you are safe, Chloe."

"God," I mumbled.

I shook my head but couldn't continue with the conversation with the protectiveness and possessiveness this man was emanating from each pore of his body, washing all over me.

And part of me was terrified that Kyle or whoever worked with him would come back to harm me, so what was I fighting against exactly?

"Do you think Kyle would try something again?"

"He might not necessarily want to, but he has K. on his team, and that makes him smart, patient, and very dangerous. K. worked for me for a long time. He was the one in charge of the investigation at Motor Holmes."

Jake raked his fingers through his hair, anger contorting his expression. "Kyle did text someone with that name."

"He did. He hid any evidence that pointed to Kyle in his reports to me. I did a second review of the raw data I had, the same you reviewed. He was good, but he was still sloppy, not realizing that there isn't one document that lands on company laptops that doesn't get backed up on my server. By the time I realized what was going on, Kyle had taken you already."

I stayed silent, eyes wide, understanding the breadth of the work Kyle had done behind the scenes to frame me. It had gone beyond simply using my laptop.

He had known about Jake all along, or early enough, to be able to taint the investigation from the beginning, and he also somehow corrupted one of Jake's employees.

"This was someone I trusted. I thought he was not just an excellent employee, but a good friend. I don't know what the connection with Kyle is; if I had to guess, K. went to him and negotiated for a piece of the pie. I put one of my best men on the job. I didn't anticipate that greed would be able to destroy his work ethic after all this time."

I saw the fury in his eyes, but he was also hurt, feeling betrayed. I itched to grab his hand to console him, reassure him. I knew what it felt like to have someone you trust let you down. But I resisted.

"He presented a seemingly iron clad case to me against you, Chloe. Even if my gut told me it wasn't you, I couldn't ignore the facts in front of me. When you ran out of your father's office like that, I fucking lost it. I had just found out that all the evidence pointed to you, of all people. I thought you used me. I was out of my mind, and I accused you prematurely, before I doubled check his work.

"I should have followed my gut, but the idea that I was falling for someone who would do this to their family, and who would be able to manipulate me like I thought you had, it shook me. I should have never talked to you like that, never."

"Jake..." I shook my head. I didn't want to hear it.

"I made a mistake. A big fucking mistake. But I need you to forgive me. I never meant to hurt you; you have to believe me."

My eyes get wet, my heart pumping, his words awakening something in me. He said he was falling for me. I was sure I heard him right. I didn't know what to do with that information, but it made butterflies flutter in my belly, making me feel all fuzzy inside.

"I'm sorry about K."

That was all I could muster.

He held my gaze for a few more seconds, then nodded, understanding that he wasn't going to get anything else from me. I opened my phone, the screen blurry, as I pretended to scroll through social media for the rest of the ride.

CHAPTER 50

Chloe

THE DAY AT THE office was worse than what I expected. There was meeting after meeting, all discussing what to do about the situation with Green Mile. The stakeholders were concerned, as they deserved to be, but my job was to make sure they remained calm and confident we would handle the situation.

Board meetings took place as well, discussing the threat posed by Green Mile going to market with a competitive e-axle to ours, putting in jeopardy certain critical contracts for the company. The concern was that the company would lose significant value with a competitor with a matching product in the market. We would no longer be trailblazers.

The shareholders feared that they wouldn't recoup the value of their investments if customers went with Green Mile. Some were pressuring the rest to sell. The company had aggressively promised a faster launch, with a product that would be cheaper but same quality. Which made sense when they didn't invest the time, cost, and effort to develop the product. They stole it, unafraid of repercussions.

I remained calm through the process, lightly touching my father's hand as he was sitting next to me, to remind him to keep his cool.

Chad was a majority owner of his family-owned business. Once we found him, this whole charade would go away. But customers and suppliers started hearing rumors, and they had been calling, inquiring, with manufacturers wondering if they also should jump ship.

At the end of one of the hardest days since I had joined my father's company, Jake, my father, and I sat down in my office. My dad was exhausted, anxiety deepening the crevasses on his forehead, tying a knot around my heart.

I wanted to end his suffering, the stress that he might lose everything he had worked so hard for. There wasn't much I wouldn't do to help him, so I accepted I would have to work with Jake if needed. All the mattered was saving the company from the hands of that jackass.

"I shouldn't have added more shareholders to my company. I should have known."

"Dad, it's not your fault. At the time it made sense; we needed their money."

"It's understandable that they are considering the offer," admitted Jake. "But we have what we need to bring Chad and his company to the ground."

"We don't," I added, turning a stern look to Jake. "We need to find Chad from wherever he is hiding."

"We will, trust me."

I did trust him with this, but my dad was breaking in front of me, and it was painful to watch.

"I hate what we are putting our customers through. They are concerned."

"We have requirements contract provisions with some of them. We can renegotiate amounts, so they don't breach. But we won't have to, Dad."

"The suppliers are all concerned that Motor Holmes won't be able to meet the take or pay provisions of their arrangements."

"We will. We did a good amount of damage control today, Dad. We will continue to do so. And we have a nuclear option in our pocket."

Both men stared at me with horror incrusted on their faces.

"I'm not dragging you or my company through the mud with a court case."

"You prefer to let it get to the hands of the likes of Chad?"

My dad got up and started pacing.

"That would mean putting you in the middle of all of this, Chloe," added Jake.

"I know, but if that is what it takes to save this company, so be it."

"No, there has to be another solution."

"This is just a backup plan. If you want to keep this company, Dad," I added as I stood up, "you have to consider it. I hope it doesn't come to that, but you must prepare yourself for that possibility."

"We are not putting you at risk, Chloe."

"This is not your decision, Jake!"

"I am on the board. It is in part my decision."

When had he gotten so close to me? I was fuming, wanting him out of my sight. But I sucked in air between gritted teeth instead and rolled my eyes. We needed him.

"Let's all calm down, please," said my father, his gaze going from me to Jake and back. "I think we all need to rest, especially you, sweetie. I am so sorry you got caught in the middle of all this. I don't know what I would have done if something had happened to you."

I held down a sob. My dad had not stopped apologizing, feeling like this was all his fault, when all he had done was try to protect me. It was my hotheadedness that had put me in harm's way.

I didn't regret what I had done but acknowledged that I had let my emotions get the best of me when I decided to play investigator instead of relaying what I had found out to Jake.

I had my reasons, but in hindsight, it wasn't the most rational thing to do. I put myself and the company in danger, a few days having made all the difference between us having the upper hand and me being locked in a basement against my will.

"No, Dad, no, I told you, it is not your fault." I walked to him and hugged him. "I should have talked to you before I acted."

"It is. Had I gotten you involved from the beginning," he said, and he straightened to face me, my hands in his, "you wouldn't have felt the need to do all of this."

I looked in the direction of Jake. Guilt was splattered all over his posture.

"It's my fault, Philip. I'm the one who pushed her away."

I wanted to disconnect from him, look away, but the pain in his voice was mesmerizing. I wanted to hit him and wrap my arms around him at the same time.

"No, son, it all goes back to my decision to keep her out of this. You are the one who got my daughter back to me; I can never thank you enough for that."

"Oh, Dad, I'm here, I'm okay, I promise."

I took my father in my arms again, letting my tears soak his suit jacket.

"Plus, I got a chance to play badass agent and record those assholes on my phone; a little light kidnapping episode was worth it."

I managed to make my dad laugh, even if he looked at me like I had just committed a crime. He was familiar with my sense of humor. Jake did not find any of it amusing.

"Okay, okay, maybe you are fine if you think this is funny."

His smile finally got to his eyes; I felt some tension leaving my shoulder.

"I am," I reassured him again.

He sighed. "Okay. Let's all rest. If tomorrow is anything like today was, we will need it."

"Goodnight, Dad, kiss Mom for me."

With that, my dad left us in my office. I leaned back on the wall next to the door, and closed my eyes, my hands folded behind my lower back.

I focused on my breathing to avoid breaking down into pieces. I was overwhelmed by all the emotions coursing through me, the danger of losing Motor Holmes palpable, more real than it had been in the past days.

"Hey, look at me Chloe."

I opened my eyes at the soft whisper. Jake was in front of me, his face just a few centimeters from mine, one hand now at my waist, the other lightly caressing my face, erasing the tear I didn't realize had rolled down my cheeks.

I could feel my body lightly shaking as I fought the sobs threatening to take over.

"It's going to be okay, Chloe, I promise. I won't rest until you're safe, and the company is safe. I swear to you. I won't let anything bad happen to you or your family."

His words warmed me up from my toes to my hair follicles. His hand traveled to my shoulder, releasing some tension from my body again. Just being close to him was enough for me to feel safe, unable to stop myself from trusting his words.

I might not want to give my heart back to him, but I knew the love and respect he had for my father. I believed he wouldn't stop at anything, even if my family wasn't his, even if this business wasn't his to defend.

When Jake ran his hand from my hips to my waist and pinned me to the wall, I didn't object. He kissed my forehead, my eyes, before he nested his head in my neck.

"Jake," I breathed out in protest.

"Let me make you feel good, baby, please. Let me take the pain away."

My brain shot warning signs all over the place, but I needed him. Every inch of me needed this man I thought was mine just a few days ago to make me feel something positive again, even if only for a second.

Jake spread my legs open and shoved his thigh between them. I brought my hand to his chest, unsure whether to push him or pull him closer. He moved his hand under my skirt, and pulled my panties to the side, sliding his fingers between my already wet lips. He groaned next to my ears.

He steadied me on the wall with his fingers wrapped around my side, as he rubbed my clit with the other. I moaned in his mouth as he grabbed my lips, his tongue demanding to be let in.

The kiss was too intimate, but when he slid his middle finger inside of me, his thumb still circling my bud, I let out a whimper and he took advantage, sucking my lips in between his, hot, possessive, as he grunted.

There was no turning back, no force of nature that could convince me to ask him to stop. He kept rubbing, holding me against him, his heartbeat as accelerated as mine.

I wrapped my fingers around his jacket lapels as I brought my face to his shoulders, the smell of him taking my pleasure to a higher level.

"Oh my God!" I moaned.

I intensified my rhythmic motion against his hand, any decorum out the door. I wanted more of him, and I was losing control.

"Oh, that's it, baby, come on my hand. I want you to come for me," he growled, intensifying his movements.

I was gazing at him with my eyes half open. What was between us, it was too strong, too intimate. The way we always looked at each other in the eyes, feeding off each other's pleasure, created a bond like no other. But I couldn't look away. I reveled in his need for me, holding on to a thin rope of self-control as he breathed fast.

His hard dick was stretched against my stomach. I knew the effect I had on him, and that drove me crazy with lust and desire.

"Oh God, ah!"

I exploded all over Jake's hand, my juices dripping from his fingers. He grabbed me and held me close to him, aware that my legs were now reduced to mush.

I kept my head nested in his neck, my orgasm still coursing through me as he rubbed my back.

After a couple of minutes, I was coming back to my senses, my face reddening, conscious of what I had done, no longer blinded by my needs. He probably felt me stiffen, as I felt the back rubs stop.

I slowly moved away from him, and he let me. I leaned back on the wall, looking anywhere but his face.

"Chloe," he said after a few seconds of silence.

"We shouldn't have done this; it shouldn't have happened."

"No, Chloe, don't."

"Don't what?"

I looked up at him, pain twisting a knife in my stomach.

"Don't shut me out again."

I closed my eyes and shook my head.

"This was… this, was just a moment of weakness, a lapse in judgment. It's not happening again. Don't touch me," I said with a stronger voice as he attempted to approach me again. "Its best if you don't sleep over tonight. Keisha should be on her way to my house by now."

"You're not going alone."

"Have one of your goons take me then, but I'm not going with you."

I almost took my words back when I saw his face tighten. He looked confused, almost lost. He pressed the bridge of his nose.

"Fine. If that's what you want."

"Thank you."

I gathered the strength to walk around him and grab my purse. We headed to the elevator and stayed in silence.

Jake accompanied me to the car that was already parked by the revolving door waiting for us. He pinned me to the car before I could open the door. We were still by the office, someone could see us, but Jake didn't seem to care.

My lips parted, my eyes wide in surprise, scanning passersby to make sure our coworkers didn't see us, but he didn't budge. Those dark blue eyes searched mine for a second, his jaw clenched, his breathing accelerated.

"I know I messed up; I know I hurt you. You can push me away as much as you like, but I know you want me as much as I want you. I know you need me as much as I need you, and I'm not going anywhere. I am not losing you."

My breath came out strangled as he got off me, not waiting for an answer. I took a few seconds to break from his gaze, as I remembered where we were, where I was, leaned on a car in front of my dad's company.

I stared at him for one more second, trying to convince myself that I didn't just feel the earth and the skies vibrate inside my soul. I finally found it in me to open the door, fumble into the car, and let myself be driven away from Jake.

When I got to my house, all I wanted to do was sleep, but the bodyguards had to do an inspection of the place before I could get in. I needed Kyle to get caught, desperately, not only for my safety, but having guards all the time reminded me that my life had been in danger, and I felt suffocated.

Keisha got there within five minutes. We spent an hour watching TV before I caved in and fell asleep in my bed, with Jake haunting my dreams.

CHAPTER 51

Chloe

I SHUT THE DOOR once Keisha's Uber took off. Spending so much time with one of my best friends was doing me good, calming me, reminding me that the world wasn't full of evil.

We had finally informed Iris and Amelia of what had happened. They almost booked flights that same night, but I asked them for a few days, hoping that perhaps by then, things would settle down, Kyle would be found, and I'd be able to go back to my life again.

I jumped when I heard my doorbell. I saw Jake's face on my phone. I rolled my eyes but couldn't deny the excitement that rose inside of me from knowing that he was there.

I opened the door to let him in.

"Good morning," he said as he removed his sunglasses.

It was a sunny day, with the slight cool air announcing that fall wasn't far off, even if it was only July.

"Good morning."

He removed the caramel iced latte from the tray he was carrying and handed it to me.

"Thank you." I tried to hide my smile, but how could I when he had my favorite cheat day coffee with him?

We walked to the kitchen. I wanted to complain, ask him what he was doing here, but I couldn't bring myself to say anything. He set the Dunkin Donuts bag he was carrying on the kitchen island and proceeded to remove what looked like bagels and donuts.

"Have you heard anything?" I asked.

"Yes, it's part of what I wanted to discuss with you this morning," he explained. "We found Chad."

"Oh my God, finally. Where is he?"

"We got him back in his condo here."

"Got him back? You mean you found him and forced him to go home?" My brows furrowed.

"Something like that, yes."

I didn't want to get any more details.

"Does my dad know?"

"Yes. We plan to meet at Chad's house at three."

"I'm joining."

"Your father won't be happy about this."

I raised my chin in defiance. "I don't care."

"I know." The side of his mouth lifted as he shook his head.

"I'm going to change."

I had opted for a light-yellow dress that was now too relaxed for the meeting we were about to have.

"Eat some breakfast first," Jake pleaded.

I was going to retort when I heard my stomach growl, blatantly calling me out. I sighed but sat next to him, accepting the everything bagel with cream cheese that he handed to me.

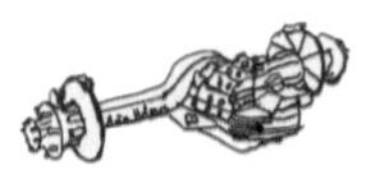

Jake and I met with my dad for two hours in the morning so we could prepare and strategize for the meeting with Chad, if one could call holding a man in hostage in his own home that. I had worked on editing my stock purchase agreement form to conform to the deal we wanted to present to Chad, purchase his company at a discount, with him signing an ironclad non-compete, as strong as Illinois law permitted.

The way Jake talked though, it seemed like that document would just be a formality, Jake assuring Chad won't ever be able to hold any meaningful position at any company ever again once he was done with him.

We arrived at his condo in Lincoln Park at 2:50 p.m. sharp. A suited man opened the door for us. Clearly the house was surveilled by Jake's men.

We were led directly to Chad's opulent dining room. I got more and more upset with every step we took. This man lived a lavish life, with a gorgeous house, and from the pictures I could see, a beautiful wife and a son.

Yet, his ambition got the best of him, leading to stealing and endangering my life. And now, his life as he knew it was going to be destroyed.

I had never met Chad in person outside of when Kyle took me, and then he was wearing a mask. The man in front of me was a bald forty-year-old, staring at us with rage coming out of his deep blue eyes. He was wearing a green cardigan and a pair of blue jeans. His lips were busted.

I stopped in front of the chair across from him, with Jake on my right and my father on my left. Chad didn't get up to greet us. All the fears I had, they all took a back seat as I stared my enemy down.

A smile slowly spread across my face. We were here to annihilate him, and I was going to have a lot of fun doing so.

"Pleasure to see you again, Mr. Gorbel, although, nice that I can see your face this time around."

I could feel the tension emanating from Jake and my dad. I hadn't given them a heads up about my plans to let this man know I both saw and recognized him. But my plan was to start strong, to destabilize him. Chad eyes widened.

Jake had informed us that once he found him, he told him we had enough evidence that he had stolen proprietary information. When he refused, jake had and he had gotten him back to Chicago at gun point.

"I... I don't think we've ever met."

I sat down, followed by Jake and Philip.

"I'm a little offended, Chad. I thought we were friends."

I saw Jake smirk on my side.

"Anyways, we are not here for a friendly reunion. We want to make you an offer, on behalf of Motor Holmes," I said simply.

I slid down the purchase agreement we had prepared earlier. Chad skimmed the papers, his nostrils flaring, small beads of sweat glistening his forehead. He shoved the document back to me.

"Fuck you. I am the one buying your little shit company, not the other way around. If this trash is the reason you forced me back to my house against my will, you can shove it up your ass and leave."

"Chad, stop playing games here. You are lucky we even bothered to be here, pretend that we are negotiating with you. You stole our IP; you know the game is up. There is no scenario where we let you have my company."

My father's voice left Chad visibly disturbed. I didn't understand how he thought he was going to get out of this. While he didn't quite know about the recording, he knew I had been rescued at his home; he had to know Kyle was on the run and that Motor Holmes knew everything.

"Your other shareholders are very interested in the premium per share price I ȧm offering. It's a good deal for them. For all of you. I don't—"

"Chad, stop fucking around," growled Jake as he hit the table so hard, I felt it vibrate.

Even my blood chilled at the icy tone in Jake's voice.

"We have all the proof we need. This can go one of two ways, your choice. You agree to our terms, you sign the purchase agreement Chloe drafted right now, today, with your counsel on the line of course, or we go public with this. As I am sure you know, we wouldn't be here if we didn't have proof. We will ruin you and your company in court, destroy everything you've built in the blink of an eye," explained Jake.

"This is personal, Chad, you and the piece of shit Kyle put my daughter in danger. Destroying you will be our lives' mission, regardless of what happens to Motor Holmes. You would go to prison."

"I don't believe you. You wouldn't risk the bad press. All the customers who would walk away from both of us due to the scandal. That would be mutually assured destruction. And considering you hired an investigator in secret, I know you don't want a scandal, you don't want your name or your daughter's name associated in any public feud. I'm not stupid."

"Try me," challenged my dad as he bolted to his feet.

Chad stood up as well. Jake followed, closing his suit button after he did. I remained seated, just smirking at Chad. The man didn't know where to look, but it was clear to me that my calm and smiling demeanor confused him.

And that was the point. The tension in the room was palpable, invading every inch of my body, but I fed off it, relished in it. Maybe I should have been a litigator, I thought.

It was time for me to put an end to this charade.

"Your first mistake was trusting someone like Kyle to do your bidding, Mr. Gorbel, and he left so many breadcrumbs it's pathetic. Now, this is the purchase agreement we've put together."

I pushed the seventy-page document back towards Chad.

"It's pretty straightforward, quite buyer-friendly frankly, but I am sure you understand, given the circumstances. We can give you a couple hours to discuss with your counsel. After all, we want to make sure you make an informed decision, with all the legal advice you desire.

"You are the majority shareholder, so we trust that you can convince the rest to follow suit if need be. We can do a bifurcated sign and close, but it won't be for more than a few days in between."

"Are you not hearing me, little cunt?! I am not signing this."

"Don't," I said as Jake started to move towards Chad, the man taking a step back in fear. "I can handle it," I said as I looked in his eyes.

Jake looked almost possessed, his gaze as lethal as blue fire, but this was my battle to fight.

"I don't know what Kyle did or didn't do. You have no proof I was involved in anything!"

"I saw you there. As a matter of fact, we all know I was held hostage at your house, Mr. Gorbel."

I thought the man's eyes were going to fall out of his eye sockets.

"No, you weren't."

"Oh, why are you making this so time-consuming?" I breathed out as I rolled my eyes. "We have all the proof we need to show that you misappropriated our trade secret maliciously and willfully, I might add. The part where we show you used it won't be hard to prove in court. We already have conversation showing how you intend to use it in the first place."

"Please, you don't. You can't show I had access to whatever Kyle stole from you. You can't show that anyone at my company used it."

"That's what discovery is for."

"Fuck you. Fuck all of you! I am not signing any of this! You don't think I have money? You don't think I also have access to the best law firms in the country? My company is older and more lucrative than yours; I will prevail, I will make you spend every dollar you have by delaying this lawsuit as much as I can. You will lose because I have the means to play the long fucking game.

"I assume the authorities were not involved when you gathered whatever it is you think you fucking have. My team will make all your evidence inadmissible in court. You will fucking lose this!"

I just started laughing. My father and Chad gawked at me like I was losing it. But Jake gave me that look, like he knew exactly what I was about to do.

What I said I would do as a last resort.

"How long do you think is jail time for kidnapping and false imprisonment Chad?" I drawled.

"I don't know what you are talking about."

"Oh, Chad, but I have such fond memories of your deciding that I might have one hour left to live; I'm disappointed to see that such moments meant nothing to you."

I could feel Jake and my father's fury, but I was going to play this my way. Because Chad was right. We didn't want the scandal, or the damage a long and tedious litigation could do to our business. I slowly rose up, preparing to play my last card. I pulled my cell phone out and played the audio at the exact part where Chad came in the room. The horror that drew on his face was one for the books; it was an expression I would never forget.

It was the face that had a chance to help me heal. The contortion of his lips, the droplets of sweats, the shaking hands. I knew I had won.

"You can't use it; I didn't consent to being recorded!"

"Well, Mr. Gorbel, I didn't record this in Illinois now, did I? I recorded it in Wisconsin, not a two-party consent state for recording surprisingly. This is admissible in court."

Chad gripped the chair next to him for support. I barely had the time to relish in my victory when Chad launched at me from across the table, with a strength and agility I had not expected.

Jake was quicker, though, as he forced me out of the way and grabbed Chad by the throat, slid him on the table, and lifted him on his toes as he hit him violently on the wall.

"Don't you fucking dare, you fucking piece of shit. If you ever touch her—no, if you or anyone connected to you even so much as breathes the same air as her, I will destroy you family, and you, I will bury you alive, twenty feet underground."

I was shaking, my body cold and hot at the same time. The lion inside of Jake was fully out, bold, beautiful, wild, and oh so strong, so powerful I felt heat pull between my legs.

Every single muscle on his body was contracted, making the room feel way too small for Jake to be in it. Chad fought to be set free to no avail.

"That's enough," I said.

Jake slowly put Chad down, but he didn't take his hands off him.

"Call your fucking lawyers, Chad. And now you have an hour to sign this."

Chad nodded his head, finally acquiescing. Jake let him go but positioned himself between Chad and me until Chad made it back to his seat. He dropped down, taking his face in his hands.

The man was crying, finally recognizing that there was no way out. He had lost his company because even after all he had accomplished, his greed had gotten the best of him and destroyed everything he had built.

And Motor Holmes would gladly take advantage of the wreckage.

CHAPTER 52

Jake

WE SETTLED IN THE living room while Chad was reviewing the agreements with his lawyers. I was still fuming, putting all my energy in resisting the urge to beat the shit out of Chad.

He had put Chloe in danger, whether he intended to do so or not. And he had the audacity to think that he could hurt her in my presence.

I bolted up from the couch and started pacing.

Chloe sat next to her dad. She held her head high and didn't let an ounce of her pain show. That power that had emanated from her, it matched every rhythm of mine. She was a lioness, and she was mine. My need for such a strong and powerful woman had never been satisfied, hell, I hadn't even known the was the type of woman I needed until I met her.

The gratification of being with a woman like Chloe came with the need to also possess every inch of her, body and soul. I just had to get her to see it, to see that no one else could make her squirm and explode the way I did. I needed her forgiveness, for her to trust that I would never ever doubt her again, I would never hurt her again.

Philip was trying to seem calm, but I spotted the vein beating on his temple. I saw Chloe caress his arm every now and then, trying to reassure him.

Philip was a friend, a mentor, and the father figure I never had, and just for that, even without Chloe in the picture, I wanted to squeeze Chad's neck until I saw his eyes pop out. But murder wasn't going to help us; there was a bigger picture.

The silver lining in all this was the unique opportunity to acquire a company three times our size for barely anything, use their channels and manufacturing plants to expand much faster in the market.

For the sake of avoiding a scandal for Motor Holmes, as the new owner of Chad's company, I couldn't kill him. Not yet. But I was going to keep tabs on this man and his family for the rest of his life. To make sure he never even thought of going back after Chloe or her father.

After the torturous hour was over, Chad walked in the living room. He threw the documents on the glass coffee table, loathing all over his face.

Chloe smirked at him with satisfaction, leaned down, and took her time to flip through every single page of each of the documents to make sure nothing was amiss.

Once done with her review, Chloe slowly stood up, that smug look on her face making me desperate to feel that smart mouth wrapped around my cock.

"Nice doing business with you, Mr. Gorbel. You got the full shareholder consent in an hour? I'm impressed."

This man would definitely be watched. The fire that emanated from his eyes was intense, and he directed every bit of it toward Chloe. But she wasn't fazed, or if she was, she didn't let it show.

Philip appeared relieved. His finally looked as if he took a deep breath, the tension in his shoulders eased.

"This is not over." Chad's nostrils flared.

I saw Chloe's body slightly flinch, probably unperceived by him, but I knew that body well enough to catch it. Her poker face was slightly shaken by the threat.

"It *is* over," snapped Philip. "You stay away from my family, Chad, my company, and me. We won't be negotiating with you next time you mess with us; I can promise you that. There is nothing I won't do to protect my family. Remember that."

I was pleased with Philip insinuating he would take any measure necessary to protect his family. But he wouldn't have to; that was my job, and I would gladly oblige.

"Well, shall we?" offered Chloe.

"Let go," Philip said with a nod.

"Give me a few minutes. I'll meet you outside."

My eyes never left Chad. Chloe frowned and hesitated, but her dad grabbed her by the arm and led her out.

Philip knew that I wasn't above taking drastic measures when it came down to it. I waited until I heard the front door close before I allowed all the fury I had inside to show.

"Chad, you went against the wrong family."

"Why are you so involved in this, Jake? I don't know you, but I know you were hired to investigate. Why do you fucking care about this? Isn't your job done here?" he sneered.

I laughed, a slow rumble that didn't reach my eyes.

"My services are extracurricular at times. In this case, it's personal. I know you signed a non-compete." I took a few languid steps until I towered over Chad. "But that piece of paper wasn't needed because not only will you never work in this industry, but you will never work in any high-level capacity, for the rest of your life."

His eyes widened. "You can't."

I punched him so hard the impact radiated all the way through my shoulders.

"Fuck!" screamed Chad, his hand holding the blood pouring out of his mouth and broken nose.

"Do not interrupt me when I am speaking. Want to know why? Because I could wipe you off the face of this earth, and not a single person would question where you went. I have money and power beyond your comprehension. And believe me when I tell you this, I will use those very resources to make your life a living hell if I ever so much as hear your name again."

Chad flinched, fear finally clouding his face. I had him right where I wanted him.

"You now have a target on your back, for the rest of your miserable life. There isn't a corner of the world where you can hide from me. I will always know where you, your two sons, and your new wife are at all times. The same goes for your grandson."

His eyes widened in confusion, the effect of my words telling him that I was not to be messed with.

"Yes, your daughter in law is pregnant. Just two months. She will get the test results in an hour. Congratulations."

He swore. "You fucking bastard."

"I'm not a bastard, Chad, I am your worst fucking nightmare. Don't provoke me, and you can live a pretty normal mediocre life like any other average Joe. You come within a mile of that family, or I find out that you are trying any illegal bullshit, I will have to reconsider. And you won't get a warning, you won't get a second chance like you did today.

"The people you love will just start dropping from the face of the earth like flies. This... is your first and last warning. I am not stupid enough to repeat myself. Next time, it won't be a warning. There will be blood."

Chad's body was shaking, a mix of horror and anger fueling him. From the look on his face, I knew that my message had hit home. But it's only when Chad would confirm he was about to be a grandfather that he'd understand the breadth of my reach.

I walked out of the room, satisfied, but my surveillance system on this family would stay in place. I wouldn't hurt an innocent person, but it was all about how you presented information to people to instill fear.

I put my sunglasses back on and joined Chloe and Philip in the car where they were waiting for me.

"Everything good?" asked Chloe, looking more anxious than I had seen her all day.

"All good," I answered, under Philip's understanding gaze.

We proceeded to Chloe's house to finalize the next steps of the day. The Motor Holmes board had a meeting in the morning consenting to the acquisition after Philip had exerted pressure. They didn't believe the deal was real, though; it was too good to be true, yet here we were briefing both the board and shareholders over Zoom.

We explained that the hostile takeover offer led to the start of certain investigations. Kyle had confessed to having provided Green Mile with confidential information just yesterday. We had to act quick and in silence to secure what really was the deal of the century for us, to acquire the business of a competitor.

Part of the closing conditions negotiated what the issuance of company stock to Chloe and me for all the work we had done to secure the deal, as well a seat on the board for Chloe. It was still a risk for Motor Holmes to approve and close so quick on the transaction because we didn't know what liabilities we were assuming. We didn't have time to do diligence, but time was of the essence, and Chloe had put in all the bells and whistles indemnification provisions could provide should we need to sue the sellers for any liability.

We explained that Chad, even if forced to sell, wanted his business to be in good hands, and wanted his employees protected, and he trusted no one better than us. Once they had heard the entire story, they were on board for whatever we decided to do to move forward.

Although unusual for a seller to insist that certain buyer employees get stock in the parent entity, this was the deal. The shareholders, seeing the potential of going to a bigger market and at a faster pace than anticipated, consented, giving the Holmes family back majority control of the business.

This was a weird play, but Philip never wanted to risk losing his company again just because some of the shareholders might want a short-term profit.

He was going to make it his mission to strategically reduce their owner-ship even more during the coming year. We spent a good three hours on the calls, but by the end of the day, the acquisition was formally announced on the media. Chloe's dad was in heaven, the only shadow on the celebration the fact that Kyle was still out there with K.

"Okay." Philip got up once we were done with dinner. "It's getting late, and it's time for me to go home. Your mother is planning dinner tomorrow. See you both at six?"

Chloe tensed a bit, but she sighed and accepted.

"We'll be there," I answered, ignoring the daggers I could feel her shooting my way.

She walked us to the front door, and I accompanied Richard to his car.

"Are you coming?" he asked holding the handle to the back seat.

"No, I need to talk to Chloe a bit more."

He nodded in understanding.

"So, you and my daughter huh?"

"Yeah," I answered, holding his gaze.

"I should have seen that coming."

"Even I didn't," I admitted.

He clasped my shoulder, his eyebrows raised.

"Well, I think she's too good for you." He smirked. "But I think you are just what she needs."

"Thank you, Philip. If she forgives me, that is."

"Hm, yeah. Well, that's a problem. Just hang in there. I'm sure she'll come around."

He sighed and got in the car and drove away.

CHAPTER 53

Jake

I CLIMBED BACK THE stairs and went back in the house and joined Chloe in the kitchen. She was pouring herself some coffee.

"Long day," she said as she handed me a cup.

"I know. I couldn't take my eye off you today." Fuck, I was so proud of her, so in awe of her. I closed the gap between us.

She sighed. "Thank you. Thank you for helping us with all of this."

"It's my job."

"Technically, your job ended once we discovered it was Kyle."

"You mean when he had you tied in a basement? That's when I should have been done?" I scoffed.

"You are a PI, Jake, not my bodyguard."

I wrapped my index finder under her chin and lifted it so I could see her face, my eyes drawn to those plump lips of hers.

"I protect what is mine, Chloe. No matter what, I would give my life to protect yours if I had to."

Her mouth parted; it took all the restraint I had to not take those inviting lips in mine. God, I wanted to devour her. But my priority in the moment was to make sure she was okay.

She drew away from me. "Yes, I do. Good night."

"Good night."

Every time she stepped away from me like that, I felt my heart tearing apart, the knot in my stomach intensifying the furthest I was from her. The idea that she might never trust me again was threatening to drown me.

I opened the fridge to grab a beer. I couldn't afford to think this way. Considering going back to a life without her felt like a nightmare. *This* was a nightmare.

I couldn't lose her. She was mine, plain and simple.

A life without Chloe would be no life at all.

I knew she was still attracted to me, considering how she had let me make her come in her office just last night. My dick got hard just thinking about it. I knew how her body reacted to me, but what I couldn't tell was how much territory I had gained in her heart before I ruined things between us. I didn't know if I could fix what I had done.

I chugged the rest of my beer and proceeded to the guest room, preparing for another sleepless night.

I woke up to a shriek, the sound of fear traveling through my spine. I shot up in my boxers and rushed to Chloe's room. I calmed down a bit when I confirmed she was alone, bundled on the left side of the bed, but she wasn't resting. She was twisting in bed.

"Please no, no!" she cried in anguish.

I was by her side in a second. I sat next to her, caressing her face and hair, hoping to wake her up.

She was sweating, her eyes fully shut, but her face distressed. My stomach tensed up; she was in pain, stuck in a nightmare Kyle had put there.

"Jake!" she screamed.

"I'm here, baby, wake up."

I didn't want to startle her more than she was already, but perhaps if she could hear my voice, I could bring her back to me.

"Don't hurt him, Kyle," she mumbled.

"Mein leibling, come back to me. I'm here, I'm fine, you're safe."

She let out another screech and propelled herself up on the bed, eyes wide open, her breast barely covered by her silky sheets, her chest heaving up and down.

"I'm here, baby."

She looked up at me with big round eyes, a couple of tears rolling down her beautiful face, the moonlight coming from her window accentuating the shadows on her face.

My heart was breaking to see her like this, and I was enraged, wanting to destroy anyone who had contributed to her being haunted in this moment. She started sobbing.

I cradled her into my arms, her head resting on my chest, her left arm on my back. I could feel her fear and desperation in the strength she used to hold me close.

I was fuming, desperation making me feel useless, wanting to do whatever it took to take her pain away, make it mine so she could smile again. The bruises on her body killed me but also reminded me just how strong she was.

I ran my fingers softly through her damp curls and down her naked back, my right arm holding her close. My cock twitched; I couldn't help it. She was naked against my bare chest, our skin separated only by those soft sheets. I could feel her nipples rubbing against me through them.

The nightmare she was having, while it pinched at my heart, also made my pulse quicken. Because just like when she was in danger, in her dreams, she was trying to protect me, of all people, from Kyle.

She didn't sound worried about her own safety, but about mine. The thought warmed me up, intensifying my desire to put her on her back and get inside of her. Show her I was there, with her, for her. Remind her that she was mine. Fuck her silly until she trusted me again, until she forgave me. Make her come until she opened up to me again, thrust into her until she was ready to embrace what I knew she had to feel for me.

"I'm sorry if I woke you," she whimpered as she lifted her head to wipe her tears.

"You have nothing to apologize for. I am here to keep you safe, even against your nightmares," I murmured.

She sighed, straightening her core a bit, pulling away from me. My jaw twisted from the loss of her warmth on my torso. She pulled the sheets tighter around her round breasts.

She was getting back to her senses, and that meant she would take her distance from me again. The thought felt like a rope was tightening around my neck, each rejection pulling tighter.

"What were you dreaming about?"

She looked up into my eyes, hers still glistening with tears.

"Kyle." She swallowed hard.

"And?" I prompted.

"He, uh, he had a gun pointed at you. I couldn't stop him, and..." Her voice got strangled, caught in her throat.

"Shh," I soothed, grabbing her face with both hands. "He can't hurt me, Chloe. Look at me. He can't harm me, and he can't hurt you. We will find him, I promise you. But you are safe now. This house is surrounded by guards and surveilled 24/7.

"I've made it alive so far, and trust me, I have dealt with people a lot more dangerous than Kyle in my line of work. I have this under control."

"Okay. Okay, I trust you."

Her words made my heart pound. I knew she didn't mean romantically, but that was a step in the right direction. For her to trust me with her safety, to stop fighting me every time I wanted to reinforce security or take measures to protect her.

"Thank you," she whispered.

I searched her eyes, those dark brown eyes that had looked at me with amusement, confidence, and desire. They looked so unsure now. How did I fuck this up so bad?

"Do you want me to stay with you?" I whispered.

I held my breath, unable to move a muscle as I waited for her to answer. She nodded her head.

My heart accelerated, because I honestly didn't think she would let me, but I was more than happy to oblige.

I stood and rounded her bed, under her watchful gaze. I saw her eyes widen as she admired my broad shoulders, my traced stomach. Her eyes traveled down to my boxers and widened.

I got under the sheets. She laid back down, facing me. What I would give to bring her head closer to mine to open her lips with my tongue and take what I couldn't help but feel was mine. But I restrained myself with the sliver of reason I had left when she looked at me with so much hunger.

All I wanted to do was be there for her, for what she needed. This wasn't about me, but my dick had a mind of its own.

"Why would you put yourself at risk like that? Why come get me?"

"Chloe, how could I not?" I asked, a bit exasperated that she would even think I'd consider another option.

"You could have sent someone else."

"I wouldn't trust your life with anyone other than myself. If I didn't have the skills, sure, if it meant you would be in better hands. For something like this, it needed to be me. Time was of the essence."

"You've trained for this?"

"I have. My line of work is not supposed to be dangerous. But sometimes it is. When I used to do the field work myself, I had to infiltrate the nest of very dangerous people a few times. I had to be ready for anything if they caught wind of what I was doing."

"So, it's just part of your job? Is there like an extra package people pay to add physical protection on top of discovering misappropriation of IP or insider trading or something?"

She was teasing me, her sense of humor coming back. I let out a sigh, feeling the tension behind my ribcage lessen a bit.

"No. The purpose of those skills were to protect myself. And what or who I care about."

She bit her lips.

"Do you tend to... sleep with your suspects on the job to get information?"

I frowned, clenching my teeth. There was that tension again. This was my chance to explain myself. I would go as far as she would let me.

"No. Chloe, I didn't sleep with you to get information. There was no need; the moment access to your computer was needed, there are a million ways I could have gotten to it."

"Such as?"

"Making it crash so you had to bring it to IT would be one. Which is likely what happened when they took it from you the first time."

Her eyes went wide, but she nodded her head in understanding.

"I didn't realize it could be so easy." She lightly scratched her throat. "When did you take my laptop?"

Fuck. I was going to hurt her again. But I couldn't lie to her. My secrets were what got us there in the first place.

"In Michigan."

She tensed. "When we were on the yacht. She knew. It wasn't a question.

"Yes."

"So you planned that day, to get me out of the house."

"Yes."

She closed her eyes and shook her head. I saw her lips quiver, even in the dark. I gritted my teeth.

"Okay, well, thank you for the honesty."

She was starting to roll over, but I grabbed her arm so she could continue to face me. I moved my body a little closer to her, as I felt her hold her breath.

"I'm not done. I don't sleep with suspects or anyone on the job when I am on an assignment. That is unprofessional and adds an unnecessary layer of complication. Which was why I fought so hard to resist you. To deny us. I tried to stay away. But since the first time I laid eyes on you at the bar, I haven't been able to get you out of my mind."

I caressed her arm and slid my hand to her face, putting some of her unruly curls behind her ear.

She tightened her hold of the blanket around her breast.

"Jake..."

"I wanted to tell you, Chloe, I did, but it was my job to keep this quiet until we got further in the process. Your dad didn't want you involved. And it wasn't personal, but for you not to be on the list of suspects would have been reckless. Then I got to know you, and while I believed you innocent, it was still inappropriate for me to be with you. But there was no force, no ethics strong enough to keep me away from you. So I broke one of my rules.

"When we were at your father's birthday party, that's when K. called to tell me that Kyle was clean. I panicked that day, because it was starting to look like it could be you. The list of suspects was getting smaller, and you were still on it. I hadn't given the green light to search your files; I didn't want to because I knew you would be upset once everything got out into the open. But when finally, it was just down to you, I had to let my team do their job."

"I understand. I just got caught in the middle of a shit show."

She grinned, but it didn't reach her eyes. I had the words at the tip of my tongue, my heart desperate to tell her, desperate to hear her say it back.

"We both did. But I need you to understand that you weren't just some adventure for me, Chloe, some temporary fuck while on the job."

"Maybe not. But you still lied to me. You tainted every single one of our times together with deceit."

"It doesn't mean I wasn't dating you because I wanted to. It just make it a bit murky. But I didn't sleep with you for information. I did because I needed to have you Chloe. I spent time with you because I was fascinated by you."

Her eyes darkened, her posture stiffening. I was losing her again. Desperation took possession of me as I got closer to her, my face just a few inches away from hers.

"Don't. Don't come any closer Jake."

"Mein leibling..."

"No. You still played with me. You were dating my cousin."

"That was a frustratingly unfortunate coincidence, Chloe, I didn't know about you when her and I dated. I don't deny that she and I had something, but—"

"Please, Jake. I just want to sleep right now. I don't... I don't want to talk about this anymore."

My whole body tensed, sorrow threatening to take over. I searched her eyes again, but the door had closed. Even if I was breaking inside, I needed to be patient. Chloe was a prideful woman, and I had hurt her.

She needed time, and as much as it tore me apart, I would give it to her. This wasn't optional; I couldn't afford to lose her.

I grazed her lips with mine, and she let me.

"Good night, mein leibling."

She didn't respond, but she closed her eyes and let her head slightly rest on my chest. It took everything I had in me not to pull her closer and flush her body against mine.

Instead, I kissed her hair until she fell asleep against me.

CHAPTER 54

Chloe

I held my breath when I felt a hand tightly wrapped around my stomach, under the sheets.

Yes, Jake had spent the night in my bed. I was naked, and that naked body was right against Jake's. I could feel his erection in my back through the thin boxers, the strength of it awaking my senses.

My body, always the traitor, instantly responded to his proximity. I couldn't help the need that started to build up within me. I needed friction to take the edge off, to ease the throbbing in my core.

I started to rub my ass on him, feeling his erection grow. I needed him.

But my mind soon caught up. The pain of having him so near but being unable to let him in felt like a heavy pit in my stomach.

Last night, when he came to my room after that horrible dream I had, I hadn't been able to let him leave.

But I knew I would only be hurting myself. While I couldn't stand being away from him, I couldn't see myself pretending like he hadn't torn my heart into shreds just a few days before. The exception I had made for him, trusting him, letting him see the hidden parts of me, sharing my insecurities with him, had proven to be a mistake.

It wasn't that I didn't understand his explanation, but I couldn't let go of how much it had hurt when he accused me.

Being vulnerable, letting someone else's whim impact mine, was the thing I feared most. And he had reminded me of why, painfully so.

I saw something in his eyes, the way he looked at me the last night, telling me that he cared about me. I felt him on the verge of saying a lot more, of saying words he couldn't take back. Words I couldn't un-hear.

I had cut our chat short, panic invading me at the thought of what it would mean to forgive him. My heart was bleeding, but my brain told me to run. I had done such a poor job listening to it lately when it came to Jake, I wanted to rein it all back, take back control of myself, my emotions and my life. No one else was supposed to have the code to what made me tic.

I slowly tried to remove his hand from my waist, but he squeezed me in further when he felt me move.

"Stay," he asked in a rough voice, "please, mein leibling."

I felt his warm breath in my hair and neck, the sensation sending a shiver down my spine, all the way between my legs. My body was melting at the thought of morning sex.

Why couldn't I just walk away from him for good?

He glided his fingers down my stomach, while his lips left trails of kisses down my neck.

If I didn't pull myself away in the next second, I was done for.

But that hand, that wonderful hand of his, was already parting my thighs open, one finger positioned directly on my clit, sending a surge of electricity through my body.

It was already too late, his wet finger making circles on my bud. I moaned, the sensation so powerful, so primal, I started arching my back so I could be even closer to Jake.

"Hm, fuck, you're always so ready for me, baby," I heard him mutter in a guttural tone, fueling the desperation in me.

His other hand traveled from my stomach to my breasts, stroking them one after the other, teasing the sensitive nipples up. His lips continued kissing and sucking the back and side of my neck, and that spot behind my ear.

"Uhn, hmm…"

"That's it, baby."

I moved my left hand behind him, needing to feel more of him. I grabbed his plump and firm ass, pushing him to me, as he grinded against my back.

My heart was pounding at a thousand beats per hour; I was in a trance.

I wasn't going to last much longer, his fingers having reached that spot that made me feel like my body was being lifted from the bed, gravity unable to hold me down.

I slowly lost myself in the sensation, the present, past, and future merging into one moment in time, one eternal, glorious moment. I screamed his name while the explosion of my orgasm took possession of every single part of my being, shattering me into a million pieces.

Jake continued to hold me close to him, keeping his hand between my legs as I slowly drifted back to earth.

But he wasn't letting me all the way down, his hands still toying with my nipples. I could still feel him rock-hard against me.

I wasn't satiated.

I couldn't tell if it was the sense of self, the sense of control over my being, that was shaken by my kidnapping, or if I just missed him, but I was not done, desire taking back its place in my veins.

I rubbed my ass against him.

"Fuck."

The breathy deep sound from his lips fueled me, the need to feel him throbbing in me, to fulfill my fantasy of the night before, stronger than any reasoning my brain had tried to subject me to.

I rolled around to face him, losing myself in the intense blue pools looking at me. I grabbed his face and kissed him.

He hesitated for a moment, but it was replaced by a sudden urgency as he leaned forward to claim my lips, his tongue sliding inside of my mouth, taking all my moans to him.

He grabbed my ass and drew me closer.

"I need you so much, baby."

I closed my eyes harder to stop the tears his words had incited in me, his want for me finding a mirror image in my soul. But that wasn't what this was about.

I ignored the tinge in my heart and let myself focus on the physical need, my pussy perfectly aligned with his swollen penis. I lowered my hand to bring his boxer down. He lifted his body a bit and helped me remove it.

His teeth clenched, and he let out a groan as I wrapped my hand around his fully erect cock, but he refused to take those piercing eyes away from my face. I moved my hand up and down, as I studied the contraction of his muscles, his strong arms rubbing my ass and my back.

"Show me. Show me what you want."

He knew me. He could tell from the devious pinch of my lips that I wanted control. I would show him just how much.

I shoved him until he was fully on his back. I lifted my body and straddled him, his hungry eyes devouring me. I grabbed his cock and positioned it by my entrance as I lowered myself on him.

I held his gaze as I moved up and down, riding his cock like I owned it, and oh I so wanted it to be mine and mine only. That thought angered me as I rode him more and more aggressively, my hands on his muscled chest, stabilizing him down.

"Fuck, baby, what are you doing to me?"

There was no answer needed; he knew exactly what I was doing.

My eyes rolled in the back of my head as he squeezed my hips. I needed to be closer to him. I leaned my body on his chest until my breasts dangled in front of his face.

He understood what I needed, as he grabbed one by the hand, and wrapped his lips around the other. I thought I was going crazy.

"Oh, Jake!" I screamed his name, intensifying my rhythm, and lost all self-control or sense of reality with every stroke of his tongue around my nipple. He switched breasts, stealing another moan out of me, his eyes closed, his forehead creased as he growled and grabbed my waist more aggressively, moving me violently against him.

Watching a man that was such a force of nature slowly coming undone under me fueled me to no end, knowing that I was driving the lion wild with desire and need for me, for my body, for my thrusts.

The fire in his eyes, the way he grinded his teeth and bit his lips in between breast sucking was more than I could handle as a high-pitched sound tore out of me, the liquid gold pleasure blazing through me until I emptied around his dick, feeling him do the same inside of me.

CHAPTER 55

Jake

I WAS A POWERFUL man, respected by most and feared by many, but that woman brought me down to my knees.

While the thought used to concern me, I would gladly give up some control if it was her holding the reins.

The way she rode me this morning, confident, strong, demanding, bossy, it made my dick throb again just thinking about it. That was the Chloe that drove me wild, although when she was vulnerable, or hurt, it enraged me to no end.

I would burn the world if that meant she was safe and happy.

After the way she shamelessly used me, she went to shower, and I followed suit. As much as I wanted to join her, I could tell that having her strength back in place would make her a little more challenging to be convinced.

So, I just sat on the bed and Penny joined me. I petted the furry creature I had gotten so attached to in such a short period of time. She seemed to take pity on me.

I didn't want to rush Chloe. Last night, when I stared into those hesitant hazel eyes, I almost told her how I felt, but she stopped me. It was only a matter of time, though. Because there was no losing her, especially when I got a glimpse of how much better my life would be with her in it.

I got ready as fast as I could, to catch up on work and touch base with my team as to the whereabouts of Kyle and K. Questioning the IT specialist who was now fired from Motor Holmes didn't lead to much. He was just a man paid to do the job, clearly not involved with the rest of the big picture.

He had been promised a position at Green Mile, but now he was fired with no job in sight. I would make sure he never managed to get an IT job ever again. Vermin like him were not needed in the profession.

I got dressed and headed toward the kitchen to make coffee while I waited for her. I was taking Chloe for a checkup at the doctors. I had made them open the office today, wanting to make sure nothing was amiss after the mild concussion she had.

That kitchen had a lot of memories, mostly of me thrusting into her with her bare ass on the island counter. I planned on trying to do so again hopefully tonight, after the dinner we had been invited to at her parents' house. This was my chance to redeem myself in the eyes of the Holmes family.

I knew that just like Chloe, they were vacillating between gratefulness for me saving her, and resentment for how I had treated her, putting her in harm's way in the first place. But her parents seemed more forgiving than she was. Eric, on the other hand, had proven to be as stubborn as his sister. With Keisha on the guest list, though, I expected him to be distracted.

She finally joined me, wearing a long sleeveless light pink dress. Her golden skin reflected a pink hue brought up by her dress. God, she was beautiful.

"Figured I'd get ready for dinner since they want us there early," she explained as if feeling questioned by the way I was undressing her with my eyes.

"Makes sense," I managed to utter as I got up to bring her a cup of coffee.

"Thank you," she answered as she took a sip.

I wanted to discuss last night, take a chance and see where that left us, but she chugged the brown liquid and returned to the living room where she slid on her high heel sandals, then grabbed her purse and a cream sweater.

"Ready?"

"Ready," I said as we proceeded to the garage.

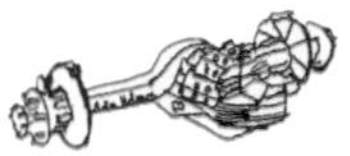

According to the doctor, Chloe was fine and didn't seem to still have any signs of her concussion. I was relieved.

The appointment done, I drove us straight to Philip and Yasmin's house.

"Welcome!" exclaimed Yasmin as she hugged me and then Chloe.

"Thank you for having me." I shook the hand Philip was offering.

"Of course. Glad to see you."

Philip looked a lot more relaxed now that his company was not only safe but ironically in a much better position than if Chad hadn't tried to destroy it.

"I love the dress," complimented Yasmin, admiring her daughter with adoring eyes.

"I love *your* dress!" Chloe replied with a smile.

I wondered how I even thought for a second that Chloe would hurt these people. The love emanating from this family was beautiful, just like the relationship I had with my mother and my brother, even if I hadn't seen him for a few months now. We were due for a catch-up.

We all proceeded to the living room, with Chloe sitting next to her mother.

"How was everything at the doctor's?" asked Philipp.

"All good. I am all healthy," answered Chloe with a smirk, trying her best to reassure her family.

"Her attitude is back, Phil. I think she's fine," teased Yasmin.

"Mother, where the hell is the alcohol?" Everyone laughed, with Chloe feigning to be horrified. "What a faux pas, I'm going to go get some wine."

Chloe left the room as if a fire was chasing her. With her absent, Philip turned a grave look towards me.

"Any news on Kyle?" he asked.

"Not yet. He had the help of an expert in the field. But I will find him, even if it's the last thing I do."

"Don't put yourself in harm's way, though," Yasmin counseled, a shadow of concern washing over her face. "You know we see you as a member of our family, Jake. We want you to stay safe. Chloe would never forgive herself if something happened to you either."

"You might be overestimating how she feels about me right now," I answered, sadness making my voice sound rough.

"She needs some time," explained Yasmin in a softer tone, looking to make sure her daughter wasn't back in the room. "Chloe is very prideful. That man she dated when she was in law school, well, he did a number on her. She doesn't trust easily. And she trusted you. She's just... scared."

I could tell Philip was getting uncomfortable by the conversation. After all, he was now confronted with the fact that I, a longtime friend of his, wanted his daughter.

But he nodded his head, agreeing with his wife.

"Son, when I begged you to help me, the last thing I had in mind was that you and my daughter... well, you know. But don't think I didn't notice how you always follow her around with your eyes at the office. I recognize that look."

He grabbed Yasmin's hands in his, making his wife blush.

"My daughter always reserved her brightest smile for you, too. I hadn't seen that lightness in her gaze in a long time. This is... partly my fault, I put you in an impossible situation."

"It's all my fault Philip. I—" I shook my head to try to push down the knot in my throat. "I should have handled things differently. But I love her.

I am fully and irrefutably in love with Chloe. I will wait for as long as it takes, but I will win her back."

Yasmin looked up behind me, her eyes round. I felt my heart drop in my stomach as I pivoted. Thankfully, it was only Eric.

He clearly had heard at least part of the conversation considering how his gaze was bouncing from me to Philip to Yasmin. We all got up as he walked in the room.

He headed straight to me, holding my stare. I wasn't sure what he wanted from me, but I gave him my hand to shake.

"She's the most stubborn member of this family, so I wish you luck."

I raised my brow as I shook Eric's hand.

"Thank you."

I didn't know what else to say but knowing that Chloe's family didn't hate me and was rooting for me gave me hope that maybe if they could forgive me, so could she.

She soon rejoined us, carrying a tray with two decanters full of the burgundy red liquid, and a few glasses of wine. She also brought the bottle of scotch and a couple whiskey glasses with ice.

The evening was going great, and Chloe lit up even more once the surprise of the evening arrived. Keisha, and her other friends Iris and Amelia who had flown from California, joined the party. Chloe spent the hours before dinner with the three of them on the patio.

Dinner was finally served. Yasmin prepared a feast, featuring all of Chloe's favorite dishes. My heart felt warm, seeing how happy and relaxed Chloe was, almost as if nothing had changed.

But every time our eyes met, I lingered for as long as she would allow, the knot in my stomach twisting as her smile wilted when it was for me.

But I was determined to weather the storm. She was worth it.

After dinner, we all proceeded to the backyard. The outdoor area was spectacular, with long couches enough to sit twelve as we enjoyed the cloudless night and the nicer temperature.

Yasmin had served a homemade chocolate cake for dessert. I sat next to Eric, who was doing a poor job at pretending that he could in fact take his eyes of Keisha sitting with her friends on the right side. Philip and Yasmin were seated on the sofa to our left.

I felt more relaxed when Chloe finally looked at me with less sadness in her gaze. If all remained the same, perhaps by the end of the night, I could find time to be alone with her, tell her what she meant to me, take those lips in mine, remind her of just how good I had made her feel just a few hours ago.

I shifted my position, feeling myself get hard at the memory of how she rode on top of me this morning, her firm breasts all exposed and bouncy, until she brought them down to my mouth so I could feast.

I gave her that knowing smirk. She bit her lips and turned her head around, but I saw how her cheeks got a bit of a hue. Perhaps today she would be more amenable to giving me a second chance.

If I had to fuck her into forgiveness, I would gladly oblige.

"I am so sorry we are late!"

I tensed instantly as the high-pitched voice that could only be Linda's. She joined the group with her husband next to her and Lauren right behind them.

FUCK!

Linda proceeded to hug Philip, who had gotten up to greet them. I focused my gaze on Chloe, seeing her stiffen, her earlier relaxed attitude gone and replaced by coldness and a determined lift of her chin. I knew what that meant.

Philip had mentioned he had invited his brother, but they never confirmed attendance. Everyone had been somewhat relieved at their absence since they hadn't been told about what had happened with Kyle.

While there were suspicions that he got fired, no one else outside of the group previously seated knew the truth or what he did to Chloe.

Lauren blew a kiss to everyone and sat herself on the sofa between Eric and me.

"One of us took two hours to get ready," huffed George half-jokingly as he took a seat next to his brother. "Congrats again on the merger, man, great things ahead."

"Thank you," Philip replied, a bit nervous.

He likely could tell Yasmin was forcing the smile currently on her lips.

"How are you, Eric? It's been so long!" said Lauren as she hugged her cousin.

"I'm great."

"I hear you are moving back here?" inquired Linda as she took one of the solo chairs to Eric's right.

"I am, for a little bit anyways," confirmed Eric as he glanced in Keisha's direction.

"Nice to see you," whispered Lauren to me as she hooked her elbow around mine.

"Nice to see you, too," I answered as I extricated her arm as nicely as I could.

She frowned at the gesture but didn't protest.

"Oh, I would love to have some cake!" she said, observing everyone with their plates. Jake, would you be a doll and get me some?"

"I'll bring some," Yasmin said quickly as she got up.

I sent a grateful look her way as she patted my arm. I got up and sat to Philip's right, taking Yasmin's place. I saw Amelia smile as Keisha shot daggers in Lauren's direction. Iris was the most discreet of them all. Chloe focused her attention on her phone.

This was going to be a long night, but I knew I had one and only one goal: win my woman back, no matter how many other hearts I had to stomp on in the process.

CHAPTER 56

Chloe

OF COURSE, I KNEW this was a possibility. I knew my cousin better than anyone else. When my dad said he had invited my uncle, who knew Jake would be in attendance, I braced myself for this.

But the hours went by, and one glass of wine at a time, surrounded by my best friends, I relaxed and allowed myself to enjoy the moment. To savor the view of Jake sitting amongst the most important people in my life, eating his cake the way I wanted him to eat me.

It didn't help that my group of friends was currently inhibited, drunk with the happiness of being together again.

But I sobered up quickly when Lauren arrived in her short pink dress and plopped herself next to Jake. I knew I had no reason to be jealous, but this wasn't a rational reaction, the need to scream at her that this man was mine.

I had no right; I had rejected him, but it didn't negate the feelings I still had for him. Our morning activities didn't help me get past how I felt about him either. Instead, the sex had confused me even more.

I came alive everytime we were together, but was it worth it?

The back and forth between my heart and my mind was killing me.

"We can leave whenever you want," whispered Iris, her deep blue eyes softening as she looked at me.

"That goes for both of you," Amelia said, staying strong under the burning gaze her comment got out of Keisha.

I hadn't been the only one suffering tonight; Keisha was trying her best to keep her composure, but the effort she was making to avoid Eric was palpable.

It didn't help that Eric was not as diplomatic as he thought he was either.

"I'm fine, really," I lied.

I wanted to go, but I wasn't going to give Lauren the satisfaction of making me leave a dinner in my parents' home, that was organized in my honor.

Jake stood up once my mother went for more cake and sat next to my dad, his intense gaze tracking my every move.

I grabbed my phone to keep me occupied and managed to block out most of the small talk surrounding me.

Lauren was doing her best to engage in conversation with Jake; the flirt turned to the highest level. She kept bringing up all the parties they had been to, trips they had taken together, my stoic face becoming harder and harder to control.

I didn't realize how long this supposedly on and off relationship had lasted. I didn't know they had spent so much time together, including trips. Lauren was twisting the knife currently in my stomach every time she brought up those memories.

Jake changed the conversation as best as he could, but Lauren was a master at manipulation.

"Do you remember Acapulco?" she teased. "Such a great trip. I will never forget when you rented that boat, and we spent all night—"

"Lauren, enough!"

The annoyance from Jake was emanating out of his every pore.

The gasp of both Lauren and her mother was followed by a deafening silence, the air crisp with tension and unease.

Even I was shaken but the cutting tone of his voice.

Silence fell on the group. My eyes went wide, not sure how to react to the outburst.

I almost pitied for my cousin, but when I remembered how she had soiled my name, told Jake that I had stolen from my parents, my sympathies disappeared.

Lauren shot up, her face red, her eyes slit, not at Jake, but at me. I raised a brow, challenging her.

Apparently, it was the day to come clean, and I was in the mood for mayhem. Lauren jetted out of the room, with Linda angrily gawking at Jake.

I wasn't going to let Lauren leave without giving her a piece of my mind, so I also stood up and rushed after her.

"Lauren!"

We came to a halt by the front door, with me blocking the exit with my body.

"What do you want?" she demanded.

"Next time you want to spread lies about me to someone, I would urge you to think twice. I have protected you all these years; I never told anyone but my mom that it was you who stole my dad's money and framed me when you were about to get caught."

"I didn't—"

"Shut up. I don't have time for more of your fucking lies. If you *ever dare* to tell your made-up story to anyone else ever again," I threatened between gritted teeth, "I will fucking destroy you."

She snorted. "Please, no one would believe you."

"Watch me. You have no idea who I am. I have friends with accounts three times the size of yours; it wouldn't be hard to spread the news around in a matter of minutes."

I finally saw her lips thin, taking my threats seriously.

"This is all about Jake, isn't it?"

I stiffened, and Lauren started laughing.

"Of course. I knew you had the hots for him. I saw how you glared at him when he talked to me."

I wanted to rip that satisfied smirk off her face.

"He will never be yours; you aren't his type."

"That's where you're wrong, Lauren."

We both jumped at the guttural sound that came behind Lauren. My eyes went wide as I saw Jake standing there, staring just at me, making my blood run faster through my veins.

Jake walked next to Lauren and straight to my side, grabbing me by the waist. I noticed my friends, my parents, and Linda also were in attendance not too far off, giving us space, but from the glare coming out of Linda, likely able to hear everything.

"I am sorry if I was harsh earlier, but it was really inappropriate for you to keep bringing up very old and very forgotten adventures we had at a family dinner like this. I've made it clear that it's all in the past."

Lauren lifted her head in defiance.

"I wanted to remind you of all the good times we had. You seem to have forgotten, all because that little bitch—"

"Watch your words, Lauren," warned Jake.

I tried to keep my face expressionless, but my heart summersaulted at the intensity in Jake voice. I didn't need him to defend me or fight my fight. It didn't mean I didn't enjoy it when he did.

Lauren launched at me, but thankfully Jake was faster and held her away before she scratched my face. My heart twisted a bit for her. We used to be good friends but ended up at opposite ends of the spectrum.

And my cousin's tantrum was likely just spanning out of hurt.

That was what happened when you trusted someone with your heart, and they didn't want it.

I knew Lauren wasn't innocent; she was manipulative, and part of her sorrow was likely because Jake hadn't fallen in line like all the other guys she toyed with. But it didn't mean she wasn't in pain.

The rest of the crew joined. In a cloud of chaos, Lauren and her parents left the party.

"Was she always like that, showing up uninvited to people's houses?" asked Keisha as she got closer to me. I was shaking.

"No. No, she wasn't. We used to be friends. Ugh, I want to leave now," I said, sadness invading my senses.

The girls started saying their goodbyes to Jake and my parents. I hugged them as well. I didn't know what to do with Jake. He hadn't stopped staring at me, as if there was no one else in the room, going through the motions, but only focused on me. I wanted to run as fast and as far away as possible.

What was his plan, I wondered, seduce me back to him with agonizing proximity? Just staying around, so I would cave?

Was it working? No, it was not. Because every time I stared in his eyes too long, I saw his face on the day he accused me. The day he ripped my universe apart, reminded me why I had written off putting all my trust into a man before.

"I won't let her bother you or make you uncomfortable, not again, I promise."

Those had been his words, but the next day he had kissed her in front of me. I should have felt vindicated, but seeing Lauren suffer didn't give me any comfort, it just terrified me even more.

Everyone gave us space without us having to ask. Jake made it more than clear that he wanted some alone time with me by his reticence to budge.

Alone, we just stared at each other for a few agonizing seconds. I couldn't decipher what I saw in his somber expression, his frown, his tense jaw. I wanted to caress his face, to remove whatever was tormenting him, but that would mean something I wasn't ready for.

"I never meant to come between you and your cousin."

"Yeah. Just another one of those unfortunate coincidences, right?"

I felt my eyes burn. I closed them, trying to bring the tears back down.

"Yes, believe it or not. Had I known, had I predicted us, I would have never let things with her get so murky for so long. Chloe, look at me. It's been months since anything actually happened between her and I."

"Months? When exactly did it end, Jake? After you started working for Motor Holmes? When?" I rasped.

That was irrelevant really, I knew that, but the questions left my lips before I could stop myself.

Jake pinched his nose and shook his head.

"I was already at Motor Holmes. But it stopped very shortly after."

Jealously coursed through me like wildfire. I knew I had no right. Even after we met, it was weeks before anything happened between us. But still, the part of me that wanted to own this man, to have him all for me, was livid.

"You know what, Jake? It doesn't matter. There is nothing left between you and I, nothing. My cousin was never really the problem, it was you, your lies and deceit, and your accusations."

"Chloe, please—"

"No, don't touch me. I... I need you to stay away, to stop being around me all the fucking time. It's suffocating. You're suffocating me."

The tears were rolling down my face, my lies hurting me as they left my lips. I did need space to think, but to say that he was suffocating me when he was helping me heal was dishonest and ungrateful.

Jake's eyes slit, and his nostrils flared. He took a step back from me as if my mere presence harmed him. He shook his head.

"I need you to not be around me Jake... I, I just, I don't... you broke me, I don't want you near me. You can't sleep in my house anymore. We need another arrangement; I can't keep seeing you."

I felt my heart constrict as the words left my mouth, my gaze on the floor. If I took another look at Jake, I would break into pieces.

After a few seconds of silence, Jake finally spoke up.

"Okay, Chloe. I will give you the time you need, the space you want. I will leave you alone, not because it's not killing me, but because it's what you need, even though we both know that's not what you want."

Jake closed the distance between us in two strides. He lifted my chin to meet his gaze, his heated eyes burning his words into my soul.

"But know this: there is no force of nature, there is nothing in this world, that can keep me away from you. When you are ready, I promise you, I will be there. Because you are mine, and I am yours, and there is nothing that can change that. Not even you."

Jake took my parted lips in his aggressively, branding me, making every inch of my body vibrate against his. Without warning, he let go of me and stalked out of the house.

I closed my eyes and leaned against the door for support, his words tormenting me further, making me wonder if I was making a mistake.

CHAPTER 57

Chloe

I COULDN'T THINK OF a better place to be than cuddled on my rooftop couch surrounded by my best friends, Penny, and the champagne bottle we had consumed in record time. We were having a much-needed sleepover.

Amelia had managed to escape from Alejandro for the week, even if he was in town presumably meeting with Jake and Mike to see what he could do to help track Kyle. I was sure Jake would be livid having someone question his decisions and process, but I didn't really have a choice in the matter.

Alejandro would do anything to remove any sliver of concern out of Amelia's life, and clearly my kidnapping had shaken her a bit. I was amused as I realized that perhaps the issue was that my situation was bringing back some not so tasteful memories for them.

My head laid on Iris's lap while she fiddled idly with my hair.

"Please never stop playing with my hair," I teased, eyes closed.

"We should just all get a massage this week," suggested Keisha.

"Yes! My back is killing me from the flight!" added Amelia.

"Must suck having to fly coach," Keisha teased, and Amelia threw a pillow at her.

"Shush! I didn't want to wait one more second before being here, Alejandro be damned."

"I mean, he's not wrong," Iris said, a small smile on her lips.

"I love how spoiled we all are," I laughed.

"And she's not even joking," Keisha chuckled, shaking her head.

"Or ashamed," I added, as I leaned up to chug the rest of my drink "Even if Mr. Cunningham had apparently been even more suspicious of me due to my 'lavish lifestyle.' Fuck him."

Silence fell in the room. It was the first time I had brought Jake up since we got back to my house.

"Well..." started Keisha, avoiding my sharp look. "He knows how to do math, Chloe. He didn't know about your other lucrative career."

"Why do I feel like you are all on his side?"

I shot an accusatory glance to all my friends. They needed to be angrier at Jake than they were. I wanted someone else to tell me I wasn't overreacting.

"We are not on his side, sweetie," started Amelia.

"Sometimes people deserve second chances," dared Iris.

"Especially when they do things to redeem themselves," said Keisha.

I rolled my eyes and pressed my forehead in my hands.

"He likely acted out of guilt."

"I don't know about you, but I wouldn't put my life in danger 'out of guilt'."

I glared at Keisha. That's the problem when you have friends that are more like sisters. They don't feel like they have to walk on eggshells around you. While that was one of my favorite things about my friends, in this moment, I was not appreciating it very much.

"Chloe, trust me. When Alejandro put himself at risk for me, there was no doubt left in my head. It took me a little bit to catch up, granted, but I couldn't deny that he loved me, not after he showed me that life without me wasn't worth it for him.

"Jake put himself in harm's way for you; he had people shoot at him, just to get you safe. You told me something like this, remember?"

"Okay, okay, okay, I don't want to talk about that anymore. This is girls' night not Jake's night."

"Meeaoooww!" I could have sworn my cat was agreeing with my friends.

"Ice cream?" suggested Iris to try to diffuse the tension and the sadness in my eyes.

"You don't have to ask twice. Sorry I am so snappy," I apologized, doing my best to retain my tears. "I'm not ready to trust him again. I don't know that I ever will be. I'm scared—no, I'm fucking terrified."

My friends came to me and hugged me as tight as they could.

CHAPTER 58

Jake

THE WORDS, "WAIT AND HOPE" had been etched in the dark leather walls of the Kratos Society for as long as I could remember.

Kratos was a very exclusive social club I had been lucky to join over ten years ago, invited by my client. It was originally created as a gentlemen's club, and the decor was still consistent with that, but now it was one of the most coveted social clubs in the world, where successful professionals came to mingle.

The group offered a collection of fully equipped hotels, resorts and events its members could enjoy across the world. But the best value was in being part of the most elite members of society. The meetings that took place between those walls could make or destroy a nation.

For the members of Kratos, nothing was unachievable, one just had to have the right connection. I had strategically built my network there since I stepped foot in the place. It had done me well.

I was seated at the table furthest in the back of one of the restaurants, with a breathtaking view of Lake Michigan. I hadn't been very social since Chloe asked for distance, but this meeting was long due.

"Sorry for the delay," said Alejandro as the server walked him in.

"I was early," I acknowledged as I got up to shake his hand. This was our first time meeting in person. The man was dressed in a sleek gray suit and a black t-shirt that made it obvious how much time he spent at the gym.

Eric walked in a few minutes later, in a blue three-piece suit and a tie. I had lost mine hours ago. They shook each other's hand.

"I haven't been here in forever," Eric remarked.

"You're a member, I take it?" Of course he was. Eric was an intense asshole who liked the finer things in life from what I could tell, and I meant that as a compliment.

"I am. I usually go to the New York chapter."

"I see."

"I never really understood the point of these stuck-up establishments," contributed Alejandro.

"I know where you're coming from," I admitted, "but rich people love to flash their fortune and use it to separate themselves from the rest of the world. Some of us play the game, because it's good for business. They respect you more if they know you run in their circles."

"Some of the most powerful people in the world are sitting next to us," said Eric in lower tone. "This is a hell of a network of people to rub shoulders with."

"Welcome to Kratos," said Bart, my usual waiter, to my guests. "I'm Bart. And I'll be here to serve you for this evening. With me I have our Macallan Anecdotes of Ages Collection, as requested."

A petite woman we hadn't noticed moved from behind Bart and set our drinks at the table, accompanied by an assortment of charcuterie.

"Cheers," I said as we each picked up our glasses. "Alejandro, thank you for helping me get to Chloe."

"Thank you," added Eric.

"My pleasure."

We each took a sip, letting the oaky liquid coat our tongues and warm our throats. I closed my eyes for a second, to savor the sensation.

"Wow," said Alejandro. "I guess I can be swayed."

Eric raised a brow as he took another sip. We were drinking some of the finest scotch the world had to offer, after all.

"We'll work on making you a member," I announced as I clinked my glass with his again before taking another sip.

Alejandro had allowed me to use his men and resources, and did it quickly, something that I both admired and respected. The least I could do was buy him a three-thousand-dollar-a-glass whiskey and introduce him to the life of the elite.

I had a pretty good idea of who he was. I had done a bit of research on him. He had been involved with some gang leader in Mexico. Alejandro was a rich man, and those diamonds that mysteriously disappeared after the death of that drug dealer led me to believe he might even be richer than he let on.

That didn't mean his and Amelia's businesses couldn't benefit from rubbing shoulders with the patrons of the Kratos Society.

"So, you're engaged to Amelia?" asked Eric.

Alejandro slowly set his glass down. "I am."

"Hm. How did you meet?"

A smirk lifted Alejandro's face, but I could tell he tensed a bit at the question.

"What do you really want to know?" asked Alejandro, his gaze challenging Eric.

"I'm not the enemy," said Eric, lifting his hands in the air. "I'm just protective of who is around my sister, that's all. And you can't blame me for being a bit curious how you came into all these... resources. You seem to be a very well-connected man. Plus, the girls are not always as discreet as they think they are. I heard some things. I've known Amelia for a while now, as she is one of my sister's best friends."

Alejandro shot him a death stare. I wanted to say something, ease the tension, but I stopped myself. They needed to figure this out if those meetings were going to become a regular thing.

And Eric knew we still needed all the help we could get to find Kyle, so pissing off Alejandro had to have its limits.

I wasn't concerned, though. Considering the lengths he had gone for Amelia, he wouldn't stop helping me simply because she wouldn't let him.

"All you need to know is that I would never harm her."

"I believe that," added Eric. "And she has never looked so happy. Congrats, man, you got a good one."

Alejandro's shoulders slightly relaxed. "Thanks, man."

"What about you, Eric? What's the deal with Keisha?"

Eric's head spun so fast I thought he pulled a nerve.

"What are you talking about?" he spluttered.

"Oh, come on, background checks are second nature to me, you know that by now." I offered a sly smile.

"And me," added Alejandro.

Eric leaned back in his seat, seemingly flabbergasted, looking from Alejandro to me, disbelief stretching his features.

"In my defense, it's literally my job," I added.

"I needed to know everything there was to know about people who were around my fiancé," explained Alejandro as if that was an acceptable, normal answer. I liked the man more already.

"If we didn't cross a few boundaries, we wouldn't have found Chloe so fast." I shrugged.

From what I could tell, Eric seemed to be a pretty strait-laced attorney who liked to do things by the book. But I also knew that just like his father, there wasn't a line he would cross for people he cared about. He loosened his tie and chugged the rest of his drink.

"Hey! this is meant to be savored!" protested Alejandro. I laughed.

"Fuck it," said Eric. "I need liquid courage if this is where the night is taking us."

Fair point.

"Anything else I can get you?" asked Bart as he made his way back to us.

"We're going to need a bottle," I requested.

"And some cigars" added Eric.

I wasn't in need of new friendships. I was a man who kept alone except for certain social settings and my best friend from college. But this was a group of men I could see myself making an exception for.

CHAPTER 59

Chloe

A WEEK WITH THE girls had been energizing, the therapy I didn't know I needed after the weeks I'd had. They spent every single day at my house, with Keisha and I managing to work part-time to spend the rest of our time together.

Amelia and Iris were able to continue working from my place as well, finalizing the details for the launch of Amelia's new hotel line.

The first was set in Mexico, a mini resort focused on experiencing local cuisine and boasting local artists work on the premises for the clients to purchase.

It was Amelia's little jewel addition to her company, in partnership with Alejandro. Amelia's fiancé had also joined us for dinner at my place one time.

I used the next few weeks afterwards to recharge, focus, and do a lot of self-reflection. Now that I finally had a seat on the board, I had reduced my legal duties by a lot, slowly transitioning into a more supervisory role in that side of the business, so I could focus on strategy and business operations at a higher level.

That arrangement gave me a good salary bump and ironically more time to dedicate to my writing career.

I had come clean to my family. While I kept my pen name, I had let them in on my secret. My mother had been quite offended that I hid something so important and special to me from my loved ones. But I explained that I hadn't wanted my writing career to intersect with the legal one, especially when I was in the law firm.

Now, I cared a lot less. If I learned anything from the experience with Green Mile, it was to take life by the horns and live it, really live it, and be whoever I wanted to be, unapologetically.

It was a weight off my back, really. I even took pleasure at seeing my dad's face redden as he read some passages of one of my books.

My favorite part of it all though was the bonding experience with my mother. Once she got past the awkwardness of reading smut written by her daughter, she opened more than I could have asked for. She even joined me and the girls at one of my book signings, the first one I hosted in Chicago, proud with tears in her eyes when she saw the line of people who came up to see me.

The merger with Green Mile had caused a lot of work for the company, as now we had to blend certain resources across the company and essentially integrate Green Mile as seamless as possible in our organization, considering the rush of the transaction.

As I had expected, we didn't have too much trouble getting the required consents from Green Mile's major customers and suppliers. We had used the merger as leverage to negotiate more advantageous contracts as well.

Green Mile had been the gift we didn't know we needed, or rather, we didn't even know we could have, and aside from the headaches of diligence and unplanned integration, it sped up the process by which Motor Holmes was establishing itself a leader in the industry. With the infrastructure of Green Mile, and the fact that they had indeed started manufacturing e-axles with our IP, we were able to capitalize on that to plan the launch our products to market a lot sooner than anticipated.

Speculations were running wild in the market as to the cause behind the merger. Motor Holmes had strategically taken control of the narrative, while letting rumors circulate but controlling the rumor mill, so that Motor Holmes was painted as David winning against Goliath when Goliath tried to take them down, sending the message that we were not to be messed around with.

Mike had been working at Motor Holmes now for over a month, loving his job and his salary bump, but also bringing some much-needed IT changes to both companies. He and his girlfriend were back together, with no future breakup this time I hoped. I wanted to believe that his new position would make his in-laws less wary of him.

And as for Jake, he had done exactly what I had asked him to do, for better or worse. He had texted, sent flowers, chocolates, books, but I had held firm. Slowly, the gifts diminished, the text messages got scarcer, and the midnight calls stopped.

I thought I would feel relieved, but I was distraught. I threw myself into my new position on the board and my writing career. Of course, the bodyguards he had forced on me were still there.

He had ignored my attempts to pay for the service, but every day I was driven around by security. They had a rotation in front of my doorstep, and to this day, they still inspected the house every time I had to go back in it, unless someone stayed behind to guard it.

Jake was no longer in the office since he resigned from the board. It felt a bit weird without him there.

The season was changing, the fall breeze making its way to cool the lake, change the leaves and the fashion around town. I caught myself a few times looking at that picture of Jake and I at my parents' house, just twenty-four hours after the first time we met. It stopped my heart every time, as I wondered if back then, I was already in love with him.

Yes, I still loved him. I had admitted it, at least during sleepless nights when I ached for him. I had contemplated calling him, but every time I remembered that Friday in Michigan, the pain of seeing Lauren in his arms, how fast he had dismissed me when he should have trusted me, I stopped myself.

How could one be so terrified of giving it all to another, while feeling half alive in their absence? Was protecting my heart worth the agony I felt?

Was avoiding a heartbreak worth the tears I shed when my body felt like it was going through withdrawal at 1 a.m. when I craved him?

I missed those strong arms, those lips crashing into mine. But mostly I missed his company, the hand holding, the possessiveness, the charm. The way he made me feel naked around him, and the way I had started enjoying letting all my strength and flaws just be. I missed the thrill my brain got when we talked about legal issues. I missed his smart answers, that smirk he had when he knew he was winning.

There wasn't anything about the man that I didn't miss. But every time I picked up the phone, I cried and put it down.

CHAPTER 60

Jake

A Reasonable Amount of Groveling Time Later

IF I HAD BEEN told that my last assignment would turn into me stalking the daughter of my client, I would have waved the thought away as ludicrous. Yet, against all odds, there I was parked on her street, waiting on her, as if I didn't have businesses to run.

She had asked me for space, and against my better judgment, I had given it to her. She had accepted my security, even when she had travelled a few times in the past months for her book signing.

Chloe fully embracing her writing career was the most beautiful thing I had ever seen, especially the few times I had been unable to resist the urge and flown to where she was, staying in the back, hiding in the shadows so she couldn't see me.

Those were her moments, and I didn't want to ruin them, but that didn't mean I had to stay away, either. That smile that lit up any room, the way she shined surrounded by others that shared her passion for romance novels had made her look like a source of light.

When I couldn't attend, I required daily reports, because even if I was staying away, I still had to protect her, make sure she was safe.

We still hadn't been able to find K. or Kyle, so that danger was still looming over us. That was until one of the bodyguards who was assigned to Chloe full-time informed me that Kyle had had the audacity to write to her, the letter having arrived an hour ago.

My soul had practically left my body when I had been notified. It was all made worse when I had the guard search her mail while she was at work, and he found that the letter was the third one Chloe had received during that week.

That explained her sudden shift in plans. Her schedule had her in NY, then in California during the week, but she had cancelled her flights and her book signings at the last minute. In the past week, she had only left her house once this morning to go to an in-person director meeting.

Kyle threats were affecting her life, and the thought enraged me, knowing that Kyle was still torturing her, and I hadn't been able to do anything to stop it. In those messages, Kyle had threatened her, saying that he was running out of money, and that he would kill me and then her if she didn't send him anything.

The notes had gotten creepier, with Kyle sending her pictures taken at some of her signings, or when she was out with friends, indicating that he was following her.

I had my team searching every inch of Illinois for traces of Kyle and K. In the meantime, I wasn't going to take any chances with her safety.

In this moment, that meant rushing to her house to wait for her as she got home, and inevitably piss her off.

CHAPTER 61

Chloe

I SHOULD HAVE KNOWN the semblance of peace I lived in for the past few weeks wouldn't last. I'd manage to shove Kyle in the back of my mind for a bit. But he started sending me notes, threatening me, asking me for money. I had still managed to keep a strong front, but the last one shook me.

So, I hibernated in my house the past week for the most part and cancelled my upcoming book signings. The only reason I had left the house was for an in-person work meeting I was coming home from.

The driver pulled behind a familiar black BMW. I considered staying in the car. After all, it was warm, comfortable, and more importantly, free of Jake's intoxicating smell.

Shit.

Jake Cunningham dressed all in black, lips curled, chest heaving, palpable anger emanating from his every pore, even under his calm and composed demeanor, got out of the backseat of his car, and stomped all the way to mine.

I gulped hard, his crisp blue gray eyes piercing through the black glass and straight to my soul. I was overwhelmed by the flow of emotions invading my senses. The thought of Jake still haunted me, my chest tightening every time I thought of him.

Time hadn't healed anything. I didn't understand how I could feel so empty without him, when I had managed to lead most of my life not knowing him. And seeing him again after so long was more than I could handle. I gathered all the courage I could muster and stepped out of the SUV to face him when he opened the door.

"What... what are you doing here?" I managed to ask, the colder air sneaking under my coat.

"We need to talk."

My body was shaking.

"You could have just called."

Jake bent his head to the side as he took a deep breath, his teeth clenched so tight his jaw was protruding.

"Not for this."

"Jake, I am busy."

"I don't care. Get in the car. We are going to my place. We're not having this conversation on the streets."

"Let's just go upstairs," I suggested. I didn't want him in my space, but the last thing I wanted was to go with him.

"No. You're not sleeping here anymore. You're coming with me, where I can make sure no one associated with Kyle makes it to your fucking doorsteps."

"Jake, there is no need for this." I felt a slight tremor in my hands, as I feared I had gotten caught.

"I'll be the judge of that."

"I'm not going anywhere with you," I snarled at him. He grinded his teeth and gave me an exasperated look.

"Get in the car, Chloe."

I was inhaling as much cold air as I could, trying to keep my composure. He must have found out about the letters. I wasn't going to win this one.

The worst was that part of me was relieved to see him here. Even with the guards around the house, I still got startled everytime I heard a random noise. It got a lot worse since the notes. I sighed, admitting defeat. But the idea of sleeping in close proximity with Jake again didn't make me feel any safer.

"You know, you don't have to be so rude."

I glared at him but stomped away from him and towards his car. I violently swung the car door open and climbed in. He stepped in right after me and closed the door. Roger made eye contact with me in the rearview mirror briefly before he pulled the partition up to give us some privacy.

We stayed silent for most of the drive as Roger glided through Lake Shore Drive, while I mostly tried to lower my heart rate.

I had an overwhelming urge to both slap Jake and sit on his lap. The shock to my system, after not having seen him for what felt like an eternity, was unbearable, all my pain and frustration coming at me in waves.

We made it all the way to his apartment, in the loudest silence. I didn't know what to do with myself. We headed to his living room. I sat down, but Jake was pacing back in forth in front of me, a hand on his waist. He hadn't removed his black coat.

It had been a while since I'd sat in his luxurious apartment. The view of the city was even more breathtaking than I remembered.

"You lied," he finally said, stopping in front of me.

"Me?"

"Yes, you. Why didn't you say that Kyle had reached out? Why didn't you mention, even to Roger, that he had been sending you letters?"

Jake looked so angry, I swallowed the snappy answer that came to my mind. I could see his nostrils flaring, the darkness of the night in the background making him seem so ominous.

"Jake, I, I didn't think it was necessary. Those are just silly threats."

I hoped to God he couldn't tell I had been petrified since I received the first message.

"Is that why you're cancelling your signings?"

I sighed. What was I supposed to say? I was terrified.

"I'm just postponing them."

"Of course. Well now you are going to stay here with me until we catch them."

"No. There is no need for this."

"Kyle, or K. or someone who works with them hand delivered a letter to you, no postage. And you hid it from me. Just like you hid the others you had received. So, now, you're staying here. It's that simple."

"Oh my God, Jake, extreme measures are not needed. I am fine in my house," I said, bolting to my feet.

Jake didn't back down; he was standing right in front of me, his boots touching mine.

"Extreme? You were fucking reckless, Chloe. You asked me to back down with the security, and I did, on the condition that you'd inform me of any changes. You hid that Kyle had contacted you, had sent you pictures of him tracking you for fuck's sake. Why on earth would you do something like this?"

"I don't need to explain myself to you!"

Was he right? Yes. Would I admit it? No.

Jake grabbed my arm.

"Yes, you do. Do you not get it? If something happened to you, I, I don't..." His tone was deep, heavy.

My heartbeat accelerated when he stopped, tensing his jaw, shaking his head. He was concerned for my safety, and here I was, acting like a spoiled child, refusing to admit that he was right. The truth was that I hadn't really slept since those letters started coming in.

His phone rang. With a frown on his face, he let me go and picked it up.

"Are you in the security room?" Good. I want the team on every single floor, and around the clock surveillance of the building. Set up the surveillance in the apartment next to mine. Send me a message immediately when it's done," he snapped as he turned the phone off and slid it in his pocket.

"What are you doing?" I asked.

"Updating the building surveillance protocols."

"How do you have access to that?"

"I bought the building."

"You did what!?"

I stared at him, eyes wide open, fire practically shooting out of them.

"I needed access, and I needed to monitor the perimeter," he explained as if he was talking about the weather. The man had spent what was easily in the hundreds of millions of dollars to make sure he could control the building. All for my safety. I couldn't act as a brat no matter how angry I still was with him. I owed him an explanation. I sighed.

"I should have told you. I just didn't want to go back to a few months ago. I didn't want him to control my life, where I go, what I do. I didn't mean to annoy you. And yes, I was scared, Jake, of course I was. That's why I cancelled my trips, like a fucking coward."

I saw the rage in him disappear. I was trying as hard as I could to stop the tears that threatened to take over me, so I took a few steps back, avoiding his gaze, but it was to no end. I felt the warm liquid go down my cheeks before I could stop it. Jake closed the distance between us in a second and grabbed my face in his hands.

"Please, don't cry, because then I'll be forced to find that son of a bitch and snap his neck in two."

Jake gently wiped the tears off my face. I leaned into his touch. God, I had missed him so much. I could barely believe he was right in front of me, in one of those long black coats that made him look like the secret agent he was.

"He can't harm you, mein leibling, I promise you. I would never allow that to happen, do you hear me? You are safe here; you don't have to be scared.

"I am sorry it's taken so long but I swear, we will find them. K. will slip the more they run out of money, and when he does, I will find them."

"Thank you."

My body was starting to melt in his hands, my heart constricting at hearing him call me mein leibling like he used to.

I thought putting some time and distance between us would have lessened the ache I felt all over my body, the tightness in my heart since I let him walk away, but it hadn't. My fingers were itching to run through his thick hair.

"But promise me that you will tell me everything. Please. I can't protect you if I don't know. We could have increased supervision, tried to catch whoever was delivering those documents for him and use that person to lead us to him."

"Okay." I nodded, my throat thick.

I couldn't help feeling like a teenager getting reprimanded. I knew I should have told him, but that would have made the threats real.

But now, the cause of my sleepless nights and uncontrollable desire was standing right in front of me, those blue eyes burning through every inch of me, heating up my skin and warming up between my legs, my need for him having only increased since I last saw him.

"I'm sorry," I finally said, his hands still framing my face and wiping my tears. "What do we do now?" I sniffled.

"Well, I've increased the building security so we should be good. You can do whatever you want, but there will be an additional car following us around."

"Us?" My eyes widened at his words.

"Yes, Chloe. I am not leaving your side. That's not up for discussion."

I sighed. Every instinct was telling me to run away as fast as I could. But I didn't have the energy or the willpower.

If I was being honest, I didn't want to be away from him either. I had done enough of that.

"I need clothes. And Penny."

"My team is bringing her and your clothes here as we speak."

Of course. "Do you plan on... sleeping here?" It was a stupid question considering the size of his apartment.

He raised a brow. "Do you want me leave?"

This man and his questions, tugging at my heartstrings. Being around him after a few months felt like no time had passed at all. As if it was yesterday that I let him go, and possibly made a mistake.

It wasn't that I regretted my decision, but I was no longer sure that the way I ached to be with him was worth protecting my heart against anymore.

Did I want him to stay? Of course. Was it wise? Not in the slightest, not if I still wanted to stick to my decision of moving on.

But I had to admit that as much as I had tried to relax, Kyle's letters had put me on edge, especially at night, when I had trouble sleeping, imagining that Kyle would get past the guards and get to my bedroom while I slept.

I couldn't utter the words, but I shook my head, agreeing to spending the night under the same roof as Jake Cunningham.

CHAPTER 62

Jake

I FELT THE TENSION that had tied my back into knots reduce significantly. She accepted to stay.

I was ready for a fight, because there was no way in hell I wouldn't remain on the premises, but I was prepared to sleep in the unit next door, if that was what it took to keep a close eye on her.

She was looking at me now, her arms wrapped around herself, putting her guard up and trying to fight the fact that she was glad I was here. I knew she was.

God, I wanted to kiss her, bring her body close to mine, feel her breathing on my neck.

I missed her so damn much. She wasn't fighting me with as much fervor as I expected, and as relieved as I felt, I missed her fire and wanted to slowly squeeze Kyle's neck for taking that away from her.

"You can sleep in the room next to mine" I said tenderly, running my palms on her arms.

"That works for me."

She shivered a bit, even if she was still wearing her coat. Her hair was longer and slightly darker than before, her beautiful face laced with concern.

"I'm sorry to barge in like this after you specifically asked me to stay away."

She closed her eyes for a second. "I should have expected it, to be honest."

She gave me a small smile, almost as bright as the ones from before the day I changed our fate in Michigan.

"Okay, see you tomorrow."

She looked hesitant for a second but then turned around and walked towards the stairs to the second floor.

I desperately wanted to follow her to her room, lift her up to the bed, ravage her lips until she could barely breathe, tell her I loved her, and fuck her to submission, until she admitted that she was in love with me as well. But, as much as my dick pulsed its protest in my pants, that would be for another day.

I proceeded to my room where I changed and got into my bed. Buying control of the building had cost well into the nine digits, but if she was to stay here, I needed complete control of the premises.

For the past months, while I monitored her every move through my team, I had been a tortured soul, a crankier shadow version of myself, an empty shell going through the motions, out of my body, unable to be present without that stabbing pain caused by the absence of the only woman who made me feel whole, who had made me realize a piece was missing, only to then take it away.

But now that she had accepted to stay with me, it was my chance to win my woman back, and this time, I would stop at nothing to win her heart.

We had gotten into a semi-routine. I usually woke up before her to make coffee. I made sure my chef had breakfast ready by the time she woke up.

After about an hour of me roaming the halls on calls or working on my laptop on the kitchen island, she would show up down the stairs, wearing tight shorts and a crop top t-shirt, heading to the gym room, while I got a hard-on seeing how round her ass looked. She would then head back to her room for about an hour and come back down around 10 a.m.

She'd prance in the kitchen with a book and her laptop in hand. She'd say hi, grab a coffee and a pastry, and proceed to the library, with her faithful cat purring next to her. I'd hit the gym but otherwise try my best to stay in any room but hers.

Eventually, my feet would take me wherever she was typing or reading or managing her social media. I'd work in silence next to her or across from her. Penny would jump back and forth between us, maximizing on the cuddles she could get.

Chloe wasn't uncomfortable with silence, that I knew, but she was an extrovert, so she couldn't help but start conversation with me.

I cherished the opportunity to spend time with her. It felt normal, natural, and she had seemed to forget about her reservations towards me. This gave me hope that she would eventually come around to the idea of us being together... for good.

Because damn, I wanted to kiss her. Especially after we had a few bottles of wine at dinner, and Chloe would rest her head on my shoulder as she fell asleep in front of the TV.

We had caught up on what we had been up to since the dinner at her parents' house. She had been quite curious about my day-to-day in the private equity word, while I enjoyed seeing how much more relaxed she was now transitioning to the business side of Motor Holmes, her writing career out in the open.

Friday rolled in at a fast pace, the nights getting darker earlier as fall made its way in.

Chloe was cuddled up on a loveseat with her usual blanket, while I worked on the office table next to her. Penny was sleeping in her bedroom. Other than the colder weather, the late evening wasn't any different than the other ones we had spent staying in, except that although I knew exactly what she had been doing the past few weeks, she was telling me about some of her next projects. I was enjoying the sound of her voice, and how her brown eyes lit when she talked about her writing.

"It's just nice to not have to worry about someone recognizing me at signings anymore, you know? But it was a little weird when Jane's mother, Kyle's girlfriend, introduced herself when I was in Wisconsin," she explained, as she got off the chair to plug her laptop charger in the wall.

"She seemed quite enamored with you, though."

Chloe immediately stiffened. I realized my mistake, but it was too late. Her smile was gone, and her eyes were round, understanding seeping in as she stood straight.

"You've been following me?"

I sighed. My lies and accusations had come between us before; I wouldn't let history repeat itself. I slowly lifted from my chair and sat at the end of the table, bringing myself closer to her.

"No, I wasn't following you. But I did pop up at some of your signings every now and then."

"Why?"

We stared at each other in silence. I got off the table and walked towards her so I could stare into those caramel eyes, to make sure she internalized every one of my words.

"Because I needed to make sure you were safe. Because I fucking missed you, and while I wanted to give you your space, I also couldn't stay away from you for so long. I needed to see you, even from a distance. So, I compromised."

I felt relieved when she only shook her head, letting me know she didn't consider me a stalker at this point.

Instead, a small smirk graced those beautiful lips, the knot in my stomach slowly untying further, as it had been bit by bit that week, the more time we spent together. I felt like I was slowly getting her back to seeing me as someone she could trust. She glanced at my bookshelf spotting my collection of Chloe Holmes books. I had caught her staring at them a few times, but she never brought it up.

"You have all my books."

"Yes."

"You read them."

"Yes." Of course I did. I would have given anything to have a piece of her those first weeks. Her writing gave me a better look into that beautiful brain of hers. They made me feel closer to her.

Having her so close to me, tempting me all week, I could no longer stay far from her. I needed to touch her, smell her, hold her, feel her warmth. That need fueled me as I closed the distance between us, wrapping my fingers around the back of her neck to bring her closer.

"Jake," she said softly, a warning lacking the strength from her protests a few months back.

I lowered my lips to hers but stopped right there, just lingering for a few seconds, feeling as she held her breath. I slowly trailed kisses down her jaw and then put some distance between us. She looked confused and a bit frustrated.

Frustrated was good; frustrated it meant that she wanted me as much as I wanted her. But I resisted and left her in the room as I proceeded to the kitchen to finish some of the work I had to do still for the day, telling my now awakened cock to take a hike.

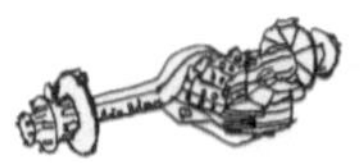

It was 8 p.m. when I finished working. I found Chloe cuddled up in one of the corners of the huge L-shaped couch in the family room. The room was lit only by the light coming from her computer screen.

The blanket had slipped down some, and I could see that she was wearing that silk negligée I had almost torn off her a few months back. One of the thin straps on her shoulders fell down her arm as she pushed her straight hair back. I felt my dick stretch my sweatpants, a plague that had been torturing me every time she moved.

I knew how little coverage that outfit had, I could imagine her nipples hardening below the fabric with every bit of friction she encountered.

She looked up when she heard me coming, surprise in her gaze. "I thought you went to bed."

"No," I answered as I stopped right in front of her, "I was still working."

She studied me, her gaze traveling down my blue t-shirt and my black joggers. I saw her eyes widen a bit when she spotted my erection just before she lifted them back up to my face, her mouth lightly agape as she bit her lips.

I didn't hide it because I wanted her to see what she was doing to me. I wanted her to witness the pain I was in at needing to be inside of her every goddamn second of every goddamn day.

"Want to watch something?" I offered.

"What? Oh, um, yes." She blushed.

I went to the kitchen to pour her some wine, get some scotch for myself, along with some cheese, grapes, and crackers for us to share. I set it all on the glass coffee table and sat at the other end of the couch. She grabbed the remote and put on the next episode of a show called Younger.

I would never admit it, but I had taken an interest in the show as well. But tonight, I couldn't focus.

I chugged my scotch and filled it up with the bottle I had parked next to the couch. I couldn't stop eyeing her, her bare legs tempting me. I wanted to run my hand on her lotion-ed up soft skin, all the way up those soft shorts.

She wasn't unbothered by my presence either. That much was obvious by how much she kept fidgeting, glancing in my direction every now and then. I was bracing myself for another night of blue balls when I heard her sigh.

"I think I'm going to go to bed," she announced.

I wasn't ready to sleep; I was much too agitated for that, so close to the source of my every desire, to the woman I loved but hadn't touch in months. Not being able to show her how much I needed her, unsure if she felt the same, was torture, and I wasn't looking forward to yet another sleepless night.

"I'll stay here a little longer."

"Okay."

She got up, the blanket slipping off her body and onto the floor. She bent down to pick it up, giving me an unobstructed view of her braless, perky breasts. I muttered under my breath as I rubbed my face.

Chloe folded the blanket back on the chair and walked right in front of me, between the couch and the coffee table. Before I could stop myself, I raised my hand, grazing her right leg, stopping her mid track. I could no longer hide behind my stoic behavior, all the frustration and pain I had been holding inside boiling to the surface. I needed her to put an end to my suffering. Now.

When she looked at me, I waited for her to tell me to stop, but she didn't, so I trailed my hand from her shin to her thighs, and pulled her between my long legs.

My right hand traveled to her hips and squeezed, turning her slightly so she could face me fully.

Eyelids half closed, I buried my face on her stomach, kissing her belly over the silk. I felt her lean into me. Her eyes closed and her head slightly bent backwards. She let out a shaky breath.

"Chloe, baby, how long are you going keep punishing me for?" I lamented.

"You hurt me, Jake," she whispered, her voice cracking.

"I know. I'm sorry. I'm so sorry."

I lifted her shirt with my nose, craving direct contact with her soft skin. I kissed and sucked, as she moaned and arched her body towards me further.

"I need you to forgive me," I begged, as I sucked lower. "You have to forgive me," I grunted, pulling her even closer. "Fuck, baby, I fucking miss you. I don't know how much longer I can hold it together without you."

My voice shook, but I wasn't even ashamed. I was a desperate man.

I hadn't realized my face was wet until I felt her thumb caress under my eye. She pulled my face up, those amber eyes scanning my face with a confused frown.

She didn't look scared like before; she looked worried and overwhelmed.

"Don't cry," she whispered.

She bent her head towards me as she crooked mine to meet her lips. That was all I needed to wrap both my hands around her hips.

I moved my ass at the edge of the couch and pulled her closer to me, positioning her further between my thighs. I sucked every inch of her belly. My hands dipped into the hem of her shorts, and I lowered them to the ground.

Once they hit the floor, I raised each of her feet to step her out of them.

Fuuuck! She wasn't wearing anything under them. God, she was a literal dream.

I didn't wait, too afraid she would change her mind. I needed to taste her. I sucked her fully waxed pussy and she moaned, as her hands grabbed my hair.

"Open wide for me baby, I want to suck that pussy," I ordered against her cunt.

She immediately obeyed, her gaze on me. She was already panting, so ready for me to fuck her with my tongue. I gladly obliged, sucking on her clit harder.

She moaned, and I felt it all the way to the tip of my dick. I needed more access, so l lifted her left leg on the couch next to me.

She was so fucking wet for me already. I ate her up slowly, torturing her the best I could, as my dick throbbed in my pants. She was growing frustrated, needing more, pushing my face further into her sweet cunt. I wanted nothing more than to bury myself in there. My cunt. Mine.

"Oh," she whimpered as I put my tongue inside her tight hole. I could not get enough. Her body was shaking in my hands, and she was fucking herself against my face.

"Put your weight on me, mein liebling, don't be shy."

She did as she was told, her movements desperate. "Please, Jake."

I smiled. She was a goddess who brought me to my knees. I fucking loved the effect I had on her, her desperation for me to fuck her.

There was no sweeter sound in life than Chloe coming for me.

I brought my right hand up and slid my index finger inside of her. I raised my head to look at her face as I added a second finger, curving right where I knew she liked it.

"Unh," she whimpered as she lost some of her balance.

I steadied her with my other hand, my mouth open, cherishing her gasps, her tightly closed lips, her tits now almost out of her shirt, her nipples hard.

I bent her towards me until I could wrap my lips around that right nipple that had been driving me crazy all night.

"Jake!"

My cock twitched every time she moaned my name, desperately wanting to give her what she wanted.

I took my time, still slowly fucking her with my fingers, while I sucked on her other breast. I grabbed more of it in my mouth, sucking everywhere like a mad man.

I lifted my thumb to her clit, rubbing it just the way she liked it.

"Jake," she cried, "Oh God, Jake, please, please!"

As much as I wanted to draw this out all night, I felt like I was going to come any minute. So, I pushed myself back on the couch as I pulled her down to me until she was straddling me, my throbbing dick perfectly lined up with her pussy.

She let out a little scream, her fingers lacing in my hair, as I intensified the kiss, wanting to taste every inch of what she had to offer.

"Oh, Jake."

"I know, baby. I need you, too."

I lowered my face to kiss and suck her neck, her shoulder, traveling down to her nipples. I devoured her, circling the tips lightly with my tongue, stealing a moan out of her.

I sucked on it, while my other hand traveled to her other breast.

"Oh God," she whimpered, her head bent back, eyes closed.

My hand traveled down her back until I cupped her ass and rubbed her further again my hard dick. With shaky hands, she started to pull at my sweatpants, demanding that I take them off.

We both worked to shimmy them down, my dick springing free, ready to be deep inside her.

I moved my head back a little bit, wanting to stare at those flushed cheeks, the parted lips, and those hungry eyes as I helped her reposition herself. She was desperate for me and impatient.

I paused at her glistening entrance, enjoying her thirst and desperation for me. It was clear that she had been as starved as I had.

"Please," she begged. "Jake, I need you, I need you so much."

Her plea was my undoing, as I slid myself inside her, both of us moaning at the explosion of feelings exhaled from our lungs.

She was rhythmically moving; her wet, tight pussy clenching around my dick was what heaven felt like. God, she felt so. Fucking. Good. I wanted to be buried inside of her over and over again. There couldn't possibly be any better sensation in the world than that.

"Fuck, baby, you take me so fucking well."

"Uhn, Jake, oh God, Jake."

I removed my shirt and hers. I held her neck and her ass, bringing her perfect body flush with my body, refusing to leave any space between us. Her nipples rubbed against my bare chest.

Our lips brushed but remained opened, all our strength focused on the movement of our bodies against each other.

"I will fuck you into forgiving me, mein leibling, because I know you have me under your skin," I rasped by her ear. "You. Belong. To me. You. Are. Mine," I growled.

I felt her rhythm intensify; her breathing quickening. I wasn't going to be able to hold back for much longer, pre-cum already leaking from my tip and soaking her further, the combination driving me wild to the point of losing whatever sliver of restraint I had left.

I grabbed her hips, trying to slow her down, but she wasn't having it. She continued to move against me, surprising me with her strength.

"Jake!"

"Yeah, baby, tell me what you want. Let me hear it."

She was growing more and more frustrated, my grip hindering the diabolical twist of her hips. She gritted her teeth, her eyes staring at me with annoyance, and I smirked.

"Tell me. Tell me, and I will let you get there," I whispered against her lips, my eyes half closed but still gazing into her burning swirl.

"I want to come all over your cock. I want to feel you come inside of me Jake. Oh, Jake, I need you so much."

Oh, fuuuck.

Dirty talk coming out of that fiery but classy mouth of hers was my kryptonite. I still held her but relaxed my grip, letting her take the reins again.

Her movements intensified, her eyes rolled back in her head, those perfectly manicured nails digging into my shoulder.

"I'm coming!" she screamed, my body responding to her like clockwork, my throbbing shaft releasing inside of her while her cum engulfed me whole.

She kept moving, her silent cry carrying us both until there was nothing left of the intoxicating wave we rode on. We both hit the peak at the same time.

Finally, she slowed down and lowered herself to me, resting her head in the crook of my neck, our breathing short and heavy.

I gently rubbed her back, holding her close, while we slowly got back to earth. I felt her slightly shiver against me. I held her closer and lifted the both of us up. She barely moved; her legs securely tightened around my torso.

I carried her to my bedroom and onto the bed, where I proceeded to slowly kiss her. Her greedy fingers reached out for my dick again.

I smirked against her lips, already feeling my dick pulse. I hadn't lied when I promised to make her come so many times, she wouldn't be able to walk away from me ever again.

I took her nipple between my lips while I slid a finger inside of her. She moaned with pleasure. I would gladly fuck my woman until morning.

CHAPTER 63

Chloe

JAKE HAD MADE ME come two more times when he took me to his room. My resolved hadn't withstood the man. The slight shake of his voice when he admitted the pain he was in broke me, the horror and guilt I experienced when I felt the face of this man who usually exerted so much self-control wet under my fingertips was more than I could bear.

So, I gave in to what we both had craved so desperately, sat on him, and gave us both the release we so needed.

I closed my eyes and took a deep breath at the memory of my mind-blowing orgasm, the feeling threatening to course through me as I sat in the cafe in his building. I shifted my position, to distract my body.

I had ached for him for so long, I didn't know if I could go back to not having him in my life. But I was conflicted; this was becoming too real.

I sneaked out of his bed that morning like a coward, and went to the restaurant in the building. I needed some distance. Jake, I knew, wasn't going to be okay with things going back to before. And I needed to make a decision.

As if I could be next to him and not want his hands all over me.

But doubt still ate at me. If I forgave him, if I let him in again, I would put myself and my heart at risk. I had barely survived the past months.

How did one just decide it was ok to give themselves fully to someone else, putting their happiness and sanity at another person's will?

I shook my head, trying to get back to typing. It was already dark out. I knew my time was limited.

CHAPTER 64

Jake

I HAD TO LEAVE the apartment that morning, for meetings that needed to happen in-person. Chloe slipped out of my bed sometime before dawn, taking advantage of me finally getting a full night's sleep since the dinner at her parents, and left me waking up to a cold and empty bed.

After the night we had, I knew there were only two options: she had either fully forgiven me and was ready to let me in, or she would freak out and push me away.

I knew she was as crazy about me as I was about her.

I just needed to figure out a way to convince her that she could be with me.

What if she never forgave me? What if it was too late for forgiveness? What if me giving her the space she had asked for had been a mistake?

Giving her enough time to realize that she probably could do so much better than an asshole like me? What if she had moved on? I closed my eyes and grabbed the side of the kitchen island for support.

No, I couldn't think that way; I couldn't allow for this debilitating fear to take control over me, the fear that I had already lost the only woman I wanted, no, needed. The woman I didn't know how to breathe without.

While I had managed to distract myself with work during the day, the night had descended at a fast pace, and now there was nothing distracting me.

The suit I wore all day was now feeling like a restraint, anxiety creeping its way back inside of me.

I furiously headed to the door and swung it open but stopped in my tracks when a startled Chloe let out a small squeal, gazing at me with rounded brown eyes, Roger behind her. I stepped to the side to let her in and dismissed Roger with a head nod.

I followed her to the living room. She kept her back turned to me.

I saw her shoulders tense as she took a deep breath and removed her sweater to reveal a tight black shirt with long sleeves and those black silky leggings that shaped her ass to perfection. She ran her finger through her long brown strands. I felt my body's reaction to the movement, but I cleared my throat, trying to get my head on straight. We needed to talk.

She turned around to face me, her eyes looking anywhere but where I was standing, five feet from her. She looked small, a bit distraught. She looked like she would rather be anywhere but here with me, as if all she wanted was to find an escape and keep that distance she so wanted between us.

My jaw tensed, the idea that I was causing her anguish, that she would rather be anywhere but with me was destroying me. But I couldn't avoid this, because I was dying inside.

But giving her space was no longer an option.

"I'm sorry I left."

She spoke first, unusually uncomfortable with the silence between us, only perturbed by the sound of the wind hitting the windows, the storm picking up in intensity.

"I needed... to think," she continued, looking at the floor.

I caught myself holding my breath. That demeanor of hers, it wasn't a good sign. I took another step towards her; she took two steps back.

"Did last night mean nothing to you?"

"Of course it did." She sighed as her lips quivered a bit. She looked like she was trying to keep her emotions under wraps to have a conversation she had been preparing likely for a good part of the day. But she was doing a bad job at it.

Chloe wasn't one to do a bad job at anything. I didn't know if I should further panic, or feel a bit of hope. But the pain on her beautiful face was more than I could bear.

Before I could stop myself, my hands reached out for her, pressing her body against mine as my lips crushed against hers, the frustration I had kept for the past few months pouring out of me like lava.

"I'm not going to let you run away again. You heard me? I know how you feel about me. I know you were upset with me for accusing you like I did, but I know you don't care about that anymore. You are too rational to let something like that still stand between us. Which means you are using that as an excuse to cut me off, to run away from what you feel for me, how you feel about us."

"I know" she admitted. Something cracked inside of me. This was my chance.

"Take me back, Chloe, I need you to take me back."

"I don't know what I want."

"You do. Chloe, I love you."

Chloe's eyes glowed amber under the light of the skyline.

The light from the electric fireplace turned her skin almost golden. Her cheeks were flushed, her breathing was accelerated. Her eyes warmed up, as she swallowed hard.

God she was beautiful. I couldn't go back to living without Chloe. This was it.

I stole another kiss. She whimpered in my mouth, eliciting a groan in response. She wrapped her hands around me, holding me closer.

I let out a curse when I felt the vibration of a phone against my legs. My phone.

"Damn it."

I reluctantly parted from her to check it. It was Roger. As much as it pained me, I knew Roger wouldn't be calling at 11 p.m. if it wasn't important.

"I have to take this," I explained as I stepped out of the room.

CHAPTER 65

Chloe

I WAS LEFT CONFUSED and heated as I watched him pick up the phone and step out of the living room, feeling like my heart was about to jump out of my chest. I just stared at where he just stood.

Jake came back in the room after a few minutes, with a frown on his face, his jaw stiff and his lips thinned. I felt a weight drop in my stomach. I could tell this wasn't going to be good.

I raised an eyebrow at him, and he shook his head.

"We found K."

The blood left my face, my worse fear taking shape in front of me.

"And Kyle?"

"Not yet, but K. will crack; I will make him talk."

"Do I want to know your methods for getting that information?"

Jake raised a brow at me. "No, you don't."

"Okay." I swallowed hard. I wasn't going to start defending people who had put my life in danger.

"I have to go."

"Now?"

"I'm not missing a chance to catch those assholes, Chloe, not after all they put you through."

"Can't someone else handle it?"

"No."

"Jake, it's not worth it, please; you already have people on his tail, you don't have to go."

Jake grabbed my face between his hands and planted a kiss on my lips. I knew it was his way of reassuring me, but I couldn't help the nagging feeling deep in my gut.

I grabbed each of his arms, trying to keep him close to me. The idea that he would go find K, a dangerous man who had managed to keep both him and Kyle hidden for so long, was more than I could bear.

What if he got hurt, or worse?

I wanted him to stay here, with me, where I knew he was safe. I held him with all my strength, but he eventually pushed me back.

"Promise me you won't kill them."

His silence horrified me, leading to me digging my nails in his arms.

"I can't promise you that."

"Please, don't."

"I don't plan on killing anyone, Chloe, but I can't promise you that they won't get hurt."

I sobbed again, the idea of Jake in a dangerous situation overwhelming.

"Jake, please, don't go." I let out a small whimper as I buried my face in his neck.

Jake kissed my forehead and trailed more kisses along my jaw, stopping by my ear.

"Falling in love with you was never part of the plan, Chloe, but I did. And I'll be dammed if I stay here while those bastards continue to terrorize you. This is my fault, and I will fix it."

"Jake, please, I can't loose you."

"Oh, baby, you won't."

Jake kissed my forehead one more time, peeled me off of him, and left the room. I heard the front door close behind him.

My heart rate accelerated, my breathing choppy, his words unleashing a wave of emotions inside of me. He had told me those words I had whispered to him late at night, with no one to hear. He loved me.

I dropped to the ground, my hands covering my face, the sobs taking over my body, the sound of the wind outside pulling at my heart.

My resolve to move on had dissipated little by little ever since he picked me up in front of my house. Being with Jake felt like a breath of fresh air.

And now I was certain. I couldn't deny him any longer. I would be his forever, or at least until he walked away from me.

Because I would never leave his side if I let him in any further, if I admitted to myself that my life without him was empty, that happiness for all I had accomplished was usually followed by a hollow feeling, because I couldn't share it with him.

And if what I wanted was proof of his devotion, proof that he would put me before all else, proof was staring at me right in my face again, with him risking his life just for my mental peace.

If Jake got hurt, I would be the one to murder both K. and Kyle. Because at this point, there was no denying it; a life without Jake wasn't worth living.

CHAPTER 66

Chloe

I HAD BEEN PACING the halls of the house for what felt like an eternity, my phone held in a tight grip. Jake had been gone for over three long and painful hours during a thunderstorm.

Three hours during which I had cried and broken a lamp. Three hours during which I regretted pushing him away, regretted not forgiving him sooner, regretted the time wasted, not cherishing even second of every day with him the past few weeks.

Roger was my lifeline at this point. He knew exactly what Jake was doing and reassured me he had everything handled. He also had explained that him and some of the men were still around the premises, making sure that no one came to the house just in case.

He had promised to keep me updated, and after texting him ten times, I had tried to back off. I didn't want to text or call Jake, not wanting anything to distract him from whatever it was he was doing.

I missed him, deep in my bones, the idea of anything happening to him sending me in a spiral of madness.

The clock kept ticking at the slowest speed imaginable, as the storm grew stronger outside, the wind hitting the windows at full speed, my anxiety unmanageable.

I aimlessly paced. I couldn't lose him. I wouldn't survive it. After having him again, none of it really mattered. I didn't care that he doubted me because I probably would have done the same in his shoes. I wanted him, just him, only him, safe.

What choice did I have when even the sound of the wind carried his voice to my ears? When my sheets felt cold when I woke up to realize his hands on my body had only been in my dreams?

I needed him, body and soul. I needed him to come through the door, alive, his heart still beating for me.

It was 3 a.m. when I finally heard a noise coming from the entrance. I ran towards the door from the back of the house barefoot, my face puffy. I stopped in my tracks in the hallway, mouth agape, red eyes focused on the man who had just walked in and closed the door behind him, his coat soaked, his darkened eyes trained on me.

I let out a trembling sound, my hand on my chest, trying to slow down my accelerated heart rate. Relief coursed through me, relaxing my shoulders and overwhelming me all at the same. My eyes swelled with new tears as we closed the distance between us, my lips finding his, my fingers laced through his cold, wet hair. I ran my hands under his coat, helping him remove it.

He wrapped his arms around me and lifted me up, my legs wrapped around his waist, and walked us to his room.

I could barely breathe, the need to feel him inside of me making my body shake.

As he dropped me on the bed, his gaze never left mine as he removed my shirt and my leggings. He remained standing, his gaze ravaging every inch of my body.

I held a breath as he removed his clothes; I never tired of that sculpted body and those broad shoulders.

The storm outside, the sole source of light, threw shadows and light on his torso, accentuating the crevices between his traced abs.

This man, this god among mortals, was mine. He wanted me, and accepting that thought was overwhelming. Tears filled my eyes again as he slowly laid himself down on top of me, both hands grabbing my face, tenderly wiping my tears.

"Say the words, baby," he breathed as he searched my eyes. "Say the words and I'm yours." Hopeful, hesitant, worried, I saw all the emotions on those now gray-looking pupils, scanning my face with all the tenderness and intensity I never knew was possible, a match to all the turmoil I felt inside.

I brought my hand to his face, my thumb tracing the small hollows under his eyes, the light crinkle around his eyes.

"I love you, Jake, I—"

I couldn't finish as he crushed his lips into mine, stealing a moan from me.

"I want to hear it again," he grunted.

"I love you."

"You love me," he repeated, almost to himself.

"I love you," I reassured.

"I love you, Chloe. I am so sorry I hurt you, baby. You have no idea how much."

He was kissing me all over my face, holding me so close to him as if he wanted my body to merge with his and become one.

"I will never hurt you again, mein leibling. I'd rather die than ever hurt you again."

"No, no don't say that. You can never leave me. Don't leave me, Jake."

"Oh, baby."

I heard the tremor in his voice, my heart cracking a bit at all the love I felt emanating from his every pore.

"Make love to me, Jake. I need you."

He growled, positioning himself between my legs and sliding inside of me with no hesitation.

I moaned and the incredible feeling of completeness I always felt when he was in me, the feeling that nothing else was missing, my broken heart mended, held tight by the love and support I felt from him. My soul was at ease, at peace, as he thrusted inside of me over and over, pouring all his strength and frustration in every pulse, my body, matching his one for one.

"I love you, baby," he said as he slid inside me over and over again.

I wrapped my fingers around his ass, encouraging him to destroy me, reek havoc over me, let all his need, all his frustrations out each time he pumped deep inside of me.

My legs were holding him tight, so that there was never any distance between us, even when he pulled back to grind inside of me again.

"Ugh, Jake, I'm gonna come!"

"I know, baby. Chloe, look at me. I want to watch you come. I want to see what I do to you."

I opened my eyes and stared into his. "Jake!"

"I love how you unravel for me, baby, fuck!"

I could tell he was as close to the edge as me. The maddening desire and pressure oh so evident in the way he parted his lips.

His breathing was fast, and his eyes blazed with fire as he watched my dazed eyes, and my mouth open as I called his name over and over again. The pulsing inside of me driving us to ecstasy until we had nothing left but satiation.

CHAPTER 67

Jake

SHE WAS STILL SLEEPING, her soft face laid on my right shoulder, her arm across my chest. The necklace was back around her neck, where it belonged. The sight took me back to that day at her parents' house, when I tasted her for the first time. I couldn't have her then, but still, some primal part of me wanted to brand her with something from me, plain and simple. It was low, but it was the truth.

I was facing the usual conundrum of wanting to feel her just like this, cuddled in my arms, but wanting to catch a better look at those long lashes and that slightly open mouth, loving how relaxed and angelic she looked when she slept in my arms.

I moved her away from me ever so slightly to take a look at her. Her hair was a messy combination of curly and straight strands, just the way I liked it, a chaotic mess reflecting my woman, the one who was so strict rational and disciplined, but unwound in a fiery tiger: wild, passionate, full of life and fire when life demanded it.

Last night had been more than I had been ready for. Meeting with K. had been frustrating, as he wouldn't talk. The amount of hatred he had for me was palpable, and I couldn't help but be affected by that.

A man I had treated with respect and deference wanted nothing but pain and turmoil for me. Jealously was a drug, and that was all it seemed K. had felt during the years we had worked together. In the confrontation, K. had managed to get a hold of a knife, and through the struggle, I had no other choice but to kill him.

I hadn't felt any remorse, just sadness and disappointment.

We had gotten to Kyle's whereabouts, but Kyle hadn't put too much resistance. He had gotten arrested and had been taken back to Chicago.

I didn't like the idea of what promised to be a painful process of charging him and getting him in prison. Some problems were better addressed by ending a life.

But those were punishments I had only used for heinous situations, and even if I wanted to cut Kyle into pieces for daring to put a finger on Chloe, I knew she didn't want me to. That meant I was able to keep my promise to Chloe and limit the damage I needed to do. A displaced nose and a couple broken limbs were the worst of it for him.

I was doing all of this to keep her safe, but to also bring her peace of mind, so I couldn't break my promise to her. No amount of revenge, for how satisfying it might be, was worth a frown on her face.

After we had both let out our frustration and need for each other, she had timidly asked me questions to find out what happened. She looked relieved. She understood the coming mess at having to put Kyle in jail.

And I knew that for as long as Kyle was alive, I would have him supervised, in and out of jail. He could always retaliate, even in twenty years, and that wasn't a risk I was willing to take.

I had almost lost her; that thought still hit me hard, how close I had gotten, but I was determined to spend the rest of my life earning her trust again, getting her to see that I was hers as much as she was mine. Let her understand that she was above all else for me, no matter what. There wasn't a force on earth powerful enough to tear us apart.

She made a little whimper as her eyes slowly opened. She closed them back immediately, a smile creasing on her lips as she let out a happy sigh.

I brought her closer to me as she moaned. She buried her face in my neck. I felt my dick's immediate response to the friction of her naked breast grazing my chest.

She giggled as her hand slid down my stomach and grabbed my dick. She sucked on my neck as she ran her fingers expertly up and down my shaft.

"Hm, Chloe?"

"Yes, baby?"

My dick twitched at those words on her lips, enjoying my nickname. The woman was my undoing. "We need to talk," I tried.

I had to make sure she wasn't going to run away from me again. I wanted to be certain that even if she had doubts, she would give us a chance, a real one. But Chloe wasn't in the mood for conversations on this rainy Sunday morning.

"Do we?" She licked my neck again as she grazed the top of my dick with her thumb.

"Yes, we do," I managed to let out, my eyes tightly shut, trying to control myself.

I tried to remove her hand from my protesting dick, but she took advantage of the move and threw her right leg over my waist, turning us both, me on my back, and her on top of me, straddling me.

I let out a grunt as my dick found its favorite place in between her wet folds. "Fuck."

"That's right," she teased, a smirk on her lips, as her eyes started to glass over. She slowly moved up and down my dick and moaned.

I had to let the words out, I had to. Otherwise, she would make sure we fucked all day, without giving me the peace of mind I needed.

"Chloe," I let out between gritted teeth as she worked on positioning my dick for entry. "Promise me that you will never leave me again. We will fight, we will struggle sometimes, but there is nothing we can't talk through, what we can't do is close each other out."

She put the tip of my head at her entrance and slid herself down it slowly.

"Fuck!" I growled between clenched teeth, barely able to keep going. "Promise me you will never close me out, promise you will never leave."

"I promise."

She made that little grind she did when she twisted her hips to music, and I shut my eyes, the sensation too intense for me to utter another word without exploding inside of her before she was ready.

She moaned as she put both her hands flat on my chest and concentrated her energy on where our bodies met with my treacherous cock letting her do whatever she wanted to do with it.

I opened my eyes to watch her. Her eyes were dazed, her head bent slightly back. Her lips were parted as moans spilled from her. And those gorgeous, full breasts were heaving up and down as she rode me, her perfect, erect nipples on display.

My mouth watered, needing to taste her some more.

I grabbed her hips and started sliding her up and down my waist as I knew she needed it, creating friction for her clit as she pulsed my dick inside of her.

She brought her head down, all the way close to mine. Her thirst turned into tenderness, as she grabbed my face with her hands, pulling me toward her until I was in a seated position, with her still straddling me.

"I love you," she whispered.

The proximity to her body, not an inch of skin not touching the other, was going to make me come so hard I swore I felt my dick stretch another inch.

"I tried a life without you, Jake, I really tried. There wasn't a night I didn't sleep with you name on my lips, there wasn't a morning I didn't cry for not having your arms around me. I love you, baby, I love you so much I chose to walk away, because I knew if I didn't, there was no saving me.

"But all I got was tears and heartache. All I got was emptiness, loss, desperation. I can't... oh Jake, I can't live without you."

God, yes. Finally. I lifted us up and pinned her on her back. She was mine, body and soul. I fucked her, deep, possessive, desperate.

I grunted as she continued to make my dick pulse with her soft movements against me, as if she was trying to get more of me inside of her.

I thrusted inside of her with more force, pumping so fast I was holding my breath.

"Jake!"

"I love you so much, baby."

"Oh!"

"Yes, mein leibling, let it go. Let it all go, baby, let this take over."

And she did; she lost herself and took me with her. We flew through another universe, beyond the concept of time or space, present in every inch of ourselves while being totally absent, floating through a feeling so powerful there was no longer a concept of life or death.

ABOUT THE AUTHOR

Stéphanie is an author of angsty love stories with assertive female leads, who go toe to toe with alpha heroes. Stephanie's love for romance stems from her teenage years, when she was secretly reading her grandmother's Harlequin books under the covers, coupled with spending every weeknight avidly watching telenovelas with her mother.

Stéphanie grew up in the Caribbean and currently lives in Illinois. She enjoys spending time with her cat, a romance book in hand.

Want to read more? Check out the first book of the Game Series (link on next page)!

Game of Revenge Link!

Sign up for my newsletter!

@INBOOKS.ILIVE

*Follow me on Instagram for
more!*

Please also stop by Amazon and Goodreads to leave a review, we LOVE
THOSE!